AWAKE AT
dawn

awake at dawn

WILDFLOWER SERIES
BOOK 2

AMELIE RHYS

Published by R. H. Publishing

ISBN: 979-8-9893446-3-5

Cover Design: Caitlin Russell

Character Art: Alie Reighard at alies_artwork

Copy Editing: Sandra Dee at One Love Editing

Developmental Editing: Ink and Quill Publishing

This book is intended for an 18+ audience. Awake at Dawn contains explicit sexual content. It also focuses on the pregnancy journey and the side effects that go with it (ie mentions of vomit) and contains discussions of consent in the context of a drunken one night stand. One night stand is not depicted.

playlist

Delicate — Taylor Swift
Glue Myself Shut — Noah Kahan
Selfish — Justin Timberlake
Honey — Troye Sivan
Be Someone — Benson Boone
Home — Good Neighbours
I Can See You — Taylor Swift
Heaven — Niall Horan
Souvenir — Selena Gomez
Walk — Griff
Quiet — Camila Cabello
Hey Daddy — Usher
Sunrise — Kygo & Jason Walker
The Alchemy — Taylor Swift

To anyone who's started over or had to find a different way in life. I hope your path is filled with wildflowers.

Especially tiger lilies.

eight years ago
NOAH

Julian's sister was coming to visit tonight.

He made me swear not to go near her.

For the record, he also made our other roommates swear the same thing.

They swore they wouldn't.

So did I.

But that was before I saw her.

CHAPTER ONE

noah

I T TOOK SOME effort to maneuver my arm out from under
her, but after a minute of strategic finesse, I thankfully
managed.

Doing it without waking her up was a different story, though.
As soon as I sat up in bed, she mimicked me. *Fuck,* of course
she did.

I rolled out of bed anyway. And big surprise—she moved to
follow me. Flashing her a look, I dropped my voice. "Stay."

My command seemed to do the trick. For a moment, anyway.
And then she looked like she was about to do the exact opposite
of it.

"Don't you fucking dare move from that bed."

Soft brown eyes blinked up at me as she settled onto the blankets again. I smiled, satisfied. Fuck, she was too cute for her own
good.

"Good girl."

Happy with her obedience, I turned on my heel. And that was
when I heard the sound of puppy paws hitting the hardwood
floor.

"Oh goddamnit," I sighed. So much for obedience. When I
peeked back over my shoulder, Winnie was sitting at my heels,

her tail thumping on the floor excitedly. And there were those brown eyes again—those big, puppy dog eyes. "So much for staying in the fucking bed."

Winnie continued to stare at me eagerly.

"Fine," I groaned. "You can come with me to the bathroom."

"*I* don't want to come with you to the bathroom." My friend's deep laugh echoed into my ear from my wireless earphones, making me jump. I almost forgot Julian was still on the call, let alone that he was the reason I'd gotten up in the first place. Normally, nothing could drag me out of bed this early on an off-season Sunday. I supposed that made Jules special—not that I'd ever tell him that.

"You wanted me to check my calendar to see if that weekend was free, didn't you?"

"Your calendar is in your bathroom?"

"Yes, my calendar is in my bathroom. It's when I have the most time to schedule my life."

"I think you need to adjust your diet if that's the case, man."

I ignored him, maneuvering through my apartment with Winnie on my heels. From the moment I brought her home a few weeks ago, she'd been attached to my goddamn ankles. I took a step; she took a step. I went to the kitchen; she went to the kitchen. I was afraid I'd trip over her tiny, wiggly body one of these days.

"Yeah, that weekend should work," I said after flipping through the Minnesota State Fair wall calendar my mom had sent me to "remind me of home." The only thing it did, though, was remind me of all the fried food I couldn't eat. Despite Julian's teasing, my diet was annoyingly healthy. Although...if cheese curds presented themselves, I sure as hell wouldn't pass them up.

"Excellent." Julian's voice cut into my thoughts.

"What's the plan? Vegas? Miami?"

Julian sighed, and I knew he was about to ruin all my fun party ideas. "I was thinking we'd just...I don't know. Hit up the Bellflower."

"It's your *bachelor party*, Jules. Come on," I groaned. "You go to that bar all the time. Now's your chance to think outside of the box. Where's the spirited college captain that I remember?"

Julian Briggs was the reason I was an NFL quarterback. He pushed our college team to new heights and helped shape me into the player I am today. And while he could have also easily gone pro, he'd made the wild decision to go to law school instead and now worked his ass off as an associate attorney at a law firm here in Boston.

"I told Grayson he could decide," he said with another resigned, lawyer-y sigh.

"Oh *sure*, let the dad who doesn't drink and will complain about missing his wife the entire time plan the bachelor party."

"Well, he's the best man."

"Way to rub it in." I rolled my eyes. Not that I cared. Grayson, another one of our college teammates, had a different sort of bond with Julian than I did. When he got married right out of college, Julian had been *his* best man. When his son was born shortly after, he'd asked Julian to be his godfather. And when he'd considered filing a medical malpractice lawsuit because the hospital missed his son's congenital heart defect, he'd asked Julian to be his attorney.

I wasn't the friend people counted on for things like that. I was the friend who made sure everyone laughed and had a good time. I got that.

Which was why I should at least be able to help plan the bachelor party.

"Remember when you took my fiancée on a date?" Julian drawled.

"I took her out for dinner as an apology. It wasn't *even* a date," I corrected, tossing my trusty calendar onto the counter and retreating from the bathroom, nearly tripping over Winnie. "Besides, she wasn't your fiancée or even your girlfriend at the time, and I knew you'd finally fix that when your possessive panties got in a twist. You're *welcome*."

"Yeah, yeah." Julian's dry chuckle told me he'd gotten over the stunt I'd pulled last year. "That's why you'll be standing with me on my wedding day, too, London."

I nodded, knowing I should have felt happy to be included. But something still nagged at me.

Maybe it was just Winnie, who was attacking the bottom of my sweatpants, tugging on them with her tiny teeth. She didn't let go, even as I stepped onto the rug in my living room, which was covered in dog toys and ripped cushions. I swore under my breath at the sight in front of me. Within the last two weeks, my luxury apartment had turned into a puppy playground.

"What?" Julian prompted.

"My little shadow is going to be the death of me," I muttered.

"Well, you might need to work up to *don't you fucking dare move from that bed*," Julian quoted. "I would suggest starting at the beginner level and teaching her *sit*."

I wiggled my leg, getting Winnie to release her piranha teeth. "Aren't you a fucking smart-ass today."

"Have you found a dog sitter for your away games?" he asked, ignoring my comment.

"No. You know...*you* could—shit." My phone buzzed, indicating another incoming call, and I sighed. "You're saved by the bell, Briggsy. My sister's calling."

Julian snickered before hanging up, and I rolled my eyes before swiping across my phone screen to accept the call.

"Hey, Nat."

"Noah." Her frantic voice made me stand up straighter, worry falling into my gut. "I just got called into surgery. Can you please, pretty please, do me a favor?"

"What's the favor?"

When it came to my big sister, Natalie, otherwise known affectionately as one of the three Dr. Londons in the family, I knew better than to say I'd do anything without knowing the details.

"Pick Chloe up from skating practice. It ends..." She paused like she was checking the time. "Well, now."

I could *hear* the wince in her voice, but I just shrugged. Of all the things she could have asked me to do, picking up my niece, aka the coolest eight-year-old on the planet, from the skating rink ten minutes from my apartment wasn't a big deal.

"Yeah, Nat. I can pick our little skater up. We'll grab some lunch and head back here. You can swing by my place whenever you're done."

"Thanks, Noah. You're a lifesaver."

I snorted. "You're the trauma surgeon, so I think that's actually you. But..."

"What?"

"The season's coming up," I reminded her. "I won't always be able to be your backup plan, Nat. As much as I wish that weren't the case."

"Wow, way to stress me out right before I'm about to cut someone's chest open," she snapped, the tension in her voice rising.

Shit. She was right; it was a dick move bringing this up before her surgery. But it had been weighing on my mind lately, and I was stressed about what Nat would do when I was out of town this season for away games. Ever since her dickhead husband left her for his secretary, I'd picked up his slack.

Not that it was a burden. Actually, I liked that I could be there for at least one of my siblings. The rest of them—and my parents —still lived back home, and my schedule kept me away more than I liked. Plus, I could count on Chloe to play with Winnie all afternoon and wear this puppy out so I could get some uninterrupted sleep tonight. I wasn't used to losing sleep for any other reason than orgasms, and being a dog dad had come with some adjustments.

"Sorry, sis. Go kick ass and all that jazz."

She huffed another thank-you before hanging up, and I

swooped Winnie into my arms to bring her to her cozy crate so I could head out to pick up Chloe.

I looked down at Win and the tongue that flopped out one side of her mouth. "You're cute, but you're a pain in my ass."

Her lips pulled back slightly, making it look like she was smiling. It made *me* smile.

Until she sneezed in my face.

A few months ago, Chloe decided she wanted to be a figure skater. And since my sister was determined to give her daughter every experience possible in order to make up for her long work hours and lack of a present father, she immediately signed Chloe up for lessons.

Lo loved skating practice, but especially the last two weeks— ever since she got a new instructor. She always talked my ear off on the way home, detailing everything that happened on the ice, and it usually revolved around Coach B, who was the *best ever*.

Uncle Noah took some offense to that, honestly.

Typically, I didn't go into the rink when I picked her up, opting to hang on the bench outside instead. While ice sports and football were played on different fields, sports still attracted sports. And I didn't like getting recognized and pulled into conversations about my job when I was just trying to pick my niece up from skating practice.

Today, the July heat was blasting up my ass, though. I couldn't think of anything better than stepping into the rink to cool off while I waited for Chloe.

Relief washed over me as I walked through the front doors and crisp air hit my skin. The sound of skates cutting through ice added to the somewhat delightful chill running down my spine. Stuffing my hand in the pockets of my athletic shorts, I wandered around the curve of the rink, making my way to the stands, where a group of parents were helping kids remove their skates.

I caught Chloe's eye and waved at her. Her face lit up when she saw me, flashing a smile. Then she ducked her head again, focusing on her skates. She didn't need help, and I knew better than to offer it. Getting put in my place by an eight-year-old wasn't on my to-do list for the day.

Leaning against the wall surrounding the rink, I twiddled my thumbs. Lo kept getting distracted every other second by talking to the girls on the bench, but I didn't mind. She switched schools when Nat moved into her own apartment last year, and I knew it had been hard for Chloe to make friends. It was nice to see her so happy here.

"I really can't impose on you like that, but thank you."

A warm, sugary voice caught my attention, and I turned slightly to see a woman leaning against the end of the stands, her back to me. It was a nice back—a back covered in wavy, coppery hair and skintight clothes. She still had skates laced on her feet, one foot propped up on the toe of her blade. She wiggled it almost nervously.

"Seriously," another woman replied. Dressed in a similar outfit, she sat in the stands as she faced the redhead. "My couch is always free."

"I can't sleep on your couch for five months," the other woman groaned, and I heard her voice more clearly that time. Recognition blazed its way through me, as well as shock.

I wasn't shocked to see Gemma Briggs at a skating rink; I knew she did this for a living. But I was definitely surprised to see her at *Chloe's* rink.

"Is that how long you think you'll need?" Her friend winced.

"To save up enough to find a new place around here?" Gemma sighed, and my feet automatically started moving toward her. "Yeah. Even with my bare-bones budget, I think it will take at least that long."

7

Gemma kept talking, even as I crept up behind her, feeling like...well, a creep.

"I love working here..." She glanced around the rink, letting me see her side profile as her eyes landed on the kids packing their stuff. Her lips turned up in a soft smile. "But the paychecks definitely aren't the same as they were at St. Maverick's."

"Well, let me know if there's any other way I can help," the other woman said, dragging Gemma's attention back around. The two of them shared a quick hug, and then Gemma was left standing alone. Her forlorn expression chased concern around my brain. I'd never seen this side of her before.

Not that I knew her that well, despite *trying* to get to know her better on more than one occasion.

God, I was about to do something rash, wasn't I?

I flipped my ball cap—the one I usually wore low to stay incognito—around, wearing it backward instead. And then I cleared my throat.

"You're looking for a new place?"

Gemma spun at the sound of my voice. I watched as the worry that had been coating her expression morphed into surprise and then something else I couldn't put my finger on. Her cheeks flushed, though, giving me a hint of what it might be.

"Noah," she said breathlessly.

I usually hated when people recognized me in public, but boy did I like how my name just fell out of her mouth like that.

"What are you doing here?" she asked, and I realized I'd been staring. It was hard not to when she ran her fingers nervously through her hair like she was doing right now. The color reminded me of a tiger lily—vibrant with darker streaks speckling it.

My eyes flicked to Chloe on the bench. She was standing now, all ready to go but chatting with her friends. A grin stretched over my face. "Picking up my niece."

Gemma followed my gaze. Her brows lifted. "Chloe Abrams is your niece?"

My lips twisted at the reminder that Lo still had her asshat dad's last name. But I nodded in response, watching from the corner of my eye as Chloe started bounding toward me, her limbs awkwardly long for an eight-year-old.

"Coach B! We want to learn forward crossovers next week!" Chloe called, her eyes shining as she looked at Gemma, and all the pieces clicked together in my head.

Gemma was Coach B. Of course she was, and of course Chloe thought she was the best.

I thought she was the best, too. Always had, but there was only one problem.

Gemma Briggs was Julian's sister. And out of all of my friends, Julian was by far the most wildly protective and ridiculously smothering. Talking to Gemma was strictly against the rules. Hell, even *looking* at Gemma was against the rules.

I'd definitely broken that rule before.

Promptly deciding to ignore all the warning bells in my head, I rounded on Gemma to ask her again about her living situation.

Because her dilemma might just solve one—or even two—of mine.

CHAPTER TWO

gemma

E MBARRASSMENT TRICKLED DOWN my spine.
Noah London just overheard that I was flat-out broke.
Of all the mortifying things that could have happened today, this
one had to involve my brother's too-hot-for-his-own-good friend
and former college teammate. Considering I had to pack up all my
belongings into as few boxes as possible, I hadn't exactly expected
a *good* day, but I definitely didn't think it would be a *Noah London
knows your greatest failure* kind of day.

If that wasn't causing my cheeks to flame enough, now the
quarterback of the New England Knights was giving me an odd
look while crossing his tattooed-covered arms over his chest. He
leaned back casually as his eyes skirted to Chloe, who'd gotten
sidetracked by watching the older skaters glide out on the ice.

I loved the passion in her eyes—like she was determined to
get where they were. Finding out that she had professional
athleticism in her veins made sense.

When I felt a prickling on the back of my neck, I looked back
to find the reason: Noah's sharp gaze had returned. When he
stared at me like that, the air grew thick. Humid. Hell, I wouldn't
be surprised if the ice started melting on the rink—Noah just had

that effect. I wasn't ashamed to admit the truth, but I *was* ashamed to be blushing so furiously about it.

He cocked his head to the side, considering something. "Does Julian know you need a place to live?"

I swallowed a groan. Great, we were back on this subject. And of course he had to bring up Julian.

"No, and you're not going to tell him," I said pointedly.

Noah's brows rose in response, and I realized that maybe I was being a *touch* defensive.

"I'm not going to tell him," he said, and the honesty in his reply made my tense body relax. A bit, anyway. There was still the way he was looking at me, after all. "But I am curious why *you* won't tell him."

"If I told Julian, he would either insist on giving me money that he's saved up to pay for his wedding, or he'd demand I move in with him and Juniper."

Noah frowned. "Moving in wouldn't be so bad, would it? I mean, Juniper *is* your best friend."

"Exactly," I said, lifting a finger to emphasize the point he'd just made. "Do you think I want a front-row seat to my brother and best friend's love life? Absolutely not."

A low chuckle slipped from Noah's lips. "I suppose when you put it like that..."

I lifted a brow as if to say, *See?*

I'd considered an exhaustive list of options when I realized I couldn't continually afford my apartment in the suburbs, but never once had I considered asking Juniper or Julian for help.

Noah nodded like he understood, and I appreciated the validation. Sadie, another Back Bay Skating coach, had implied that not asking my brother for help was ridiculous. But Noah didn't try to pressure me.

Instead, he changed the topic.

"Chloe loves you."

I immediately warmed at the comment. It always made me feel good to hear things like that. I wanted to make the rink a safe place where kids felt excited to come and try new things. There had been moments when it hadn't always been like that for me, and I never wanted that for my skaters.

"I've really enjoyed getting to know her," I said honestly. "She's always the one who gets me laughing on these weekend morning practices."

"Yeah?" He rocked forward, taking a step closer. Despite the cold air swirling around us, heat continued to rocket through me. Noah London was startlingly attractive. And staring at me funnily. And incredibly unavailable. His lips curved, and his eyes danced with mischief. "That's good to know. And how do you feel about dogs?"

"Dogs?" I repeated. Had I heard him correctly, or had my preoccupation with the light brown twinkle in his eyes distracted me?

"Dogs," he affirmed. "Of the young variety."

Okay, yep. I was lost.

"I like dogs," I said slowly. "Of all varieties."

Growing up, I'd begged my parents for a dog, but they never caved, saying they opted for more kids over pets. They had a point; Julian aside, I also had four other sisters. There wasn't really anywhere to put a pet in our house.

Noting my confusion, Noah laughed.

"Well, I wanted to make sure before offering you a place to stay," he explained, and I stiffened. In shock? Heatstroke? I wasn't sure, but I suddenly had the urge to face-plant on the ice. "I got a new puppy a few weeks ago."

"What?" I began to backpedal. Not literally, because I was standing with my back to the metal stands and still had my skates on my feet. But figuratively, in my brain, I was doing a whole lot of backpedaling. "Noah, I—"

He didn't let me protest. "I have an extra room that's not being used at home, and it would be great if someone was around to hang out with Winnie when I'm gone at away games this season."

"Is Winnie your...girlfriend?" My stomach turned uncomfortably because that just sounded...strange.

Noah's lips twisted in amusement. "Winnie's my dog, Gemma."

"Right."

Yeah, that made a lot more sense.

Not just because what he suggested would be weird and awkward but also because Noah London didn't have girlfriends. He had girls, of course. But he didn't have *girlfriends*. Everyone and their mom knew he was one of the NFL's biggest playboys.

My cheeks were officially on fire, probably matching the shade of my hair.

"Think about it," he said, his eyes skirting to the side to see Chloe approaching us. He jerked his head toward her. "I've also been worried about Chloe."

Dread dropped into my stomach. "What's wrong with Chloe?"

Noah's eyes darkened, and the relaxed version of him I'd grown accustomed to was suddenly gone.

"She has a dickhead for a dad." I let out a breath as Noah went on. "My sister works odd hours at the hospital, so Chloe often ends up at my place. Her dad isn't in the picture, and I don't know what Nat will do when I'm traveling over the next few months. But maybe if *you* were there..."

His voice grew quieter as his niece neared, and all I could do was blink back at him, struggling to keep up with everything he was saying. And especially his tone, which indicated that he was serious. He genuinely wanted—or needed—me to move in with him.

"I know it's a lot to ask," he whispered, shrugging. "Too much, probably. But I'd pay you, of course."

"Pay *me*?" I shook my head in disbelief. "I was going to ask how much you wanted me to pay *you*. For rent?"

It was his turn to stare blankly. "Nothing," he said after a moment. "I don't want your money, Gemma."

Was this a dream? He wanted me to live in his apartment free of charge, play with his dog when he was gone, and hang out with his niece, who I already adored. This was absolutely too good to be true. And absolutely too dangerous—as noted in Noah's growing smile. He probably didn't do it on purpose, but he always had this wolfish, wicked grin that made me think things I shouldn't be thinking.

"Julian would have a fit," I hissed under my breath.

There, that was a responsible thought.

"I thought you weren't telling Julian about this," Noah said, that grin of his full-fledged now.

He had a point. But still...

"Noah, you can't be serious."

"Oh, I'm super serious," he said as Chloe snuck into his side, giving him a giant hug around his middle. He squeezed her in return, casting a warm look in his niece's direction before returning his attention to me.

He didn't look serious; his lips formed a twisted smirk. But I'd learned from meeting Noah over the years that he never really looked serious.

"Let me give you my number," I said hurriedly. "Maybe sleep on it, and then let me know if you're *still* serious."

I put my hand out, and Noah unlocked his phone and placed it in my palm. His lips did that thing again, twisting further like he was suppressing something, some emotion he didn't want me to see. While I put my number in his phone, I heard him quietly tell Chloe about how we knew each other.

I mean, we didn't know each other. Not that well, anyway. And I suspected that wouldn't be changing.

Noah London was a famous professional athlete, and I taught kids how to figure skate while living paycheck to paycheck.

We lived in different worlds.

Yet, he wanted us to share an apartment. And I just wasn't so sure how that would work.

I paced around my living room, knowing I needed to pack. My mug collection was scattered haphazardly around my living room, colorful little mementos waiting to be put into boxes. I wasn't going to, but I really *should* donate some of them because there was no way I'd be able to bring everything with me—not that I even knew where I was going. Even though I had to be going *somewhere* really soon.

I hadn't been able to stop thinking about Noah.

Well, not Noah like the *person*. I wasn't just sitting around daydreaming about Noah and his sleeves of tattoos and the way he wore his hat backward with his light brown hair curling out beneath the sides—

No, I wasn't thinking about *Noah*. I was thinking about *his proposition.*

No, not his proposition. That made it sound...dirty.

His *idea.*

There, yeah. I was just thinking about his idea.

Mentally exhausted, I threw myself onto my couch and tipped my head back with a groan. I missed working at St. Maverick's College. It was well paying and prestigious, and I loved the girls on my team to death.

But it also came with a boss who manipulated his way into my bed after taking me out for drinks—way too many drinks. And that drunken one-night stand resulted in the cutest little sweet pea.

That was what the internet said: at six weeks pregnant, the embryo was the size of a sweet pea.

Silas, my boss, was the athletic director at St. Maverick's. I'd never really know what his intent was when he kept buying me drinks that night, but I knew I accepted them because he was my boss. That, and I'd never minded Silas before. He'd always been moderately nice to me, and apparently, I was easily manipulated by people who smiled at me and also held my job in their hands. It made it hard to say no.

Maybe he'd been trying to get me into bed from the start, or maybe both of our judgments had been skewed by alcohol. I didn't remember consenting, but I also didn't remember *not* consenting. I hated that I couldn't remember, that only bits and pieces of that night popped up in my brain, and while none of them were particularly good, it could also have been so much worse. It left me feeling slightly traumatized by the *what-ifs*. What if something worse could have happened? What if something worse *did* happen? What if I never really knew?

It was a vulnerable feeling, one I hoped I never experienced again. And once I finally started to get over the experience of that night, a new emotion overwhelmed me: shock.

Because I was pregnant.

Silas took the news of my pregnancy about as well as I expected. There was denial, first—it couldn't be *his* baby. When I informed him that it quite literally couldn't be anyone else's, he threw a lot of hateful words at me before implying that there was only one solution, and if I didn't take that solution, he didn't want to be involved.

Suddenly, Silas Taylor turned into a boss who was anything but nice.

Imagine that.

I didn't take the solution he wanted me to. Being a mom was something that I'd always dreamed of, and despite the turmoil of it happening in such a craptastic way, I didn't want to give up on that dream. I was scared beyond belief, mortified to my core, but beneath all that, I was excited—in a terrifyingly beautiful sort of way.

But I couldn't keep working with Silas, let alone *for* him.

Feeling uncomfortable and out of my depth, I quit St. Maverick's. I could have fought for my job and fought with Silas about what happened that night after our supposedly harmless round of drinks, but I needed out. I needed to never see or work with Silas ever again.

Since Juniper and Julian were both attorneys at a Boston law firm, the smart move would have been asking them for legal advice first before quitting. But that would have meant telling my brother I was pregnant.

To put it mildly, I was *terrified* of how Julian would react. He would undoubtedly jump into big-brother overdrive and do exactly what I told Noah earlier: uproot his entire life with Juniper to support me, insist on giving me money, or force me to move in with them.

I couldn't do that.

Not telling Juniper had been so much harder. I'd needed her the last few weeks. I'd needed my best friend more than I ever had. But I couldn't ask her to keep this secret from Julian, so I'd kept it for myself. At least until I came up with a plan that I could tell them to prove I had everything figured out.

I didn't have everything figured out.

Moving in with Noah was an absurd idea. While I liked Noah, we barely knew each other. We'd met a handful of times over the years, mostly at parties that revolved around Julian, like when I visited my brother in college or when we'd celebrated his law school graduation. But we didn't *know* each other.

Not well enough to live together.

But he lived ten minutes from Back Bay Skating.

He'd already texted me the address and information about the building, not even waiting to sleep on it like I told him to. He lived in the perfect location. In a highly secure penthouse that was close to *everything*. I wouldn't have to take the commuter rail to get into the city, and not paying for a T pass would save me a good chunk of change each month. The more I could save, the better.

Plus, it was temporary. A few months so I could save up for this baby, help him with his puppy and Chloe during the football season, and then I was out of there. Besides, while I didn't know Noah well, of all my brother's friends, he was my favorite. He'd played the ultimate wingman to force Julian and Juniper together, and despite all my efforts to get those fools to realize how in love they were, he was the real MVP who made it happen.

I liked Noah London.

But that thought came around again, the one that reminded me how he was a famous all-star, and I was a single-mom-to-be.

I could like Noah London.

I just couldn't like Noah London *too* much.

That wouldn't be a problem...right?

eight years ago

NOAH

Julian hadn't stopped pacing.

I watched him, ignoring my phone buzzing in my pocket—an unwanted reminder that I'd missed my brothers' combined grad school graduation party last night. My mom kept sending me pictures of the two new family doctors, one medical while the other had a PhD in something I didn't even begin to understand.

Meanwhile, I had a final today that meant I hadn't been able to fly home. I probably failed it, too. It was for some low-level Chem class that both of my brothers would have aced.

I sighed, focusing on Julian and his pacing.

Back and forth, back and forth across the living room of our slightly dilapidated college rental house. He'd stubbed his toe twice on the dumbbells Grayson left lying on the floor earlier, and the second time, I thought he might pick them up and chuck both out the window.

I must be missing something.

I'd always gotten the impression that Jules was really close with his sister. Or sisters. He had a lot of them. Four? Five? I couldn't remember. I didn't know which one was visiting tonight, either, just that Julian Briggs—our normally calm and collected football captain—was stressed. More than I'd seen him for any game or any of his pre-law exams.

Our end-of-semester party was in full swing by the time she actually walked through the door.

I immediately forgot about Julian and why he was acting so weird. I didn't give a damn about that.

I didn't give a damn about anything that didn't involve getting closer to the one girl in the room I should absolutely steer clear of.

CHAPTER THREE

noah

J ULY TWENTY-EIGHTH. I was going to mark it on my Minnesota State Fair calendar—the day I finally got Gemma Briggs' number.

I'd asked Julian for his sister's number repeatedly, on more than one occasion and over the span of more than a few years. But today, I finally got it.

I wasn't delusional, though. Gemma gave me her number because she needed something from me, and I needed something from her. It was transactional, practical, and it needed to stay that way.

Did I just shoot myself in the foot where Gemma was involved? No doubt about it. Despite having her number, I just moved her further into the off-limits territory by making her my roommate-dog-sitter-part-time-niece-nanny.

But Gemma needed help, and this was a way I could help her. I *wanted* to be someone that could help people. Julian might not like that I was doing this behind his back, but I hoped in the long run he would see that I was trying to support his sister in the same way he might. In the same way I might support my own siblings if more of them were here.

"Are you going to date Coach B?"

I sighed, watching as Chloe licked the rim of her ice cream cone, desperately trying to keep it from melting down the sides despite the sun blasting on us as we walked back to my apartment.

"No," I said decisively. "I'm not going to date Coach B, Little Lo."

She wrinkled her nose. "I'm not little anymore."

"You're little to me."

Chloe scoffed before turning her chin up and giving me a stern glare. "Why?"

"Because I have a couple feet and a hundred some pounds on you."

"No." She groaned dramatically. "Why aren't you going to date Coach B?"

I should have known it wouldn't be that easy to escape the subject of Gemma and our number exchange.

"Coach B doesn't want to date me."

Coach B wanted a place to live—that was it.

"Have you asked her?" Chloe persisted.

"Well, no," I admitted.

"You should ask her," Chloe said with the definitive note of a girl who had spent far too much time as an only child.

"We'll see, Lo," I laughed. "Don't count on it."

I thought about telling her what I *did* ask Coach B but decided against it. There was a good chance Gemma would say no to my idea, and then I'd have to let down a hopeful Chloe. Nothing was worse than that.

Gemma told me to sleep on it, but I didn't need to. Hell, I'd already sent her my address so she could look up the location and told her to let me know if she wanted to come over and see the place. She hadn't responded—not a good sign.

With a glance down at my niece, I stifled a laugh as she tried to clean her sticky fingers on a napkin that was making more of a mess than helping. Luckily, we were only another block from home, and as soon as we entered my apartment, I pointed at the sink. I already had puppy paw marks all over the place; I didn't need sticky kid hands, too.

"Where's Winnie?" she asked excitedly as soon as her hands were clean.

"I've got to take her out," I said. "Wanna come?"

Chloe nodded with enthusiasm as she followed me to get the little rascal. I let Lo harness Winnie and take the leash as we wandered to the pet area on the rooftop of my building. We stayed up there for an hour, letting Winnie run free before the heat became unbearable, and we retreated into the air-conditioned building again.

Deciding that was enough activity for a Sunday, I threw on the TV and kicked back while Chloe continued to play with the furry tornado in my living room. Periodically, I checked my phone and shoved down the disappointment whenever I saw that Gemma hadn't replied to my text yet.

When my sister showed up around five o'clock, she noticed my preoccupation.

"Waiting for a text?" she asked, leaning against my kitchen countertop in her scrubs. With her honey-colored hair falling out of her messy bun and her dead-tired expression, you'd think she'd be too exhausted to give me shit. But no, of course that wasn't the case. "A girl?"

"Yes," I drawled, "technically, I am waiting for a text from a girl, but it isn't what you think."

Nat pressed her lips together with a little hum of disbelief.

I sighed. After a glance at the living room to check that Chloe and Winnie were still passed out on the couch together, I asked Nat what she thought about my idea to have Lo's skating instructor move in for the football season.

To say the conversation came as a shock to Nat was an understatement.

"Wow," she said once I was finished. "I didn't realize you knew Gemma."

"I didn't realize she was the same person as Coach B until

today," I replied with a shrug. "I usually wait for Lo outside the rink."

Nat nodded, and I could see the wheels turning in her head while she quietly considered what I'd told her. It was making me nervous.

"What's going on in that head of yours, Nat?" I asked when I couldn't bear it anymore.

My sister heaved a sigh. "Well, I think Gemma's pretty great. I mean...I don't know her well, but I've watched her at Chloe's practices the last couple of weeks. She's definitely worlds better than the lady who was coaching when Lo first started. And knowing that she's Julian's sister makes me feel that much more comfortable with her. If she's willing to help out with Chloe, that would be amazing. I don't have a lot of other options right now."

Relief spread through me, more palpable than I would have thought. I really didn't want Nat to hate my idea. And her liking Gemma was a step in the right direction. Although, there was still something Nat wasn't saying.

I raised a brow. "I'm waiting for the *but*."

Nat pinned me with a look. And then she started drumming her fingers on the countertop.

"She's also very pretty," she said finally.

My stomach soured.

"I'm aware," I said, trying to keep that sourness out of my voice.

"Oh, I'm sure you are," Nat laughed dryly.

Great. If my own sister didn't even trust me to keep it in my pants, could I even really blame Julian when he tried to keep me away from his sister? Jesus.

"It's not like that," I grunted. "It's just a mutually beneficial situation."

"Uh-huh." The corner of Nat's mouth tugged up in a half-smirk. "I know of other things that can be mutually beneficial, too."

"Well, we're not going to do those things, Nat," I said through clenched teeth. "She's Julian's sister."

I wasn't sure what bothered me more: that I had to commit to not touching Gemma Briggs for the next few months or that I had to convince my sister that I was capable of it.

"Okay." Nat nodded, her voice taking on a singsongy quality. "If you say so."

I rolled my eyes.

"I say so."

After keeping me waiting for a whole twenty-four fucking hours, Gemma texted me back.

> SHE'S JULIAN'S SISTER, NOAH: Thanks for sending that information over!

> Are you always this notoriously bad at texting, or are you reserving that for me?

> SHE'S JULIAN'S SISTER, NOAH: What are you talking about?

> I sent you that an entire day ago.

> SHE'S JULIAN'S SISTER, NOAH: That was actually a pretty good turn around as far as I'm concerned.

> So you ARE notoriously bad at texting. That makes me feel better.

> SHE'S JULIAN'S SISTER, NOAH: I was giving you time to sleep on it.

I don't need time to sleep on it.

SHE'S JULIAN'S SISTER, NOAH: Well, maybe I needed time to sleep on it.

You could have slept on it after texting me back.

SHE'S JULIAN'S SISTER, NOAH: Are you always this notoriously argumentative, or are you reserving that for me?

I don't think argumentative is the word you're looking for.

More... impatient.

SHE'S JULIAN'S SISTER, NOAH: Ah, not used to having to wait for girls to text you back, huh?

I winced at her reply and how it was, well, true. When I texted girls, they typically replied immediately. And then they usually never left me alone, as was evidenced by the slew of unread text messages in my phone from just today.

I don't know how to reply to that without sounding like a cocky asshole.

SHE'S JULIAN'S SISTER, NOAH: I think it's too late.

Damn. So... how would you like to live with a cocky asshole?

SHE'S JULIAN'S SISTER, NOAH: I was thinking we should talk some more first.

Sure. Why don't you come on over, and then you can see the place, too.

SHE'S JULIAN'S SISTER, NOAH: Okay, yeah. That sounds good.

Tomorrow morning?

SHE'S JULIAN'S SISTER, NOAH: You really are
impatient.

8am? 9am?

SHE'S JULIAN'S SISTER, NOAH: You're lucky I'm an
early riser, Noah.

8:00 it is.

I couldn't say why I was so impatient to solidify this deal with
Gemma, but I wanted her to agree to our arrangement really
fucking bad. It would just be nice to have someone I trusted
around so I wouldn't have to worry about Winnie or Lo when I
was out of town. That was it—nothing else.

I had no other reason, absolutely *no other reason*, for really
wanting Gemma Briggs to move in with me.

Winnie bolted for Gemma as soon as I opened the door, and it
saved me from having to form a coherent greeting.

Just one look at her, and I was rethinking everything.

Maybe this was a terrible idea after all. Maybe, although I
hated to admit it, Nat was right; Gemma was way too fucking
pretty to be allowed anywhere near me. This morning, she wore
an airy white sundress that made her look like a goddamn angel.
Her long, coppery hair looked so soft as it fell around her shoulders, and fuck, I just wanted to bury my fingers in it.

I was so screwed—so wildly screwed.

All I could do was gape at Gemma as she entered the apartment. Luckily, she didn't seem bothered, flashing a wide grin at
me before dropping down to coo at Winnie and scoop the
wiggling puppy into her arms.

"Oh, I *love* her," she laughed, her smile lighting up the
goddamn room.

27

I cleared my throat. "She seems to love you, too."

Gemma's eyes rolled up with that little bit of sass I'd seen from her before. "She's a puppy. Pretty sure she loves everyone."

"Nah." I shrugged off the lie; Winnie definitely loved everyone she'd met so far. "I made coffee. Want some?"

"I would love—" She stopped midsentence, wincing. "No, that's okay."

"You sure?" A chuckle slipped out of me at her mixed message. "You know, if you're that worried I'm trying to poison you, that might be something we should discuss before you move in."

"No." Gemma shook her head, and I was grateful to see her smile emerge again. "That's not it."

I frowned, considering what else it might be. I tried again. "Well, if Julian told you I'm bad in the kitchen, he was lying through his teeth. I made his ass dinner all the time in college, and he wasn't complaining then."

Winnie took that moment to lick the side of Gemma's face, and the beauty in my front entryway responded with an adorable peal of laughter that trailed into her words. "Believe it or not, Julian has not mentioned your skills as a chef or a barista."

"Well, that's a relief," I mumbled before leading Gemma to the kitchen. She set Winnie down on the ground while I grabbed a mug from the cabinet and filled it up. Then I watched her pointedly over the rim of the coffee cup as I let the black drug slide down my throat.

Gemma stared, not backing down from the tension that suddenly simmered up, her gaze bright as she lifted one brow and tugged her bottom lip between her teeth. Heat coiled in my gut.

"Are you trying to prove it's not poisonous right now?" she asked finally.

"Maybe." I swallowed hard, putting the cup on the counter again. "Did it work?"

"Pretty effective technique," she said with a nod, her eyes flicking to my mouth as if assessing whether my lips were about to turn blue or if foam would appear. Or maybe there was another reason; I couldn't be sure, and I didn't want to think too much about that. "But I'm trying to...cut down on my caffeine intake, and I'm guessing that's not decaf."

"You would be right," I admitted, a twinge of regret coating my reply. "What about something else? Let me grab you a water at the very least."

"Water would be great." She smiled politely, and I rushed to pour her a glass, setting it in front of her. She took a sip, and my eyes swept over her, curious.

"An early morning riser without even a lick of caffeine, huh?"

"Well..." Gemma fidgeted, twirling her thumbs between her clasped hands. "I actually wanted to—" She broke off again, her eyes growing wide this time with alarm. With *panic*. She clapped a hand to her mouth, muffling her one-word plea. "*Bathroom?*"

"Shit," I sputtered, jumping into action as I ushered Gemma down the hall. I flung up the toilet cover as we dove into the bathroom, thanking the Lord I'd cleaned my porcelain throne before she came over because, sure enough, a second later, Gemma's face was buried inside it as she purged whatever breakfast she had this morning.

By the sound of it, it wasn't much. Actually, it sounded a lot like she didn't have anything in her stomach at all. Poor girl.

I stepped into the bathroom behind her, pulling her hair back from her face and ignoring the way she slapped at my legs to try to make me leave. When I'd thought about burying my fingers in her hair earlier, this wasn't exactly what I'd had in mind.

With her head still in the toilet, Gemma flung a few garbled words at me—ones I ignored because they were telling me to get out. I couldn't get myself to do that, not when she had a white-knuckle grip on the toilet bowl and a trickle of tears streaming down her face. I wasn't squeamish. It was sort of a trait in our family, considering how Nat and Blake cut open bodies for a living.

With a gentle hush, I dropped to the floor behind Gemma, stroking her back. She shivered before leaning into my touch slightly, trying to catch her breath. It took a minute or two before she finally lifted her head and peeked back at me.

I flashed her an apologetic look. "I really hope you believe me when I say I didn't poison the water."

"I believe you." She laughed weakly, wiping at her eyes before attempting a smile. It was wobbly at best. "Because there's something I actually wanted to talk to you about. You know, in case you don't want to share your apartment with a girl who spends most of her mornings sitting in front of a toilet."

I felt my eyes grow wide. "Are you...sick?" I asked before biting down on my tongue because, obviously, she was sick—in some way, shape, or form. Hopefully not in a serious way, though.

Or maybe not, considering how Gemma immediately shook her head with a wry twist of her lips.

"No, I'm not sick."

She blinked up at me, and her watery eyes seemed extra blue all of a sudden.

"I'm pregnant."

CHAPTER FOUR

gemma

I WISHED I could have an interaction with Noah London that wasn't wholly mortifying. But here I was, sitting on his bathroom floor while hugging his toilet. I'd flushed it and closed the lid, but that didn't mean it wasn't a stark reminder of how I'd vomited into it a minute ago.

Meanwhile, all Noah seemed to be able to do was blink at me.

"Pregnant?" he repeated, slack-jawed.

I nodded while gripping the toilet, afraid that nausea would return if I moved too much.

"Okay...well...we can, we can work with that." The way Noah stumbled over his words while rubbing the five-o'clock shadow on his jaw was sort of adorable. He was usually such a smooth talker. "But it's...up to you, of course."

Despite his obvious surprise, Noah was calm, and after a beat or two of silence, he returned to stroking my back. The creaking of a door was the only sound that echoed in the bathroom, followed by the pitter-patter of paws. Out of the corner of my eye, I saw Winnie slump onto the cool floor tiles, her tongue hanging out of her mouth. Meanwhile, Noah continued to rub my back. His hands were firm, strong.

It felt manipulative to let him take care of me like this. Noah put on a cocky smirk in public, but I knew from what Juniper had told me that he had a sweet, kind side. I was sure he wanted nothing to do with me but likely didn't know how to extract himself from the situation.

Sighing, I closed my eyes for a moment. I'd let him rub my back for just another minute, and then I'd return to reality—a reality where *nothing* really felt like it was up to me.

"I wish the baby's dad had reacted this well," I mumbled, more to myself than anything.

Noah stilled. The soothing circles on my back stopped.

"How did he react?" he asked, his voice strained—like it was being forced out through clenched teeth.

I appreciated that Noah skipped the obvious question. I didn't intend to keep the baby's dad a secret, but I didn't love talking about him, either.

"By telling me he didn't want anything to do with us."

It wasn't just me anymore. It was us—this baby and me.

"What a piece of fucking garbage." The intensity in Noah's low voice startled me, but I didn't hate it. Silas *was* a piece of garbage. A trickle of goose bumps rose on my skin. "Julian broke all his goddamn bones when he found out, right?"

It was my turn to still as I bit my tongue, looking down at the closed toilet lid. I heard Noah's quick intake of breath behind me before he said my name in a gritted sort of warning.

"Gemma..."

I pressed my lips together, still trying to hold on to the truth for a little longer.

At this point, Noah sounded pleading. "Gemma, please tell me your brother knows you're pregnant."

"I can't..." I tapped the top of the toilet lid absently while biting the inside of my cheek. "I can't do that."

"Christ." Noah heaved a sigh, and I peeked over my shoulder to see him leaning back against the bathroom wall, running a hand through his hair. When he caught me looking, he met my gaze and held it. "So to recap, *I'm* going to kill the human piece of garbage who left you alone after getting you pregnant, and then your *brother* is going to kill *me* when he finds out that I knew about it first?"

I swallowed past the lump in my throat, unsure if it was from the fiery look in Noah's eye or the guilt in my gut from dragging him into this.

"I'd rather just avoid all the killing, please."

He shook his head, still running his hand aggressively through his hair. "Might not be possible," he mumbled.

God, coming here had been such a mistake. I should have thought it through more. Slept on it for a few more days. Realized that Noah would never go along with it after he knew all the details.

The problem was that I didn't have a few more days, and I should probably stop wasting my time sitting here on Noah London's bathroom floor.

"I think I should just go," I decided before pushing myself off the ground. Or rather, *attempting* to push myself off the ground. Noah didn't let me get far before he wrapped a powerful arm around my middle and brought me back to the tiled floor, where he was straddling me from behind.

"No, wait." His soft sigh breezed through my hair as he held me captive against his chest. "Why?"

"What?" My brain was too jumbled from our position and all the ways we were touching for me to make sense of what he was asking.

"Why do you want to leave?" He slowly released his grip, his hand falling to my thigh instead—my *bare* thigh that my dress hardly covered as I straddled the toilet in the same way that he straddled me. *Christ.*

I kept my eyes trained forward, reminding myself to keep breathing while Noah's thumb started moving in soothing circles on my thigh. "I haven't told Julian because I don't want to mess up his life, and I don't want to mess yours up, either."

Noah scoffed, his breath fanning the back of my neck while his hands fell to the ground. I let out a breath that contained both relief and disappointment. "You're not messing up my life," he insisted. "You're here because we can help each other. Unless you're no longer interested?"

I floundered for a second, debating if I should insist I wasn't, even though I was. But I couldn't find it in me to lie. I was so tired. "No, I'm interested."

"Okay, then let's have that talk we were going to have." Noah's eyes flicked around the bathroom. Although it was updated and sparkling with a brightness that made me wonder if Noah employed a housekeeper, it wasn't very large—clearly, just a half bath meant for guests. The only decor was an out-of-place looking wall calendar hanging above us. "Should we stay here or move somewhere else?"

"Move somewhere else," I said, feeling the tight knot in my stomach dissipate. I needed to put a little space between the off-limits NFL player and my currently overactive hormones.

With a decisive nod, Noah pushed to his feet before holding his hand out to help me up.

Deciding there was no turning back now, I took it.

Noah guided me to the couch, keeping close and not moving his eyes from me while we walked. He seemed afraid that I'd pass out any minute, and honestly, fainting wasn't out of the realm of possibility. I couldn't keep down any food this morning, and my stomach was completely gutted.

Once I was settled into the corner of his massive cloudlike sectional couch, Noah brought me a glass of water, which I sipped gratefully.

"Is there anything else I can get you?"

I shook my head.

"Are you sure?"

"Just sit down, please. I'm fine, don't worry."

I'd gotten used to the morning sickness routine over the last few weeks.

"Seems like *someone* needs to worry," Noah muttered grumpily as he sank onto the couch next to me and crossed his arms over his broad chest, making his biceps pop. Internally, I groaned.

"I don't want anyone to worry," I pressed. "That's why Julian doesn't know."

"I was thinking more about the man responsible for putting you in this position." Noah's handsome face dipped into a scowl. "He's a fucking asshole for not worrying. How could he—"

"It's okay, Noah."

I really didn't want to talk about Silas.

Noah opened his mouth, undoubtedly to protest, but I cut him off, changing the subject.

"When do you have to start traveling for the season?"

I had a feeling there was still a buffer of time between when Noah would need me to move in and when I would have to be out of my apartment. I was running out of time, and if I needed to figure out a place to stay for an interim, I should get on that.

He sighed, giving me a look that said he wasn't done with the topic of Silas, but he'd let it go for now.

"My first trip is in a couple weeks, and then I'll be on the go a lot. It probably won't even feel like we're roommates." He relaxed a little, uncrossing his arms. "I have a guest suite over there," he added, pointing to a door off the kitchen. "So you should have a good amount of space to yourself if you decide to move in."

I nodded, taking that in. Noah was trying to reassure me that I'd have privacy and free rein most of the time, even though this was *his* luxury apartment with high-end appliances, sweeping views of the city, and enough space in his living room to fit my entire unit. God, this place was amazing.

"Are you sure this isn't too imposing?" I asked, still feeling uncertain. The last thing I wanted was to take advantage of his generosity.

"The opposite—it would be a relief." Having followed us out of the bathroom, Winnie took that opportune moment to jump into Noah's lap, and he chuckled, looking down at her. "That is if you're still willing to keep an eye on this wild child."

"I would be more than happy to," I rushed to confirm. "And if Natalie ever needed someone to watch Chloe when you're not around, I'd love to help."

Working at the club had and would give me experience around children, but being their skating coach was entirely different from taking care of them at home. And I would take any practice in that department that I could.

Noah smiled at the mention of his sister. "You've met Nat, then?"

I nodded. "Just in passing at practices."

I ran into Natalie on my first day working at Back Bay, shortly after learning I was pregnant. I accidentally mistook another parent for Chloe's dad, and Natalie was quick to let me know I'd never see his cheating, good-for-nothing face around the rink. It gave me a sense of...camaraderie. She was a single mom, and soon I would be, too.

"You know, I'm surprised that you left St. Maverick's," Noah said, considering me carefully. "I know how renowned their skating program is. Haven't they won like every championship in the last five years that there is to win? I assume the pay was higher, and considering the pregnancy, I'd think it would be worth..."

My mood must have leaked into my expression because Noah's words melted away at the look I gave him.

I cleared my throat and dropped my gaze. It wasn't Noah's fault; he made a good observation. I should have stayed at St.

Mav's so I could afford this baby. So I wouldn't be in the position I was in now. But I acted rashly—with my hurt heart and not my level head.

I came here today knowing that I'd need to be up-front about, well, everything. There was no reason to keep secrets from Noah, and honestly, he should know exactly what he was getting himself into. I could only imagine how having a pregnant, lonely roommate might cramp his style. So I sighed and prepared to tell him the truth.

"You're right," I said. "It's a great program. So many of my former skaters have gone on to be in professional ice shows and have great careers. But..." I sighed before admitting, "the baby's dad is the athletic director at St. Maverick's."

Noah's eyes hardened. I imagined this was similar to his game face, and right now, the opponent he wanted to obliterate was Silas. "You've got to be fucking kidding me."

"I wish I was kidding."

I chewed the inside of my cheek as I thought about *how much* I wished I was kidding. What I would do to go back in time and never go for drinks with my boss. Not because of the pregnancy, but because I'd have to live with the half memories forever, the wondering. That, and the consequences of having to uproot my entire life. I was still struggling with how to handle everything. The last few weeks had been a mess. I was a mess. A mess sitting on Noah London's plush couch in his fancy apartment.

I wanted this pregnancy. I *really* did. But I didn't feel equipped to handle it right now, and I needed to change that. I was *going* to change that. Because I was on my way to becoming a twenty-eight-year-old single mom, and I had to be ready to do this on my own.

Sure, I'd have my family to lean on. I knew my dad, in particular, would do anything to help me. Both my parents, of course, but I'd always been closest with my dad. Still, though...it wouldn't be the same as having a partner, and I didn't expect to change the *single* part of my new title anytime soon. What guy would want to sign up to play dad for another man's baby? I couldn't imagine there'd be many takers on that account.

"Did he *make* you quit?" Noah pressed. Whether he realized it or not, his body leaned toward me, intensity rolling off him in waves.

"No, I just couldn't stand being around him anymore. He was someone I looked up to, someone who I thought shared my values. But now I know he's just a manipulative dick who wanted me to lie to everyone about how I got pregnant. I couldn't stay there and pretend that everything was okay. That it was okay for him to do that."

"Were you—" Noah broke off with a quick inhale, shaking his head. His arms returned to their crossed position, his hands flexing into fists. His jaw clenched as though he was physically forcing his lips to remain locked, refusing to let his question out. "Never mind. It isn't any of my business."

I didn't say a word for a long minute, debating whether I should give Noah the details he was looking for. Noah was the only person I'd told about this, and it felt good to let the secret out —at least to someone. But I really didn't want to talk or think about Silas. So I settled on giving him different details.

"I quit the same day that he made his feelings about the baby clear," I said after swallowing past the emotion in my throat. "I took the first job offer I got the next week and started immediately at Back Bay, knowing I wouldn't make enough to stay in my apartment. But risking being unemployed was worse."

I sank further into his cloud couch, wondering if I could disappear inside it and never come out. "I've applied for more part-time gigs but so far haven't gotten lucky."

Noah grunted as he started stroking a hand down Winnie's back absently. And maybe with too much force, although Winnie seemed perfectly content as her eyes drifted shut. "Well, now you have one."

"What?"

"A part-time gig. Watching Winnie. And maybe Chloe sometimes, too."

I stared at him. I'd learned that staring men straight in the eye usually spooked the hell out of them. Working in collegiate sports taught me how to do that and do it well. But Noah was a different breed, and he returned my stare, not backing down.

"You *really* don't have to pay me," I finally said. "Having a place to stay is more than enough. It's already incredibly generous, Noah. I can find some retail job to bring in some extra money."

Noah appeared slightly affronted that I even suggested the idea. Although, if I worked another job, that meant less availability for Winnie and Chloe.

"No."

Okay, maybe not a little affronted. Very affronted.

I opened my mouth to assure him that I would absolutely work my schedule around his away games so that I was available when he was gone, but he beat me to it.

"You can't work yourself into the ground, Gemma," he said in a long, loud exhale.

I clucked my tongue. "Seems ironic for you to say, considering you literally get worked into the ground at your job."

"Only when my offensive line sucks."

I laughed, but Noah didn't crack a smile.

"But seriously, it's not the same," he added as if his flat expression didn't give away just how *serious* he was.

I flashed a doubtful look, and his jaw clenched—again.

"You're *pregnant*, Gemma."

"Believe me, I know." Heat spiked beneath my skin, the indignation and hurt burning inside me. "I'm very aware of just how *pregnant* I am, Noah."

My harsh words left a wake of silence in the apartment until Noah broke it.

"Listen, I'm sorry." He dragged a hand over his face, lowering his voice. "Of course you know that. I just...I'm trying to think like

Julian would, you know? He's going to be pissed if he finds out you're working your ass off like that while you're growing a whole human inside you. You need to take care of yourself."

The fire drained out of me as I took in the consideration and concern on Noah's face. But I wasn't entirely convinced it was for me.

"Admit it." Winnie stumbled off Noah's lap, across the couch cushion, and onto mine. I tucked her into my arms. She was so soft and sweet—the perfect golden puppy. "You're just scared of Julian and what he'll do if he finds out about our arrangement. More than me, I think."

"Pfft. Afraid of Julian?" Noah grumbled but then stole Winnie back from me—almost like he needed her to be his emotional support animal at the thought of Julian getting anywhere close to this situation. "No way."

"He did break Greg Kennedy's fingers in high school. Ruined his whole football career, likely," I said thoughtfully. "But that was over Juniper because he'd cheated on her. Not me, of course."

"Yeah," Noah cut in dryly. "He was *that* obsessed with your best friend, but he didn't let himself have her until ten fucking years later. And you know who *that* was over?"

I winced before he could say it.

"You."

He was right; I shouldn't have implied that Julian didn't love me or wouldn't protect me as much as he did his fiancée. It was just different.

"Yeah, so...I think we've just settled why Julian never needs to know about all of this," I concluded lightly. "For the sake of everyone's fingers."

Noah sighed, his lips twisting wryly. I knew he disagreed with me.

"You won't be able to hide the pregnancy forever." He stared at my stomach pointedly. I grabbed a pillow to hide behind, hugging it to me, and his eyes immediately lifted guiltily.

"No, I won't," I agreed. "But I can hide it until I have a solid plan. By the time your season is over or close to being over, I'll have enough money saved up to find my own place. And then when I tell Julian and the rest of my family, they won't need to worry about a thing because I'll have it all figured out."

"You're sure this is what you want to do?"

I nodded. I had to be sure. This was what I *had* to do.

"I'm sure." I flashed him a smile that I hoped looked more confident than I felt.

"Okay." Noah set Winnie back on the floor and stood, careful not to step on her as the puppy danced at his heels. "Let me show you around the rest of the apartment, then."

I followed Noah through the kitchen to the guest suite he'd mentioned earlier, which was at least twice the size of the only bedroom at my current apartment. I eyed the massive bed longingly before Noah led me to other parts of the penthouse, including an office and a state-of-the-art home gym.

Yeah, I wasn't going to find a better deal than this.

Eventually, we wandered back to the front door.

"So you said your first trip was in a couple weeks?" I clarified.

He nodded. "When do you need to be out of your apartment?"

"Oh, um. I think like, in a couple weeks as well."

"You're a shit liar, Gemma." The corner of his mouth lifted in a crooked smile. "Text me your address, and I'll swing by tomorrow to help you move stuff."

"What? No, Noah—"

"Text me your address, or I'll call Juniper to ask for it," he amended, changing tactics.

"You can't call Juni," I panicked. "That girl doesn't know how to keep anything from my brother these days."

"Then you should probably just text me your address." He shrugged, opening the door for me with a growing grin. "For the sake of my fingers, Gemma."

I glared at him. "You're way too used to getting what you want, Noah London."

That twinkle I'd grown accustomed to seeing in his eyes

returned as I stepped out of the apartment. "I don't know how to respond to that without sounding like a cocky asshole," he said.

"Too late," I called back on my way down the hallway.

Even though he couldn't see my face, I still tried to hide my smile. And then when I got back to my apartment, I texted him my address.

Guess I was moving in with Noah London.

CHAPTER FIVE

S ILAS TAYLOR. WHAT a motherfucking sleazeball.
   I stared down at the picture of St. Maverick's athletic
director on my phone, wishing I could wipe that smug expression
off his face. The only thing keeping my pissy mood in check was
the knowledge that Silas Taylor wouldn't be looking at *anyone* like
that once Julian learned he'd knocked up his sister and then told
her to fuck off.

God, I couldn't wait for that day. I hoped to hell that Julian
would let me tag along.

A flash of copper hair caught my attention, and I shoved my
phone into my pocket, snapping into action. Gemma had a
teetering pile of boxes in her arms as she slipped through the
front entrance of her apartment complex.

I swore, racing forward to grab the load from her arms. She
was reluctant to let me help; I felt the stubborn resistance in how
she gripped the boxes, but she didn't say anything.

"When you said you were coming down, I thought you meant
you were letting me in so I could come up and *help* you."

"I just figured I should bring a load if I was coming down."
She wiped a few beads of sweat off her forehead. "Save some
time."

"You brought a load, alright," I muttered, maneuvering her piles of boxes into the back of my SUV. They weren't light. "Fuck. How much can you bench, Gemma?"

"Oh, I don't know," she said, waving the comment away and turning on her heel to lead me back into the apartment complex. I wasn't fooled, though. I saw her eyes light up when she saw my home gym yesterday. I'd bet anything Gemma had all her PRs memorized.

I followed her through a foyer, noting how the old building seemed to have been recently renovated. But then she brought me to an elevator that didn't seem nearly as new as the tile in the entryway, and I half wondered if we should have gone with the stairs instead.

"Did your doctor mention any restrictions for the gym or the rink?" I asked, deciding not to comment on the state of our ride to the fifth floor.

Gemma froze, giving me a funny look.

"Was that an obvious question?" I chuckled, nervous I'd said the wrong thing. "I obviously don't know the first thing about pregnancy."

I still hadn't completely wrapped my head around that— Gemma being pregnant. It bothered me more than I cared to admit, but mostly because it meant that a sleazeball named Silas had fucking touched her. I hated that. I hated how he'd treated her and how I couldn't shake the urge to treat her better when it wasn't my place. I hated that she'd forfeited her job—her whole goddamn livelihood—to get away from him.

Although if that hadn't happened, we wouldn't have run into each other, and we wouldn't even be here.

Gemma relaxed again, her lips twitching as those dazzling blue eyes swept over me. We stood on opposite sides of the elevator, her leaning against one wall and me leaning against the other. The space between us seemed to stretch forever, and I resisted the urge to lessen the distance.

"Well, Noah. When sperm travels through the cervix and into

the uterus—" She broke off with a grin at my expression, and then her sparkling laugh drifted into a sigh that sounded almost sad. "I considered making a speech about how when a man loves a woman...but clearly, that isn't necessary to make a baby. So the technical version will have to work."

Gemma looked pointedly down at her stomach at the last words, and before I could conjure up a response, the elevator dinged, and the doors slid apart. Gemma slipped through them as fast as she could, and I had to quicken my pace to keep up with her, watching her long, shiny hair fly behind her as she damn near sprinted down the hallway.

"Eager to get out of here?" I teased when Gemma stopped in front of a door labeled 512.

She grimaced as she glanced back at me over her shoulder. "I told my landlord I would be out of here by eleven."

"It's 10:39, Gemma."

The door clicked open, and she raced through it. "Why do you think I was trying to save time earlier?"

I ran a hand down my face. "Jesus, you should have told me to come like two hours ago."

"I didn't want to inconvenience you more than I already am."

She started stuffing blankets into a bag, and I paused in the doorway to her apartment, taking in the pile of boxes and worn, weathered flooring. The space was decently sized, the walls painted in pastel colors that reminded me of the girl packing her things. A pang of sadness hit me as I realized what she had to give up, and then anger came crashing in, too. Just another thing that I hated about *him*.

"Gemma."

She ignored me, wandering through her packed belongings like she was looking for something. I was sure she was just using it as an excuse not to look at me, though. So I followed, weaving through the piles until she was within reach. "Gemma," I repeated, wrapping my fingers around her forearm.

She stilled, her breaths labored as she kept her eyes downcast.

"If we're going to spend the next six months living together, you can't do that."

"What?" She blinked, her long lashes sweeping up so I finally had her eyes. They sucked me in until I felt trapped—but in the best way possible. This was what living with her would be like, wasn't it? Hell, I might not make it.

"You can't keep things from me because you don't want to bother me," I clarified.

"But I *really* don't want to bother you, Noah."

"Are you afraid I'm going to rescind my offer? Because I won't," I assured her. "I promise. I wouldn't do that to you."

"I just feel like such a burden," she whispered.

The anger kept rolling in, spreading through me like wildfire. Silas Taylor was such a fucking dead man. Gemma was doing me a favor by moving in, but she couldn't see that at all. And there had to be a reason for her worries.

"You're not a burden, and this isn't charity. You're helping me. I'm helping you. It's a two-way street." She bit down on her lip, and I could tell she wasn't totally buying what I was saying. "This is because of what he said to you, isn't it?" When I realized I was still gripping her arm, I let it go. "He made you feel this way. When you told him—"

"Noah, it's fine." She shook her head, but I didn't miss how her eyes glossed over before they darted away. "It doesn't matter. *He* doesn't matter."

I pursed my lips but didn't argue the point. If Gemma needed to get her stuff out of here as soon as possible, then that was what I should focus on. I could worry about how to deal with Silas Taylor another time.

But there *would* be another time.

46

I tossed Gemma the bag with blankets in it when we arrived back at my place, specifically picking something light for her to carry. The idea of watching any girl break their back when I wasn't the one doing it didn't sit right with me. Gemma rolled her eyes like she knew what I was doing but didn't say a word about it.

In fact, Gemma was unusually quiet on our way up to my unit, meaning it was our second unsettled elevator ride of the day. And the lingering awkward tension only worsened when we ran into my neighbor Summer.

"This one's moving in already, huh?"

She was clearly about to enter her apartment but just *had* to take time out of her fucking miserable life to harass us. I wasn't sure what I ever did to Summer, but she hated me.

Okay, that wasn't necessarily true. I had an idea of what I did to her, but I still didn't think it warranted the attitude she gave me on a daily basis.

"*This one* has a name," Gemma snapped before I even had a chance to consider what Summer said. Usually, I let her snide little comments go in one ear and out the other.

Summer opened her mouth to reply, and I quickly added, "And we won't be telling you what it is."

I didn't want word to get around about Gemma. If the media caught a whiff, it would only be a matter of time before Julian found out. And while I didn't particularly like the idea of hiding this arrangement from my friend, the last thing I wanted was for him to find out from someone other than Gemma or me.

"Hm, protective," she murmured as we walked past her. I guided Gemma to the opposite side of the hallway than Summer, blocking her from view. "Interesting."

"No, it's called common decency," I called over my shoulder. "Because my friends don't deserve to be harassed by you."

"Friends?" she laughed. "Is that what we're calling them now?"

I gritted my teeth but pressed on, motioning for Gemma to ignore her and keep walking.

47

But we didn't make it all the way into my apartment before Summer conjured up something else to say.

"I'm not the one who uses women for—"

I slammed my apartment door on the end of her sentence, but I knew what it was. It was always the same.

"Fuck, I'm sorry about that," I said immediately, setting the heavy boxes on the ground and moving to take the pillows and blankets from Gemma. My insides sank as I realized what she likely thought after Summer's spewings. "I promise the rest of my neighbors aren't so..."

"Jealous?" Gemma finished for me, cocking her head slightly with a lopsided grin.

"I was going to say hostile."

Gemma shrugged. "I think she's just jealous she's not invited to the slumber party."

That squeezed a laugh out of me. "I don't know about that, but Summer never used to be like that until I rejected her."

"See? Jealous." The expression on Gemma's face remained neutral, but it didn't make me feel a lick better.

"Look, about what she said—"

Gemma held up a hand to stop me. "You don't have to explain anything, Noah."

"Right." My lips twisted. "I forgot my reputation precedes me."

"I just meant that it isn't my place to have an opinion on what your sex life is like."

Oh, great. We were really having this conversation, weren't we?

"I don't use women for sex," I said flatly, feeling like she missed that point.

"That's good." She considered me, lazily assessing my face like she was looking for a lie she knew wasn't there. "I didn't really think you did."

I picked up one of the boxes again, needing something to do with my hands. "You have more faith in me than a lot of people, and you barely know me," I muttered, slipping away from Gemma to put the boxes in her new room.

"My brother wouldn't be friends with someone who used and abused women," she called after me.

But it made me scoff as I slid the box into the room and returned to grab another. "You do remember his reaction when he thought I was going on a date with Juniper, right?"

I wasn't sure why I was arguing against her about this. Of course I didn't *want* her to think that I used women for sex, but she was giving me the benefit of the doubt when I wasn't sure I deserved it. Everyone, even my own sister, thought I was a fucking player. There was no reason for Gemma to have this much faith in me. I might be doing her a little favor, but I didn't want her looking at me with stars in her eyes. I'd only disappoint her.

That was the last thing I wanted, even though I was terrified it would happen. I really wanted to be someone Gemma could count on right now when she felt like she had no one. In reality, she had a million people in her life that would be a better support system than me, but until she was ready to tell them, I wanted to step up to the plate. I hoped to hell I wouldn't mess it up, but I didn't really know what I was doing. I didn't know anything about pregnancy, hadn't lived with someone else since college, and had never even had a girl sleep over at my apartment. No one was allowed to stay the night.

And now Gemma was going to be here every night.

And every morning.

"Because he was *in love* with Juniper," Gemma emphasized, bringing me back to our conversation as she crossed her arms over her chest.

"And for some reason, he still worried I'd take her home with me afterward," I grunted, grabbing the next box.

"Did *Juniper* seem worried about that?"

"No." I shook my head with a shrug as I returned to where Gemma stood. "She seemed to know that it wasn't a real date. Just a dinner between friends."

Gemma raised her brow as if to say, *See?* But I shook my head again, waving off her reassurance. And that was when she moved closer.

"Noah, I told myself I wouldn't trust men who didn't deserve it. Not after...you know." Her hand moved over her stomach, which was still flat—no hint of pregnancy. But I did know.

"I know I come off as desperate, but I'm not *that* desperate," she continued. "I wouldn't be moving in if I thought you were an ass. And please don't let me being here keep you from living your life. If you have girls over or whatever, I won't say a word. I'll gladly hide in my room or leave for the night. You can do the good ol' tie-on-the-door thing."

Great. So she wasn't delusional, and she did think I was a playboy. Just a *nice* playboy. Somehow, none of that made me feel better.

"I'm not going to bring girls over while you're here," I said gruffly.

"Oh, you're practicing abstinence now?" she asked, looking wholly surprised.

I gritted my teeth together, her shock making the next words fall from my mouth for no reason other than the need to lash out. "No, I'll just use my away games for that."

"Oh."

Gemma didn't seem to know what to say to that, so I added, "You can have guys over if you want."

As soon as I said it, I bit down on my tongue to keep from taking it back. Watching other guys flirt with Gemma in my apartment was not how I wanted to spend my free time. And the thought of that happening when I was out of town? Fuck that.

Luckily, Gemma quickly brushed my offer aside with a sad smile that made my stomach turn. "I don't really think dating is a priority for me right now, but thanks."

"Dating is different from sex," I pointed out.

Why? Why did I point it out? I had no fucking clue besides the fact that I knew the distinction between sex and dating incredibly well. But the smart thing to do would be to end this conversation.

"Yeah..." Gemma winced, reaching to grab the pile of blankets again. She balled them in her arms as though she could hide behind them. "The thought of casual sex isn't appealing at the moment, considering the recent memories," she admitted.

My hackles rose up, my hands automatically balling into fists at the tone in her voice. "Did he hurt you?"

"No...not physically."

Her expression grew sullen, making me wonder exactly what happened that night with Silas Taylor. I probably wouldn't ever know, but that didn't stop me from wanting to. Mostly so I'd know how badly Taylor needed his ass kicked.

The silence fizzled, stretching between Gemma and me. She cocked her head to the side, assessing me again. And I needed to know why.

"Why are you looking at me like that?"

"Because you just proved why I don't need to worry about you." The small, sad smile reappeared. She walked to her room, throwing the blankets inside it before returning. "Come on, why don't we go get another load? It'll give me a chance to flick off your neighbor if we see her again."

I fought a grin at the thought of Gemma giving Summer the finger. I'd never had anyone fight for me before. To be honest, I wasn't sure I liked it.

Mostly because Gemma was wrong. She thought I was someone I wasn't; she had no idea I'd spent the last handful of years waiting for my chance to take her home and make her scream my fucking name.

Now she was living with me, and that chance had gone out the goddamn window.

But that didn't mean I knew how to stop myself from thinking about it.

eight years ago

NOAH

It took me approximately thirty-eight seconds after his sister walked through the door to realize that Julian was not stressed about her coming to visit.

No, the reason he'd paced the living room for the better part of the afternoon had to be almost entirely attributed to the girl who came with his sister.

I had no idea what her name was, but her hair was pulled up into a high ponytail, tied with a bow, and it swished dramatically as she snapped back at everything Julian had to say.

I couldn't help but grin at whatever was going on. I'd never seen anyone give Julian a run for his money like this. No fucking wonder he'd been stressing. I momentarily wondered who she was and why his sister had brought her but then decided I wasn't going to spend too long trying to figure it out. Not when I could be using Julian's preoccupation to my advantage.

Because while he was squaring off with the brunette, his sister was standing idly to the side, looking slightly out of place. And if Julian wasn't going to do it, I'd happily be the one to make her feel right at home.

CHAPTER SIX

I'D SPENT THE last week adjusting to the new normal that was living with Noah London.

For the most part, we stuck to our own spaces while we were home. But there were a few exceptions, including Winnie walks, where Noah taught me everything I'd need to know to puppy sit, and Chloe visits, when I'd come out of my room to hang out with Chloe and Uncle Noah while they waited for Natalie to pick her up.

I wanted Noah to see how seriously I took my side of this arrangement so he could be worry-free when he was out of town this season. Besides, spending time with Chloe and Winnie was not the chore that he was concerned it would be. Living at Noah's apartment—dog, kid, and hot NFL player combined—had been great.

That didn't mean *I* was great, though. The unsettled feeling in my gut had nothing to do with Noah or our living arrangement and a lot to do with the embryo the size of a cucumber seed growing in my belly.

I knew there were things I should be doing to prepare, but I was, for lack of a better word, frozen. The biggest hurdle in this mess had been finding a place to live, and the stress and panic of it had kept me moving. The past few months had been a blur of decision-making that was imminent, and now I felt...lost.

Noah and his offer had given me a sense of stability. I should have been able to breathe, relax, and refocus on my next step. I just couldn't seem to figure out what that even was. There were so many decisions I needed to make. *So* many. But they all swam in front of me in an endless stream of consciousness, and I didn't know which to pick first. On more than one occasion, I'd picked up the phone to call Juni, desperately needing someone to wade through the options with me, but I'd ended up texting about her bachelorette party instead.

She was so happy, so settled. I didn't want anything to ruin that.

I would be fine. Everything would be fine.

After all, I had a home gym at my disposal that I could use whenever I needed a distraction, which was exactly what I was doing now.

I usually listened to the same playlist while I worked out—a mix of songs from my skating routines over the years. The nostalgia was enough to get my adrenaline going and my blood pumping, but I had to be careful about which memories I pulled from. I didn't want to think about anything involving St. Maverick's right now. I didn't want to think about my skaters. Or about my colleagues, like my friend Kayla, who had posted new skating pictures online from a training she'd gone to. A training I was supposed to have gone to, too.

I shook my head, trying to clear it. And then, luckily, it was wiped blank. *Blank.*

Because I walked into Noah's home gym, and for the first time, Noah was in there, too.

And he was sweaty.

And wearing a cutoff shirt that showed *so many* of his defined muscles, so much of his glistening skin, tanned by the summer sun.

And all of my hormones that had been on overdrive? Oh, they were loving this.

Noah, with two massive dumbbells in hand, immediately caught sight of me in the mirror that covered the entirety of one wall.

And *I* immediately turned to leave.

"I'll come back later," I called over my shoulder, catching a glimpse of Noah dropping his weights, popping off his headphones, and shaking his head.

"You don't need to do that," he said between ragged breaths.

Because of course he wasn't just sweaty and exposed; he was also panting, his chest heaving as he worked to catch his breath.

Biting down on my lip, I spun back around to face him.

To say my body reacted viscerally was an understatement. Noah *had* to have noticed. But if he picked up on the fact that every inch of me was starting to sweat just by looking at him, he didn't say anything.

"It's not a big deal," I said, wishing my voice didn't sound so fucking hoarse.

"It's also not a big deal for you to stay and work out with me," he tossed back at me.

I raised a brow. "With you?"

"In the same room as me," he amended dryly, sweeping his gaze down and away from me.

"Of course." I walked back into the room, trying to brush off my nerves. "I wouldn't dare try to keep up with the likes of Noah London, New England Knights' finest, while in the gym."

He rolled his eyes but still refused to look at me. I glanced at my matching spandex set, wondering if I had a hole in my crotch, but I didn't notice anything.

"Oh, I don't know," Noah chuckled. "I think you could keep up just fine. I saw you handling those heavy boxes like they were filled with air."

"Your body can do amazing things when given a deadline by your landlord."

Even though his expression was downcast as he put his weights back on the rack, I could still see how it soured. "I'm still mad you didn't tell me about that."

I shrugged as I walked over to the treadmill. "It all worked out."

Noah was unimpressed with my answer. I caught a glimpse of his scowl before he used the bottom of his shirt to wipe the sweat from his face, giving me a view of his cut abs. My mouth ran dry, and Noah's next words startled me back into reality.

"From now on, let's focus on *not* putting your body through extra stress." His shirt fell back into place, and somehow, I recovered enough to reply.

"Physical activity is good for pregnancy," I argued, knowing full well that wasn't the kind of stress on the body he was talking about. It was the emotional panic he wanted to avoid, which was ironic because I felt stagnant without it.

Noah's eyes finally lifted to look at me, and then he *really* looked at me. "It is, huh?"

I nodded because I couldn't figure out how to talk.

I was usually pretty good with guys. I was good at talking to them, flirting with them, and even dating them on occasion— even though I'd never really had a serious boyfriend.

But there were guys, and then there was Noah London.

"So you don't have any physical restrictions from the doctor?" he pressed. "You never did answer that question the other day."

Noah was back to looking at the floor as he walked around the gym, grabbing resistance bands from a hook on the wall. He had to talk louder to be heard over the whirring treadmill I'd started at a walking pace.

I bit the inside of my cheek, knowing I needed to answer his question this time. I couldn't skirt around it forever. "Well, the internet says I shouldn't go downhill skiing, horseback riding, or off-road cycling. Lucky for me, I'm too uncoordinated to have any interest in those."

That wasn't exactly true. Years on the ice had resulted in

excellent coordination, and Noah surely knew it. But I'd rather he argued with me about that than the alternative.

Noah stilled, resistance band in hand. He turned slowly, his eyes narrowing as they settled back on me, and I knew I wouldn't be so lucky after all.

"Gemma..."

I looked away. I knew where this conversation was going and didn't want to have it.

But my lack of interest didn't stop Noah.

"Gemma, have you not seen a doctor yet?"

I shook my head and then increased the speed on the treadmill, intent on drowning out Noah's question.

He strode over, his expression hard as he leaned against the treadmill. God, he was incredibly *hard* to ignore. Sweaty and gorgeous and so very close to me. With one of his lightly veined, tattooed arms, he reached over the top of the treadmill and lowered the speed. My eyes traced over the inked images of nature. Flowers mixed with waves of an ocean, all surrounded by evergreen trees. It was a good reminder that even though Noah lived in the middle of a city now, he'd lived in different places and had different roots.

"You can tell me if I'm wrong, but isn't that kind of important?" he asked, looking up at me.

His brilliant green eyes drilled into the side of my head, and I reluctantly turned to acknowledge him.

"I know I'm pregnant, Noah. I have about fifty home tests and multiple weeks of morning sickness to prove it."

He nodded patiently, wiping at the sweat that kept dripping from his brow. "Again, I'm not an expert or anything...but I'm pretty sure there are reasons to go to the doctor besides confirming the pregnancy."

"Well, I had to wait to get my new insurance information after switching jobs," I explained, throwing out the only real excuse I had. I increased the speed on the treadmill back to where it was before.

"And do you have that information now?"

"Yeah," I admitted regretfully.

"Then you're going to the doctor," Noah confirmed as if he had any say in the matter.

"I was planning on it. I was. There was just a lot going on, and I read online that you just need to go in the first eight weeks, and I don't think I'm there yet, and...yeah."

"This week," Noah insisted, although his expression softened with understanding. "I'll go with you."

My mouth momentarily gaped open. "You don't have to go with me."

He sighed. "Well, you shouldn't have to go alone. And since Silas Taylor is useless, and you're not telling your brother or your best friend, I guess I'll have to do."

I blinked at him at least three times before finding my voice. "You know his name?"

Noah shrugged as he went back to his resistance bands. "I looked him up. Wanted to see what the asshat who ran the athletics at St. Maverick's looked like."

"Oh?" I couldn't help the smile that emerged from Noah's attitude toward Silas, especially considering how much Silas obsessed over the Knights. If only he knew what their star player thought of him. "And what conclusion did you come to?"

"He looks like a guy who doesn't know how to eat a girl out properly," Noah said without looking at me, assessing his form in the mirror as he did bicep curls with the band.

"I can confirm that."

Noah grunted, but I couldn't tell if it was in response to my comment or because of the heavy weights.

"It's honestly better off that he's not interested in being involved in my life," I added. "I have no interest in experiencing that a second time. I'd rather be single and alone than have anything to do with him."

"His loss," he muttered, his eyes meeting me in the reflection of the mirror. His voice sounded clipped, likely because he was in the middle of a set of curls. "And you're not alone. Especially not for your doctor appointment. I'm coming."

I didn't say anything. As much as I knew I should protest him coming, the thought was comforting. Noah possessed a self-assuredness that made decision-making look easy. And that was the type of energy that I needed at the moment. Even just talking to him for a few minutes gave me the direction I had been looking for.

There were a million things I knew I should be doing to prepare for this baby, but now I knew what I'd be doing this week: going to the doctor. One thing at a time, right?

"Do you have a doctor or hospital in mind?" he asked.

I shook my head. The clinic I used to go to was now out of network with my new insurance.

Noah nodded. "Go to Suffolk County Medical Center, then. Nat works at SCMC. She's said before how good their OB-GYN department is."

"Okay," I said, thankful that yet another decision had been magically made for me. Of course, I'd do my own research before actually making an appointment, but this gave me a place to start.

Noah seemed pleased that I was agreeing and went on to rattle off his schedule for the week before saying, "You know what, I'll just add you to my calendar so you can see for yourself. You should have my season schedule anyway so you know when all my away games are. I'll need help with Winnie for all of them."

He gave me an almost sheepish look like he hated to put that on me, even though that was the whole reason I was here. "But it's harder to say about Chloe. Natalie's schedule is all over the place, but she did promise she'd come with Chloe to my Minnesota game because the rest of my family will be there. So you don't have to worry about her for that one."

I smiled, trying to reassure him that I was ready to help out as much as needed. "That'll be fun to have your whole family there to watch."

Noah nodded, a mix of eagerness and anxiety shining in his eyes. "It'll be great to see everyone. I don't get home as much as I should."

"Well, you're a little busy."

He shrugged, clearly unwilling to take the excuse. So I raised a brow and added, "You know, I figured you just planned your life around that state fair wall calendar in the bathroom."

"That's the preliminary calendar," he said, suddenly boasting a serious expression I didn't believe for a minute. "And then when the new month rolls around, I transfer all my events into my phone. I know it's weird, but it works for me."

"Noted."

"My mom always sends me wall calendars," he added, still serious. "So I have to use them."

I smiled. "Aw, Noah London is a momma's boy."

He didn't deny it, shrugging, and I laughed.

Noah cocked his head to the side. "What?"

"I just didn't expect that about you," I admitted.

"I'm sure there's a lot of things you didn't expect about me." The cocky grin was back. "You'll just have to try to keep up."

I considered him for a moment, ignoring how my heartbeat started picking up. It had nothing to do with exercising and everything to do with how he was looking at me.

That, and how he'd promised to go with me to the doctor like it was the most normal thing in the world for two roommates who barely knew each other to do.

"I guess I will."

CHAPTER SEVEN

noah

"WHAT IF SOMEONE recognizes you?"

Gemma hadn't stopped talking or asking me questions since we left the apartment.

"Oh my God," she groaned. "What if they think *you* knocked me up? It's going to be all over the media and—"

"No one is going to recognize me," I said reassuringly while throwing my hoodie up over the ball cap I was already sporting. She walked a few paces ahead of me on our way into the clinic as if that small distance would lead people to believe we didn't know each other. "No one will be paying any attention to us. Except, of course, your doctor."

"Oh, Noah, you don't have to come in with me," she rushed on to say, glancing over her shoulder with wide eyes.

I gritted my teeth, annoyed at her persistent attitude of not wanting to *bother* me. Going with her to the doctor didn't bother me. If it had bothered me, I wouldn't have insisted on coming. What bothered me was how there was no one else to do it.

Besides, when Julian finally discovered that his sister was pregnant and that I knew about it, he'd only kick my ass harder if I left her to do all this herself. She shouldn't have to be here on her own. I was only doing what he would.

"If I don't come in with you, there's a higher chance that someone will recognize me and connect the dots about why I might be sitting in the waiting room at the OB-GYN," I pointed out, thinking she couldn't argue with that.

Then again, I'd learned recently that Gemma Briggs and I didn't agree on a lot of things. She thought it was smart to keep her pregnancy from her brother. I thought it would come back to bite all of us in the ass. She thought we shouldn't try to get Silas Taylor fired. I thought that was only the start of what we should be doing. She thought I didn't need to worry about how she could barely keep food down. I thought we needed to bring that up to the doctor. She thought I needed to mind my own business a little more.

She was probably right about that.

But again, my ass was dead if I didn't make sure *someone* was taking care of Gemma. And that someone was going to be me.

Gemma halted and turned around. "This was a bad idea. Maybe you should just wait in the car."

"I'm not waiting in the fucking car." I bristled. "How will I know you actually went to your appointment then?"

"I don't know, maybe you'll just have to believe me."

She scowled at me, and I glared back.

At least today, she wore a loose-fitting sundress that fell below her knees. It was nice being able to look at her without risking a hard-on, unlike the other day when she walked into the gym wearing a spandex set that was designed to destroy me from the inside out. Not to mention when she came out of her room this morning in the tiniest pajama shorts that had me imagining things I had absolutely no business imagining.

Living with Gemma Briggs would be damaging to my sanity —that much, I was sure of.

The squeal of tires echoing in the parking garage was the only interruption as we faced off. Determination flashed in her gaze as she realized I wasn't backing down. It came as absolutely no surprise that Gemma had a streak of stubbornness, considering who she had as an older brother. But what did surprise me was the vulnerability that leaked into her expression as our eyes remained locked.

"Noah, please," she whispered after a beat of silence. She twisted her hands in front of her, a ball of nervous energy. But while her body fidgeted, her words fell slowly from her mouth—like she was reluctant to let them out. "I just...I need to do this."

I didn't like it, but I held up my hands as a sign of defeat. "Fine, I'll stay in the waiting room."

"The car," she argued. "If someone sees—"

"The car," I agreed before she could work herself back up. It clearly made her anxious to be seen in public with me, and I wasn't here to cause her more stress. "I'll be in the car."

She nodded wordlessly.

It was my cue to leave, but my feet didn't budge. It seemed impossible—mean, cruel, uncaring—to walk away when Gemma's eyes sparkled with unshed tears. I stepped forward. Awkwardly, I might add, even though I'd never been awkward around women before. But I'd certainly never been in this kind of situation before, either. And I had no fucking clue how to navigate it.

Gemma didn't leave me many options; as soon as I moved closer, she retreated, backing toward the clinic.

"Do you want me to call Juniper?" I asked hoarsely because she looked like she wished someone would swoop in and save her from doing this alone. And she clearly didn't want it to be me.

I mean, why would she? I could hardly blame her for that.

Her eyes bugged out as she shook her head in immediate refusal. Still no words, though.

I lifted my hands again—another show of defeat. "Okay. Then...I guess just call me if you need anything."

She gave me another nod before ducking her head and hurrying into the hospital. Sighing, I retraced my steps and did precisely what I told her I would.

I waited in my car.

I couldn't wait in my car any longer.

Rationally, I should have left. I should have gone anywhere, done anything but stay in this parking garage. After all, someone *could* spot me. But I couldn't get myself to drive away, not when I was the only person Gemma might call if she needed anything right now.

It had been well over an hour, and while I didn't know from experience how long it took to confirm a pregnancy, I figured Gemma had to be wrapping up her appointment soon.

I fought the urge to text her and ask for an update, but Gemma had already convinced herself she was a burden, and I didn't want to fuel that fire anymore. Yes, I was impatient, but not because I minded waiting. I was just anxious to hear how it was going.

I had half a mind to go in there and find out, but I'd never figure out exactly where she was in the maze of exam rooms. And considering I wasn't the father of the baby nor related to her, I was sure no one would tell me if I asked.

Mostly, I hoped she was okay.

Fuck, of course she wasn't okay. In fact, it was a miracle just how "okay" Gemma had been acting since moving into my apartment. I suspected there was a lot she tried to hide, but still.

Sighing, I drummed my fingers on the wheel of my Audi to keep them from picking up my phone and texting Gemma. I was about to finally give in when I heard the buzz.

> SHE'S JULIAN'S SISTER, NOAH: I'm sorry it's taking so long. I can get myself home. It looks like it's only a twenty-minute walk.

I bit down on a foolish, silly grin at Gemma referring to my apartment as *home* and then immediately frowned when I fully comprehended what she was saying.

65

. . .

> You're not walking home, Gemma.

> SHE'S JULIAN'S SISTER, NOAH: I don't want to
> make you wait. I know how impatient you are.

Of course she was trying to use my own words against me. And I
didn't even have it in me to find it amusing.

I had to remind myself that Gemma grew up in a big family
like me. I understood the ingrained sense of urgency, of ensuring
you never take too much time. From sharing one bathroom
between five siblings to sharing our parents between Little
League games and recitals, it was a balance I knew all too well.

But Gemma didn't have to share me. I didn't have anywhere
else I needed to be today, and the only one waiting for me or
counting on me was Winnie.

> I don't mind waiting. Are you still in your
> appointment?

> SHE'S JULIAN'S SISTER, NOAH: I'm just finishing
> some stuff. Be right out.

My frown deepened because she didn't really answer my
question. But sure enough, a few minutes after she texted me,
Gemma tapped on the windshield, and I unlocked the car so she
could get in. She kept her head down, letting her long hair shield
her face as she buckled herself into the car.

And that's when I heard the sniffle.

"Sorry it took so long." Her voice was thick, sounding stuck in
her throat, and my heart sank.

"You don't need to apologize, Gemma. I just started to worry."

"I already told you not to worry about me," she murmured,
looking out the window while continuing to hide her face
from me.

I took a deep breath as I pulled out of my parking spot,

knowing I needed to choose my next words carefully. Gemma didn't talk as I maneuvered out of the parking garage, and the silence grew nearly unbearable until I broke it.

"Gemma...who knows you're pregnant?"

She hesitated, and I caught her wiping her face out of the corner of my eye.

"What do you mean?"

"I mean, besides the asshat athletic director and myself, who knows that you're pregnant?"

Gemma finally showed me her eyes as they flicked over to me, a look of devastation in them. It nearly gutted me. "No one."

I nodded, expecting that response. Didn't mean I liked it, though.

"Gemma, I know I'm not the person you wanted to tell about this. I know I'm not the guy you wanted to be supportive. I know I can't fill the shoes of your best friend. I know I'm not your first choice or anywhere near it...but I'm the one who's here. And I'm going to worry about you whether you like it or not."

Gemma slowly pushed her hair out of her face, revealing how blotchy and red her usually pale, slightly freckled skin was. Tired-looking eyes blinked at me. Wet lashes clumped together.

"I didn't want to cry in front of you," she whispered.

I gave her another nod, acknowledging that I understood. I understood it from the moment she refused to look me in the eye when she'd never shied away from meeting my gaze before. She usually met it straight on—unless she was hiding something.

Or trying to, anyway.

"You know, I would have been more surprised if you hadn't cried," I said honestly. "That's why I wanted to go to the appointment with you. In case..." I sighed, not sure where I was going with this. "Never mind."

I was well aware that my personality didn't exactly scream *comfort*. Not many women had cried on these shoulders. People didn't come to me for that kind of thing, so it wasn't surprising that Gemma didn't want me to join her for the appointment.

Gemma readjusted, twisting her body to acknowledge me again, and I felt the heat of her eyes as they landed on my side profile. I tried to focus on the road, not sure if I could handle the abrupt switch to being on the receiving end of all that Gemma Briggs' attention.

"I knew this would happen," she said, her voice still soft. "I knew going to the doctor would make it feel real. I think that's why I've been avoiding it."

I squeezed the steering wheel tighter. "I'm sorry if I pushed you to feel it too soon."

"No, I needed the push," she admitted, and I glanced over, noting how her throat bobbed as she swallowed. "And I suppose the worry isn't *so* bad, either." A heavy sigh punctuated the otherwise still air. "Just try not to emulate my brother so much."

A harsh laugh flew out of me, except it wasn't funny. Not really. A lump formed in my throat, and it was my turn to swallow past it. Sure, I'd taken on Julian's overprotective role in his absence...but I didn't have one single brotherly thought about Gemma Briggs.

Not. One.

"How does ice cream sound?" I asked, needing a change in topic. How embarrassing that I was using the same tactic I did with my eight-year-old niece. That showed how little I knew about connecting with women I didn't want to sleep with.

Correction: connecting with women I wasn't *planning* on sleeping with.

Unfortunately.

But Gemma didn't sound fazed. "Ice cream sounds great, actually. But be aware that I might throw it up later."

I bit down on my tongue, wanting to ask if she talked to her doctor about how sick she had been lately. But instead, I said, "Scoopies has Moose Tracks. I think the risk is worth it."

"Scoopies?" she laughed.

"It's the ice cream shop Lo and I always go to," I said, my lips curving into a grin as I looked over at her. A similar smile flitted onto her face, too, putting me at ease.

"Well, if Chloe approves, then count me in."

With that settled, I turned at the next intersection, rerouting for ice cream. I took my time, driving a few blocks out of the way to give Gemma a few more minutes to wipe at her eyes before parking in front of Scoopies.

I wasn't in a hurry. And I wanted her to know exactly how much I wasn't in a hurry. I had time for her, and she deserved that time. So after buying her two scoops of Moose Tracks, I led Gemma to a sunny spot on the patio. I didn't care how quickly my ice cream would melt sitting here; I fully planned to take my goddamn time eating it.

"I needed this," she said before licking her spoon clean a second time. "Thank you."

I cleared my throat, attempting to ignore how her tongue flicked over the tip of the spoon.

"Everyone needs ice cream every now and then," I agreed. My voice sounded hoarse as fuck, and I decided to blame it on my low water intake today and not the seductive way Gemma ate desserts. She licked her lips clean, and I tried so damn hard to look away from her mouth, but my eyes kept dipping to track her movements. Fuck, that mouth of hers. It was going to be a problem. Just her existing so close to me for so many months was going to be a problem, honestly.

"Yeah." She spoke softly, her bright blue eyes flicking over at me as she pushed her empty dish aside. "Ice cream."

The way she said those two words told me they weren't the ones she meant. And I couldn't help but hope that one day I'd hear all the words Gemma Briggs kept locked inside her head.

Maybe one day she'd trust me enough to let me hold her hand at difficult doctor's appointments, too.

"When's your next appointment?" I asked, trying to make my interest sound casual.

"Dr. Amos said I'm nearly eight weeks along right now, and I need to come back in about a month."

I nodded.

A month.

I had a month to become someone Gemma Briggs trusted so that hopefully her next appointment wouldn't end in her hiding her tears. Or having any at all.

eight years ago

GEMMA

One second, I was watching Juniper and Julian trade insults, otherwise known as their own language of flirting, and the next second, I was staring at a ridiculously attractive football player.

At least I had to assume he was a football player, considering the OSU football sweatshirt, the backward ball cap with light brown hair curling out from under it, and the cocky, lopsided grin. Not to mention the group football picture on the wall behind him that I was pretty sure he was in.

I smiled back at him. I couldn't help it. There was something about him that made my guard immediately drop.

It was dangerous. So, so incredibly dangerous, yet my feet didn't move an inch away from him.

CHAPTER EIGHT

gemma

A WEEK AFTER my first doctor's appointment, I found myself on Noah's couch next to Chloe, who blinked up at me, a giant bowl of popcorn covering most of her body.

"Is it weird living with a boy?"

This was our first night together without Noah, who was doing some kind of football-related thing. He didn't go into too much detail but said he'd be home late.

I shrugged. "Not really. I grew up living with a boy."

She gasped like I'd said something scandalous. So I clarified, "He was my brother, Chloe."

Her expression relaxed again, her eyes rolling up. "Well, that's different."

"Not that different," I said, trying to be convincing with my lie.

Chloe saw through me immediately. She cocked her head to the side, lifting a brow. "Isn't it, though?"

I looked away so my face wouldn't give me away.

It was completely different. My brother was, well...my brother.

And Noah was decidedly *not* my brother. He was my incredibly hot roommate.

Temporary roommate, I reminded myself. This was temporary —all of it was temporary.

Except for the raspberry-sized embryo in my belly, of course. That was the only real and permanent thing about this entire situation.

"Do you want to take Winnie to the roof to play?" I asked, purely because I knew it would shift Chloe's attention. She loved playing with Winnie, and I didn't want to continue our conversation. Why did kids always have the uncanny ability to see right through us?

As expected, her face lit up, and the bowl of popcorn was pushed to the side, forgotten. Chloe sprang into action, running through the apartment to get Winnie from where she was napping in her kennel.

Not only was this my first night alone with Chloe, but it was also my first solo gig with Winnie.

Not that I was nervous about either. Winnie, from my understanding, was a remarkably easy puppy. She was good at sleeping, nearly entirely potty-trained, and only *occasionally* tried to chew the corners of the couch. And Chloe was hardly a troublemaker.

I watched the sunset from the sidelines as Chloe ran around with Win, happy to let the two have their fun.

While I felt relaxed and comfortable being alone with Chloe and Winnie, I had to admit how much I missed Noah being here. I liked seeing him as an uncle and a dog dad. It felt secret or private, getting access to that side of Noah London—the side that joked with an eight-year-old and let a puppy climb onto his shoulders and fall asleep.

When the sun had fallen entirely in the sky, I decided it was time to usher Chloe and Winnie back to the penthouse. We passed Summer on the way, who narrowed her eyes when she saw me with Chloe, and then Noah's other neighbor, Matt, who was always much more friendly. He'd made sure to introduce himself one day when he saw me coming out of the apartment with Winnie, and if he'd thought it was a little odd that Noah

London, famous NFL player, would have a platonic roommate, he didn't say anything.

I suspected if we put on a movie, Chloe would pass out in no time. Noah told me she didn't have a strict bedtime, but that was usually what they did when she was here on weekends. Chloe would excitedly pick out a movie and fall asleep within fifteen minutes of watching it.

"Do you know what makes a movie and popcorn even better?" I asked Chloe as we strode back into Noah's living room.

"What?" she asked, her upturned eager expression making me grin.

"A fort."

"A fort?"

"Yes, a fort!" I laughed before walking back to the kitchen and grabbing a barstool. I noticed the other day that they had the perfect sort of knobs on top for blanket securing. "Look, Chloe."

Setting the barstool down near the couch, I snatched a blanket—one of the ones Noah usually let Winnie use, so I knew it wasn't too high-quality—and then yanked the elastic band from my hair. Chloe watched as I dragged the blanket over the barstool and wrapped the band over the protruding peg. Then, I did the same thing to the other side with the extra band from my wrist.

Chloe just stared, confused.

"My brother and I are the oldest in my family," I explained. "Sometimes, when we had to babysit my younger sisters growing up, we'd do this in the living room. My parents hated how big of a mess it made. While we were good at making forts, we weren't as good at taking them down."

I smiled at her, but Chloe curiously cocked her head. "How many sisters do you have?"

"I have four sisters," I said.

"My mom has four brothers," Chloe said as she watched me bring another barstool over. This time, she joined in, helping me tie the blanket to the chair.

"So you have three other uncles?" My brows rose, surprised I didn't know Noah had such a big family.

"Yeah, but I don't see Uncle Theo, Uncle Sully, or Uncle Blake very often. They live in Minnesota with my grandparents."

"I heard you're going to go see them soon. And that you're all going to Uncle Noah's game."

"Yes!" Chloe's entire face lit up and then promptly dimmed as she added, "I hope Mom's work doesn't mess it up like it usually does."

"Your mom has a very important job, Chloe," I said, even though my heart ached for her. "But I'm sure she'll do her very best to make it work."

"I know," Chloe acknowledged, and I could tell she *did* know. But I was sure it didn't make it any easier to have her mom gone a lot.

I gave her a reassuring smile as we continued to make the fort. After a minute of working in silence, she sighed heavily.

"I wish I had brothers or sisters."

My heart panged again.

"My best friend Juniper was an only child, too," I said. "She felt the same way, so she practically lived at my house growing up. And now she'll officially be my sister soon."

Chloe paused, looking at me with wide eyes. "How does that work?"

I gave her a soft smile. "She's marrying my brother."

"So now she has a really big family, too?" Chloe asked before scowling. "Lucky."

I worried my lip, wondering if I'd said the wrong thing.

"We're lucky to have her," I said, trying to placate the eight-year-old. "Just like Uncle Noah and your mom are lucky to have you."

Chloe nodded, but I could tell I didn't really make her feel better. We worked without talking for a bit, and my thoughts drifted to my son or daughter. To my little raspberry. Would they grow up feeling like Chloe and Juniper? Because there was no way in hell I'd be procreating with Silas more than once.

"Oh my God, it's like a tent!" Chloe suddenly exclaimed as though she understood my vision of why we were doing this for the first time.

"Yes!" I laughed, throwing some other spare blankets and pillows on the floor. Winnie pounced on them immediately, sinking her sharp, tiny teeth into a cushion, which I had to scoop away before she destroyed it. "Climb in."

Chloe bounced to the floor, picking Winnie up and snuggling her to her chest as she settled beneath the blanket canopy we created. I grabbed the TV remote and the popcorn that had been pushed to the side earlier before crawling in to sit next to Chloe.

"Do you like it?" I asked, noting how she was examining the fort from the inside.

A smile stretched over her face, and she nodded enthusiastically.

Good.

I switched with Chloe, passing the remote and popcorn to her and taking Winnie in return. The puppy rolled around in my lap for a few minutes before finally settling in. Chloe picked an animated movie to watch, and before I knew it, she was asleep.

I tipped my head back with a smile.

"Come on, Little Lo."

Noah's hushed voice broke through the barrier of sleep.

Asleep. Oh my God, I'd fallen asleep. On the job. While I was supposed to be watching Chloe and Winnie. And Noah was here.

I blinked to see him scooping Chloe up from the ground. It seemed he was trying not to wake her, and she certainly wasn't stirring. He carried her off, and my eyes drifted shut again, reluctant to open.

A bit later, Noah returned, and I remembered that I was supposed to be awake. Or at least acting awake.

I started to push myself upright, but Noah put a gentle finger on my shoulder and pushed me back into the blankets and cushions. And then he surprised me by climbing into the fort and taking Chloe's spot beside me. Winnie jumped off my lap, happy that her dad was home. She started crawling all over him, her tail wagging excitedly.

"I can't believe I fell asleep," I said with a groan. "I don't know what happened. One minute, we were watching *Moana*, and the next, you were here."

Noah's soft chuckle drifted into the space between us. He hauled Winnie into his tattooed arms, and her dog tags chimed as they hit each other.

God, the sight of them. Noah was handsome enough on his own, but when he held a goddamn puppy in his toned arms like that, my insides turned to mush. I knew I shouldn't keep lusting over my roommate like this, but he made it incredibly hard, and it honestly wasn't fair.

"I'm sorry," I whispered.

"No need to be sorry, Gemma. I'm sure you're exhausted."

"All I did today was play with Winnie and Chloe."

"And that's exhausting," he acknowledged. I made a face, and he added, "Also, it's normal to be tired during your first trimester."

I turned on my side, facing him as I snuggled into the sea of pillows. "How would you know?"

Noah mimicked me, flipping on his side, too. The only thing between us was Winnie, but I couldn't think about the dog right now. Not when Noah was so close, his body radiating heat. I wanted to dive into his warmth.

"I looked it up," he said matter-of-factly.

I raised my brow, and he stared at me for a long moment, long enough that I felt my heart rate pick up. His gaze dipped, and I licked my lips before realizing what I was doing. I needed to be more careful not to give myself away, but it was too late. Suddenly, his attention sizzled, like we were sitting in a sauna instead of a blanket fort.

It was amazing how acutely I felt his presence when he wasn't even touching me. I couldn't imagine what would happen if he *did* touch me.

Fuck, I *shouldn't* imagine that. I really shouldn't.

"Still..." I said, finding my voice, "I made a mess in your living room and fell asleep while babysitting."

"I'm not mad about either of those things," he said, a slightly amused curve to his lips. Shit, now I was the one looking at his lips. "In fact, I think we should just keep the living room like this."

"I bet it'll impress all the girls when you bring them over," I teased before immediately regretting my words.

His expression hardened, and his eyes flicked away from mine. "I already told you I'm not bringing girls home while you're here."

I frowned as I wondered if Noah missed it—missed living the lifestyle he was used to. And if he was ever annoyed that I was keeping him from it.

"Have you ever dated someone?" I asked, curiosity getting the better of me.

Noah shrugged, turning onto his back again. "In high school."

I struggled to hide my surprise. "Not since then? Really?"

He shook his head, throwing his Winnie-free hand behind his head to brace it. His arm flexed, and I hated to admit how much that position did it for me—the look of a relaxed, cocky jock. But his eyes told a different story of a different attitude as they stared at the fort's ceiling.

"What about Juni?" I asked.

Over a year ago, Noah agreed to take Juniper to her half sister's wedding as her fake boyfriend, and they'd gone on a few date-like outings beforehand. Juniper said it was just so they could get to know each other better, but still.

Noah looked over at me. "What about Juni?"

"You seemed willing to go on dates with her."

Something churned in my stomach at the memory, something I didn't let myself acknowledge. I hadn't then, and I couldn't now.

"Juniper is easy to go on dates with," Noah answered simply, not giving anything away from his expression.

"So, was it hard to give her up?" I pressed. "To back out on being her fake boyfriend for the weekend?"

Noah chuckled. "You mean so Julian could finally get his shit together and volunteer to take her to the wedding himself?"

I nodded.

"No," he replied easily, "it wasn't hard."

"You didn't like her?"

"Of course I like her. But just as friends." He grinned as he thought about Juniper, and my stomach churned again. *Ugh.* "It was easy talking to her, and I was happy to help. But we never really had that spark."

"She said you almost kissed her once," I argued—for some goddamn reason.

"It wasn't like that." He shook his head. "I wanted her to know that she deserved to be kissed. I know how girls overthink things if they don't get a kiss at the end of a date."

"But you're not disappointed you didn't take her to the wedding?"

I wasn't sure why I needed this to be so clear, but I did. This wasn't the first time I'd wondered about Noah's intentions and feelings toward my best friend.

Noah cocked his head to the side like he was curious why I cared so goddamn much. Truthfully, I wanted to know, too—why I cared. I shouldn't care. But despite his curiosity, Noah answered me honestly. Or at least, it seemed honest.

"I was slightly worried that Julian wouldn't go through with it and she'd be stuck alone," he replied. "But no, I wasn't disappointed. We would've had fun, but it would have been as friends. It wouldn't have become anything."

"Why not?"

"I'm not the kind of guy that girls date, Gemma." He said the words firmly, finding my gaze and holding it. It seemed purposeful, and my cheeks burned.

"Why aren't you the kind of guy that girls date?" I couldn't help but ask.

"Because if you date a girl, you're making a promise to give them something." Noah's voice lowered to something strained. "I never saw myself giving Juni what Julian does."

"And what's that?"

"Love. A relationship. A future."

"You're trying to tell me you're incapable of love? Unwilling to love?" I scoffed. "Somehow, I doubt that."

Noah clearly loved a lot of people. Maybe not in a romantic way, and maybe not in an outward fashion. But his actions showed how much he cared for the people around him.

He just shrugged, and even though I wanted to probe further, I bit my tongue. I'd asked for a lot of answers tonight, and I knew I should have stopped talking a long time ago. But the person everyone told me Noah London was...seemed far different than the person lying beside me in a poorly crafted blanket fort.

And I wanted to know what this version of Noah was all about.

"What time does your practice end tomorrow?" he asked, switching subjects. "I'm supposed to pick Chloe up afterward."

I cleared my throat. "It ends at three, but you should come a little early and watch. Chloe has made a lot of progress, and I'm sure she'd love for you to see."

Noah's gaze warmed.

"I'll be there."

CHAPTER NINE

gemma

N OAH'S FACE APPEARED on the other side of the tempered glass in the last twenty minutes of practice. His lips pulled into a frown as he watched me with Chloe's class, and I wondered what that look was for. I thought he'd be happy to see how good Chloe was doing.

As soon as I stepped off the ice, he didn't waste any time telling me.

"That cannot be safe."

Noah leaned against the boards, similar to how he did a couple weeks ago when we first met here. But he wore an entirely different expression this time.

"What?"

"You," he said stiffly. "On the ice."

"What did you expect? That I was coaching from the side of the rink?"

His brows tugged together as he scowled at me. His arms flexed as they crossed over his chest, and I found my eyes wandering the lines of his tattoos, like usual. "I don't know what I expected, but I didn't think you'd be flying around like that."

"Here at Back Bay Skating, our rink is incredibly safe, Mr. London," I said, forcing my gaze away from his arms.

That scowl deepened. "Mr. London? Really?"

After ensuring all my skaters were busily unlacing their skates as they lined up on the benches, I walked toward the NFL player that all the moms in the building were staring at.

"Just being professional. You *are* here to pick up one of my skaters, aren't you?"

"Professional?" Noah raised a brow, questioning me again. "We live together, Gems."

"My brother calls me Gems. I told you not to emulate him."

"We live together, *Em*," he amended without missing a beat, his voice ghosting over the first and last letters of my name even though his lips seemed to form the whole thing.

"Shush," I muttered once I got closer, realizing that more than one or two people had turned their heads in our direction. I wasn't too worried about repercussions—Back Bay wasn't that serious. It wasn't a competitive club, just a place to come to learn. No one would care that I was living with a family member of a student, but I still didn't feel the need to broadcast it. "People are looking, Noah."

He lifted one shoulder, eyes smoldering as they wandered over me.

"I'm used to people looking."

I mock gasped, lowering my voice. "You *are* a cocky asshole."

"Don't sound so surprised," he teased, his lips curving upward for the first time since he showed up. "We've been over this."

"You're right," I said, switching to mock seriousness, "I should have known."

Noah seemed to be surveying the stands behind me, not paying attention to my retort. His lips quickly descended into a frown, and with two quick strides, he switched his position to stand on the other side of me. I had to turn to keep facing him, and he gave a satisfied nod at the reorganization.

I cast him a confused look. "What was that?"

"You were right that people were looking. There was a row of dads staring at your ass."

"They were not," I argued, resisting the urge to look behind me and see for myself.

"They were, and I didn't like it," Noah grumbled. "I also don't like *this*."

He pointed at my feet, but my brows pulled together in confusion. "What?"

"This." He waved his finger around again, still pointing at my feet. "This whole thing."

"My skates?"

"Yeah, and how you wear them on ice." He took his backward hat off, raking his hand through his hair before putting it back on. "Jesus Christ, it's an accident waiting to happen."

"I've been figure skating since I was Chloe's age," I laughed.

"Yeah, but now you're pregnant," he said, lowering his voice.

"And I have an excellent track record with very few accidents," I replied.

Noah narrowed his eyes. "Did you tell your doctor what your job is?"

"Yes," I said honestly. "She was not concerned. There isn't a concern until—"

"So there *is* a concern."

"Again with the emulation of my brother," I sighed, exasperated. No wonder Julian and Noah got along.

"Oh, your brother would have already carried you out of here if he realized you were walking around on the ice with tiny little blades on your feet while pregnant."

"He would *not* have."

That was a lie. He probably would have.

Which was another reason that Julian couldn't know about my situation. He'd try to convince me to find a new job, and I didn't want a new job. I loved working on the ice, and I loved being at Back Bay more and more every day.

"Ah, so that's it. You just don't want to get in trouble with my brother."

Noah pretended to consider it. He was still trying to act annoyed, but the one thing I'd learned about Noah London was he didn't know how to stay mad for long. "I can't deny that it would be terribly bad for my career if all my fingers were broken."

I clucked my tongue. "And here I thought you cared about me."

His smile fell. "I sure as hell care about you more than some people."

He hissed the words *some people,* and I knew precisely which *some people* he was referring to.

Or person.

I took back my earlier thought—Noah did know how to stay mad and hold a grudge. It just depended on the person.

I sucked in a breath, put off-kilter by how Noah looked at me. The intensity of his glare had returned, and even though I knew it wasn't directed toward me, I still didn't like to see it. I was a much bigger fan of seeing him smile.

"I'm going to keep skating until my bump is large enough to put me off-balance. Which will be months yet," I explained, trying to put him at ease.

It didn't work.

"Oh, so one day, you're just going to topple right over, and that's how you'll know?" Noah readjusted his hat again, fidgeting. "Sounds like a great plan."

"We can get ice cream on the way home, right?"

Chloe jumped into our conversation, which was probably good because the longer it continued, the more I felt like strangling her uncle's neck.

"Of course we can get ice cream on the way home," Noah said, his body visibly relaxing as he switched roles—from cocky alpha athlete to chill uncle in less than thirty seconds. "You deserve it after how amazing you did today, Lo. You should ask Coach B if she wants to come with us."

Chloe's eyes darted between me and her uncle, pure mischief in them. "Why don't *you* ask Coach B if she wants to come with us?" she shot back before giggling and disappearing into the throng of eight-year-olds gathering their stuff.

Noah sighed heavily, his attention swiveling back to me. I had a feeling this wasn't the first time Chloe had dropped some hints —ones that Noah obviously had no intention of picking up.

"Would you like to come with us to get ice cream?"

"Ice cream with the infamous Noah London twice in one week? I'm starting to feel special."

He looked tempted to roll his eyes but didn't. His lips twitched, though. I couldn't tell if it was amusement or irritation. "I'll even get you a triple scoop if you want."

"As tempting as that sounds, I have another class in fifteen minutes."

Noah nodded. "You'll be home after that?"

"Yeah, I don't have anything going on the rest of the night."

"Good. I'll see you then." He started to back away, but that didn't stop him from assessing me with a critical eye. "Be careful out there on that ice, Coach B."

"I always am, Mr. London."

His eyes narrowed in response, but I spun around before he could say anything. If he wanted to glare at something, he could glare at my backside.

Despite it being early evening when I walked home, the sun still shone bright and warm. If I could walk anywhere, I usually did. Juniper and I got into a car accident in high school, and ever since, I walked or biked whenever I could. I didn't have a car anymore; I sold it as soon as I found out I was pregnant because one, I needed the money, and two, having a baby to keep safe only increased my anxiety around driving.

Neither Juni nor I had been badly injured in the car accident. I'd suffered a bad concussion and a broken collarbone, and she'd only needed a few stitches. But the ordeal spooked me all the same. If I could avoid planes or cars, I did. And if walking or biking wasn't an option, I tried to take the commuter rail. It was definitely the best of all the choices, with it being on a set track, whereas planes were the worst. They made me feel trapped.

I walked into the apartment to find Noah in front of the stove. I wasn't surprised, but I started salivating all the same. As if my hormones needed another reason to rage, Noah liked to cook. More specifically, he liked to cook for me. He'd made it his personal challenge to find foods I could stomach, and I appreciated it more than he could ever imagine.

Noah frowned at the chicken on the stove before swiveling his attention to me.

"How's your nausea today?"

"It's surprisingly good," I said honestly, sliding onto the barstool to face him. There hadn't been any impromptu breaks during my lessons today, no rushing to the toilets to toss my cookies. It gave me hope that maybe the nausea was lessening.

"Are you up for a little stir-fry?" Noah asked. I nodded, and he added, "Spicy? Or is it too much for your stomach?"

"Noah, I desperately need some spice in my life," I laughed. "Add the spice."

His eyes twinkled with humor, but he didn't say anything. He nodded and moved to the fridge, pulling out the veggies.

"This meal should be rich with folic acid," Noah explained. "They say that's important in the first trimester."

"They?" I questioned, raising a brow. I already knew the answer, though.

"The internet," he said, a bit sheepishly. He shrugged, and I had to bite down on a smile. "I learned only a little bit about pregnancy when Nat had Chloe—not as much as I probably should have. I was finishing college in California, and she was on the East Coast finishing med school when she was pregnant. I should have tried harder to be there for her, especially now that I know how poor of a support Chloe's dad was."

"I think you've more than made up for it with how you're here for her and Chloe now," I assured because it sounded like he needed it. "Can I help cook?"

"No," he said simply. Like I knew he would. "Here, eat some peanuts while you wait."

Another laugh burst out of me as Noah slid the largest container of peanuts I'd ever seen across the counter.

"Who on earth needs this many peanuts?" I exclaimed, struggling to tame my amusement.

"You do," he said, pointing at me with the knife he'd pulled out to cut vegetables. "They're a good source of folic acid."

I shook my head with a smile as I screwed off the lid of the container. I wasn't about to argue with him while he was waving that kitchen knife around like that. But before I could dig into the peanuts, my phone started vibrating in my pocket, and when I pulled it out, my smile vanished.

It was Silas.

Silas Taylor was calling me.

I let it ring, staring at his name on the screen until it vanished, going to voicemail. Relief spread through me, but then my phone lit up again.

Across from me, Noah froze. His frenzied cutting ceased.

"You don't have to pick it up," he said, his voice suddenly cold.

"This is the second time he's called," I said hoarsely, watching as the phone went to voicemail again.

No more than three seconds passed before he was at it again, calling for a third time.

"Do you want me to talk to him?" Noah offered. "I'd be happy to tell him to back the fuck off."

I shook my head while sucking in. No, I had to do this. Like it or not, Silas and I were now tied together, and I'd have to learn how to deal with him.

I accepted the call.

"What do you want, Silas?" I sighed, ready to get to the point and get this over with.

"Finally," he exclaimed, irritation coating his voice. Somehow, it was satisfying. "Would you open your goddamn door?"

I stiffened. "My door?"

"Yes, your door. I'm outside of it."

"At my apartment?" I clarified, my thoughts racing at what he was implying. He'd gone to my *apartment*?

"*Yes.* Jesus Christ, Gemma."

How dare he have the audacity to sound annoyed when he showed up at my apartment without any warning or indication that we would stay in touch. He was the one who said he wanted nothing to do with me—with us.

"I'm not there," I said coldly.

"I can hear voices inside," Silas replied flatly.

"I moved."

My eyes flicked up to Noah's, which was a mistake. His gaze was nothing short of murderous as it trained on my phone. That look of his made my stomach flip, my heart race.

"You moved?" Silas exclaimed before swearing under his breath. "Well, where are you? We need to talk."

"I don't think there's anything we need to talk about," I said, mimicking his flat tone from earlier, which annoyed the hell out of me. "You said you didn't want to be involved. So go be uninvolved, and don't fucking bother me again, Silas."

With that, I hung up the call, my hands shaking as I put the phone back on the countertop. I stared at it, waiting to see if he would call back.

He did, of course he did.

The ringtone was jarring. I saw Noah jolt out of the corner of my eyes at the sound. His hand flexed like he wanted to grab the phone himself, but I beat him to it, silencing the call.

And when several slow seconds had passed without seeing his name pop up again, I let my shoulders relax slightly. Let my heart rate return to its normal tempo.

Until a voicemail notification popped up, and my stomach turned.

"A man like that shouldn't be allowed to procreate," Noah grunted before resuming his task of chopping vegetables. He seemed to be using extra force as he slammed his knife through a bell pepper.

"Agreed," I muttered, swiping to open the notification and reading the transcript of the voicemail, which mostly detailed how Silas wanted to ensure I was going to keep my mouth shut about our situation. Fuck him. I threw my phone back down. "There should be some kind of rule that a guy has to at least be able to get a girl off before he can impregnate her."

Noah chuckled softly, that spark of humor slowly returning to his eye. "That bad, huh?"

I shrugged, having blocked the entire night out of my brain. There definitely hadn't been any mind-blowing orgasms, though.

"Never settle for someone who can't find your clit, Gemma," he said with a little tsk.

Noah London saying the word *clit* made my cheeks flame.

"First, I didn't plan on sleeping with him," I said hotly—though I couldn't help a smile. Not when Noah smirked at me like that. "Second, how was I supposed to know he couldn't find it? It's not like I give guys a questionnaire before going out with them."

Noah stilled slightly at my first comment but didn't say anything other than, "Maybe you should."

"I doubt they'd answer honestly."

"It might still give you some insight," Noah offered, but I saw that teasing crease around his eyes.

"I'll work on developing that, then. You can review it for me and give me some feedback."

"Well, it's all about *your* personal sexual priorities," he tossed back, eyes skating over me, making me feel hot from across the countertop. By the time his gaze connected with mine, I could barely breathe. "And since I don't know those, I might not be of much help."

He said that last sentence like he wouldn't mind finding out, but I was sure that was just Noah being Noah. He had a playfulness to him that I found overwhelmingly confusing at times.

"Eat the peanuts, Em," he demanded, jerking me out of my thoughts.

That was the second time he'd used a nickname today, and I couldn't help but feel a bit fuzzy and warm at the familiarity. Noah's head tipped down as he concentrated on the vegetables, so I didn't bother trying to hide my smile as I scooped out a handful of peanuts.

I might not be getting any action these days, but I did get a front-row view of Noah London cooking me dinner. And that was a hell of a lot better than sex with Silas Taylor or any other guy I'd slept with.

I popped a peanut in my mouth, and Noah looked up with a smile.

"Good girl," he muttered.

My poor hormones never stood a chance.

"I'm getting together with Julian soon," he said, almost like a reminder to both of us that my brother was one of his best friends. And maybe we shouldn't be talking about my sexual priorities. "Juniper said she needs help keeping him busy when the two of you go to her bridal fitting. He's trying to tag along."

"Of course he is." I rolled my eyes.

"I think we're getting brunch. It's going to be weird," Noah said, keeping his eyes on his cutting board. "Not telling him about this."

He didn't have to explain what *this* was.

"I know," I acknowledged. "And I'm sorry. It's weird keeping things from Juni, too. I'm a little nervous about seeing her."

Noah's gaze lifted, and even though it shone with understanding, I could also tell he didn't quite know why I was insisting on keeping everything a secret.

"Her bridal fitting should be all about her," I explained, pleading slightly for him to get it. "Not my surprise pregnancy."

"Okay." He nodded. "We'll get through it, then."

And once again, Noah's assuredness made me believe it.

We'd get through it.

eight years ago
GEMMA

"Jenny?" he asked before lifting a finger like he had a second thought. "No, Julie."

I pressed my lips together, trying not to laugh. "Jenny is my mom, and Julie is my next-door neighbor."

"Shit. I'm on the right track, though. Aren't I? It starts with a J."

"It starts with the same sound, yeah."

He leaned against the wall, putting a hand in his pocket. "Put me out of my misery and tell me what it is so I can put a name to your pretty face."

I blushed. Fiercely.

"Gemma Briggs. I'm Julian's sister."

I bit the inside of my cheek, wondering why the hell I added the last part when he obviously knew I was Julian's sister.

But he just tossed me a smile as he leaned forward playfully. "Had a hunch you might be."

"And that's Juniper," I added, looking for something else to say.

"Ah, another J name." He nodded, raising a brow. "But she's not a Briggs."

"What gave it away?" I laughed. "The hair?"

"No, I was just really hoping Julian didn't look at his sisters like that."

Our gazes both flicked to Julian and Juniper, and I withheld a groan as I watched them make pointed jabs at each other. Heatedly. Passionately. Julian's eyes were roaming over my best friend, drinking her in. When the hell would they stop fighting and come to their senses?

"Definitely not a Briggs," he confirmed.

"Yet," I added.

CHAPTER TEN

"**D**OES THIS DRESS make me look pregnant?"

Noah looked over at me from his place on the couch, eyes wandering down my body and making me feel things I shouldn't.

"I feel like this is a trick question," Noah said dryly. I tried to ignore the goose bumps his gaze gave me, but as usual, I wasn't very successful. I wondered if he knew how much heat he radiated. I was sure he didn't mean anything by it; he was just effortlessly smolderingly attractive, and his attention simply had that effect.

"I don't want Juniper to suspect anything today."

Noah's expression soured, and I knew it was because he disapproved of me hiding my pregnancy from Juniper. "She's not going to suspect anything," he said definitively.

I nodded before taking my turn in assessing him. He looked... tired. Worn-out. Which wasn't all that surprising since he'd had training camp every day this past week, leaving the apartment before dawn and not returning until dinner time. I tried to take on some of the cooking responsibilities, but Noah always insisted on jumping in and helping me once he got home. He said it relaxed him, so I didn't argue too much. But all our conversations this last week had been short and to the point.

"Where's the bridal shop you're going to?" Noah asked as I walked over to the front door. "I'll make sure Julian stays clear."

"It's in Beacon Hill." I checked the time on my phone. "The appointment isn't until noon, but I'm walking, so I want to give myself plenty of time."

Noah's smile vanished. "Why are you walking?"

"Because parking is a hassle, and as we've previously discussed, exercise is good for pregnancy."

Noah didn't know I'd always pick walking over anything else. I should probably tell him and explain why if this was going to be a common conversation, but I didn't have time to dive into the past at the moment.

"I'll drop you off. I was planning to head out to meet Julian soon anyway," he said, ignoring my second point. "I just need a few minutes to change out of my sweats."

My eyes lowered as I unconsciously gave myself permission to check Noah out—specifically, how a pair of gray sweatpants was riding low on his hips. When I caught the faint outline of something I definitely shouldn't be staring at, my eyes snapped up again.

"I really don't mind walking," I blurted out, hoping he wouldn't notice where my attention had strayed.

"I mind."

His words marked the end of the conversation as he strode toward his room. I considered walking out the door anyway, but a part of me had an inkling that would actually hurt Noah's feelings. And that was the last thing I wanted to do.

So I waited, and within ten minutes, I was sitting snug in Noah's Audi. I didn't mind riding in cars nearly as much as I minded driving them. Especially when it was Noah behind the wheel, who buckled me into the car himself when I didn't move fast enough. His fingers lingered on the seatbelt afterward, like he needed the reminder that it was there. My skin warmed from the proximity of his touch, making me ache for more of it.

I blamed the hormones.

And the way Noah backed out of his parking spot with one hand.

Okay, yeah, I definitely didn't mind riding in a car with Noah.

He radiated confidence as he maneuvered the vehicle, and it was hard not to trust him. More and more, I was trusting Noah London. Not to mention, a cute puppy buckled in the back made the ride more fun than usual. Apparently, Winnie was going to brunch, too.

"Drop me off around the corner," I instructed as we neared the bridal boutique. "So Juni doesn't see."

He nodded, pulling up to the curb so I could hop out after thanking him. I strode into the sparkling all-white shop and wasn't surprised when I immediately ran into my best friend. She was always early for everything.

"Hi!" She greeted me with an enthusiastic hug, squealing in my ear. "I feel like I haven't seen you in forever."

"I know," I groaned, guilt immediately flooding me. "I've been so busy with my new job. I'm so sorry."

"No need to apologize," she said, waving away my comment. "How are the little ones? Is it a good change from college kids?"

I'd told Juni and my family that I wanted to change jobs because I needed something new. Plus, working at St. Mav's involved too much travel. The second part wasn't a lie; we traveled a lot for competitions, and it wore on me. Especially considering how much I didn't enjoy the *travel* part of traveling.

"It's been a lot of fun," I said honestly. "And guess who's in one of my classes?"

Juni cocked her head to the side. "Who?"

"Noah's niece, Chloe."

"Noah?" Juni repeated. "Noah London?"

I nodded. I'd already decided to tell Juniper about running into Noah at the rink. I figured it was harmless and could help explain if I ever slipped and mentioned him to her. Or vice versa with him and Julian.

"I don't think I even knew he had a niece," Juniper said with a frown. "Now I feel like a bad friend."

"He seems kind of private with his family life."

Juniper nodded but still looked bothered, so I was happy when the bridal consultant interrupted us. She led us to the fitting rooms before bringing out Juniper's dress, and I settled into a plush cream-colored armchair while Juni changed.

My jaw dropped when she emerged from the fitting room. Her dress fit her perfectly, hugging her curves—the ones I had always been jealous of—in a sexy but classy way. The glam and glitz was the perfect combination for Juniper, and Julian would probably pass out when he saw her in it. That was likely why he'd wanted to come today: to spare him the embarrassment of fainting on his wedding day.

Juniper covered her hands over her mouth, muffling her tiny scream.

"I love it," she breathed softly, her smile radiant. It lit up the entire store.

"It's beautiful, Junes," I agreed.

The consultant bent down to inspect the hemline, adjusting her dress so that it barely hit the floor. When she ran to get a few pins, I took some pictures, and Juniper checked her phone to find a slew of texts from an impatient Julian.

"Speaking of Noah, he's with Julian at a brunch place on Tremont," she said, still looking at her phone. "Julian says we should meet them there when we're done."

"Oh, sure." I forced a smile, realizing that I should have expected this might happen. But I couldn't say no when Juniper looked so excited about the idea. In fact, she seemed *really* excited about the idea. "I don't have anything else going on today, so that sounds good."

I spent the rest of the fitting and the entire walk across Boston Common coaching myself on how to act neutral around Noah and *not* like we'd been living together for weeks. I felt confident that I would be able to do it. But the one thing I didn't account for?

Winnie.

As soon as I spotted Noah and Julian's table on the patio of Trémugs, Winnie spotted me. And she went *wild*.

Juniper stood ahead of me, and she gasped like everyone did when seeing an adorable puppy. But when she bent down to greet Winnie, and Noah gave a little slack on the leash so Winnie could say hello, the puppy darted right past Juniper and straight to me.

Winnie leaped into my arms when I bent down, squealing and wiggling with the excitement you'd expect from a dog being reunited with its long-lost owner.

"Well, she's excited to see *you*," Juni laughed, watching as I tried to corral Winnie and get her under control. Noah tugged her back, but when that wasn't enough, he swooped in and picked her up.

I smiled, hoping Juni couldn't hear the way my voice wavered slightly as my brain searched for an excuse. "Noah sometimes brings her with him when he picks Chloe up from skating. I guess she must remember me."

"That's so cute." Juniper didn't look suspicious as she slid into the chair next to Julian.

But my brother's hawkish gaze alternated between me and Noah. "What's this, now?"

I sat in the last empty chair as Noah cleared his throat and answered.

"Gemma is my niece's skating coach."

Julian's eyes narrowed. "So you're a big fan of going to skating practices now, huh?"

I ducked my head, pretending to be preoccupied with the menu when really, I didn't want my expression to betray anything.

"My sister isn't always able to pick Chloe up, so sometimes I do it," Noah explained dryly, unfazed by Julian's pointed questioning.

Julian grunted in response before turning his attention to his fiancée. "How was the fitting, Juni baby? Did you take pictures for me?" He picked up Juni's hand and brushed his lips over her knuckles like the lovesick sap he was.

"Gemma took pictures." Juni's eyes twinkled, full of mischief. "But they're not for you."

Julian frowned. "Who are they for, then?"

I pulled my phone out. "I was thinking that Noah might like to see them."

"Oh, *hell* no." Julian swiped at the phone but missed, and I tucked it back into my pocket with a laugh.

"No pictures for either of you," I said diplomatically.

"Fine by me," Noah said, chuckling as he lifted one hand in defense while the other stayed on Winnie's back. She'd settled back into her usual curled-up position on his lap.

Julian's expression told me it was not *fine by him* that he was still in the dark about the dress, but he would have to deal with it. He'd thank us when he finally saw Juniper in it on their wedding day.

My brother sighed, giving up on seeing any pictures, and directed his attention to Noah.

"Have you found a puppy sitter yet? You've got your first preseason game coming up, right?"

I tensed, wondering how Noah was going to respond to that and considering if I should just jump in and tell a partial truth— that *I* was puppy sitting for a little extra cash. But Noah answered before I could make up my mind.

"Yeah, first game is this week, but Nat's going to help me out," he said, shifting uncomfortably in his chair. The lie came out easily enough, but I could tell he wasn't happy about saying it.

Julian nodded, accepting his answer. "Isn't she going to your Minnesota game, though? I know the whole family usually goes to that one. If you need help while you're both gone, let us know."

"Thanks, man." Noah smiled, relaxing a little. "I'm sure I'll figure something out, but I'll let you know if I can't."

Julian nodded again, and the conversation descended into more wedding talk, which was perfect, considering I only wanted to make it through the rest of this impromptu brunch without talking about myself or puppy sitting or anything related to our situation. As far as I cared, all the attention could stay on the happy couple.

It definitely made it more convenient when my stomach started to reject the strawberry-topped waffles I'd wolfed down, and I had to slip away from the table discreetly. I wasn't really sure *how* discreet it was, but my primary focus was getting to the bathroom as fast as possible before emptying the waffles back onto my plate.

Although I'd gotten used to the waves of nausea, I still hated the upheaval, the feeling of my stomach emptying until nothing remained and all I could do was gag.

I didn't have time to close and lock the stall door in the bathroom before dropping to my knees in front of the toilet, so I shouldn't have been surprised when I felt a hand at the nape of my neck, pulling my hair back.

Great, I was going to have to think of something to tell Juni now that she'd seen—

"I brought you water when you're ready."

The deep voice wasn't what I'd expected to hear in the ladies' bathroom.

"Noah," I choked, wiping at my face. "You shouldn't—"

"Shh." His hands were doing that soothing thing they did the last time we were in this position. *God*, why did we have to keep ending up like this? "Just have a little bit."

He put a glass in front of me, lining the straw up with my mouth so I could easily take a sip. And because the feeling in my mouth was making me want to vomit again, I obliged, sucking up some water to rinse the horrid taste.

"I told them I was going to check on the bill," he said as if he could read my mind. The next words out of my mouth were going to be worries about what Juni and Jules would say. "Just take a deep breath."

I hadn't realized that my chest was still heaving violently. The combination of nerves, nausea, and the exhaustion that plagued me lately made it hard to catch my breath. My knees shook, and I dropped my ass back onto my heels while kneeling on the cold bathroom floor. My eyes squeezed shut, and I felt Noah's body drop to the ground behind me, cradling my own. He pressed his chest to my back and wrapped an arm around my waist, lightly settling his hand over my belly.

"You have to breathe with your stomach," he murmured, his words fanning across the nape of my neck. He sucked in, his torso expanding against my back as he took a deep breath. "Feel it here," he said after blowing the air out again. His hand was still on my belly, his thumb moving in those soothing circles.

I nodded and slipped my hand beneath his, feeling my stomach expand as I took breaths in time with Noah. I could feel his whole body moving with mine—a slow, deep rhythm that worked my nerves down into something I could manage.

"That's it, Em," he encouraged softly. "You're okay."

"I'm okay," I repeated, the words barely a whisper.

"You're okay." He said the words stronger this time. Like he wanted me to believe them. "You are."

"I am," I agreed, and my eyes gradually fluttered open.

We stayed like that for another few moments, breathing in and out. Eventually, I nodded, trying to indicate that I felt better —maybe even okay. But Noah seemed reluctant to move away. He probably thought I'd start dry heaving again any second.

"I should probably go back outside before they start wondering if something's wrong," I said, clearing my throat.

"They're too busy flirting with each other," Noah countered, but I felt him back away regardless. "Plus, I left Winnie with them as a distraction. But I'll head back now, and you can follow in a minute."

"Okay." After wiping at my face again to ensure no residual

vomit lingered around the corners of my mouth, I turned toward Noah. His eyes swept over me in a quick assessment before he gave a nod of approval. I thought that would be it, that he'd leave, but I was starting to realize that I never knew what to expect when it came to Noah London.

Slowly, as though I were a skittish animal, he lifted his hand, tucking a strand of hair behind my ear. His touch heightened the awareness that already fizzled inside me from our proximity. And it only increased as his fingers slid down the strand of hair, all the way to the tip, where he gave it a little tug.

Afraid my cheeks were blossoming with color, I cleared my throat and wiped at my face again. "I probably look like a mess."

"Never." Noah shook his head, his lips crooking sideways in an adorable smirk. "You're not a mess, Gemma." He paused, his green eyes glittering as they took me in. Then he swore under his breath. "But fuck, I sure am."

Before I could ask what the hell that meant, he was gone.

eight years ago

NOAH

"I'm Julian's roommate, Noah," I said, desperate to keep our conversation going.

Gemma beamed, and fuck, I understood now why Julian warned us to stay away.

Because Christ, Gemma Briggs was gorgeous. Creamy skin, pretty freckles, bright blue eyes, and vibrant hair that reminded me of summer —of the hot sun and sprouting flowers. The orange kind with coppery speckles. Lilies. Tiger lilies.

"It's nice to meet you, Noah," Gemma replied, unaware that she was blasting me away with that smile of hers. She leaned closer and muttered, "I'm so sorry you have to live with my brother."

I laughed.

She was sweet, but I could tell she had little claws.

I liked that.

Gemma Briggs was a tiger lily.

And I was becoming a fucking poet.

God, what the hell was wrong with me?

CHAPTER ELEVEN

noah

"**G**REAT GAME, MAN."

Phoenix Jones, our kicker, clapped me on the shoulder as we walked into the locker rooms.

"Thanks, Jonesy. You, too. Way to come in clutch on that last field goal."

I meant it. He'd won us our first preseason game tonight. If there was one thing I could count on during a Knights game, it was that Phoenix would pull through for us when we needed him.

"You good?" He gave me a quizzical glance as we trailed through the locker room to find our bags. "You've seemed a bit off today."

Playing for the same team for six seasons meant the guys on the roster knew me too well. Which was great when it came to our work on the field but not so great when they saw right fucking through me.

I sighed. "I think it's just taking a bit for me to gel with the lineup this season."

"I didn't mean you seemed off on the field," Phoenix said, cocking a brow. "And I think you knew that."

Goddamnit. He was right; it had been a cop-out response. The team played surprisingly well tonight, and I felt great about our chances this year. We had a few rookies, but our starting lineup was solid.

Honestly, I should be on cloud-fucking-nine right now. It was the start of a new season, and the anticipation and high hopes usually made me jittery with excitement. The adrenaline of getting back onto the field and hitting those plays just right usually gave me a high that extended long after I left the turf for the night. But my mind kept drifting to the scene right before leaving my apartment. Gemma and Winnie sitting on the couch, both looking slightly...dejected.

I didn't expect this. I didn't expect Gemma to give a fuck when I left for my games because that just wasn't something I was used to—having people around to miss me. And rationally, I knew she likely didn't miss *me*. With everything she was going through, she probably just didn't want to be alone. And while she had other people she could rely on, she still insisted on keeping them all at arm's length.

Which meant I'd left my lonely, pregnant roommate to sit at home with my dog while I was in another state getting pats on the back for a few good plays. What if she got sick like she did at the restaurant the other day? What if something happened? Something with the baby, and she stubbornly refused to call anyone for help?

I thought leaving Winnie would be my biggest worry. But Winnie had someone taking care of her. My question was...who was taking care of Gemma?

She would say she didn't need anyone to take care of her, and she didn't need anyone to worry. She was capable, independent, and incredibly strong. She was. But everyone should have *someone* to lean on.

"Just getting used to being on the road again," I finally said to Phoenix because it was the closest thing to the truth.

Phoenix nodded in understanding. Being a professional athlete was often glamorized. The money, the women, the fame, the game. It left little to complain about, and I fully knew that, but traveling wore on a lot of the guys. It always left me feeling ragged by the end of the season. But I was already feeling that way in the preseason, which was new. And not a good sign for the few months ahead.

"You'll be back home to your girl soon," Phoenix said as he sat on the bench lining the lockers.

I'd been about to shuck off my jersey when I paused, whipping my head around to look at him. Did he know about Gemma? Because that sure as fuck wasn't good, considering our arrangement was supposed to be a secret.

"You got a puppy, right?" Phoenix clarified, mimicking my confused expression. "Winnie? I assumed it was a girl."

"Oh, yeah." I nodded, giving him a half grin as a bucket of relief crashed over me, making my shoulders slump. "My friend's sister is watching her while I'm gone."

Friend's sister. Gemma was my friend's sister. It would do me good to fucking remember that every once in a while.

"Yeah?" Jonesy perked up with interest like he did whenever a member of the opposite sex was mentioned, and I gritted my teeth. The two of us usually hit up the bars together, taking turns playing wingman, and I hoped he didn't ask me to play wingman for Gemma. Because like hell was that happening. "Which friend?"

"Julian," I said, wishing I hadn't mentioned anything about Gemma. "We played at OSU together."

"Briggs, right?" Phoenix asked, as perceptive as fucking ever. "It's a damn shame he didn't go pro."

"I know," I agreed because it was the truth. Julian could have had an equally successful career in the league.

Phoenix went off, talking about Julian and college ball, letting the conversation drift away from Winnie and Gemma as we changed. He thankfully forgot about them. Me, on the other hand...I annoyingly couldn't get them off my mind.

Once Phoenix wandered away to chat with some of the other guys, I pulled out my phone, tempted to text Gemma. A different kind of nerves twisted inside me at kickoff tonight, knowing she might be watching, might see my every move on the field. I wondered if she turned on the game at home.

Sure enough, I unlocked my phone to find a picture of Winnie in front of the TV, the game on in the background. My stomach turned, making me feel like I was free-falling for half a second.

> Hmm, I only see Winnie in this picture. Is she the only one who watched the game?

Was I fishing for a picture of Gemma Briggs so that I had one on my phone that no one else did?

Maybe.

But a second later, I got one.

And goddamnit, it was a good one.

It was a selfie—a little blurry with shitty lighting, but her smile was as bright as the sun. And she was wearing my fucking green-and-white jersey while sitting on the couch in my apartment. Our apartment.

My cock twitched in my pants. Life would be so much easier if I weren't so undeniably attracted to her. Why couldn't my cock twitch that easily at the first look of the girls Jonesy tried to set me up with when we went out for drinks earlier this summer?

> Ahh, there she is.

Did she already own that London jersey, or had she bought it recently? Or did she go into my closet to find something to wear? All of those options pleased the fuck out of me. I needed to know the answer, but I didn't dare ask.

> SHE'S JULIAN'S SISTER, NOAH: She's here, and she's proud of you for kicking ass tonight. It was a great game.

My chest warmed annoyingly, and I struggled to find a response. People often gave me compliments, but it was usually because they cared about the Knights. They cared about the stats and the numbers and anything that would make those two things look good—like me. And since people didn't typically care about the preseason wins or losses, people didn't usually watch. They didn't bother talking to me about these games. Because what I did didn't really matter all that much. I mean, it did to my coaches and my teammates, but that was it.

> SHE'S JULIAN'S SISTER, NOAH: We should get Winnie a little London jersey. That would be so cute!

I had mixed feelings about that one.

> I'm well aware of my cocky asshole status, but don't you think dressing my dog up to look just like me would take it a step too far? I don't need people thinking I'm that full of myself, Em.

> SHE'S JULIAN'S SISTER, NOAH: Oh, come on. I'll just have her wear it when it's just us at home watching the games.

> Is this game-watching going to become a regular occurrence?

While my chest tightened at the thought of continuing to leave her and Winnie at home over the season, I did like the idea of having a cheering squad just for me in my own living room.

> SHE'S JULIAN'S SISTER, NOAH: Of course. I always watch the Knights games.

> SHE'S JULIAN'S SISTER, NOAH: My dad got us into football young.

Ah, so it wasn't about me, then. That made sense.

> Good man. See you when I get home, Em.

> SHE'S JULIAN'S SISTER, NOAH: Safe travels, Noah.

Our plane landed on the tarmac in Boston well after midnight, and my limbs felt sluggish as I made it to my car. It was a struggle to stay awake on the drive home, but I woke the fuck up as soon as I walked into my apartment.

Low, desperate-sounding moans filtered through the door off my kitchen. Gemma's door. Those mewling whimpers were *her* noises, and it was unmistakable why she was making them.

My dick immediately stood at attention as I listened to a high-pitched gasp, sharp and needy. And then it happened again...and again, and I realized that I was about to listen to Gemma come. I couldn't get myself to *stop* listening, either. I should walk away, give her some privacy, but her moans were the hottest fucking thing I'd ever heard, and I desperately wanted to know what she sounded like when she hit her peak.

A brief but intense cry pierced the air, and I knew that was it.

God, what I wouldn't give to see her pretty face right now. To see lips parted in ecstasy, to see her lost in her own orgasm. I bet she looked so goddamn good.

It wasn't until the apartment grew quiet that a sickening realization hit me. I'd been so consumed by listening to Gemma that I didn't stop to consider who was responsible for making her sound like that. For making her come like that.

I whipped my head around, looking for a pair of shoes by the front door or anything that might indicate she had someone over, but before I could further my investigation, she emerged from her bedroom.

Shit.

Gemma jumped when she saw me, letting loose a tiny scream. I couldn't blame her; it was the middle of the night, and I stood in the dark kitchen, my hands gripping the barstool as if holding on for dear life. I hadn't even realized I'd moved this far into the apartment, too busy being drawn by the sex-fueled noises coming from my roommate's room.

Once she realized it was me, Gemma quickly stepped back into her bedroom like she was hiding something, and my suspicion flared.

"Do you have a guy over?" I asked abruptly.

Too abruptly.

God, what the hell was wrong with me? I sounded mad. I hated that, considering I'd told her she could have guys over. But I didn't know how to withhold the burning in my chest from the thought of another man making Gemma moan like that.

"No," she murmured before blushing furiously.

"No?" I parroted.

"Hello to you, too, Noah." Ignoring my question, she ducked her head before finally committing to leaving her bedroom. A dim light filtered out of the door behind her, illuminating the kitchen well enough that I could see the small pink hearts on the pajama shorts and button-up top she always wore. She walked briskly to the cupboard, grabbing a glass to fill with water. "You could have given a girl a heads-up. I didn't expect you to already be home."

"Sorry, we usually fly back right after a game," I explained before circling back to the conversation I wanted to have and trying not to pay attention to how her shorts kept riding higher. "No one's over?"

"No guy," she confirmed, focusing on holding her cup beneath the faucet.

"Girl?" I questioned. Didn't hurt to check.

She shook her head before finally meeting my gaze. It was hooded, that drowsy postorgasm look. But her irises burned bright, even in the dark. She stared at me, daring me to continue my questioning. And man, did I want to. Because if no one else was over—thank God—that meant Gemma had been doing that to herself, and fuck did I like picturing that scene.

And with that thought, I realized my cock was still tenting my sweatpants.

Luckily, I didn't think Gemma could see it from where she stood.

"So..." I ventured, trying to choose my words carefully.

But Gemma understood me regardless.

"Yeah," she said, still daring to hold my gaze, refusing to back down. "Sometimes you just have to take care of things yourself, Noah."

The air in the kitchen sizzled, crackling between us, reminding me of all the recent times we'd cooked together. Except this time, I felt like I was the one at risk of burning. It took everything in me to withhold my offer to *take care* of things for her. I'd fucking love to take care of her all night long.

"I'm sorry," she continued, misreading my silence. Her eyes finally broke away from mine as she took a sip of water, and I sucked in, able to breathe again. "I'll...make sure I'm alone next time."

I gripped the barstool harder. "Next time?"

Her head shot back up. "You're not asking me to break up with my vibrator, are you?" she asked, her lips twitching now with slight amusement. She seemed to have gotten over the embarrassment and decided to simply fuck with my head instead. "It's the only reliable thing I've got these days."

"No," I said dryly. "I'm not going to make you break up with your vibrator."

God, how I would love to be the one to reliably give her orgasms. I mean, we could keep the vibrator around for fun, too. But she'd be begging for my tongue instead if I just gave her a taste of what it could do.

My jaw clenched. I stepped back from the barstools, putting some distance between us as I realized my control was slipping. I was so close to saying something I shouldn't. Or worse, initiating something I shouldn't. Gemma's slight grin fell as she watched my tense reaction, her eyes flaring as if she understood the war in my head.

She couldn't.

Or maybe she could.

Because then her eyes flicked down, zeroing in on my painfully stiff cock. Without the barstools to hide behind, it was more than apparent how turned on I was.

"How long..." Gemma's voice suddenly sounded hoarse. Her cheeks flamed as she tore her gaze away from my erection. "How long were you listening to me?"

"Only about a minute before you walked out here."

I could hardly get the words out with how tight my throat felt. I hadn't felt desire like this in a long time, and it was doing things to my body I didn't entirely understand. I didn't feel like I could move, could walk. That was how intensely this girl made me feel, especially as she folded her arms over her chest, inadvertently making a button pop open on her top.

Oh hell, this had to be a fucking test.

If the sudden amount of cleavage wasn't enough to drive me wild, her nipples had peaked, too. I could see through her shirt how fucking hard they were, and I had a guess why. What I wouldn't give to suck each one into my mouth until she made those hot sounds again. Until she made them for *me*.

Goddamnit, I was losing it.

"Gemma." I pushed her name through my gritted teeth. "I need you to go back to your room."

She sucked in.

And then took a goddamn step *toward* me.

"Noah, I—"

"*Now*, Em. Please."

I didn't like the idea of resorting to begging, but I liked what was happening here even less. I refused to cross a line with her. We had a good thing going here, and I needed it to last until the end of the season. I didn't know what she was thinking as she looked at me with those big blue eyes, but I knew better than to find out.

After a long, heated pause, Gemma nodded.

And then she disappeared into her room.

I sighed heavily, hating the look of rejection on her face as she walked away.

I'd make it up to her in the morning.

Maybe not how I really wanted to, but I'd figure something out.

I had to.

I still had months left of living with Gemma Briggs, and if I didn't figure something out soon...I simply wasn't going to survive.

CHAPTER TWELVE

gemma

"WINONA!"

Noah's loud, booming voice jerked me awake.

I wasn't sure I'd ever heard Noah yell before, and it startled me so much that I threw the covers off and bolted to my bedroom door...only to find a scene that had me holding in laughter.

Winnie, covered in what looked like flour, ran in circles around Noah as he tried to catch her before she spread more mess in the kitchen. It was a lost cause, though. The counters and floor looked as though they had been through a snowstorm.

When Noah finally snatched Winnie up, he stood and visibly stumbled back at seeing me in the doorway to my room. His eyes on mine, dancing with unspoken words, brought me back to last night.

When he'd heard me orgasming loudly while I imagined things I had no right imagining.

When he'd told me to go back to my room.

When he'd had a tent in his pants that I tried not to think about because of how *big* it was.

Oh hell.

My cheeks, I could feel them heating up. And the ache...the

ache between my legs that I'd tried to assuage last night was returning.

Noah was the first to clear his throat.

"I'm sorry for waking you. I was..." His eyes wandered around the kitchen before he let out a heavy sigh. "I was trying to make you pancakes. To make up for..." I waited, wondering if he would come right out and say it, but finally, he just said, "Last night."

Yeah...last night.

He went on without further elaboration. Not that it was needed.

"But Winnie jumped up and tugged on the towel beneath the bowl of pancake mix like it was one of her rope toys, and, well..."

Another deep sigh fell from his lips as he gave a hopeless perusal around the kitchen.

Despite the tension rolling in my gut, I smiled.

"You didn't have to do that, Noah."

"I also, uh..." He scratched the back of his head, ignoring my comment. "Bought you flowers." Noah gestured to a vase filled with tiger lilies on the kitchen counter, sitting safely away from the pancake mess. "I don't know if you're a flower girl, but I saw these when I was out getting the pancake ingredients and picked them up."

I bit my bottom lip, trying to keep my grin from growing even more and giving away how he was making my insides turn to mush.

"For the record," I said when I got a hold of myself. "I *am* a flower girl. I'm not good at growing them or keeping them alive like Juniper is, but they're pretty, and I like looking at them."

"Yeah." Noah blinked without looking away from me. "Pretty."

"Thank you for getting them." Fuck, I hoped the heat in my cheeks wasn't too noticeable.

"You're welcome. We should maybe put the vase somewhere away from Winnie, though. She's been getting into everything, and I haven't had a chance to research what plants are dog safe."

"Good idea," I said before repeating, "Thank you, Noah. You didn't need to do that."

I didn't want him to think I was mad. I was embarrassed, flustered, and unsure how to act, but I wasn't mad. Noah didn't seem like the type of person who would *try* to sneak up on me. He probably assumed I would be sleeping when he got home.

Little did he know that I *couldn't* sleep. Sleeping alone in his apartment was weird, and I absolutely hated it. Sure enough, his arrival home last night chased away my restlessness. Even with my embarrassment, I'd returned to my room and fallen into a deep sleep that only Noah's bellowing had been able to break through.

Speaking of...

"Winona?" I questioned, leaning against the doorframe. "I didn't know this princess pup had a full name."

"I named Winnie after the town my parents met in," Noah explained before looking down at his dog covered in pancake mix.

My heart squeezed. Noah didn't talk about his family much, and I so badly wanted to ask a follow-up question and dig a little deeper, but given his expression, I doubted he was in the mood.

"At least it was just the dry ingredients," I offered up.

Noah nodded, but he didn't look consoled. So with a deep breath, I foraged into the snowstorm and held my hands out for him to hand over the puppy.

"Here, let me go clean her up."

As though coming to the reluctant conclusion that nothing would salvage his surprise, Noah nodded and handed Winnie over to me.

"If you bring her into the bathroom, I'll grab her dog shampoo," he said. "Just don't let her go. She'll run right out. She's a menace in the bathtub, so we'll have to do it together."

My pulse ticked up at the notion of being in such a confined space with Noah, especially after last night. But I needed to get over it if we were going to continue to live together. This was as good a way as any to do it.

Just dive right in.

To the bathtub.

I didn't think that I would *literally* have to get into the bathtub, but I soon learned that Noah wasn't kidding when he said that Winnie was a menace to bathe. In order to keep her from escaping, I had to squat behind the soaked dog in the tub, holding her from both sides so that Noah could scrub shampoo all over her silky golden coat.

It would have been fine if it weren't for Noah's fingers brushing over mine as we worked together in silence. It made it impossible to trick my mind into thinking that the heat in my body was from the warm, sudsy water covering my legs.

It had nothing to do with the water. All I could concentrate on were his hands, letting my mind wander to places it shouldn't be. The result? Feeling jealous of a goddamn puppy. I bet Noah London knew just the way to work those hands, knew just the right places to put them, knew just the right pressure to use.

Shit.

Maybe I shouldn't have gone back into my room last night.

Maybe I should have walked right across the kitchen, just to see what he would have done—what he might have let *me* do to ease the tent in his pants.

As Noah rubbed Winnie down, she seemed to accept her fate, her body relaxing beneath my fingers. Enough that I loosened my grip.

That had been my first mistake.

My second mistake was to use my body to block her when she attempted to escape over the side of the tub, meaning it wasn't just my legs that were wet anymore. It was the entire front side of my body.

"That was close," I laughed as I plopped Winnie back into the center of the tub and tightened my hold again.

When Noah didn't say a word in response, I looked up to find him unsmiling. Not a lick of amusement surfaced on his face. In fact, his jaw clenched, ticking in an almost angry way that made me frown. Was he mad at Winnie? Was he mad that I almost let her escape to trail soap all over his fancy penthouse apartment? That didn't really seem like Noah, but maybe—

"Gemma." His voice came out hoarse as he jerked his eyes away from me. "*Christ*, Gemma."

"What?" My laugh was more tangled in confusion this time, feeling hurt from whatever had caused the intensity in his eyes. Plus, Noah had stopped washing Winnie, focusing instead on grabbing a towel from the rack behind him.

"Your top," he rasped, throwing the towel at me.

"What?" I repeated, my half-smile fading.

"It's white," he said tightly, his nostrils flaring. "And wet. And *fuck*—"

He interrupted himself, ducking his head as he stared at Winnie. Meanwhile, I clutched the towel to my chest with one hand while keeping the other on top of Winnie to hold her in place.

Noah wasn't mad. And hell, after last night, I should have realized what was happening sooner. Something warmed in my chest as realization bloomed. And I had to admit...I kinda liked it.

Noah London, notorious playboy and star NFL player, was struggling to maintain composure...because of *me*?

I draped the towel over my shoulder, clearing my throat. I'd try to keep the towel there for his sake, but personally, I didn't care. He could stare if he wanted to. I was sure it would only make the heat in my veins grow hotter, and it felt so good as it was.

"Is it just because of last night?" I dared to ask when I found my voice.

Noah's abrupt laugh was rough, lacking humor. "Are you

asking if I just noticed you're an attractive woman because I heard you come last night?"

"Yes," I admitted, pushing through the embarrassment of the question because, as a matter of fact, that was exactly what I was curious about. "That's what I'm asking."

"Em, you've got to be kidding me with that," Noah groaned without lifting his eyes from Winnie. He had the showerhead in his hands now, using it to rinse her coat, and I found myself wishing he'd use that showerhead on me, too.

Oh my God, I was a mess.

But I might as well embrace it.

"Fine, then," I huffed before tossing the towel onto the bathroom floor. If he wanted to make me suffer, I could do it right back.

Noah lifted his head to see what I was doing, and I could tell he immediately regretted it. He bit back a groan, pressing his lips shut as his eyes drifted lower. I could feel them like a hot caress on the curves of my breasts, which my shirt clung to even more now that I'd pressed the towel against me. Seeing as I didn't sleep with a bra last night, my pajama top stuck to my bare skin, and this time, Noah was unashamedly eating it up.

"I've always fucking known," he finally said, voice husky as he forced his eyes to my face. Then he scooped up the towel from the floor and tossed it back at me. "But I'm also trying to ignore it."

I gulped, wanting desperately to shuck the towel again and see what might happen. But Noah seemed tortured enough, and I didn't want to make it worse for him.

I bit down on a smile and wrapped the towel tighter around me.

Okay, so there *was* attraction between us.

It felt good to have that finally established and know it wasn't just something in my head.

But Noah didn't want to acknowledge it, and there must be a reason. It was likely that it overcomplicated things, and Noah was an uncomplicated guy.

Well, that wasn't entirely true. I suspected that Noah *wanted* to be uncomplicated, though. And acknowledging the heat that transferred between every little touch of his fingers and mine would definitely hinder that for him.

So I sighed and resigned myself to helping him finish rinsing Winnie. And when she was clean enough that he could scoop her into his arms, wrapped in a towel like a baby, he nodded at me as I stood in the tub, watching him.

"Thank you for your help," he said, his voice scratchy. "I'm sorry that...I'm sorry about everything."

I shook my head. "You don't need to apologize, Noah."

He pursed his lips like he didn't entirely agree with that.

"Can I still make you pancakes before I have to head to the gym?"

Something told me that making me pancakes would make Noah feel better, so I nodded.

"I love pancakes."

"Good."

He smiled before striding out of the bathroom with Winnie in his arms. Each step he took away from me caused me to sink further into a feeling I didn't fully understand. I should be relieved to put a little distance between us, to break away from whatever was happening in that bathtub.

But relief was definitely not the feeling coursing through me.

And I didn't know what the hell to make of that.

When I opened the door to let Natalie into Noah's apartment the following weekend, she was looking back down the hall behind her with a frown on her face.

"Is that neighbor always so prickly?" she muttered as she turned toward me.

"Summer?" I wrinkled my nose, stepping back to let Natalie into the apartment. "Prickly is a lot nicer of a word than I would use."

"Every time I pass her, she glares at me."

I nodded, unsurprised. "I'm sure she thinks you're another one of Noah's conquests, and she's jealous it isn't her. Noah said he rejected her, and she's been a terror ever since."

Natalie made a gagging noise. "Please never say the words 'Noah's conquests' in my presence ever again."

"Sorry," I laughed. "My best friend talks about my brother in suggestive terms all the time, and it makes me want to invest in a good pair of earplugs, so I should know better."

"Oh God." Natalie walked past me, dropping her purse on the countertop in Noah's kitchen. "I am *so* sorry."

"It's okay." I shrugged. "I basically forced them to realize they're in love with each other, so I only have myself to blame anyway."

She cocked her head to the side, a smile playing on her lips. "That's kind of adorable."

"Disgustingly so," I agreed before sighing and pointing to the couch, where Chloe was passed out, buried in a pile of blankets and pillows. "She fell asleep while we were watching Noah's game. Don't tell him she missed his quarterback sneak. She was really fighting to stay awake but eventually gave in sometime in the fourth quarter."

Natalie's eyes softened as they landed on her daughter. "She loves her uncle so much. I'm glad she has him to look up to, especially considering how absent her dad is. But I wish..." She shook her head. "I shouldn't have to rely on Noah, or you, so much."

My stomach turned as I thought about my own son or daughter and the people I might have to rely on because they wouldn't have a dad in their life. I knew Julian would be an amazing uncle, but he'd have his own kids soon. And the last thing I wanted was to become a burden for someone who had already spent his entire life sacrificing things for me and the rest of my sisters.

I blinked sudden tears out of my eyes, determined not to let Natalie notice what her words had brought on.

"I'm always happy to hang out with Chloe," I said reassuringly. "It's nice to have company, especially on nights when Noah is gone. It's a big penthouse for just me and Winnie."

"Thank you," Natalie whispered as she nodded, her eyes still on Chloe. But I knew that it wasn't really about me. "Thank you so much. I'm sorry to get sappy, but I appreciate it more than you know."

"I'm okay with sappy," I said, my throat a little tight. All the pregnancy hormones meant that seeing Natalie get emotional was making *me* emotional. I'd always felt a connection with Natalie because of our circumstances, but tonight, it felt stronger than normal.

"You know..." Natalie started thoughtfully. "As much pain as her dad brought me and as hard as it is to be a single mom, if I could go back in time, I'd still marry him just to divorce him down the road. Because he gave me her."

She turned, looking at me directly as she murmured the last words, and I instinctively palmed my stomach. Natalie looked down but didn't look surprised. I'd never talked to her outright about being pregnant, but either Noah told her, or somehow she must have guessed. I didn't mind. In fact, there was something comforting about Natalie knowing. It wasn't the same as my own sisters knowing, but it was a start.

She gave me a soft smile, her eyes flicking back to mine. They weren't quite as green as Noah's, but they were equally stunning. "Sometimes it's hard to remember, but the only thing that really does matter is that Chloe's loved by so many people. And we've never, ever been alone."

Her words were about Chloe, but she said them to me.

I smoothed my hand over my belly.

She said them to us.

To me and the little one inside me, who I was going to get to see for the first time soon. Really soon.

My first ultrasound appointment was this week, and a mix of excitement and anxiety swirled within me.

This baby was going to be so loved.

And I couldn't wait to get my first glimpse of them.

CHAPTER THIRTEEN

NOAH'S LIVING ROOM boasted massive wraparound windows, and since he lived on the twentieth floor, there was a clear view of the sprawling greens of Boston Gardens from where I stood, looking out as the sun finished rising.

A mug of decaf coffee warmed my fingers as I leaned against the exposed brick beam that separated the floor-to-ceiling windows. Music softly played from the TV; I'd turned on reruns from the most recent Winter Olympics because watching other people skate was comforting, in a sense.

Noah's end of the apartment had been quiet this morning. He was undoubtedly tired from his away game this past weekend, the same one he'd grumbled about going to.

It surprised me. I always assumed that games were what athletes lived for, but Noah had shown little enthusiasm for leaving on the weekends. The only away game that seemed to excite him was the one coming up in Minnesota, and that was only because his family was going.

After Natalie left with Chloe on Sunday, I headed to bed, attempting to sleep. But as usual, I didn't manage to drift off until I heard Noah's footsteps enter the apartment in the middle of the night, his deep voice greeting Winnie.

I couldn't make sense of it—why sleep evaded me unless he was home. I'd lived alone in my last apartment and never had a problem sleeping. In fact, after years of sharing a room and a bathroom with a handful of siblings, I loved living by myself.

Sighing, I sipped my coffee and watched the cars nearly bump into each other on their morning commute twenty floors below.

God, I missed caffeine. Maybe that would help me shake the deep-seated exhaustion that followed me no matter how much sleep I got. I supposed I could bring that up at my doctor's appointment today. I *should* bring it up. Along with the other million questions I wanted to ask.

When I wasn't skating, babysitting, dog-sitting, or planning Juniper's bachelorette party, I was doing pregnancy deep dives on the internet. It was hard to say whether all the research was making me feel better or worse in terms of preparedness. In rare moments, I found myself thinking that I'd actually be able to do this thing. But sometimes, it made me feel like I'd never know enough to raise a child alone.

With pregnancy worries swirling in my brain, I didn't hear footsteps approach until a gruff voice interrupted my spiraling thoughts.

"Morning."

Noah's simple greeting made my worries temporarily vanish. He stood beside me, his own cup of coffee in his hand, looking adorably tired.

But also ridiculously hot. Of course. He wore a plain white T-shirt, but it was thin enough that I could see how his tattoos swirled up to his shoulder beneath the fabric.

I looked down at my pajamas, the ones I always wore. Maybe I should invest in something nicer to wear to bed, considering how often I bumped into Noah in the morning. And in the middle of the night.

"Morning," I echoed, shooting him a soft smile. "I figured you'd still be sleeping since it's your day off."

Yesterday, he'd been gone all day, doing whatever things football players did the day after games. But I knew his Tuesdays were usually much more flexible, his duties optional.

Noah gave me a sideways glance. "I have plans in a bit."

"Oh?"

I shouldn't be surprised that he'd come home just to turn around again, but I couldn't help the small pinch of disappointment.

Before I could ask him about his plans, Noah nodded at me, his eyes trained on my hands.

"You're always holding a different mug, and yet I've never seen a single one in the cupboard. Where the hell do they come from? Is there some sort of Narnia portal in my pantry where you're hiding your stuff?"

"No, but I wish there was," I laughed. "Then I'd have somewhere to hide my sex toys."

That woke Noah up. His eyes flared as they lifted from my *Criminal Minds* mug to my face. An easy smirk slid across his features. "So you've got more than one, huh?"

"Maybe." I shrugged, trying to play it cool. Noah always exuded so much confidence, and I was determined—especially after the tension of the last week—to match his attitude. And his teasing. But I struggled to figure out what else to say, so I reverted to our original subject. "As for the mugs, I keep them in my room. In a tote under my bed."

I could tell the turn of conversation gave Noah a bit of whiplash. His head jerked sideways in confusion. "Why?"

I took a sheepish drink of my coffee. "Because I have a lot. And you don't need to see *just* how much I like Spencer Reid."

"How many is a lot?"

"Like...a lot. I know it's super cheesy, but I sort of collect them. Not like *seriously* collect them. More like, *casually* collect them."

Noah chuckled. Then he considered me for a second before coming to a resolution. "You're putting them in the cupboard. And I want to see them. If they don't fit, I'll buy a new shelf."

Shit.

"That's *really* not necessary."

"Yes, it is," Noah concluded before turning his attention toward the TV, curiosity in his eyes. "Did you ever have a skating partner like that?"

I followed his gaze, watching the ice dancing routine unfold. It was a sensual, dramatic performance. The two skaters had a lot of chemistry, the tension palpable even through the screen.

Out of the corner of my eye, I saw Noah narrow his gaze.

"Yeah," I said, thinking back on my experience in college. Noah's attention shot back to me, surprising me with its intensity. "I actually had the same partner for a couple years. His name was Liam."

"Liam," he repeated stonily. His eyes flicked back to the screen, taking in the rotational lift the pair was maneuvering that resulted in her sliding down his front to return to the ice. Noah crossed his arms over his chest, watching so carefully I almost laughed. "Did you ever—" He cut himself off, pressing his lips tightly together before trying again. "Did you keep in touch with him?" he asked without taking his eyes off the TV.

I shook my head. "No, Liam and I didn't end on a good note."

Noah snapped his gaze back to me. "Did he do something to you?"

"No," I assured him. "Just differences of opinion on our senior year performance. We got through it, but I think we were both glad when it was over and we could move on to different things. I transitioned into the coaching world, and he started performing in ice shows."

"Got it." Noah nodded, his tense body relaxing. "I'd be interested to learn more about your skating career sometime, Em." He said the words like he truly meant them before checking his watch and adding, "Fuck, I have to take Winnie out and then get ready to go."

He walked off, and I sighed.

I had to get ready, too. But I'd bet his plans were a hell of a lot more fun than mine.

"Gemma, c'mon!"

Halfway through tying my shoes, I stilled at Noah's voice.

"We're gonna be late!" he added, and that sure as hell got my attention.

"We?" I questioned, stepping out of my room, hopping because one of my shoes wasn't on yet.

"Yes, *we*," he said, exasperation thick in his voice. He leaned against the front door, sporting his usual casual look on days when he didn't have football commitments. Today, his ball cap was facing forward, ready to be tugged low.

Because apparently, Noah intended to come with me to my doctor's appointment.

"*This* was what you had planned today?" I choked out.

"Yep." He acted nonplussed by my sputtering.

I balked at him, struggling to believe that he was serious. But he was unfazed by my stare.

"God, I should have never shared my schedule with you," I muttered.

"I don't know." Noah shrugged. "I think it's been working out pretty well for us."

"You really don't have to come with me," I said, deciding that I didn't want to think too much about just how well our shared little life had been going. Instead, I focused on fixing my shoe. A trickle of sweat rolled down my back from rushing to get ready and the rising anxiety of the appointment.

"Nah, we're done with that," Noah replied casually, drawing my attention again.

"Done with what?"

"We did it your way last time, and I don't think it went well for either of us," he explained. "We're done having this back-and-forth. You're not going to this appointment alone, and since I'm the only one who knows, I'm going."

I sighed, finding it hard to argue with that. Finding that I didn't really *want* to argue. I liked the idea of Noah coming with me more than I should admit.

"You can't possibly want to spend your day off going to my prenatal appointment," I stressed, even though I honestly liked the idea of having Noah's support today. I didn't want to be even more indebted to him. He'd already helped me more than enough.

"I'm not doing anything else besides getting in some weight lifting later," he said, straightening as he twirled his car keys around his finger. "If you didn't want me to come, you shouldn't have scheduled it on a Tuesday."

I lifted a brow. "I'll keep that in mind for the next appointment."

Noah narrowed his eyes but then snapped out of it. "We have to go."

Too tired and in a hurry to argue, I followed Noah to the garage and let him usher me into his car. We didn't talk much on our way to SCMC. I was too panicky, and Noah was too intent on getting us to the clinic in time.

Amazingly, he did it. We arrived in the waiting room with a few minutes to spare, and to my huge relief, we were called back for my ultrasound within a minute of sitting down.

At this point, I didn't even argue that Noah shouldn't come with me. Mostly because the longer he sat in the waiting room, the more likely someone would recognize him. If he insisted on being here, he might as well wait where fewer eyes were around.

However, I immediately regretted my decision when we walked into the imaging room to see a long wand-like probe resting near the patient seat. And, of course, it didn't escape Noah's notice, either.

"Does that go where I think it goes?"

I could tell by his low voice that he'd only meant for me to hear him, but the sonographer answered.

"Probably," she laughed. "That's an endocavity probe, which we use for transvaginal ultrasounds. At almost twelve weeks,

Gemma should be far enough along to have an abdominal ultrasound, however."

Noah continued to eye the probe as we sat, me in the reclined patient bed and him in a chair beside it.

"Stop staring at it," I hissed, flicking him in the arm to get his attention.

His round eyes jerked away from the medical instrument. "I just feel like it can't be good for the baby to have something of that size shoved up there, ya know?" he muttered.

"Don't worry. Something of this size is more than safe," the sonographer answered for me, trying to keep the humor from her voice but lifting a brow at Noah all the same. And unless I was seeing things, there was definitely an innuendo in her expression.

Noah nodded as he crossed his arms over his chest, satisfied with her answer. "Good to know."

Maybe having Noah come with me today had been a mistake after all. Because I couldn't stop the rising flush that worked its way up my neck. I felt it spreading to my cheeks, heat spearing through me.

As if he could read my embarrassment, Noah fell quiet after that. The sonographer walked me through the ultrasound, directing me to bare my abdomen while explaining how the gel would feel cool on my skin.

I clenched my hands into fists at my side as she pressed the flat head of the abdomen probe to my stomach, but not because it was uncomfortable. In fact, I desperately needed the gel's cooling effect at the moment, thanks to Noah.

No, my clenched fists were due to nerves. Not the nerves that were currently going haywire because of sexual innuendos but the nerves that were working overtime because I was about to see my baby.

I jumped when I felt fingertips graze my arm, just below my elbow. They paused momentarily as if waiting to see if I'd brush them away, and then they continued, gently caressing a path down to my clenched fist. A fingertip tapped my thumb, wanting entry. I eased my fingers apart, and the other hand invaded mine until we were entwined.

"Squeeze my fingers instead of your own," he said softly, his lips brushing the shell of my ear. I hadn't realized he was so close, but I was grateful for it.

I was thankful that someone was here to help me pick up my pieces if I broke down into them.

I squeezed his fingers, and when the sonographer smiled at the screen she was watching, I smiled nervously, too. That was good, right? It had to be good.

When she twisted the monitor toward us, I held my breath. And when she started explaining what the hell I was even looking at and how that tiny blip on the screen was my little plum, tears pricked my eyes.

It was real. This was really happening, and I couldn't put my feelings into words, couldn't decipher through the waves of emotions to find anything accurate to describe them, but it didn't matter. Noah had the only words I needed.

"You're going to be an amazing mom, Em," he whispered. "Just amazing."

All I could do was squeeze his hand harder as the sound of the baby's heartbeat filled the room.

This was real.

I wanted to protest when the sonographer swiveled the monitor away, but then she reassured me that I'd be sent home with prints today, and I nodded regretfully. I wasn't done looking at my plum.

I'd have to wait, though. We were ushered back to the waiting room a few minutes later until a different nurse called me back for my follow-up with the doctor. Similar to the sonographer, if the nurse recognized Noah, she didn't say anything as we settled into the two seats in the exam room.

Instead of commenting on my NFL roommate, the nurse took my vitals. She smiled sympathetically when my blood pressure came back high as a fucking kite and told me that she would retake it in a bit after I'd had a minute or two to relax.

I wanted to laugh. There was a fat chance that I'd feel relaxed anytime soon.

Despite my high blood pressure or the way my pulse hammered inside me, I answered her routine questions with surprising ease and realized that this reality felt more and more...normal.

Yes, I'd been experiencing morning sickness. Yes, I'd been experiencing exhaustion. Yes, I'd been taking my prenatal vitamins. Yes, I'd been continuing my exercise regimen. Yes, I was taking my iron supplements and folic acid. Yes, this. Yes, that.

My last visit here, I hadn't felt prepared. Sure, I knew they would tell me I was pregnant—the millions of at-home tests had assured me of that. But there were things I hadn't even thought about. Did I want to get tested for sexually transmitted diseases? Which diagnostic screenings did I want? What was the father's health history?

I still didn't know the answer to that last question, but I'd been working myself up to figure it out. As much as I hated it, I'd have to contact Silas soon. I wouldn't let my discomfort outweigh the health of my baby.

It seemed to last forever, but finally, the nurse came to the end of her questionnaire and slipped out of the room, stating the doctor would be in shortly.

"Do you want me to pretend to be the father?" Noah asked as soon as the door clicked shut.

I turned to face him, my lips parting wordlessly. *What?*

When I just stared blankly at him, he went on in a softer voice. "I realized when we were doing the ultrasound that they probably assume I am. I just want to know what you'd like me to say if the doctor asks."

Having Noah pretend to be the father sounded absolutely dangerous. I had little doubt he would do exceedingly well at playing that role. He would put on a brilliant performance, but it would only make it harder when we left and I returned to reality.

"I already told her last time that the dad wasn't involved," I said when I found my voice.

"Well, maybe I got my shit together and decided to be involved again," he argued. "I bet that happens all the time."

"Then she's going to ask you about your health history," I sighed because he seemed determined to play this little scenario out. And while it might be nice for a short while, it wouldn't do me any favors in the long run. "You can't lie about that. Not to mention, it will be weird when you're not at my follow-ups."

He lifted a brow. "And who says I won't be?"

I could tell by the tilt of his lips that his challenge was partly in jest. As usual, he was trying to ease the tension in the room. And I let myself follow his lead.

"Well, maybe my next appointment won't be on a Tuesday, and then what?"

Noah scowled—his expression more serious this time as though he realized I was right and that he might actually not be able to come.

"Fine," he agreed. "I won't lie to the doctor."

A lie. It was a lie. It was fake. Noah wasn't the father of my baby. Noah and I hadn't had sex, let alone kissed. And I didn't expect that we would.

Dr. Amos noted Noah's presence the minute she walked in. She smiled at me first, but then her eyes darted to the man beside me with clear interest. Dr. Amos had a good poker face, I'd give her that, but she couldn't hide the flash of recognition that passed through her eyes when they landed on Noah.

We had a football fan in the house.

Regardless, Dr. Amos didn't waver from her professionalism as she greeted me and politely opened to include Noah.

"And who have you brought with you today?"

"This is my...friend. Noah."

It seemed like the best descriptor for what we were and the

safest on the off chance that his presence here today leaked anywhere.

With a continued pleasant mask, Dr. Amos held her hand for him to take. "It's nice to meet you."

Noah shook her hand, returning the greeting. Dr. Amos looked back to me after, and just by the way she leaned closer, I knew she was about to ask a slightly invasive question—as doctors sometimes had to do.

"Is our friend also dad?"

Yep, there it was.

"Just a friend," I said, the words making something swirl in my gut. "Along for moral support."

I wasn't sure what Noah and I were, but saying he was *just a friend* didn't seem like the most accurate description. It didn't feel right leaving my lips.

Beside me, Noah shifted in his chair. The movement caught Dr. Amos' attention, her eyes darting to Noah before switching back to me.

"Okay." She nodded, switching her attention to the computer screen. "I only ask because if he were dad, it would be important to input some of his health history into your charts while he's here." Her eyes swiveled to Noah, brow arched. "You wouldn't happen to know any of that information, would you?"

If I dared to glance at Noah right now, I'd shoot him an *I told you so* look. But as it was, Dr. Amos demanded all my attention, and I couldn't drag my eyes away from the withering look she gave Noah, challenging him to reveal the truth.

The truth that wasn't real, of course.

In her eyes, she probably thought Noah was trying to hide that he'd gotten some girl pregnant to save his image. Which only made my stomach turn, because he was risking that image by wanting to support me when he didn't need to.

"No," Noah said after clearing his voice. "I don't know any of that, unfortunately."

Dr. Amos' gaze lingered on him while trying to assess the situation further.

"Unfortunately," she finally said, more to herself than us. And then louder to me, "And are you comfortable with him being here for the duration of the appointment as we review your ultrasound results today?"

"I am," I said without needing to question it further.

I was comfortable with Noah. As much as I would love to have Juniper or one of my sisters here with me, Noah had an assured sense of calm that I needed today.

He knew how to take slow, deep breaths while I was taking fast ones.

"Okay, let's take a look," Dr. Amos said with a smile while gesturing to her screen.

Somewhere during her explanation, my hand ended up in Noah's. And even after she gave me the prints from the ultrasound and left us in the exam room with them, my hand stayed in his, squeezed tight.

Only a handful of months, and I'd be a mom. I couldn't believe it, and yet...I could.

The nurse returned to the exam room a few minutes later to measure my blood pressure again, as promised.

Miraculously, it was normal.

eight years ago

NOAH

"You know, living with your brother isn't so bad," I replied honestly, sliding my hand into my pocket to silence my buzzing phone, not needing more updates about my overachieving siblings. "We need someone to run the ship around here, and he does a good job."

"That doesn't surprise me," she said wryly, although I could hear the touch of love and admiration behind her words. "He loves to be in charge...boss people around...hover unnecessarily."

Her eyes flicked upward at that, looking at something just above my shoulder, and I turned around to find nearly identical eyes glaring at me.

Oh, fuck.

CHAPTER FOURTEEN

"FRIEND, REALLY?"

Shit.

I'd meant the question to be teasing and light, a break in the car's silence as Gemma and I drove home. But it came out with an edge.

Gemma swiveled in her seat. The heat of her gaze bored into the side of my head. But she didn't say anything, and not knowing what was going on in her brain, especially when I couldn't fully see her with my eyes on the road, drove me wild.

"Not even roommate or pretend boyfriend?" I added, trying to sound lighthearted. "You're just going to give me the boring label of *friend*?"

Gemma cleared her throat. "It was the least complicated option."

"She knew, Em."

She knew that Gemma and I shouldn't ever be described as friends. It didn't fit us. Not because we were *more* than friends, though. We were just something *other* than friends. It wasn't a word that worked for us, and maybe it was my fault, my face that had given it away, but Dr. Amos saw it. She saw how much I hated when the word "friend" slipped through Gemma's lips, and she'd honed in on it.

"She knew what?" Gemma questioned. "We're friends, Noah."

My grip twisted around my steering wheel as I drove into the parking garage at our building.

Even as she said the words, they didn't sound right. Because Gemma couldn't say them any more convincingly now than she could in the exam room.

Friends.

God, I wanted to show her how thoroughly wrong she was to use that word about us. But it wasn't like I knew the right word to use. I didn't expect to ever use those other words—boyfriend or dad. But I knew *friend* wasn't it. Even if that was all I ever would be to her.

It was all I *could* be.

But it still hurt to hear her say it.

"What?" Gemma repeated because I still hadn't managed to explain myself.

Mostly because I didn't think it needed explaining.

But fine. She wanted an explanation? Sure, I'd give her one. Even if I shouldn't because it wouldn't make a difference. Fuck, I was sick of holding my tongue around her, though.

"I wasn't thinking of you like a friend when I came home in the middle of the night to hear you fucking moaning."

Gemma sucked in audibly before recovering. "I'm sure you would react the same to hearing any girl like that."

No way.

Because it wasn't just the sounds that made me hard.

It was how they conjured up an image of the woman making them. It was how they formed this picture in my head of Gemma with her lips parted and head tipped back, moaning as she took me like a good fucking girl.

But if Gemma wanted to pretend that wasn't true, I'd let her. It was better if I didn't convince her. Because honestly, what good would it do? It certainly wouldn't do me any favors, not when I'd been trying to resist her.

"Yeah," I said, putting the car into my park. "You're probably right."

I was just about to turn the car off when the display lit up, showing an incoming call from Nat. And I knew that wasn't a good sign. I loved my sister, but she usually only called when she needed something.

I left the car running, answering the call with the touchscreen display.

"Hey, Nat," I said, raising my voice slightly to be heard through the car.

"Noah," she whined.

Yep, my suspicions were definitely correct.

"What's wrong, Natalie?"

"Don't *Natalie* me," she groaned. "It's not my fault. You know it's not."

I sighed and softened my tone. "I know it's not. What's up?"

"I got scheduled for surgery next week. On September twenty-fifth. Thursday. And I just don't think I can get out of it."

Realization washed over me, and then my stomach soured. "You can't come to Minnesota for the game."

"I'm so sorry," she whispered, and I knew she meant it. I knew she regretted the sacrifices she had to make for her job. "Chloe's going to be so disappointed, too. She's been talking about it constantly. It's been so long since she's been to one of your games, and she keeps stealing my phone to text Sully about how she's going to finally beat him at Candyland when we're at Mom's."

The feeling in my stomach worsened to include a crack in my chest.

My brothers never got to see Chloe. My parents never did, either. When Natalie had still been married to that asshat husband of hers, he'd always come up with excuses to keep my family from coming to visit them. But it was just a narcissistic tactic to separate Nat from everyone who could have pointed out what she was missing about her husband. Meanwhile, Natalie hardly made it back home to visit. Part of that was work. Part of that had been the asshat husband, too.

I sighed. "If I could bring Lo on the team plane, you know I would."

Gemma squirmed in her seat, drawing my attention. It would make sense if this was a little awkward for her, and I expected to find her wearing an uncomfortable expression, but she was pointing a finger at her chest, eyes wide.

I'll take Chloe, she mouthed, leaving me momentarily stunned.

But the more I thought about it, the more it made sense. The more it sounded *perfect*.

Chloe would still see my family, and I wouldn't have to leave Gemma behind for once.

"Hey, what if Gemma took Chloe to Minnesota?" I asked Natalie before I could really stop and think about what I was doing. "It would just be the two nights, right?"

"Oh, I couldn't ask that of her," Natalie rushed to reply. But I didn't miss the slight hopefulness in her voice. "She's already helped us—me—out so much. I couldn't ask her to do that, too. That's...that's a lot."

"I'd be happy to do it," Gemma jumped in cheerily, talking loud enough for Natalie to hear that this time.

"Oh!" Natalie stumbled slightly over her surprise as she realized Gemma had been listening. "Oh, Gemma. That's so nice of you to offer. But I don't know. Are you—are you sure you'd want to do that? Noah, what about Winnie?"

Shit. Right. Winnie. The entire reason I'd asked Gemma to move in with me.

That question stumped Gemma momentarily, her lips thinning as she thought. And then she perked up. "You know your neighbor Matt?"

I nodded, not sure where she was going with this. I knew Matt, but I didn't realize *she* knew Matt.

Why the fuck did she know Matt?

"He's stopped me a few times while I'm out with Winnie," she explained. "And he's mentioned that he'd be happy to watch her if I ever needed help or anything."

"He did, huh?" I raised a brow. I was sure Matt wanted to help Gemma with something, but it had nothing to do with my dog. But Gemma nodded enthusiastically as if she'd solved the problem. "I don't want to let some asshole neighbor watch my dog. Couldn't we just ask Julian? He offered."

"He's not an asshole," Gemma quickly argued. Too quick. "Involving Julian sounds...complicated."

What she meant was, involving Julian might mean he'd find out the truth. And considering how much Julian would hate the truth, it could ruin everything.

I bit my tongue, knowing I shouldn't argue this. Not if it meant Gemma might get to come to my game in Minneapolis.

"We'll make it work," I said, switching my focus to Natalie. "Why don't you think about it, and we can touch base tomorrow. Sound good?"

"Yeah." The relief in Nat's voice was palpable. She might not like being away from her daughter, but she hated disappointing her more. And she wouldn't only be disappointing Lo. She'd be disappointing my parents. Not to mention Sully, Theo, and Blake. "That sounds good. Talk then."

As soon as Natalie ended the call, I turned back to Gemma.

"You don't need to do this, you know."

"It would be fun going to your game instead of watching it on TV." She shrugged, but I didn't miss the slight tension in her smile. "And I figured with you being out of town and Natalie in surgery, Chloe would probably be hanging out with me anyway. But..." Her face screwed up as she thought hard about something, her mouth catching on air before she decided to continue. "I'll need to look into costs. I should have thought about that first."

"Costs?"

"You know...hotel, airfare."

I lifted a brow. "You won't have to pay for either. You think you're going to fly all the way to Minnesota with Chloe and I'll make you stay in a hotel? No way, Em." I chuckled, enjoying the way her expression widened, larger than life. "You'll stay with me."

"And where are you staying?"

"At my mom's house. At least the night before the game, anyway." When she looked surprised, I explained, "When I first joined the NFL, they had strict rules about everyone staying in the same hotels when we traveled. But I soon realized those rules are only strict for rookies. Anyway, my mom whined about it when I'd visit and have to stay downtown the whole time with the team. I tried to explain to her it was, you know, my job, but somehow, she always decided to overlook that part."

"Are you sure your mom will be okay with that?" Gemma asked after a moment of stunned silence. "With me staying with you, too?"

Oh, my mom was going to eat it up, getting to cater to a new person. As if her five children weren't enough, she always adored fawning over my brothers' girlfriends over the years.

Not that Gemma was my girlfriend.

I'd need to make sure Mom knew that.

"She'll love it," I assured Gemma before opening the car door.

And as I got out of my Audi, I had a much bigger spring in my step than when I woke this morning.

A few days later, Gemma was back to ignoring me at the rink, striding off the ice with a quickness that gave her away. She paused only for a few seconds to put on her skate guards and then took off.

"Em!" I called after her, checking that Chloe was pulling off her skates before turning to follow Gemma down the small hallway leading away from the ice. "That kid almost knocked you right over. How often does shit like that happen?"

Gemma didn't stop walking until we were in an office area, where she opened a locker on the back wall.

"Well, beginner skaters are...beginners, so it does happen from time to time," she said dryly.

"Can't you teach a non-beginner class, then?" I argued.

She might be playing this off like it wasn't a big deal, but I'd seen the way she almost lost her balance when that little blonde girl with pigtails barreled across the ice, and Gemma barely skated out of the way in time.

What if next time she didn't catch it in time? How long would it take for her balance to be affected by her pregnancy? When would she know? What if she figured it out too late?

"I'm perfectly safe on the ice. We've talked about this," she said with mock sternness, like she was a teacher scolding me for having to go over a rule I'd already learned. "And I'm in a hurry. Janie and Gianna are in town because they went shopping for bridesmaids' dresses, and we're all going out tonight with Juniper. Of course, it's on the one night of the week that I have evening classes, but whatever. It is what it is, but I have to get going."

Gemma's words all tumbled out of her with a rush of air, and it took me a second to remember that Janie and Gianna were two of Gemma's sisters. And then I frowned, stepping back to watch as she sat in an office chair and began removing her skates.

"Where are you guys going?" I asked.

Gemma looked up at me while still bent over her feet. If she wasn't wearing a tight spandex jacket that zipped all the way up to her chin, I would have had a clear shot of her cleavage.

I couldn't decide if I was disappointed or thankful.

"We're starting at the Bellflower Bar, but then I think we're going to hit up some other bars."

I crossed my arms over my chest, picturing the scene. And I had to admit, I didn't really like it.

"Is Julian coming?"

She shook her head. "We convinced him that it was a girls' night."

I'd be surprised if Julian was truly convinced. His overprotective ass probably planned to secretly trail them all night in case they needed something. He would pull some shit like that.

Gemma finished kicking off her skates and stood.

"I need to change," she said, looking at me expectantly. And when I couldn't get myself to walk away from her just yet, she added, "Considering how you freaked out when you saw the outline of my boobs the other day, you might want to close your eyes or something."

I scowled, and Gemma grinned.

She fucking liked getting a rise out of me way too much. Not many people were good at it, and it seemed like she knew that. She knew she could get under my skin, and she liked that knowledge way too much.

"I did not freak out," I grumbled before facing the office door. It was for the best this way. I could stand watch. The last thing I wanted was someone walking in on her unexpectedly while she was changing.

"You smacked me with a towel," she argued back.

My only answer was a grunt as I listened to the rustle of clothes as Gemma presumably undressed.

God, this was fucking torture. I fought the urge to think about the things I shouldn't be. Like the outline of Gemma's tits beneath that white, soaking wet pajama top. About how good they would look without *any* top. About how if I turned around now, I'd probably get to see for myself.

But I couldn't do that, so I took to words instead of actions. Because I needed to do *something*.

"I don't know if you realize this..." I muttered, just loud enough for her to hear me. "But you have really fucking nice tits, Em."

Her breath hitched audibly, and my lips curved in satisfaction.

"You know, they're only going to get bigger," she said before something landed on my shoulder. I grabbed it, only to realize it was Gemma's sports bra. Meaning, right now, she probably wasn't wearing *any* bra. Or a top.

I groaned. "You're gonna be the goddamn death of me, I swear."

She laughed, but it was strained with tension, and she tried to cover it with a cough that morphed into a groan of frustration.

"What?"

A pause before she finally seemed to cave on some internal dilemma. "Can you help me zip my dress?"

Fuck, did she not just hear what I said?

Death of me. She was going to be the death of me.

I turned around to find Gemma's bare back to me, the graceful curve of it on display. My steps seemed to echo in the office as I walked toward her, closing the distance between us. The dress zipper was stuck halfway up her back, and I tugged it up the rest of the way slowly, savoring her proximity.

And also subjecting myself to the torture of it.

"Thank you," Gemma whispered, and I knew that was my cue to step away.

But just as before, I couldn't get my legs to work.

Gemma turned, looking up at me. And God, I wish she hadn't.

I didn't have a lick of fashion sense, but the dress Gemma had on must have been designed simply to destroy me.

The bottom flared from her waist, flowing over her stomach to effectively cover the tiniest bump she'd started to show. I'd noticed it earlier when she was on the ice and immediately wanted to pull her off it. I wanted to wrap my arms around that little bump and protect it from the world, and holy hell, that feeling had terrified me.

The bump and the skirt covering it wasn't what was destroying me now, though. No, what got me was how the flowery, blue fabric of her dress loosely ruched around her tits, accentuating their natural shape while drawing them together with a string in the middle, tied in a little bow.

She looked like the perfect summer package that I desperately wanted to unwrap.

Gemma noticed my stare and looked down at her dress with a frown. "Does it look okay? You can't see my bump, can you?"

"No," I said hoarsely. "You can't see the bump. Looks great, Em."

Fucking inadequate words. I hated biting my tongue around her all the time.

"Thanks." She flashed a smile before spinning to grab something. I wasn't sure what because I didn't let her get more than one step away before wrapping an arm around her waist and pulling her back toward me again. She stumbled, her back colliding into my chest.

"Be safe tonight. 'Kay?" I murmured. She nodded, her hair tickling my chin. Satisfied, I loosened my hold on her. "Do you need a ride there?"

"I'm going to walk."

I grunted, annoyed. "No, you're not."

"It's fine, Noah," she said over her shoulder. "It's not that far."

Fuck that.

My hold on her tightened again. "I'll drop you off. And then you can text me when you need a ride home," I amended. "I can be discreet so your sisters and Juni don't see me."

She sighed but didn't argue, which I figured was a good sign. I let her go, watching as she cleaned up the rest of her stuff and grabbed her purse. A minute later, we walked back to find Chloe waiting for us.

I hoped she hadn't been waiting too long. And I hoped she didn't notice how I kept drifting closer and closer to her coach as we walked, wanting Gemma within arm's reach for some inexplicable reason.

But I didn't have it in me to care what Lo was thinking right now. All I could think about was how fucking glad I was that

Gemma planned to come with me to the game next week. Because dropping her off at the bar and watching her disappear from sight while wearing that dress?

Yeah, I wasn't a big fan of that.

Leaving her to go on the road had been my least favorite part about this season so far.

Now, I couldn't wait to bring her with me.

CHAPTER FIFTEEN

HOLDING BACK FROM unloading on my sisters and Juniper was the hardest thing I'd done in a long time. It wasn't just the whole pregnancy thing anymore. Or the quitting my job thing or having to move out of my apartment.

No, I needed someone to scream to about how Noah London just held me in his arms like that. How he kept dropping massive hints about being stuck in the same current of attraction that I was and how he was struggling just as much to break free of it. I needed someone to scream to about how I would get on a flight in a few days to stay at his *mom's* house.

What the hell was wrong with me? I *hated* flying.

But my big mouth just had to open right up and volunteer to take Chloe. The picture Natalie had described tore at my heart, and I couldn't help it. Especially not when I'd been dreading Noah leaving for another trip.

"Earth to Gemma!"

Janie laughed as she shoulder-bumped me. Tonight was her night off from studying for the LSAT, and she was taking full advantage of it, throwing back drink after drink. Gianna and I kept pushing food in front of her, wanting to ensure she had something to soak up all that alcohol.

"I'm sorry," I groaned, feeling like I was making a lot of apologies lately. "Practice tonight wiped me out."

Plus, a very handsome spectator kept worming his way into my thoughts.

"I didn't want you to get mad at me for saying it, but yeah, you look kinda tired," Janie said, which I might be annoyed about if I didn't know it came from a good place. "Is that why you're not drinking tonight? Is everything going okay at the rink?"

"Everything's going great at the rink," I said honestly. "But yeah, trying to keep up with all the little ones has been exhausting."

Hopefully, they wouldn't notice that I glossed over the drinking question.

"Do you have any shows or competitions I can come to?" Janie asked, pausing before she took a drink of her vodka soda. "I want to come see all the cute little skaters!"

I smiled. "We have a program in a few weeks. It's mostly just for parents to see the kiddos' progress, but you're welcome to come watch."

"Yes!" Janie exclaimed, clapping her hands together.

I loved my younger sister's enthusiasm, but I had no idea how she would fit my program into her schedule, considering her studying habits. Not to mention, she'd played Division I soccer as an undergrad and stayed on as an assistant coach after graduating last year.

Gianna grinned. "That would be so fun to go to."

But again, I wasn't sure when she'd find the time. Her second year as an English teacher had been off to a stressful start. She'd followed in my mom's footsteps, which worried me sometimes. Teaching had left my mom at her wit's end so many times over the years, but Gianna loved it so far.

So I just smiled back, watching as Gianna reached across the table and pushed the basket of fries toward Janie, moving her drink further away as she did. Her eyes slid to mine, more sober and scrutinizing. I felt Juniper watching me, too, and I knew I had to do a better job of acting...normal.

Except my life was nothing like it used to be. How I acted now was my new normal; they just weren't used to seeing it.

For a second, I wondered if I should tell them. It felt wrong to spill the news without Josie and Genevieve, my other two sisters, but the urge to get the secret off my chest was so unbelievably strong. A second later, though, Gianna started chatting with Juniper about bachelorette party plans, and I swallowed my confessions.

Another time. When I was more prepared. When I had a plan that extended beyond the next two months.

It was better this way.

Everyone was in such a good mood tonight, and I'd hate to be the one to ruin it. This was Janie's night to let loose and our season of celebrating Juni and Jules. It was a terrible time to reveal that I, their big sister they'd always looked up to, had fucked up and gotten pregnant. That I was broke and surviving on charity from our brother's friend and would probably have to work three jobs to afford childcare at some point. That I had no idea where I would be living in a couple of months. What a great example I was for them.

God, I wished I could have a real drink.

But I couldn't, so I forced myself to tune in to their conversation without liquid courage, and surprisingly, the next few hours flew by. We never did end up leaving the Bellflower. We had a perfect table in the corner where no one was bothering us, and why ruin a good thing?

"Do you want to stay with us tonight?" Juniper leaned in to ask.

I frowned, momentarily forgetting that she still thought I lived in the suburbs. But Juni mistook my frown for something else.

"I promise we won't be couple-y," she rushed to add. "I'll make Julian behave."

A laugh burst through my lips because we both knew that would never happen. Julian would be all over her the moment she stepped back into their apartment.

"It's okay, Junes. I'm good to drive home."

Or get a ride from my hot NFL roommate.

"You could stay at our hotel, too," Gianna offered, which caused Juniper to roll her eyes a little because she had also tried to get my sisters to stay with her. Like me, they didn't want to watch our brother salivate over his fiancée for longer than necessary. We were all hoping that maybe in a year or two, they'd stop acting so grossly in love all the time.

"Maybe next time," I said, sliding off my seat to hug each of them. I'd texted Noah a bit ago, and he'd be around the corner any minute. "My own bed is calling me tonight."

My own bed in Noah London's apartment.

I bit down on that little secret while I said goodbye to my sisters and Juniper, and guilt roiled in my stomach. I would tell them everything. Just not tonight.

Noah was exactly where he said he would be when I walked outside, and I quickly slid into his car.

"Are you okay?" Noah asked as soon as I'd buckled my seat belt.

Was I that easy to read, or was he just that good at it? Either way, it was a little unnerving.

I glanced over at him. He wore a Knights hoodie and sweats, making me feel even guiltier because he'd probably been in bed when I texted him.

"All the secrets are just weighing on me," I confessed. "But I'm fine."

Noah nodded silently. He didn't move to put the car in drive. Instead, he drummed his fingers on the steering wheel briefly before speaking.

"It's not too late to go and talk to them. I don't mind waiting."

He made it sound so easy.

"I should, but..." I sighed.

Noah waited for me to finish my sentence, but when I didn't, he asked softly, "What are you worried about?"

"I guess that I'm just..." I leaned my head back, squeezing my eyes shut. "I feel like a failure, Noah. Julian and I are the oldest siblings. We've always...I don't know, taken care of the others. And look at Julian. Successful lawyer, engaged to someone my whole family loves, always taking care of everyone. And me? I feel like I can barely take care of myself lately. Meanwhile, the rest of my siblings are..." I broke off with a groan because I didn't want it to sound like I wasn't happy for my brother and sisters, who were all doing so well.

When the car grew quiet and Noah didn't respond immediately, I opened my eyes.

He was watching me thoughtfully.

"I know how it feels to compare yourself to your siblings," he finally said. "But you impress me every day. And I don't think Julian would ever think you're a failure, Gemma. I'm sure your sisters wouldn't, either, but I don't know them as well."

I met his gaze across the darkened car, feeling my heart rate spike. There was just something about the way he was looking at me. There always was, but right now...something heavy, something intense, something I never imagined seeing in Noah London's eyes lingered there.

He was so much more than anyone ever gave him credit for.

"Not tonight," I eventually whispered. "I don't want to tell them tonight."

I would tell them, but not tonight.

"Not tonight," he allowed and put the car into drive. "Let's get you home."

Home. What a weird thing—that my home was now with this man I hardly knew a month ago. And soon, I wouldn't just be staying in his apartment, but I'd be staying in his hometown.

"What should I pack for Minnesota?" I asked, wanting to change the subject.

Noah thought about it while we waited at a stoplight. He

looked over at me, his eyes dragging up and down my body in a way that had me crossing my legs as soon as he moved his gaze back to the road. A dull ache had sprouted between them, all thanks to Noah's molten-hot attention.

"Not that dress," he finally said, a bit of gravel in his voice.

My jaw dropped. That had been the last thing I'd expected him to say. "You told me earlier I looked great. You don't like this dress?"

The light turned green, and Noah stepped on the gas with more force than necessary. We zipped down the road, but I didn't feel the fear I'd expected. Only an exhilaration of sorts that made my pulse race and my body ache.

And Noah's response only added to it.

"I like that dress way too fucking much to survive you wearing it around my family."

My heart thumped wildly against my chest as I smiled shamelessly to myself, looking out the window so Noah couldn't see my reaction. The lights of the city at night whizzed by, and I rolled down the window to let the early fall wind whip through my hair. Traffic zipped by around us. The roar of a motorcycle revving up was louder than the car engines. I closed my eyes, taking it all in.

"You would look so goddamn good on my bike," Noah said. The pitch of his voice was lower, sinfully smooth, and I couldn't help but imagine what it would feel like to be straddling Noah's motorcycle with my arms wrapped around his waist.

I'd seen that motorcycle so many times. Julian had worked on restoring it for over a year, and it sat in my parent's garage in Whitebridge the entire time. Motorcycles had never appealed to me. They terrified me, actually. But that was before Noah told me I'd look good on one.

I turned my smile toward him. "Take me?"

First airplanes, now motorcycles. What was this guy doing to me?

"No way in hell." He shook his head. "There's a reason I haven't already put you on my bike."

His eyes flicked over and down at my stomach, and disappointment washed over me. I would have to wait at least six more months before Noah even considered taking me for a ride. And by then, I'd have moved out of his apartment, and he'd likely have forgotten about me.

That thought made me realize how badly I needed to take advantage of the here and now. Before we got to that point where none of this existed anymore. And while I didn't know exactly what that looked like yet, I was sure of one thing.

I was absolutely going to pack this dress.

Noah's flight to Minnesota left before ours did, but he insisted on making sure we got to the airport before he left town.

He also insisted on researching whether or not it was okay to fly at three months pregnant and then questioned whether or not he should bump us up to first class. Somehow, I managed to convince him that wasn't necessary and also that it was safe to get on the plane according to Dr. Amos. Even though I felt anxious about it for my own reasons.

The result of Noah's worrying meant Chloe and I were at the airport four hours before we needed to be. And while I never had any problems with Chloe in all the afternoons and evenings we'd hung out together, four hours was a long time to entertain an eight-year-old in an airport. Luckily, Chloe was pretty well distracted by beating me in card games.

Honestly, the challenge of keeping Chloe occupied helped me forget all my other worries. Most immediately: getting on a flying metal tube.

It wasn't until we were boarding the plane that I remembered how much I hated being trapped while up in the sky. But I took a deep breath and reminded myself I'd gotten through a handful of flights before, and I'd do it again. It was too late to back out. At this point, everyone was counting on me to get Chloe to Minnesota.

Truthfully, while I didn't regret volunteering to bring her, I hadn't realized how much of a commotion it would cause.

According to Noah, his mom nearly cried when he'd told her that Natalie couldn't come because of work, and then she nearly cried again out of gratitude when he told her I'd still bring Chloe. Meanwhile, Natalie had to sign a child travel consent form for me to be able to fly with her daughter. And not only that, but she'd had to get her ex to sign it, too.

That was how I knew this must be important to her—to all of them. All I knew about Nat's ex was that she absolutely despised him. I was sure she only talked to him when she felt she had to. I mean, Silas wasn't even my ex, and I sure as hell wouldn't talk to him unless I felt it was absolutely necessary.

Along with the consent form, Natalie also sent me a whole bunch of other emergency information that I felt confident I wouldn't need but was thankful to have, just in case.

I blew out a shaky breath as Chloe and I settled into our seats.

"Are you excited to see your grandparents?" I asked her, hoping that talking would hold my other worries at bay.

Chloe nodded excitedly. "And I'm going to beat Uncle Sully in Candyland."

"That's what your mom said," I laughed.

Chloe's bright eyes momentarily dimmed at the mention of Nat.

"We'll send her pictures, 'kay?"

She looked up at me with a toothless grin, having lost one of her front teeth this week. "Deal."

Chloe looked out the window as the plane began to roll on the tarmac, and I closed my eyes, preparing myself for the worst part. My fingers clutched the armrests as I waited for the plane to pick up speed. And when it did, I squeezed my eyes shut tighter. I kept them closed until I felt a small hand on my leg and realized Chloe was trying to comfort me.

I looked over to find her worried expression trained on me like a little mirror of Noah's.

I flashed her a wobbly smile, which she returned.

"I think that was the worst part," she said, leaning over to whisper as soon as we reached cruising altitude.

I nodded, breathing out in relief. "I think you're right."

And she was, in a way.

The ascent would be the worst part of the plane ride, sure.

But I had a feeling that the rest of this trip would be far from easy.

eight years ago
NOAH

"You sure didn't waste any time introducing yourself to my sister, did you, London?"

Julian's sharp gaze narrowed on me, but I shrugged. "You were doing a poor job of introductions, so I took it upon myself to start without you."

"I see that," he said dryly, but then his gaze shifted to his sister, and his whole demeanor changed as he stepped around me and pulled her into a hug. "Hey, Gems. I'm glad you made it. I'm sorry about that. Juniper—"

"Don't even start," Gemma cut him off, pulling back to lift a hand in his face like she didn't want to hear it. Julian's mouth zipped shut, but I could tell it was painful for him to keep his thoughts to himself.

"Gemma, can I get you something to drink?" I interrupted, hoping to break the tension that clearly surrounded Julian and Gemma's friend.

Julian shot me a look. "Look at you, being a fucking gentleman all of a sudden."

I rolled my eyes. I might have a reputation as a flirt around campus, but that didn't mean I didn't have manners.

"Once again, I didn't see you offering to get her anything."

"It's because he knows I don't want his shitty beer," Gemma laughed.

Her laugh was angelic.

Hell, she was angelic.

Julian sighed. "I actually bought you and Daisy a bottle of that wine you like. I'll go get it."

And then he walked away, leaving me stunned.

He must not be thinking clearly.

There was no other reason Julian would leave me alone with his sister.

But like hell was I going to miss this chance.

Gemma's eyes followed her brother for a moment before they traveled back to me. She grinned, this time almost shyly, as she bit down on her bottom lip.

And now I was staring at her lips.

They were pink and full and...God help me.

"So you're on the football team, too?" she asked, jerking my attention away from her mouth and how badly I wanted to kiss it.

Fuck me.

CHAPTER SIXTEEN

GEMMA AND CHLOE stood on the curb outside of MSP's baggage claim, and as soon as my eyes landed on Gemma's face, I realized something awful.

I wanted to kiss her. Goddamnit. Just one look at her after a handful of hours apart, and I wanted to kiss Gemma so fucking bad. But I couldn't. And that was the awful part. What the hell was it about her that made her so hard to resist? From the very first time I laid my eyes on her, she had me. And now, seeing her nearly every day without getting to *have* her...it was slowly destroying me.

"Hey, you two!" I called after parking. With two quick strides, I pulled Chloe into my side for a tight squeeze and took Gemma's suitcase in one move. Gemma brushed past me, so close that all I could smell was her, sugary and intoxicating. Like a summer cocktail that I wanted to drown in. Like fucking heaven.

"Hop in. I've got it," I murmured to her.

Gemma gave me a look before sliding into the front seat of my dad's truck. After our team meeting this afternoon, Dad had picked me up from the team's hotel, rescuing me from a night of listening to Jonesy snoring. Then we grabbed a beer downtown before I dropped him off at Mom's and headed to the airport.

163

I always tried to schedule some one-on-one time with my dad. Once we got around the rest of the family, he had the tendency to try to fade into the background and become a man of few words. He'd sit back and watch the goings-on with an inward smile.

I had a feeling Tom London went into security years ago because he liked the solitude of working night shifts. Not to mention, getting a break from the crowded chaos at home.

"How was your flight?" I asked, looking back at Chloe to ensure her seat belt was on. She lifted wide eyes, staring at me. Those eyes were wide enough that alarm churned in my gut.

"Coach B does *not* like to—"

"The flight was really good," Gemma cut in, and I switched to look at her breathy smile. When my eyes so much as touched hers, she swiveled around to look at Chloe, humor in her expression. "You can just call me Gemma, you know."

That made Chloe's smile reappear. "Okay, Gemma."

Gemma laughed and faced forward again. I frowned.

What didn't she like?

"How far is it to your parents' house?" Gemma asked with a forced, artificial voice I hated.

"Roughly thirty minutes," I said, putting the car into drive. "And it's just my mom's house. My dad used to live there, too, but then they got divorced."

"Yeah, Grandma kicked his ass to the curb," Chloe piped in from the back seat, and Gemma damn near slapped herself in the mouth with how quickly she tried to cover her reaction.

"Hey, Lo," I said before pausing while I held in my laughter. It wasn't funny; it really wasn't. But I hadn't expected those words to fly out of my niece's mouth. "I know your mom might say that sort of stuff occasionally, but it's not like that for everyone who goes through a divorce. Grandma did not kick your grandpa to the curb. Also, Grandma's not gonna be happy if she hears you swearing."

"Yeah, yeah, I know," Lo sighed.

Nat had kicked *her* ex's ass to the curb, and I wouldn't doubt if Chloe had heard her say it, too. But my parents just...fell apart. No one kicked anyone's ass to the curb. It almost felt like they just... fell out of love. Like they simply decided one day they'd be better off as acquaintances.

Maybe there was something I didn't know, but they'd never acted mad, never made a big deal of it. It seemed like one day they were married, and then another day, about five years ago, they weren't.

I let the music fill the car, unsure of what to say. That wasn't usually a problem for me, but I hadn't introduced a girl to my parents since high school, and I didn't feel prepared for what was about to happen.

Although Gemma wasn't my girl to introduce. She was just a girl. A girl who was my roommate but who was *not* my friend.

Silence filled the car for a while, and I let it linger and mingle with my nerves. It wasn't until we turned off the highway that Gemma spoke again.

"There are so many lakes."

She wore a slow-spreading smile. Scenes I had memorized flew by the window, and her eyes were glued to them.

"It's actually all one lake," I corrected, trying not to reveal any of the weird emotions I was feeling.

Gemma's brows furrowed adorably, and I chuckled.

"This is Lake Minnetonka," I explained. "It's all connected. There are these separate pockets of water, some small and some huge. My mom's house is on one of the smaller ones. It sort of feels like a lake's version of a cul-de-sac."

I wasn't sure if Gemma heard a word I'd said. Her nose remained stuck to the window, eyes widening as we passed big lakefront properties.

"I don't want to be rude," she whispered, "but I'd like to know how your mom affords to live here so I can get in on whatever it is."

I repressed a smile because of the cute way she leaned toward me without peeling her eyes off the scenery. "My mom is the director of a pet rescue organization here in the Twin Cities, but while she's very good at her job, it doesn't pay much."

She frowned that confused little frown again. "Then how— oh, of course." Exasperation melted across her face as she finally spared me a glance. "You *would* buy your mom a mansion, you momma's boy."

I couldn't help the satisfied curl of my lip. I was damn proud that I'd been able to buy this house for my parents. We used to live a little further out in a farm-style home that barely fit the five of us kids. Even though all of my siblings had moved out, now we had a gathering place where we could all come together comfortably.

"For the record, I bought my *parents* a mansion, and then my dad decided to move out. But yeah, I'd do anything for Anne and Tom."

"Those are their names?" Gemma asked, and I nodded. She turned back to the window, wearing a soft smile. "I can't get over how gorgeous it is."

It was gorgeous. *She* was gorgeous, and the slight peppering of orange and red outside the window as the leaves hinted at fall was gorgeous, too. The sun was hitting the lake just right, making it glitter as we drove down the winding lane that eventually ended at my mom's big, white lake home.

Gemma surprised me, seeming eager to jump out of the truck as soon as I parked it in the driveway. But I caught her wrist right as she was about to open the door. Chloe had already leaped from the car, running to see my mom, but that was fine.

"I told you I have three brothers, right?"

I probably should have brought this up earlier, but talking about my family hadn't been high on my priority list.

"No," Gemma laughed. I wasn't sure why she laughed because nothing about my brothers was funny. They tried to be funny a lot, but they rarely succeeded. "Chloe told me, though. What are their names again?"

"Theo, Sully, and Blake," I said before warning, "Don't listen to a word any of them says. They think they're hilarious, but they're really not. Especially Sully. He's a software engineer, but I think he actually just sits around all day and thinks of ways to annoy me."

"So stay clear of Sully. Got it," Gemma said, clearly amused.

"He's the tallest but the youngest," I said. "Dirty-blond hair that probably needs to be cut. Blake is the oldest, and he acts like it. Then it's Nat. Then Theo, who's only a little more than a year older than me."

"I'm never going to remember that," she warned with a giggle.

"Honestly, it's better that way," I said dryly.

"Are any of them married? Have kids?"

I shook my head. "A bunch of bachelors," I said ruefully and then frowned when I noticed Gemma's smile fading.

"Do they know I'm pregnant?"

I shook my head. "No, but I could tell them. Just so they know in case, I don't know, you need anything."

They would be the ones spending time with her tomorrow at the game—not me. It would make me feel better if they knew, but I wouldn't force Gemma to share something she didn't want to.

"Sure, you can tell them." Gemma nodded after a long pause, seeming confident about it. "I think it might be nice not to feel like I'm hiding something for once."

"Okay," I said, relieved.

With that, I stepped out of the truck and around the back to grab the girls' luggage.

Time to bring Gemma into the chaos that was the London family.

My mom was the first to fuss over Gemma, which didn't surprise me at all. My dad flashed one of his genial smiles reserved for occasions like this. And then, to my massive irritation, all three of my brothers crowded Gemma and simultaneously introduced themselves in rapid succession.

Chloe was my little savior, though. She pulled Gemma out of my brother's clutches and dragged her up the stairs to show off her room, which my mom had gone all out in decorating just for this visit. I had a feeling she hoped that if Chloe loved it, Natalie would bring her home more.

The rest of my family trickled into the living room, where we usually hung out. I followed and, after glancing back to make sure Gemma was still upstairs with Chloe, turned to address them all.

"Gemma is pregnant," I said, wanting to get to the point quickly.

"Holy shit." Theo straightened in his seat, and I realized maybe I should have started this conversation differently. "You're gonna be a *dad*?"

"I knew it." Sully shook his head, a silly grin on his face as if he couldn't believe he'd guessed something right. Well, wrong. "Damn. Who would have thought you'd be the first brother to become a dad? Well, actually, considering—" I glared at him, and he cut himself off. "You know what? Never mind."

Meanwhile, my mom had slapped a hand over her mouth, and my dad put a hand out as if to steady her, even though she hadn't moved an inch. He, on the other hand, tipped to one side slightly before righting himself with his grip on Mom's shoulder.

"You need to move home," she gasped once her hand dropped. "I'm not having another one of my grandkids living on the goddamn East Coast."

I sighed, pinching the bridge of my nose. "Were none of you listening when I told you she's not my girlfriend?"

Blake scoffed, running a hand through his dark, wavy hair. "She doesn't need to be your girlfriend for you to put the you-know-what in the you-know-where."

"Immature asshole." I grabbed a pillow off the sofa and threw it at my brother.

"Just explaining to you how reproduction works," Blake muttered.

They liked to do that. Pretend that because the rest of them were in high-intellect careers and I was a football player, I didn't know shit.

"Gemma was pregnant before she moved in with me, and I'm not the dad," I said sourly. "Like I said, we are *not* together."

"Oh my God, Noah Lancaster London." My mom slouched onto the couch's armrest. "Don't—don't...*do* that."

Theo leaned back in his chair again. He was a big dude, bigger than me, and I never understood why he hadn't pursued football further than high school. But he was happy working as a professor for the U and making all the college kids swoon after him.

"So you just decided to come over here and proclaim that the girl you're bringing home is pregnant for funsies, then?" he probed.

"I'm not *bringing her home*. She's only coming because of Chloe. And I wanted you all to know she was pregnant before someone said something that made it awkward." I looked pointedly at Sully. "She's not taking shots with you before the game."

Sul cocked his head to the side in thought. "What about, like, one shot?"

"No." I glared at him. "And I need you to look after her at the stadium tomorrow." I eyed my other two brothers. "Make sure she doesn't get shoved around in the crowds, okay?"

Theo gave me a lazy salute. "We will protect the princess Gemma, the first of her name."

"Her name is Briggs, as in sister of Julian Briggs, who doesn't even know she's here. So you better protect her, or my ass is dead."

All three of my brothers chuckled at that. So typical that my friend kicking my ass would make them laugh.

"But no touching," I clarified.

Theo put his hands up, enacting innocence. "No touching. Just protecting. Got it."

"And that's the only reason you care...because of Julian, right?" Blake drawled, still stuck on the earlier part of the conversation.

I rolled my eyes at him.

"Does her baby daddy know you're gunning for his role?" Sully added, wiggling his eyebrows up and down.

"Her baby daddy is a deadbeat, so I really don't care what he thinks."

Theo leaned toward Sully, cupping his mouth to whisper conspiratorially in my other brother's ear, but he did it loud enough for everyone to hear. "Did you notice how he didn't deny the other part of that question?"

"I'm not gunning for the role," I groaned. "There, happy?"

Sully and Theo grinned widely. "Extremely," one said while the other nodded.

They didn't believe what I was saying, but I didn't care. I could hear Gemma and Chloe coming back down the stairs, and Sully was already on his feet, walking toward my roommate.

"So," he started, throwing an arm around Gemma's shoulders. My fists clenched. What did he not understand about *no touching*? "It's been about ten years since I had to live with Noah here, but I can't imagine it's gotten much better. Tell me, how's he doing about cleaning his nose hair trimmings from the sink?"

I shoved Sully just hard enough that he lost his footing, his arm falling from Gemma's shoulders.

Grabbing her hip, I tugged her back toward me slightly.

"Don't listen to a word of them says," I reminded under my breath.

But she just laughed and looked at Sully. "We actually have separate bathrooms, so I wouldn't know."

Sully pretended to ponder that like it was the biggest letdown. "Hm, probably for the best."

"Probably," Gemma repeated with a grin like she thought this whole little thing was mighty funny.

I disagreed.

"Let's bring your stuff downstairs," I said before this could descend further into madness. With her luggage in one hand and her hip in the other, I urged Gemma toward the basement stairs. "We're both staying down there tonight."

"Is your family going to think it's weird if we're staying, like, *together*," she whispered as we disappeared into the finished basement.

She said the word *together* like it was such an awful idea.

"Well, there are two separate rooms," I explained, "but I'm gonna tell you right now that my family doesn't care. I'm sure they probably think we're fucking."

And God, wasn't that the dream.

Her breath caught. She stopped in front of the full bar that faced the lakefront, where we hung out a lot when I visited during the summers. The living room walked right out onto the lawn leading to the dock, and down the hall were two bedrooms connected by a bathroom.

"*What?*" Gemma breathed with wild eyes.

"That's what they think I do." I shrugged. "I hook up with girls."

Plus, my family never missed a thing. And the way I just grabbed her away from Sully was probably all they were talking about now.

I led Gemma into the first bedroom. It was a full, sweeping suite with views of the lake and its own patio. A big bed sat in the middle of the room with a baby blue comforter spread across it. The whole room was decorated in neutral and blue hues. Modern but cozy.

I may have bought the house, but I didn't play a role in decorating it. That was all my mom, and she made this place feel like home, even if it was completely different from where I grew up.

"You can sleep in here, and I'll be in the connecting room. I'm sorry I won't be here tomorrow night since the team is flying back late after the game, but I promise my mom is so excited to have you. And she's so grateful that you brought Chloe."

Gemma blinked as she looked around the room. If she was worried about staying here tomorrow night without me, she didn't show it. I wasn't even sure if she heard what I'd said. Her mind seemed to be somewhere else, and her voice came out in a rasp when she spoke. "So am I going to need earplugs for when you hook up with the local girls?"

I rolled my eyes. "I have no plans to do that."

"No?" She arched a brow, twisting around to sit on the edge of the bed. Then she leaned back like she fucking owned the place and crossed one leg over the other. The result? Getting to see her dress slide up those pretty, long legs. "I thought that was what your away games were for. Hooking up."

I jerked my eyes back to her face. "What are you talking—"

The way she simply cocked her head to the side stopped my words. Because I did say that back when she first moved in. And what a fucking lie that was.

"I haven't hooked up with anyone at my away games this year," I said truthfully. "Not unless my hand counts."

My hand and the memories of Gemma's breathy moans had satisfied me on far too many nights this season.

Gemma stared at me, lips parting with unspoken words.

I could tell she wanted to ask. She wanted to know what I thought about while my hand was around my cock, and man, I wanted her to ask, just so I'd have an excuse to tell her.

But she didn't ask me, and I broke our eye contact, wondering if this was a terrible idea. We'd been alone for all of five minutes, and I was already ready to say things I shouldn't.

Maybe Gemma should stay upstairs.

But I didn't want her thinking she had to stay with Chloe; she wasn't here to babysit her. Her only job was to get her here. And if Gemma slept upstairs, she'd be surrounded on all sides by my brothers. And there was no way in hell I'd let that happen.

No, I wanted her next to me.

Even if it partly tortured me.

Swallowing, I kept my gaze trained on the gorgeous redhead in front of me.

"It gets cold down here sometimes, so there's a heater there if you need it." I pointed to the space heater in the corner.

Gemma nodded, but the way she was watching me told me that she didn't think she'd need it.

I didn't think I'd need it, either.

There was enough goddamn heat between us that we'd probably be able to feel it through the wall.

There was a reason I'd made it this long without doing something I'd regret with her, and it had a lot to do with the *many* walls and *large* number of square feet between my room and hers in our apartment.

But tonight?

Tonight, sleeping might be impossible.

CHAPTER SEVENTEEN

"**N**OAH!" SULLY'S VOICE cut through the tension in the room. "Stop hogging our guest and get your ass up here for dinner!"

Gemma's pretty face flushed before she got up and headed toward the door. Either she was really eager to eat dinner with my family or desperate to get away from me.

"You remember what I said about my brothers, right?" I called after her.

She looked over her shoulder, pausing at the bottom of the steps. "Not to listen to a word they say."

"Good girl."

Her cheeks grew even rosier before she abruptly turned and jogged up the stairs, which didn't help. Watching Gemma's ass bounce directly in my line of sight *really* didn't help.

This dinner was going to be torture.

And sure enough, it was.

Theo, Sully, and Blake all fought for Gemma's attention while my mom attempted to play referee as we ate. Gemma volleyed their questions expertly and with a smile, nonetheless. She had smart little answers for everything they asked, playing them like fucking fiddles. My mom loved it. My mom loved *her*; I could tell. Which was something I hadn't been prepared for.

Letting my mom get attached to Gemma was a really fucking bad idea.

"Okay," I finally said after watching my family pass the wine around the table one too many times. I'd been sitting back while they all vied for Gemma's attention for hours and wasn't sure I could take it any longer. "Some of us have important shit to do tomorrow and should probably go to bed."

"Alright." Theo lifted his beer. "Night, Noah."

Sully turned to Gemma. "Want another *non*-alcoholic beverage?"

I scowled at him, and he grinned back.

"What?" he countered. "*She* doesn't have important shit to do tomorrow."

"Grandma," Chloe hissed across the table. "I think I should get their dessert because they're swearing at the dinner table."

"I think so, too, honey," my mom whispered back.

"Thank you for the offer," Gemma said, smiling gently at Sully. So fucking polite when she didn't need to be. "But I'm actually feeling pretty tired, too."

"Mhm," Blake murmured as he slowly sipped his red wine— the one he'd carefully selected to pair with tonight's steak because he liked to pretend he was a pretentious asshole now that he'd become the second doctor in the family.

Pink colored in the spaces around Gemma's freckles as she blinked at Blake.

"Come on." I grabbed her wrist, giving a slight tug to have her follow me down the stairs. Luckily, she did, which allowed me to whisk her back into her room and shut the door before any of my brothers could follow us.

Gemma laughed to herself as she dropped onto the bed.

"What?"

She shrugged. "I like your family."

"They like you," I said with a heavy sigh. "Maybe a little too much."

"Oh, stop." Gemma kicked me lightly on the ankle as I walked by her to look out the window. The moon was reflecting across the lake. "I kinda feel like I'm intruding on your family reunion."

"You're not intruding," I said as I turned back to her. "You saved the day by bringing Chloe, and I'm—"

And I'm really glad you're here with me, I wanted to say. Even if I had to share her with my family. But I didn't need Gemma to know that I hated leaving her at home on travel days. We didn't need to go down a road that would just be a dead end.

"I'm excited to have you come to the game tomorrow," I finished weakly.

It wasn't a lie, but it only skimmed the truth.

"I'm excited, too," she said softly before standing. "I'm going to get ready for bed."

Bed.

Right.

After taking a steadying breath, I gave Gemma a quick rundown of where she could find things in the en suite bathroom, and then she dragged her entire suitcase with her, shutting herself inside.

Meanwhile, I went to my room. It was basically a replica of the room Gemma was staying in, except the color scheme boasted navy instead of baby blue. I tossed off my shirt and threw on sweatpants before twiddling my thumbs, waiting for Gemma to finish in the bathroom. A few minutes later, she popped her head out of it.

"I'm done if you need to use the bathroom," she said before flashing me a crooked smile. "Make sure you clean up your nose trimmings."

Goddamnit, Sully.

"Thanks for the reminder," I said dryly.

She laughed, and then her teasing expression turned shy. "Good night, Noah."

"Night, Em."

She lingered for just a moment longer before disappearing. I heard the door on the opposite side of the bathroom close and waited a few minutes before I went to brush my teeth. When I heard the slight creaks of the bed as Gemma lay down next door, I turned on the faucet to drown it out.

Christ, we'd lived together for *weeks* now. Why did this arrangement feel so much more intimate?

Maybe it was just me. Maybe it was simply because this was my mom's house, and I never had girls at my mom's house. That was probably it, which made me feel better because hopefully, Gemma didn't feel the same way I did. Hopefully, she'd fall right to sleep and stay that way all through the night.

My hopes for a peaceful night vanished when I startled from my half-sleeping state a few hours later to hear noises in the bathroom.

Noises that sounded an awful lot like Gemma getting sick.

Shit.

Sure enough, I peeked inside the bathroom in time to see Gemma wipe her chin off with her pajama top, making a disgusted face before she flushed the toilet. Tears streamed down her cheeks, and exhaustion riddled her expression. I'd learned that Gemma almost always cried when she threw up, which made it that much harder for me to watch.

She caught sight of me in the doorway before I was able to say anything.

"I'm sorry," she groaned, wiping at her face. "God, I thought for sure I was done with this. I didn't think the nausea was supposed to last this long."

It hurt so bad to watch her suffer like this.

"You're almost in your second trimester, so it might get better soon," I said, trying to be positive, even though I knew there was no guarantee of that. "Here, hang on."

Not wanting her to have to sit there in vomit-stained pajamas, I grabbed a spare shirt from my bag and brought it back to the bathroom. Gemma had her head in her hands when I crouched down to give her the shirt, and I ran a hand down her back, only to be surprised by how goddamn *cold* she was.

"Christ, Gemma."

Her head shot up, and I regretted the way I said her name. But holy shit, she was a fucking popsicle. And not only that but I could feel how her body shook with waves of shivers.

I put my hand to her forehead, suddenly worried she was sick.

But no, her forehead was just as icy as the rest of her.

"That heater in my room doesn't work," she said, tucking her knees into her chest and wrapping her arms around them to stay warm.

"Oh my fucking God." I checked my watch to see that it was nearly 2:00 a.m., and we'd said good night around eleven. "So you've just been sitting over there freezing for the past three hours?"

She shook her head. "I fell asleep for a little bit."

I frowned. "You can have the heater from my room."

Lifting her head, she matched my frown. "But then *you'll* be an ice cube. What if your fingers freeze off? We've already talked about this, Noah. You need those. I just need a couple more blankets, and I'll be fine."

"Nope." No way. "I'm not having you and your unborn child freeze to death in my mom's basement, Em."

"Well, now I think you're being just a *touch* dramatic," she muttered. "It's not *that* cold."

I ignored her and pointed to the shirt I brought her. "Put that on, and then get your ass in my bed."

"Noah—"

"Your ass in my bed, Gemma Briggs," I reiterated and then left the bathroom before she could argue with me about it.

Heater aside, this just felt...right.

Also torturous, but that was beside the point.

I didn't like waking up to find Gemma suffering. I'd rather be there for all of it. So if that meant that we were going to share a bed, then we were going to share a fucking bed.

I crawled back under my covers and then sat there, impatiently and awkwardly waiting for Gemma. I tapped my fingers on the bedspread while I stared at the bathroom door.

Goddamnit. I was acting like a prepubescent teen who'd never had a girl in his bedroom before.

At least Gemma was changing, so I wouldn't have to suffer seeing her in those pajamas with the little hearts on them. Or, more crucially, that top with the buttons that came undone so easily.

Yeah, a T-shirt would definitely be bet—

Gemma opened the bathroom door and immediately proved me wrong.

"Do you need shorts?" I blurted because she walked into the room looking like she was wearing my shirt and *nothing* else.

This was not better than her normal pajamas. No way in hell. She was entirely too tall for that shirt. I mean, sure, it covered her ass. But barely. And she looked so fucking good in my Knights apparel that I had to stifle a groan.

Her wearing my clothes made me feel like she was mine, and she wasn't even close to being that.

"No, no," Gemma protested, making a dash toward the bed as though everything would be okay once she got beneath the covers and I couldn't see how goddamn short the shirt was. "Some of the you-know-what got onto my shorts, too." I rolled my eyes at her aversion to saying the word "vomit," considering how many times I'd seen her do it. "But I don't need anything else. It's fine."

It was not fine.

Gemma slipped into bed, and my body immediately tightened with the awareness of hers. It didn't matter that it was a king-

179

sized bed. Every slight movement she made sent a jolt of heat through me, undeniable and intense.

Gemma, on the other hand, seemed unaffected. She flopped onto her back, pulling the covers over her with a contented sigh.

I wanted to make her sigh like that.

"Are you sure you're okay with this?" she asked.

"Yeah, I'm sure."

I was *not* sure.

"Are you?" I tossed back.

"It's much warmer in here," she said, and I could hear the gratitude in her voice. "Thank you."

"You don't need to thank me for not letting you freeze when you're the one who flew all the way to Minnesota so my niece could come to my football game."

"Well, I'm glad I came. But...I do miss Winnie," she murmured, filling me with guilt because she was over there thinking about my dog while I'd been fantasizing about doing dirty things to her a minute ago.

I missed Winnie, too. It hadn't been easy to entrust Matt to care for her when I'd been so used to having Gemma do it.

But I'd lived next to him for over a year, and he was *fine*. He had some kind of high-level corporate job and said he could work from home when he wanted to. I liked the idea that Winnie would have plenty of company. And even though I could tell he was looking around my apartment for Gemma when he came over to talk Winnie logistics, I could also tell he did, actually, seem genuine in his offer to take care of her for a few nights.

"I miss her, too," I agreed, sliding down to lie flat. "But I'm sure she's okay."

Gemma seemed like she needed to hear that last part, even if I couldn't help but worry a little bit, too.

"You said your mom works for a pet rescue. Did you have dogs growing up?" Gemma asked, peeking over at me. "Is that why you wanted to get Winnie?"

I turned my head sideways on the pillow to look back at her.

"Yeah, we always had dogs. Some were fosters, some were adopted. Mom always insisted on adopting the old dogs that no one else would take in. That was sometimes hard as a kid, to only have them for a short time. But I understood why she did it."

Gemma blinked, her expression softening as moonlight leaked through the window and hit her face. "Is that why you wanted a puppy? So you could have her longer?"

I shrugged, trying to act casual despite how hard that question hit me. "Yeah, I guess so. My mom likes to send me photos of rescue dogs available at this one organization she knows of in Boston. They rarely have puppies available, and I usually talk myself out of adopting any of the older dogs because of my football schedule. I just send in a monthly donation instead. But then I saw Winnie on their website one day, and I just...I don't know. I had to adopt her, even if it didn't make sense."

Gemma's lips curved, making the room feel lighter despite it being dark. "I bet your mom was so happy that you did."

I smiled at the memory of telling her. "Oh, she was."

"Momma's boy," Gemma teased before a shiver racked her body.

"Still cold?" I asked with a ghost of a smirk.

Gemma pulled the covers up to her chin, burrowing deeper into the bed. "I'm much better already."

She didn't answer my question, and she was hoping I wouldn't notice. But of course I did.

I sighed, knowing what I was about to do would not do me any favors.

"Let me warm you up."

She stared, eyes round as they connected with mine. Maybe it was just the darkness of the room, but her pupils looked dilated, lacking their usual brightness. Something else swam in their depths.

I cleared my throat. "Come here, Em. I don't want you to freeze. Besides, I make a damn good big spoon."

A breathy laugh caught in her throat as she relented, inching my way. Meanwhile, my pulse sped up as the space between us vanished, and Gemma's back collided with my bare chest. I wrapped an arm around her waist, tugging her closer until our bodies fit together like two perfect puzzle pieces.

Goose bumps prickled over her skin, and I desperately wanted to give her more of them. I could feel her shirt—*my* shirt—riding up between us, and the knowledge that her ass was probably bare as it wiggled against my crotch nearly did me in.

I shoved my hand beneath her rib cage, trapping it between her body and the mattress so it wouldn't start moving like it desperately wanted to. The urge to touch her was like nothing I'd ever known.

Gemma, on the other hand, hadn't *stopped* moving.

"Are you trying to give my cock a rub down with your ass, Em?" I rasped. "Because it sure feels like it, and there are consequences for that."

"Sorry." She laughed like this was fucking funny. "I was just trying to get comfortable. It takes me longer these days because of the pregnancy. But I'm not opposed to lending a hand if you need one."

Goddamn her.

"Can you not offer to give me a hand job in the same way you might offer a cup of sugar to a fucking neighbor?"

Another laugh burst through her lips, and I scowled at the back of her head.

"If it makes you feel better, I would never offer Matt something like that."

"You fucking better not," I grunted before realizing how jealous that sounded. But fuck it, the idea *did* make me jealous. And she could know it; I wasn't sure I cared anymore.

"I won't." Her voice was softer now. Sinfully soft, putting my body on high alert. As if I didn't already feel like I was about to explode. "Truthfully, hand jobs are not exactly my forte," she added.

"Oh, so are you rescinding your offer?"

That was probably for the best.

"No," she murmured huskily. "Just saying...I'm better with my mouth."

"*Fuck*, Gemma," I groaned.

Pictures flew through my brain, ones that I only let myself imagine when I was alone. Images of Gemma's pretty mouth wrapped around my cock, sucking me so beautifully.

"Was that a better delivery?" she asked, sounding breathy and...aroused?

Glad it wasn't just me. But at the same time, that made this so much harder.

Literally.

"I think that was actually *too* good," I choked.

Gemma snuggled backward as though she wanted to feel for herself how good she'd teased the fuck out of me. Her ass brushed the length of my painfully hard dick, and I tightened my arm around her, urging her to stop moving.

"Gemma, please."

She froze, making me feel guilty for my tone, which was probably too harsh. But she was killing me.

I let my hand drift lower, smoothing over her tiny bump, resting my hand there. I moved my thumb in small circles, a gentle caress. Gemma slowly melted in my arms, which had been my hope. All her tense muscles relaxed, and I tried not to think of the other ways I could make her body respond to my touch. Instead, I focused on the little life growing beneath my hand, stirring a different kind of reaction inside me, one I felt in my chest.

"When's the next appointment?" I whispered, hating how strained my voice still sounded. "You didn't put it in your calendar."

She cleared her throat. "I'm not sure it will work for you to make it."

"If it doesn't work, I'll move things around."

"I was worried you'd say that."

"Is that why it's not on your calendar?"

She nodded, her hair tickling my nose. My stomach dropped, and it took me a second to find words.

"Do you really not want me to come?"

She shook her head. "No, Noah. That's not it at all. I...I liked having you come last time."

Relief spread through my body, making it tingle. "Then put it on the calendar, and I'll make it work."

She sighed, her whole body inflating in my arms before losing air like a popped balloon.

"Noah..."

"What?"

Gemma didn't say anything for a long time. I wished I could see her face. I heard her taking deep breaths, interrupted only by one of my brothers laughing upstairs and a loon call from the lake.

"I think I'm warm enough now," she finally said, followed by a forced-sounding laugh. "You're like a furnace."

She was telling me I could let go, but I didn't want to.

I really didn't want to, and that terrified me.

She's Julian's sister, Noah.

That reminder was the only reason I allowed Gemma to slip from my arms and scoot to the other side of the bed.

I couldn't find the words to say anything else. Not even when I realized how cold *I* was without her.

But cold was good.

My body needed it.

My body also needed her.

But I had a feeling that was a battle I'd be fighting for a long time.

CHAPTER EIGHTEEN

gemma

"**Y**OU SHOULD PUT this on."

One of Noah's brothers, the tall one with wavy hair—Sully, pretty sure—dropped a purple-and-gold jersey on the table. I stared at it, confused, before I dropped my spoon into my cereal bowl and picked up the jersey.

"I was going to wear my Knights jersey to the game," I said, and Chloe nodded.

"Me, too," she said proudly.

She sat next to me at the kitchen table, keeping me company as I tried to blend in with Noah's family while grazing the breakfast bar his mom had put out this morning.

I looked up at Sully, only to note that mischief danced across his features.

"You can wear whatever you want to the game," he said before leaning in to whisper. "This is just an experiment."

"What's that?"

Noah emerged from the basement with a duffle bag slung over his shoulder, and his attention immediately trained on the jersey in my hands. The jersey that wasn't *his* jersey. His eyes blazed with annoyance, and I dropped the jersey like it was suddenly hot to the touch. Sully snatched it back up.

"Just a little hometown patronage," he said, all singsongy in his efforts to push his brother's buttons.

"She's not wearing that," Noah said flatly, staring his brother down.

"I'm not," I assured him. "I'm wearing what I always wear when I watch your games."

Noah's eyes flicked from Sully to me, and then they softened. My breath hitched. I hadn't been able to see his face last night when he wrapped his arms around me, but I imagined it looked a little bit like it did now. Tense but gentle. Like how his hand had smoothed over my stomach tenderly, even while his body had been rigid with arousal.

I woke up this morning feeling that arousal again, pressed into my back. At some point in the night, I returned to his arms. And waking up there, feeling him all around me, had sent me fleeing as soon as my eyes opened.

I needed a little intermission, a little breather to figure out my game plan.

I'd tried last night. I'd tried to get him to break, even just a little bit. But he seemed determined to ignore the parts of me I wanted to give him. Instead, he kept showing up for me in other ways, talking about my doctor appointments and giving me shirts to sleep in.

But I wondered if he realized what he was doing. He was trying to protect me from tasting something that could never be, but a hand job in the middle of the night wouldn't be what would ruin me when this was all over.

I wasn't giving up yet, though. As determined as Noah seemed to be, I was equally convinced it would be a loss to waste an opportunity. This was my only chance—probably for a long time —to feel something good in a man's arms. I knew it would be temporary. I didn't care.

Noah's lips parted like he was going to say something, but then they pressed together again when he realized his whole family was listening. So he just nodded and stepped backward toward the front entryway.

"See you all after the game."

"Wait, wait!"

His mom jumped from a kitchen barstool as she rushed to give her son a hug, muttering words of encouragement while simultaneously reminding him to be careful on the field.

It tugged at my heartstrings, especially when Noah smiled at his mom while reassuring her. Anne London was at least a foot shorter than him, which meant he had to lean down to kiss her forehead. Afterward, she stood there with her dog-printed apron and her mousy brown hair piled on top of her head in a messy bun, watching as he stepped back and waved at the rest of us.

"Go get 'em!" Theo called while Sully put his fingers in his mouth and whistled loudly.

"Can't wait to see those big plays!" Blake hollered.

Noah's smile cracked wider before he disappeared through the front door.

I crossed my legs, resisting the urge to go after him, to give him my own few words of encouragement. But I knew his family would read into it, so I settled for sending him a text.

> I'm looking forward to watching you win games in real life.

> NOAH: Don't jinx it, Em.

> Fine. Good luck out there 🩶

> That better?

> NOAH: That's the best.
> NOAH: I'm sorry I have to leave tonight.

> Don't worry about it, Noah.

It might be a little weird without him tonight, but by the time the game was over, I'd probably come back to the house, pass out, and wake up to catch the return flight with Chloe. I was more worried about how I'd spend the time between now and the game.

"Well, there he goes again."

One of the London brothers' voices pulled me out of my phone, and I looked up to find that the mood had deflated considerably around the breakfast table.

"Always leaving us to go do his big, cool things," Blake sighed, leaning back to sling an arm around over the empty chair beside him.

"Blake," Anne warned, flashing her oldest a stern look.

But Sully picked up where Blake stopped regardless. Except unlike his brother, he was looking directly at me.

"It's probably good that the two of you aren't dating," he said with this sort of all-knowing expression that unnerved me. "His ability to have a relationship extends to football and that's it."

I flashed him an unfeeling smile, feeling more prickly than I probably should at his implications. "You know so much about dating, Sully. Tell me...how's your love life doing?"

Blake and Theo wrapped their hands around their mouths, hollering their approval through closed fists before breaking into laughter. But my lips flattened as I stabbed a strawberry from my plate.

"Our family isn't lucky in love, so you're right...it's not just Noah who isn't dating," Sully said with a shrug. A light grin played on his lips, telling me he wasn't bothered much by the ribbing. "None of us seem to be built well for it. But I stand by what I said: he's always going to go where the football goes."

"California for college," Theo listed. "Massachusetts for the big leagues. I wonder if he'll ever come back home."

The words were wistful, but the delivery dripped with roguish teasing. Theo dropped his chin in his hand, elbow propped on the table to hold it up.

"Stop with the drama, boys," Noah's dad droned while he scrolled on his iPad with his glasses poised on the tip of his nose. "He'll be back later tonight."

"And he'll be two mil richer, too," Sully quipped. "Or something like that. I did the math once and divided his salary per game."

"Man, wouldn't that be nice," Theo laughed. "Two mil richer plus girls waiting to help you spend it."

"Seriously," Blake said, but his tone wasn't facetious anymore. His expression had turned slightly spiteful as he went back to eating his breakfast. "Can you imagine making seven figures in one day, and all while playing a kids game?"

"It's not even one day," Sully pointed out. "It's just a couple hours."

"Some of us actually have to work a full day to get paid," Blake muttered.

"*Some* of you seem like you have no idea how professional football really works," I snapped, putting my fork down with a forced calmness I didn't feel. "Maybe you've never asked your brother what his days are really like, but he's putting in work and time and energy into his career every single day for hours upon hours. And yet, his whole life *isn't* football. Chloe, how many nights do you spend with your uncle Noah every week?"

She scrunched her face up, her cereal spoon pausing on the way to her mouth. "Maybe three?"

"At *least* three," I emphasized. "And he picks her up from skating practice, and checks in on Nat, and takes care of a puppy he rescued, and he actually doesn't love always leaving to do his *cool, big things*. But do you know the only away game he's been excited for this season? This one. Not to mention he's—" I cut myself off before drawing in a shaky breath. My heart pounded with the adrenaline of confrontation, and I hated it. I really hated it. "Sorry," I muttered, immediately backpedaling. "Sorry, I—"

"No," Anne interrupted. "No, you're absolutely right, Gemma. Noah has worked incredibly hard to get where he is, and we know that." She glared at her other sons, muttering something else under her breath that I couldn't hear. But when she turned back to me, her expression was gentle. She had the same green eyes as Noah. "I'm very proud of him."

My smile felt wobbly as I let it inch up my face, trying to show Noah's mom that I appreciated her. I nodded and cleared my throat.

"Thank you so much for breakfast." Grabbing my dirty dishes, I stood from the table. "I think I'm going to go freshen up a bit, if that's okay."

"Of course it is." Anne jumped up, taking the dishes from me, which I let go of reluctantly. "Are you okay with going into the city early before the game? We wanted to show you the best places to eat in Minneapolis."

"I would love that."

I flashed her another smile. I didn't want the Londons to think that I wasn't grateful for their hospitality or that I was rude. I rarely ever snapped at people who weren't my own siblings, but I hadn't been able to handle it. Noah did so much for other people, and his brothers were making him sound like someone who couldn't be counted on, like someone who only cared about himself and money and sports.

I paused at the top of the stairs leading to the basement, realization washing over me.

They were making him sound like the person who Noah thought he was.

And suddenly, I understood everything all too clearly.

I spent my whole makeup routine worrying that Noah's brothers would act differently toward me after my outburst earlier, but I quickly learned my concerns were unnecessary.

It was a cold, gray day. An eerie mist trickled down from the sky, but the London family didn't let it stop them from showing me around the city. We went to a microbrewery that had plenty of nonalcoholic options and then a trendy Minneapolis restaurant, and all the while, they couldn't have been any nicer to me. Sully continued to make jokes, Theo's relaxed attitude remained constant, and if anything, Blake's cool confidence had reduced into something that resembled guilt.

And not only that, but they wouldn't leave me alone.

"I'm gonna use the bathroom quickly," I told the group as we entered the stadium and passed by a women's restroom. "I'll meet up with you all."

"I'll wait for you," Blake replied without hesitation.

"Go ahead, Gemma." Theo halted next to his brother. "We'll be right here."

Sully also stopped, agreeing with a nod.

"I can find our seats," I assured them, noting how eagerly Chloe was pulling at her grandparents, not wanting to wait. "It's really okay."

"The boys can wait with you, and we'll meet you over there," Noah's mom decided with a smile, giving in to her granddaughter's impatience as Chloe dragged them away.

"I'll be quick," I promised the brothers. Darting into the bathroom, I went as fast as possible and refreshed my lipstick before reemerging to find them all still patiently waiting for me. Blake looked flustered while his brothers were elbowing him, snickering slightly.

"Did I miss something?" I asked.

Blake shook his head. "Just saw a friend."

I cocked a brow. "A friend?"

Sully snorted. "A friend. *Okay*, Blakey."

"Delaney is as much your friend as Gemma is Noah's," Theo added under his breath.

"Hey—" I started, despite my stomach flipping at the insinuation. But Blake was too quick.

"You guys know she's engaged," he muttered, and the mood immediately dropped.

Ouch. Noah and I might not have a future, but at least I didn't have to deal with seeing him with someone else. Just thinking about it caused a stab of pain that shocked me with how strong it was.

"Come on," Blake encouraged. "Let's go."

Obediently, we all started walking in the direction of our seats, and the brothers simultaneously converged around me. When I flashed them a bemused expression, Blake's lips curved into a lopsided grin.

"Sorry, did you not realize you were getting a protection detail today?" he chuckled.

"I did not," I laughed. "And it's really not necessary."

"Our brother would disagree," Theo said before putting a hand on my back to steer me away from a concession stand I'd been about to bump right into as we walked. He dropped his hand as soon as my path was clear. "But don't tell him I just touched you."

"Oh, let's tell him," Sully jumped in, mischief sparkling in his eyes again. "Just for fun. See what happens."

"He's not going to care," I insisted as we made our way to the center of the field and descended the steps toward the first-row seats Noah had secured us.

My roommate had a clear protective streak, but it focused mainly on the baby. Plus, it was fueled partly by fear of my brother.

"Mhm," Blake hummed as he walked behind me. "You just keep believing that."

I tried to ignore his words, especially when they made my stomach jump into my throat.

When we found the right row, we filed into our seats. Chloe bounced up and down excitedly on my right side while Blake stood stoically on my left. Meanwhile, my eyes immediately started scanning the field for Noah. I found him stretching further down the sidelines, and I realized I should have gotten a drink to sip on. My mouth ran dry at the sight of his muscles flexing under all that football gear as he limbered up.

"I'm sorry about this morning," Blake said, startling me because I was so in my head about how hot his brother was. "We were acting like jerks, and you were right to call us out on it."

"I didn't mean to snap," I rushed to say, looking up to find his intense, brown eyes staring at me. He had more of his dad in him than Noah did. Darker hair, brown eyes, sharp jaw. He was equally handsome, just in a different way. There was more of a broodiness to him. "I'm sorry that I did."

He shook his head. "Don't be. I love my brother, and I'm proud of his success. I think sometimes I just get a little..." He turned to squint at the field while he tried to find the word. His eyes trailed Noah disappearing into the locker rooms ahead of the official start.

"Jealous?" I offered, flashing a teasing smile.

Because that whole conversation this morning reeked of jealousy.

"Yeah, I guess so," Blake admitted. "Sometimes it's hard not to be when your brother is famous and has it all, and you—" He winced, cutting himself off. "Sorry, it's not about me. I was acting like an ass and just wanted to apologize."

"You don't need to apologize to me," I said. "But Noah might pick up on more than you realize. He's one of the best guys I know, and I don't think he sees that about himself."

Blake nodded, a solemn understanding to it, like he really was taking my words to heart. But then a brow rose as he glanced at me.

"*One* of the best guys, huh? Tell me about these other good guys."

When all I did was laugh breathily, he shrugged. "Just trying to scope out my brother's competition for him."

"It's not like that." I shook my head. "The only other good guys I know I'm related to."

Blake suppressed an amused grin. "Good to know."

I didn't have the heart to tell Blake that it didn't matter, anyway. Noah and I...we weren't like that.

We fell into compatible silence as I replayed his words. And when my curiosity got the better of me, I turned back toward him.

"What were you going to say before? When you were talking about how your brother is famous, but you..."

"It's nothing." Blake's lips twisted ruefully. "I just dated a girl recently who turned out to be using me to get to him and dumped me when she realized it wouldn't happen. I felt like such a fucking fool. But it's not Noah's fault I fell for that trap."

"Oh my God," I murmured, wide-eyed. "Seriously?"

He nodded and then shrugged, trying to brush off the obvious pain in his eyes.

I leaned toward him with a whisper. "You know, if you ever move to Massachusetts, I have four sisters."

Blake laughed, a lightheartedness returning to his expression. "And a terrifying older brother, I hear."

"Eh." I waved that thought away. "Let me deal with Julian."

"I think you'll already have enough to deal with when he finds out you're..." He paused to clear his throat. "Living with his friend."

I groaned. "Don't remind me."

"Okay." Blake nodded with ease. "I won't. Do you want anything to drink? I think I'm going to grab a beer."

"If you see anything that's alcohol- and caffeine-free, I would love that."

"On it." He saluted and slid past his brothers, who shuffled down and started chatting with me in his absence. They didn't apologize like Blake did, but they loudly cheered their brother on as he reemerged onto the field and strode to the sidelines in front of us.

We screamed with excitement, and almost as though he could

hear us, Noah turned to look at the stands. But his eyes were on the wrong part of the row, and I bounced eagerly on the balls of my feet as his gaze traveled over faces until he eventually found us.

He smiled.

First, at Chloe.

Then, at his mom.

And then, finally, at me. And my green-and-white jersey.

Once his eyes caught on me, they seemed reluctant to move away, and I felt stunned by his attention. His *public* attention. I smiled, and he smirked, finishing his long, perusing look. By the time he turned back to the field, my cheeks were flaming. Up until this moment, I'd been shivering from our walk around an unseasonably cold Minneapolis and thankful for the dome covering the stadium. But now, my insides felt molten, warm, fuzzy, and I wouldn't mind a burst of cool, fresh air.

Sully elbowed me playfully, but I tried to ignore it, focusing instead on the game.

It was a fantastic game, even if I hated watching Noah take hits up close. He played brilliantly, though. It was honestly one of his best games. Ever.

But my favorite part wasn't watching him play for the Knights or beat Minnesota. It was watching him play for his family. It was watching him wave to his niece and glance over to our row with giddiness in his expression. It was watching him confidently stride across the field in those tight pants that made my mouth water.

Just getting to see his excitement was contagious. Anticipation ran in my veins, even after the game. My body seemed to vibrate as we returned to the lake home. I wasn't sure why or what I was excited about, but I couldn't shake it. I wasn't sure I wanted to.

So when Blake told me we were going out to celebrate at a bar nearby, I couldn't have been more ready.

Especially when I learned that Noah was on his way back to

join us. Apparently, I'd been cold this afternoon for a reason, and the light mist that had accompanied the dreary weather resulted in a layer of ice on the tarmac that had delayed Noah's flight out of Minneapolis, meaning he got to spend another night here. With his family. And me.

My body tightened at the thought of sharing a bed with him again tonight. Or would we go back to our separate rooms? I didn't know what to expect, but I did know that I was embarrassingly excited to see Noah.

"Should I change?" I asked Blake as we walked into the house. "What's the dress code?"

"The dress code can be whatever you want it to be, Gemma," Sully slid in before his brother could answer. "But if I might suggest something flirty and fun?"

"Flirty?" I repeated, pushing down a nervous giggle. "Please. I have no intention of trying to pick up guys tonight. Did you forget I'm pregnant?"

"I know one guy in particular who doesn't care that you're pregnant," Theo muttered as he brushed past me. When I looked up at him, he winked.

And that little sign of awareness made me say something I really shouldn't have.

"So...you're saying I should wear the dress that Noah specifically told me *not* to pack?"

Sully's eyes lit up. "*Absolutely.*"

This was a terrible idea, but with the other London brothers nodding encouragingly, I retreated to the basement to find the dress. By the time I'd laced the bodice up and tied the neckline into a tiny bow, a knock sounded on my bedroom door.

"Em? You almost ready?"

My breath caught in my throat at Noah's voice. Wordlessly, I grabbed my jacket to attempt to combat the cold air outside and walked to open the door.

"Fuck."

The rough word slid slowly from Noah's lips, drawn out as his eyes looked me over from head to toe. And then, almost as though it was unbearable to look at me for a moment longer, Noah hung his head, pinching the brim of his nose.

"Hi, Noah." I grinned. "Good game tonight. I knew I'd get to watch you win in real life."

"You've got to be fucking kidding me," he groaned. I wasn't even sure he'd heard what I said. He lifted his head again. "Gemma, I told you—*shit*. You have to change."

"Your brothers told me to wear it."

That had been the wrong thing to say. Noah's eyes flared.

"That is the last fucking thing I want my brothers to see you wear."

"Oh, come on. I could think of worse things."

So many worse things. Sure, this dress showed some cleavage and was on the shorter side, but it wasn't scandalous by any means. Honestly, I wasn't sure why Noah reacted so strongly to it. But I also wasn't sure if it mattered.

He stared at me, daring me to continue. To prove my point. Almost as though he *wanted* to see what would be worse.

Or he wanted me to change into sweats, either one.

"I didn't think you'd be one of those guys who tried to control the things a girl wears," I tsked when it was clear Noah intended to remain silent.

He crossed his arms over his chest. "I couldn't give a shit what girls wear."

I raised a brow. "You didn't want me to wear the Minnesota jersey this morning."

"I think my reason for that should be self-explanatory."

Part of me wanted to make him spell it out anyway. But we also needed to get back to the point at hand.

"And now you don't want me to wear this dress," I added.

"Fine." Noah ran his hand through his hair, which looked damp from his after-game shower. My eyes roamed over him, checking for injuries from the game. But he looked good. *Really* good. Especially when he gripped the top of the door and leaned toward me, intensity rippling through him. "I don't care what other girls wear. I care what *you* wear. But only because it's unseasonably cold as hell out there, and I also know how fucking hard it's going to make it for me. And I am *so* cl—"

He snapped his mouth shut, pressing his lips together in frustration.

So close.

I cocked my head to the side. "Harder, huh?"

Noah's jaw clenched as his hand dropped back to his side. "Yeah. Harder."

With a playful shrug, I looked away from his face because its intensity made it *hard* for me to think.

"Well, I don't have any other dress options, so I guess you'll just have to figure out a way to solve that problem."

I couldn't help it. My eyes sought his again. They were shining, alive with heat and exhilaration.

If I thought *I* was riding a high from his game, I could only imagine the adrenaline coursing through Noah's veins. Tonight—what was going on here—was dangerous. But I'd never been so excited to get a taste of this version of Noah.

I dared to step toward him, noting how the green flecks in Noah's eyes seemed brighter tonight. He bit down on his bottom lip, letting it slide slowly through his teeth as he considered me with a hooded gaze.

"It's okay," he muttered finally, gruff but seductive enough that I felt a flush work up my body. "Like you, I'm pretty used to taking care of things on my own."

My mouth ran dry, and just when I was about to ask Noah how, exactly, he liked to take care of things on his own, we were interrupted by a holler from upstairs.

"You two coming?"

"Yeah, be right there," Noah called without looking away from me. His voice lowered as he added, "You're not going to change, are you?"

I shook my head with a smirk before brushing past him to go upstairs and meet his brother.

Behind me, I heard him swear under his breath.

But he followed me anyway.

eight years ago

GEMMA

Noah nodded in response to my question. "Yeah, I've been playing backup quarterback for Julian for the last two years, but now that he's graduating, I'll take his place in the starting lineup. I'm a junior."

Some guys might have said those last words with a touch of cockiness, but Noah stated it casually, like it was just a fact. He didn't even really seem keen to elaborate. In fact, he immediately turned the conversation back to me.

"What about you? Do you play any sports? I remember Julian saying that at least one of his sisters was a collegiate athlete. Sorry, I don't remember which one." A slight flush colored his cheeks as though he thought he should have remembered such a random fact about my family, and it had to be the cutest thing I'd ever seen.

"He was probably talking about me. I'm a junior, too. A collegiate figure skater," I said with a smile, and Noah's eyes dropped to my mouth. It only lasted a second, but for some reason, it caused a flicker of heat beneath my skin.

"Oh, yeah?"

His lopsided grin returned as he pushed the sleeves of his long-sleeve shirt up, baring tattooed forearms, which he crossed over his chest as he regarded me with interest—like he really wanted to know more about skating.

My mouth ran dry.

I changed my mind.

Cute did not describe this man.

He was hot.

Actually, he was so unbelievably attractive that I couldn't believe he was still talking to me.

Of course this would happen.

Of course the first time in forever I find a guy like this...and he was my brother's friend.

CHAPTER NINETEEN

gemma

R EGARDLESS OF NOAH'S feelings about it, I was glad I put on the dress. The lakeside bar that Blake drove us a mile down the road to was just as upscale as the surrounding neighborhood and surprisingly busy for a Thursday night. Noah and I followed his brothers to a few open chairs by a sleek bar top, which boasted rows of high-quality liquors on the wall behind it, lit with moody, ambient lighting.

Maybe it was just the heat from Noah's eyes every time he looked at me, but the room felt stuffy. I slipped my jacket off and threw it over the back of the barstool before sitting down.

Noah sat beside me and then wordlessly reached beneath my seat, dragging my stool closer to his.

I looked over at him. "Was that really necessary?"

"Yes," he grunted before flagging down the bartender and asking for a drink I didn't recognize. Two of them.

"What's that?" I asked.

"It's a really good mocktail that they make," he replied. "I've had it before. If you don't like it, I'll get you something else."

I smiled. "Well, you must be sure I'll like it if you ordered me two."

His lips twitched. "One is for me, but if you want both, I'll get another for myself."

"Oh, my bad," I laughed. "You don't want a drink?"

"I am getting a drink," he said stubbornly. His eyes glittered like they did whenever he teased me.

"You know what I mean."

"I do. But it seems only fair since you can't drink. Also, I try to keep the alcohol to a minimum during the season."

The bartender slid two identical drinks across the counter, and I picked one up.

"Cheers, Mr. London. Congrats on the win."

He rolled his eyes, but his voice was soft when he clicked our glasses together. "Cheers, Coach B."

I lifted the drink to my lips, licking a small dribble off the side before taking a sip. Noah's eyes burned brighter as he watched me, his glass suspended midair. The cool, refreshing flavors of mint and strawberry hit my tongue, and a little moan of delight slipped out of me.

"That's really good," I said with approval.

Noah's fingers flexed slightly around his glass, his grip tightening.

"Glad you like it," he murmured before finally taking a sip of his own drink.

Sully caught his attention after that, lifting his glass and cheering his brother in a louder, more obnoxious way, and it definitely garnered the attention of the people around us. Guys from the other end of the bar flocked toward Noah, excitedly peppering him with questions despite Noah being partly responsible for their hometown losing tonight.

Deciding it was a good time to slip away, I hopped off my barstool, weaving through the crowd until I reached a darkened corner of the bar that hosted a few single-stall bathrooms.

I'd been in a lot of bathrooms lately, thanks to morning sickness and my increased water intake, but this one was by far the nicest. Unlike the bright, breezy interior of Noah's lake house, the decor here oozed moody, old-world charm while still being modern and trendy. The glow of the wall sconces was the only light, and the seductive atmosphere made me want to tug the top of my dress lower.

Just a little bit.

So I did.

Like Sully said this morning...it was an experiment.

I found myself more than curious of the results. And luckily enough, as soon as I left the bathroom, I ran right into my test subject.

Literally.

I collided with Noah's hard body with enough force that I would've fallen backward if it weren't for the arm he quickly hooked behind me. I thought he might let me go once he'd steadied me, but he didn't.

If anything, his hold tightened.

His eyes quickly assessed me, looking me up and down.

"Don't fucking do that," he said, sounding oddly tortured. His chest heaved against mine with quicker breaths than normal.

"What?" I breathed, alarmed by his sudden presence and the wild way he looked at me.

"Disappear like that. *Christ*." His head tipped back momentarily, eyes closing with emotion I didn't fully understand. "You're gonna be the death of me, Gemma."

"Sorry." I tried to swallow past the dryness in my throat. "I just had to use the bathroom, and you were busy."

Noah lowered his gaze again. His green eyes traced my face, and I wondered what they sought. We were only a breath apart.

I didn't know why he was still standing so close to me. Maybe he just wanted to melt into the shadows so no one would see us here alone, so no one would gossip if they saw him with a new girl. But the way his body cradled mine, pressing it against the bathroom door, made my knees weak.

"Blake just told me that they were being assholes earlier, and you stuck up for me," he finally said when he found words again.

I tried to duck my head as I figured out how to explain myself, but Noah caught my chin with two fingers. He tipped it back up so our gazes collided.

He didn't look mad. No, I recognized this look. He was—

"That's so fucking hot, Em." The gravel in his voice made shivers work their way down my spine. "That you did that for me."

"It was nothing," I protested weakly.

He shook his head, and even if he weren't still holding my chin, I wouldn't have been able to look away from him. His expression was fierce and untamed. Desperate. I loved it. He was consuming me with just that look alone.

"It was everything," he insisted. "And it makes absolutely none of this less hard."

"Noah..."

I wanted to tell him that it didn't have to be hard. That I knew exactly how we could make it better. But his thumb had moved to trace the outline of my lips, and I couldn't speak. I could barely breathe.

"Why?" Noah murmured as his eyes lowered to my lips, entranced by the way his thumb moved over my mouth. "Why is it so impossible to resist you?"

I leaned into his touch, wanting him to know that he didn't have to. But he seemed like he was waiting for something. For more of a response. My pulse raced in anticipation, and I licked my lips, trying to get them to form words. The flick of my tongue grazed Noah's thumb, and some unintelligible, gruff noise rose from his throat as he absently swiped across my bottom lip, coaxing me to speak.

"Don't," I managed to whisper, giving him permission. "Don't resist."

"Thank *God*," he groaned, sliding his palm to my cheek. Suddenly impatient, Noah tipped my head back with a rough move that made my stomach flip, and then his lips slanted over mine, claiming my mouth.

Noah London was kissing me.

No, *kissing* didn't seem like an accurate description. This was so much more than that. Noah's talented lips nipped and pressed and danced over mine as a sort of foreplay, and then he thrust his tongue into my mouth like he wanted me to know exactly how good he was at using it.

Less than thirty seconds, and he'd worked me into a knot of need, desperate for him to unravel me. This kiss alone, laced with hints of strawberry and mint and sex, threatened to end me.

He slid his hand down to the nape of my neck, caressing softly before tangling his fingers in my hair and giving a little tug. I gasped his name as heat flashed up my spine, and he groaned into my mouth with appreciation.

A second later, he'd flattened me against the bathroom door. The handle rammed uncomfortably into my side, momentarily distracting me from what Noah was doing to my body. I reached back and turned it, letting us tumble inside the bathroom.

As soon as I closed the door behind me, Noah had me pressed against it again. His lips reattached to mine in a kiss so deep a groan erupted from my throat. His tongue teased mine. Just enough that it left me wanting more, needing more, dying for more of him.

"Fuck, Em," he rasped, and I realized just how addicted I was to the way he said a name that was just for him when he was turned on.

"Noah," I reciprocated. "Noah, please."

I didn't know what I was begging for, but I knew he would. He would know.

And he did. Noah's hips began grinding into me, keeping me pinned in place as he rocked his erection exactly where I wanted to feel him. And oh, *God*, did it feel good. He moaned when he felt my hips tip up in response, and I needed to hear more of that. I had to.

Slithering my hand between our bodies, I trailed it down to the zipper on his jeans. But as soon as he felt what I was doing,

Noah grabbed my hand by the wrist and pinned it above my head instead. Then he found my other hand and did the same.

"Gemma," he warned breathlessly.

"I'm just trying to help," I gasped.

"It feels too good." He tipped his forehead against mine, letting his words whisper across my lips. "I need to feel you. That's all I want."

He slammed his lips back where they belonged while moving his body over mine in a slow roll. One of his hands released my wrist, drifting down my arm, making all the hairs stand on end as he brushed his fingertips over my skin. They trailed the length of my side until he gripped my waist like he was holding on for dear life.

But I liked how he was touching me way too much for him to stop.

"Feel me, Noah," I muttered between kisses.

He sighed into my mouth before dropping my other hand and sliding both of his back up my torso. He paused ever so slightly as his fingers drummed over my rib cage, but his restraint broke a second later as he roughly cupped my breasts in his large palms, all while stroking my tongue with his.

Lord, how I wished there weren't any clothes between us. I was dying to feel those hands knead my bare body like he did over my dress.

"Holy fuck, Gemma." Noah squeezed his handful appreciatively before making a low guttural noise in the back of his throat. He kissed the corner of my mouth before letting his lips trail over my jaw, nipping slightly. "You are...you are unreal. I can't believe..."

His words disappeared as he got distracted by dragging his lips over my skin. I gasped and tangled my fingers in his hair while his lips found the hollow at the base of my throat, exploring it as he discovered what I reacted to. I felt his mouth curve in a smile whenever I made a sound.

"I dream about those sounds you make all the fucking time," he murmured.

A whimpering noise slipped out of me. It was all the response I could muster.

Noah didn't seem to mind. His lips traveled lower until they brushed over the swell of my breasts, kissing the outline of my dress. I closed my eyes, letting him take what he wanted, but when his lips vanished, I looked down to find him staring up at me with the string holding my top together between his teeth.

He tugged on it—just slightly. I could tell he was experimenting with how hard he'd need to pull to untie the bow, but he was waiting for my permission to go further. His dazzling green eyes watched my face, desperation dancing in them.

"Yes," I breathed.

Noah ripped the string out of the knot with his teeth, and the bodice of my dress loosened.

"I knew it would be that easy," he muttered, sounding awed as he watched the reveal of more and more cleavage while the dress slowly fell open. I wasn't wearing a bra; the ruched, peasant dress design gave an all-natural shape that I liked. And I had a feeling Noah liked it, too. Still transfixed, he continued in a rough voice, "That's why this dress was such a fucking tease. Dangerous as hell because I knew all it would take was a little tug, and you'd be mine to see like this."

But he never got to see what he wanted to.

Not before a knock at the door caused us both to jump.

I instinctively covered myself, gathering the fabric of my dress in my hands before it could fall completely. Noah swore under his breath and glared at the door like it was his enemy. While he stared it down, I reluctantly tied my top again. Noah caught my movements out of the corner of his eye and scowled.

"I'm going to kill whoever is on the other side of that door," he grumbled before sighing as though realizing that the moment was lost and we couldn't continue to hide in here. It was suspicious, especially if people were waiting for the bathroom.

Noah gave me one more look of longing while we caught our breath and then grabbed my hand as he opened the door. Sully stood on the other side, his eyes widening as we both emerged. A goofy grin spread over his face despite his brother's glare.

"Shit, sorry." He pushed Noah back toward the bathroom. "I didn't realize. Go back in there. I'll stand guard."

"Yeah, okay. As though having you listening on the other side of the door isn't an absolute mood-ruiner." Noah pushed his brother off with a roll of his eyes. But I didn't miss how his lips curved, a grin threatening to break through. "Way to go, Sullivan."

Sully smiled apologetically before winking at me and disappearing into the bathroom. I laughed, which seemed to tip the scales for Noah. He grinned freely as he led me back to the bar, where his other two brothers sat. Since someone had taken our chairs, he squeezed us into a free space along the bar instead.

Noah let go of my hand, and I mourned the loss of his touch for only a few seconds before his arm wrapped around my waist instead, pulling me into his side.

It stayed there, too.

He didn't let go.

Not even when Blake smirked at him.

Or when Theo caught him spreading his palm over my stomach like he did in bed last night.

He didn't let go as he ordered us another round of the same drink. He guzzled his down, licking his lips and looking at me with heat in his eyes, as though the taste of strawberry and mint on his tongue reminded him of the flavor of mine when he'd kissed me.

Noah didn't even let go when two girls showed up beside him, offering to buy him a drink for the win.

I stiffened as he leaned over to mutter something to them. I wasn't sure what he was saying, but it felt like their conversation took forever, and I tried to ignore the irritation coursing through me.

One kiss, I reminded myself. We'd shared one kiss. It didn't mean he couldn't talk to other girls. But still, it wasn't until they finally walked away with disappointed expressions that I relaxed again.

Noah returned his attention to me, chuckling softly in my ear. I wanted to know if it was something to do with the other girls, something funny or amusing that they said. I'd been thinking about telling him he could go after them when he abruptly grabbed me by the hand, leading me away from the bar.

I clutched my drink in my hands, trying not to spill it as Noah dragged me outside.

"What are you doing?" I asked just as the chilly air hit my skin, and I repressed a shiver.

Noah didn't answer. He walked us across a deck that overlooked the lake, the moon reflecting across its ripples. We stopped near the railing, and he looked down at me, flashing a smirk. I frowned slightly, annoyance plaguing me because I didn't know what the hell was going on.

"If you wanted to get out of the bar, you had a few girls ready to join you," I muttered.

Noah's smirk grew. His eyes wandered my face with interest, and I shifted on my feet.

"Gemma," he muttered, amusement laced into my name. He reached out, plucking my drink from my hands.

"Excuse you," I protested.

But Noah simply tipped my drink back, downing the rest of it. His gaze glittered above the rim of the glass as he watched me.

I scowled at him. "There were clearly people in there who would have bought another drink for you. You didn't need to steal mine."

Looking down at me, Noah raised a brow. Without saying a word, he moved his hand to wrap around my throat, grabbing in a way that forced my head to tip back and my lips to part. And then, with aim as perfect as the winning touchdown pass he'd thrown earlier, he spat my drink back into my mouth.

He leaned close enough that our lips brushed as the cool taste of strawberry slid to the back of my throat. I nearly choked with surprise but recovered just as he issued a husky demand.

"Swallow like a good girl, Em," he murmured.

I did, and Noah watched with hooded eyes.

"While you're cute when you're jealous, you don't need to be," he added, slowly releasing my throat. "The only girl I want to share a drink with is you. I'd think you'd know that after how I kissed you, but if I need to drag you away from everyone else to prove it, I will."

"Sorry," I gasped when my airway cleared again. I couldn't feel the fall air anymore; all I could feel was heat unraveling in my gut. "I wasn't sure...I mean, maybe you didn't think it was a good kiss."

He chuckled, and I felt it vibrate through my body as he pressed closer to me. "Don't say shit we both know is a lie."

"Fine," I groaned, trying not to get lost in how good he felt. "I was momentarily jealous. Happy?"

"Right now? I'm so fucking happy, Gemma." Noah's voice had a delicious rasp to it that sent shivers down my spine as he wrapped his arms around my waist again. He mistook it for what it wasn't. "You're cold."

"It's not so bad," I argued.

"I wasn't thinking about anything but getting you alone when I brought you out here," Noah murmured, running a hand up and down my arm. "But I can feel your goose bumps, Em."

I didn't know how to tell him that those had nothing to do with the temperature.

"Let's go in," he concluded, stepping back.

"But—" I didn't want to go in yet. I didn't want him to step back. I wanted more.

"Inside. Now," Noah grunted, twisting my body with his hands so I was facing the door again. "We've already had this conversation about how I'm not going to let you fucking freeze. Let's go."

I adored sweet Noah.

But bossy Noah might be even better.

And that was the only reason I let him drag me back into the bar.

"Where's your next game, Noah?" Blake immediately asked when we reached him again, looking at us with a warning in his eyes. Or a reminder that we were in public, and a lot of eyes had been following us around. There was humor there, too. Happiness. But it seemed like the big brother in him hadn't been able to hold back any longer.

Noah cleared his throat, answering his brother with ease. As though nothing had just happened between us. But his stiff length pressing into the small of my back told me differently. Unable to resist, I wiggled a bit in his arms, and he tried to suppress a groan while tightening his hold on me.

He tightened it so much that my brain began to race.

I liked what was happening a little more than I should. But this was Noah London. This was a guy who straight-up told me he couldn't promise a relationship. He might be holding me like he never wanted to let me go, but he would. He might have dragged me outside to get me alone, but eventually, he *would* leave me alone. I knew he would because I'd prepared myself for that even while encouraging him to kiss me, to touch me.

So while standing in his arms like this felt more than nice, we shouldn't be doing it.

It was confusing. Not just to us—but to everyone.

"You should let me go," I whispered when there was a break in conversation. "People are going to assume things."

Noah grunted. "I don't care what they assume as long as one of those things is how you're off-fucking-limits."

"Noah, no one cares about me." I sighed. "The only reason people are looking over here is because you're a famous NFL player getting handsy with some random girl in a bar."

"You think this is handsy?" he breathed, his lips teasing the shell of my ear. "This is me making sure no one bumps into your precious cargo. Handsy is something entirely different, Em."

My breath hitched. "How about you show me later tonight?"

He groaned, but I didn't miss how he refused to agree or make promises.

It was like he'd already determined this to be temporary. Even more temporary than I'd prepared for.

Sure enough, when we returned to the house, Noah stood in the doorway of his room and stared at the bed, uncertainty in his eyes. He put his hands on his hips as he turned to survey the living room, and his gaze was careful to avoid me, even as I walked to stand beside him in the doorway.

"I think I should just sleep on the couch. I can turn the fireplace on. You can have the space heater in my room," he said. "That seems like the right decision."

"Why on earth would you do that?" I laughed, mostly because of how seriously he was taking this *decision*. "We already slept together last night."

Noah turned, giving me his heated attention as his body crowded me against the door frame. He pressed one hand beside my head and leaned in. Meanwhile, his eyes lingered on my mouth. Instinctively, I licked my lips, which caused a muscle in Noah's jaw to pop.

"Last night, I didn't know what you tasted like, Em," he said, dropping his voice. "And it's dangerous how fucking good you taste."

"Noah..." I whispered, hating the slight shake of my voice born out of pure need. I put a hand to his chest, sliding it up the front as though I hoped that would steady me. In reality, it reminded me of how amazingly hard he'd felt against me earlier, and it made me realize just how strung tight he was. "Noah, I already told you not to resist. Nothing's stopping you, least of all me."

His jaw clenched again, eyes closing momentarily until they flashed open and burned a hole through my heart.

"That's the problem, Gemma." The words burst out of him, but then he took a deep breath and lowered his voice. "You're Julian's sister. *Julian's sister.* I never meant for this to happen. I asked you to move in because I wanted to help you, to be a good friend to him and to you. Not because of...*this.* And now I have to figure out how much I care about him breaking my fingers."

Of course he was stuck on Julian. I should have known Noah didn't think we could go any further because guilt would follow him when we didn't last. I wasn't just a random girl he'd never see again. I couldn't be the kind of fling he wanted.

"This," I repeated. "I hope you know that I realize exactly what *this* is, Noah. You don't have to worry that I'm getting the wrong idea. I don't have any expectations."

How could I? I was a two-for-one package deal, and there was no way I'd ever expect Noah to be interested in that.

Noah stared at me. His eyes suddenly appeared...flat. A muscle ticked in his jaw again, and I'd never wanted to be able to read his mind more than I did right now. My words had done absolutely nothing to appease him, so I tried again.

"Julian's not going to break your fingers for kissing me," I sighed.

A husky chuckle emerged from Noah's lips. He shook his head before piercing me with a look that made my knees threaten to buckle. Brightness had returned to his gaze.

"If I get into that bed with you, Julian won't be breaking my fingers for just kissing you, Gemma. My self-control where you're concerned is slipping."

"Let it slip," I whispered.

"I want to. Fuck, I want to." His words descended into a slight growl as he pushed a hand through his hair and leaned even closer to me. Close enough that I felt his words brush against my lips. "But even if I let myself touch you, it can't be here. If I'm going to make you come, it's going to be somewhere that I get to hear you. I want to hear those pretty sounds come out of your mouth *for me* this time, and I'm gonna need you to be loud. I want you to scream my fucking name, Em."

My face flushed. I could feel the burn of my skin, heating me from the inside out. I swallowed and let my lips find Noah's ear, murmuring. "That night you heard me...those sounds, they were for you. They've *been* for you."

Noah abruptly pushed away from me, cursing as he walked into his room and snatched a pillow from the bed. "Christ, Gemma." He shook his head, walking over to turn the space heater on. "I really wish you hadn't told me that. Not right now."

"Noah..." I started but didn't know what else to say to him. His mind seemed made up, judging by how he brushed past me to throw his pillow on the couch. "Noah, I trust you."

It was the only other thing I wanted him to know.

I trusted him.

He didn't need to sleep on the couch.

No matter what happened tonight, I trusted him.

"I don't know if you should," Noah muttered as he dragged a blanket out of a closet.

Goddamn him.

"I don't want to take your bed," I said, recognizing defeat when I saw it. "I can sleep on the couch."

"No," he argued, his words clipped but his eyes gentle as they landed on me. "You're going to sleep in the bed. And you're also going to wake me up if you get sick during the night."

"Fine," I gave in but crossed my arms over my chest so he knew I wasn't happy about it.

Noah noticed the movement, but I doubted he was thinking about what it meant. Instead, his eyes lingered on my chest before jumping away as he swore under his breath.

I couldn't help a small smirk of satisfaction from slipping onto my face.

I didn't feel bad for torturing him anymore, not when he did it himself. He could have me. At this point, I was pretty sure I'd made that more than clear. All I could do was hope that by the time we made it back to Boston...his head would be clear, too.

It was only a matter of time.

That was what I told myself as I tried to trick my body into sleeping when I finally got into bed with Noah still on the couch. I twisted onto my side, wrapping my arms around me as I pretended I didn't wish his arms were comforting me instead.

Goddamn him. Playboy, my ass.

I'd given that boy a clear directive to play all he wanted, and he was out there on the fucking couch.

I sighed, shutting my eyes to the moonlight filtering into the room.

Soon, we'd be home again. And there was no way things would be the same.

Right?

CHAPTER TWENTY

noah

I COULDN'T SLEEP.

I wasn't exactly surprised. Not after the night I had.

Winning the game. Seeing my whole family in the stands. Seeing Gemma *with* my family in the stands. Gemma walking out of her room in that dress. Blake saying how she'd stuck up for me when they'd been assholes. The kiss.

God, that kiss.

The second my control snapped and my lips brushed hers, I'd been a goner. I hadn't been able to think about anything other than tasting more of her, feeling more of her, seeing more of her.

Gemma Briggs had consumed me.

But as pissed as I was at Sully when he interrupted us, I was also grateful. Because if he hadn't knocked on the door, there was no telling how I would have managed to stop with Gemma. I was seconds from stripping her down while she was pressed against a bar bathroom door. *Fuck*, what was I thinking?

I was thinking how badly I wanted her, that was what. I was thinking—and realizing—just how badly she seemed to want me, too.

There was absolutely no way. No way I'd be able to keep my hands off her now. How could I? I tried. I'd done my best, but now that I knew what Gemma sounded like when she was gasping my name? I didn't stand a chance at resisting her. And hell, I didn't want to.

But she was Julian's sister. His *pregnant* sister. Who had a lot on her plate at the moment and didn't need me to add more. She didn't need to add complications like me. I needed a goddamn second to stop and think about what was happening. The guilt caused by all this secrecy was starting to eat at me. The guilt of wanting her and knowing I wasn't what—or who—was best for her was killing me.

When the sun began to rise and bleak light filtered into the basement living room, I gave up on sleep, threw on a sweatshirt and a beanie, and snuck outside. The air was crisp, exactly what I needed to clear my head.

A layer of mist hovered low over the lake as pinkish light reflected on the water. I walked across the manicured lawn to the dock and headed to the end of it, sitting on the wooden planks between my mom's potted lilies, speckled in fall colors. Another reminder of Gemma and her gorgeous hair and the way it felt wrapped around my fingers.

The early morning loon calls echoed across the lake, and I listened in peace for a few minutes until the dock rattled beneath me, and I looked back to see Gemma walking down it. She wore a matching sweat set, her arms wrapped around her to keep her warm. And to my dismay, she looked tired. Like she'd gotten just as much sleep as I had.

Which was none.

"Sorry I woke you," I said, hoping she had gotten at least a little shut-eye.

"It's not your fault." She sat beside me on the dock, tucking her legs to sit crisscross. "I was having a hard time sleeping anyway."

Damn.

"You weren't feeling sick, were you?"

"A bit," she said, her voice soft.

I glanced over, scanning her expression. It was hard to read, but something about her demeanor told me she was lying. I just wasn't sure what she was lying about—that she was more than *a bit* sick or if she'd struggled to sleep for entirely different reasons. Or reason.

"How do you feel now?" I asked.

"I'm fine," she promised. "I'll be fine, Noah."

That confirmed it for me. She wasn't talking about pregnancy sickness. She was talking about what happened last night. She was talking about us.

Well, she might be fine. But I wasn't.

Our kiss last night would haunt me until I could do it again. Even now, my gaze lingered on how she kept biting her bottom lip. I knew she wasn't trying to do it to fuck with me, but God, it sent heat hurtling through my body. I wanted to take those soft lips between my teeth and tug until she gasped into my mouth again.

Shit.

I forced myself to look away, focusing on the water instead. I tried to think about anything that wasn't how badly I wanted the woman sitting next to me, letting my brain wander as my eyes traced the shoreline.

Gemma and I sat in peaceful silence, letting the loons do the talking for us. I caught sight of a pair gliding across the glassy surface. There was something comforting about them. They were always here, protecting their little part of this enormous lake. I didn't know much about wildlife, but I knew loons were territorial, and those loons swimming past us were probably the same ones I always saw when I came home.

Sometimes I really missed being home. And I knew my family probably resented me for not being here more. For flaking out to live my *big-shot life*.

Out of the corner of my eye, I noticed a light flick on in the house. Probably my mom waking up to make coffee. She'd always been an early riser, but I think she loved it even more now that she could sit and look out of her floor-to-ceiling windows and watch the sunrise over the lake.

Gemma must have noticed the light, too, because she swiveled and looked back at the house. Her gaze roamed over it appreciatively, and my gaze roamed over her.

So fucking pretty.

And I was so fucking screwed.

"It really is a beautiful house," she murmured.

"It is," I agreed. "We didn't have much money growing up, so it sometimes still feels weird to me. That my family lives here."

"My family didn't have a lot of money, either," she shared, turning back toward the lake. I did the same. "It's why Julian had to help my dad at his mechanic shop so much. He couldn't afford to hire more personnel but needed more hands to get through everything."

I nodded. "Julian would do anything for your family."

I felt Gemma's gaze land on the side of my face. "And you would do anything for yours, Noah."

I sighed, trying not to let her words affect me. I kept my eyes on the water, studying the ripples the loons created every time they dove.

"When I was younger, sometimes we'd rent a pontoon and come out onto the lake for a day," I said, letting my thoughts flow out of me. "We'd go by all these big houses, all the rich-ass people in their big boats, and I just kept thinking how unbelievable it would be to live here. So when I could afford it, I bought my parents this house because I wanted them to get to live that life we'd always see from the sidelines. I wanted them to have it, even if I wouldn't be here to share it with them."

Some people tried to run away from their families after graduating high school, but while that was exactly what I'd done, it had never been my intent.

"How did you end up in Boston?" Gemma asked gently.

"The draft," I said with a shrug. "I was kinda bummed that I didn't get drafted to play at home, but New England was still exciting. For one, I'd always respected the organization. For another, Nat already lived in Boston, so at least I'd have a piece of my family nearby."

"I bet Natalie was relieved to have you close."

I shrugged again. "Probably, but she was so wrapped up in her residency that I didn't see her much. That, and her ex cut off a lot of communication between her and any family members."

"I really hate that guy," Gemma scoffed.

"Me too."

It was an understatement. I fucking despised that man. Almost as much as I despised Silas Taylor.

"Speaking of assholes..." I ventured. "Has Silas reached out again?"

The question had been on my mind for a while, ever since he called when we were in the kitchen that day.

Gemma shook her head, and I was inclined to believe her this time. "No, thank goodness."

"Good."

A shiver worked through Gemma, and she drew her arms tighter around her. I wanted to tuck her into my arms, but she'd purposely put distance between us when she sat down. So I settled with taking off my beanie and shoving the hat over her head instead. Her hair fanned out from beneath it, matching the coppery-colored flowers behind her.

"Wear that," I muttered before running a hand through my messy morning hair.

"Thanks," she said with a soft smile, adjusting the hat on her head. "But I should probably head inside and get ready. Our flight is in a few hours."

I nodded, hating the regret that bloomed at the thought of her leaving. Even though we'd be together again by evening. Back in Boston.

"I have to go meet up with the team, but I arranged for a car to bring you and Chloe to the airport," I said.

"You didn't have to do that, Noah," she protested as she stood. "We could have just—"

"It was the least I could do. I would have taken you myself if my schedule would have allowed it." I looked up, letting my eyes connect with hers for the first time all morning. A rush of *something* overwhelmed me, and my next words got momentarily trapped in my throat before I managed to swallow.

"I'm sorry if you didn't get much sleep last night."

To my surprise, Gemma smiled. Her eyes flicked to the lake, then the sky, and finally back to me.

"I actually feel...pretty awake." Her grin grew in its warmth as she looked at me. "Thanks for letting me come. I'm really glad I got to be here."

She turned and walked away before I got a chance to respond. Or stand up and kiss her, which was really what I'd wanted to do.

It was probably for the best that she disappeared back inside.

And it was probably for the best that she snuck out of the house with Chloe before I even got a chance to follow her. The time slipped away from me as I sat on the dock and watched the rest of the sunrise, and I hated that I missed the chance to say goodbye before they left for the airport. Even if it was for the best.

I settled for a text instead.

> Safe travels, Em. A car will be waiting at the airport to take you home, too.

> SHE'S JULIAN'S SISTER, NOAH: What time will you land?

> Just an hour or so after you, I think.

> SHE'S JULIAN'S SISTER, NOAH: Would it be too much of a hassle for you to pick us up instead? I don't mind waiting a little bit.

I stared at my phone, shocked that Gemma was willing to ask me for any kind of favor. But once the surprise dissipated, I smiled.

Not a hassle at all. I'll be there.

I had a feeling I'd give Gemma anything she asked for. And damn, wasn't that terrifying.

Nearly as terrifying as the look my mom gave me as I walked upstairs with my bag slung over my shoulder.

"Why are you hiding outside on my last morning with you?" she scolded.

"Sorry, Mom." I strode to where she stood alone in the kitchen, wrapping my arms around her. "I lost track of time."

She hugged me back. "I would have come down and joined you, but I didn't want to disrupt your time with Gemma. And then I didn't want to miss saying goodbye to her and Chloe."

My mom peered up at me, flashing a reprimanding look. Because I *did* miss saying goodbye to them.

"I'll see them tonight," I said, even though my stomach tightened with the justification.

Sighing, my mom released me and wandered to the cabinet, pulling out a mug and setting it in front of me. "I hope their flight goes well. That poor girl."

I watched with a frown as Mom poured me a cup of coffee. "What do you mean?"

"Oh, I just feel for Gemma. She's so sweet, bringing Chloe here even though she feels that way about flying."

My stomach dropped. "Feels *what* way about flying?"

Mom leaned back against the counter, crossing her arms reprovingly as she looked at me. "Chloe said that sweet girl was terrified on the flight here. Shaking the whole time. And you

224

didn't so much as give her a hug before she left. Just let her walk away like that."

I was too busy comprehending my mom's words to care that she'd clearly been spying on Gemma and me.

"You better hug her when you get home, Noah London," my mom continued, poking me in the chest before moving around me to start putting away clean dishes. "I don't know what's going on between the two of you, but it's clear she cares about you, and I hope you're—"

"Chloe said she was *terrified*?" I interrupted.

I didn't have time to go into depth about my and Gemma's relationship with my mom. I needed to know what the hell she was talking about regarding the plane.

Gemma never mentioned that she hated flying. Why would she have volunteered to come to Minnesota with Chloe if she was terrified of planes?

"Oh, yes," my mom replied, nodding absently as she busied herself with the dishes. "Chloe told me all about their flight here when we were at the game. She was worried about Gemma. It's clear that they—"

"Mom, I'm sorry, but I have to go."

I hated leaving in a rush like this, but I hated the image my mom was painting in my head even more—the one of Gemma being terrified on a plane, alone with my niece. I didn't know how to explain it, but I had to go. I had to go *now*.

Mom paused, holding a bowl midair as she looked up at me. I was worried she'd be mad, but then a slow smile spread over her face as I hiked my bag further up on my shoulder.

"That's my boy," she said as I went in for another quick hug.

If I left right now, there was a chance I could make it to the airport in time. I'd helped Natalie rearrange the details for Gemma to take her ticket, so I had their flight number written down somewhere. I'd find it.

I'd find them.

And then I'd remind Gemma that I told her not to hide this kind of shit from me.

I'd find her.

And then I'd fucking hold her like I'd wanted to do on the dock this morning.

CHAPTER TWENTY-ONE

T HE WARMTH OF Anne London's hug had worn off by the time Chloe and I made it to the airport.

I was eager to get home. Being around Noah's family and basking in their kindness toward me, their nonjudgmental attitude toward my pregnancy, and general chaotic energy had me missing my own family. It woke something up inside me.

I needed to tell my family the truth. It wouldn't be fun or easy, but I missed being myself around my sisters. Around Julian and Juniper. And I hadn't even been able to face my parents since learning I was pregnant. They'd be the hardest to tell, but I needed to do it.

First, though, I had to get this flight over with.

I got Chloe buckled into the middle seat before sitting and fastening my own seat belt. She patted my knee in a tiny supportive gesture before craning her neck to look over the woman sitting by the window. I hadn't wanted her to sit next to a stranger, but Chloe asked to sit closer to the window, and I didn't have it in me to argue about it. Especially when I selfishly preferred the aisle.

Taking a slow, shaky breath, I wrapped my fingers around the armrests and closed my eyes, listening to the bustling around me as people gradually took their seats. When it seemed like most passengers had passed our row, I opened an eye, hoping the plane would be moving soon. But flight attendants continued roaming up and down the aisles at a leisurely pace, and I gritted my teeth impatiently.

The waiting was the worst part. The longer it took to get into the air, the longer I had to think about all the things that could go wrong.

My stomach somersaulted, and my chest tightened. Breathing felt slightly painful, which only worsened my anxiety. I closed my eyes again and spread a hand on my lower belly, smoothing it over my bump. I took a deep breath, feeling how my stomach expanded with air.

I was still breathing.

Everything would be fine.

Except everything didn't feel fine. It felt like my chest was growing tighter with every breath, and I couldn't give any rational reason why. I didn't understand why my body did this to me.

"Gemma."

Oh, God. And now I was just delusional. Because there was absolutely no way that the breathless voice I just heard whisper in my ear was real. Whoever said it sounded awfully familiar and also like they were trying to catch their breath.

But it didn't matter because it wasn't real. If it was real, that would mean—

"Em."

I couldn't help it. I opened my eyes on the off chance that I wasn't hallucinating. And sure enough, green eyes were staring at me. Green eyes and that light brown hair curling out from beneath a backward ball cap the same color as a New England Knights hoodie.

"What are you..."

I didn't even know how to form a complete sentence. My breathing picked up, but it didn't feel as painful anymore.

"Uncle Noah!" Chloe exclaimed as she swiveled away from the window. She bounced excitedly in her seat, moving the whole row of chairs. If I were coherent enough to string words together, I'd apologize to the woman sitting next to Chloe, but as it was, I just stared back at Noah.

"Hey, Lo," he said softly before turning to me again. "C'mon. Come with me." With a gentle touch, he grabbed my backpack from the ground and gestured for me to get up.

C'mon? As much as I loved the idea of getting off this plane, I had to be at skating practice in the morning. And he had training to get to.

What the hell was he *doing* here?

"Noah, what—"

"C'mon," he repeated, a murmured hush. He grabbed my hand, squeezing tight, and only then did I realize I was shaking. "I knew I wouldn't be able to get a seat next to you, so I booked new ones for us."

"You booked—"

"Chloe, can you grab your stuff?"

Chloe stopped bouncing, and I felt her rustling around next to me, grabbing her headphones and iPad from the chair's pocket ahead of her. "Where are we going, Uncle Noah?" she whispered, picking up on his quiet body language.

Noah tugged me into the aisle next to him. "To the front of the plane. Does that sound okay to you, Little Lo?"

"Yeah!"

I glanced over to see her scrambling to her feet.

"We have the whole row with two seats on both sides," Noah continued, speaking with a slow, measured cadence as he backed up so Chloe could join us in the aisle. He was watching her. "Do you think you'll be okay sitting across from me so I can sit with Coach B? You get both seats all to yourself."

Chloe nodded excitedly. "Yep, but she likes to be called Gemma, Uncle Noah."

Noah chuckled. "Hopefully, Gemma will forgive me," he

replied before grasping my hand and walking down the aisle. I followed him with wobbly legs as we made our way up to the new seats Noah had apparently bought in first class.

Of course he'd do that.

When we reached the empty row, he stopped and settled Chloe into her seat first. Once his niece was happily situated, his eyes sought mine, and they were so soft. Soft enough that it made me want to cry. Tears welled along my lashes, and I couldn't even say why. I couldn't explain why I was on the verge of crying, just like I couldn't explain why Noah was here.

"Window or aisle?" he asked, his voice just as gentle as his expression.

"Aisle," I answered, blinking my tears away. It made me feel less trapped.

Noah nodded, sliding into the window seat so I could take my place next to him. He immediately flicked up the armrest dividing our chairs once I sat. It felt like an invitation. Like he was letting me know that I could cross the boundaries and he'd be waiting.

I glanced at his face only to find that he was already looking down at me, concern dancing in his gaze.

"Noah, why are you here?" I whispered, finally getting the whole question out.

His lips tugged into a frown. "Why didn't you tell me you're terrified of flying?"

"*Terrified* is a stronger word than I would have used," I argued.

Noah squeezed one of my shaky hands briefly before letting go.

Okay, maybe I was slightly terrified.

It felt worse than usual. I'd been on countless flights over the years, and usually, my anxiety wasn't quite this awful. But something about this trip made my stomach continue to somersault.

"I'm not usually this..." I drifted off, not sure of even how to describe it. "Maybe it's the hormones."

Noah's frown maintained its place on his face. He leaned

closer, eyes dipping to look at my stomach before he spread his hand over it.

Oh, God. He had to stop doing that. It made me feel things I shouldn't be feeling.

But I didn't have it in me to push his hand away. Not when right now it was making me feel the one thing I needed to get through this flight: safe.

"Chloe told my mom that you were...that you struggled on the flight here," he admitted. "And I'm royally pissed that you didn't say anything to me."

I swallowed. "I didn't think it mattered."

I didn't think Noah's frown could deepen any more, but it did. His hand slid from my stomach. Around us, flight attendants finished preparing the cabin for takeoff, and I watched their movements with relief, knowing we'd take off soon.

"Why the hell would you think that?" Noah finally pushed out, drawing my attention back to him.

"I just mean that there's nothing anyone can really do about it," I muttered. "I just have to suck it up until we land."

Noah stared at me for a long moment before sighing. "Well, now you don't have to suck it up alone."

"I wasn't alone." I glanced over my shoulder to see Chloe already engrossed in a movie on both of her personal TV screens. She'd timed them up to play the same movie simultaneously. "I had Lo. She was very supportive on the way here. I could tell she was trying to channel her uncle Noah's energy."

"I'm not the person she should channel for things like that. My brothers said it best, didn't they?" Noah clenched his jaw. "I'm only there for them if football brings me home."

"Noah, if you keep talking like that, I'll give you the same lecture I gave your brothers."

Noah didn't reply. His only giveaway was that same tick in his jaw, and before I could go about giving him that damn lecture, the plane lurched, making me forget all about our conversation.

Wordlessly, Noah wrapped an arm over my shoulders. I

instinctively curled into him, hoping that the heat of his body would melt all my anxieties away. He moved his hand to my hair, stroking it in a steady rhythm that lulled me into a sense of security.

"We'll be home soon," he murmured against my hair.

"Are you going to get in trouble for this?"

If it wasn't a big deal not to ride with the team, Noah would have flown domestic with Chloe in the first place, and I wouldn't have even needed to come.

Noah chuckled. "No, Em. I'm not going to get in trouble for this. I just told the team I had an emergency."

"This isn't an—"

Noah silenced me with a look.

I felt like *I* was going to get in trouble for this. Because as Noah held me through takeoff, I grew more and more comfortable and relaxed in his arms. And it just wasn't fair. It wasn't fair that he felt so good when it was only temporary. He, like this, was only temporary.

The plane accelerated as it readied for takeoff, making me freeze up. Noah's arms tightened around me.

"We're okay," he breathed, his fingers caressing my upper arm in slow circles. I closed my eyes and took a few deep breaths while waiting for the plane to tip up in ascent. When it did, I held my breath, and Noah noticed. "Breathe."

I did, putting my hand back on my stomach to ensure my breaths were deep enough to get air into my lungs. I counted my breaths internally, making it to double digits before the plane started straightening out. It wasn't until my ears had finished popping that I opened my eyes to find Noah watching me.

"Juniper and I got into a car accident in high school," I confessed, feeling I needed to explain myself.

Noah's brows furrowed as he dipped his chin, telling me he was listening.

"The accident wasn't too bad," I added quickly. "I think that's what makes me feel so silly sometimes. We hit some black ice and rolled into the ditch. I broke my collarbone and had a bad concussion, but I only spent one night in the hospital. Juniper walked away with just a couple stitches."

Noah moved his hand back to my hair, tugging slightly on the ends. I wasn't sure he even realized he was doing it, but I felt those little tugs throughout my body. They sent a shiver down my spine.

Misinterpreting my sudden shudder, Noah frowned with concern as he waited for me to continue.

I took a deep breath. "I think it just made me realize how quickly accidents can happen. How a single-second mistake can change anything. It could have been so much worse, and I think about that every time I'm in any moving vehicle. Or flying metal tube."

Noah tipped his head back against the seat as understanding washed over his face.

"That's why you walk everywhere." His eyes fluttered shut with regret. "And I'm the asshole who forces you to get in a car."

I nudged him, wanting him to open his eyes again and see the honesty in my expression. He did, green eyes flaring. "It's not so bad...with you," I admitted.

A rush of air left his lips. "Yeah?"

"Yeah. I trust you, Noah," I said, repeating the words I said last night. I'd say them over and over again until he believed them. "I feel just as safe as I do when Julian's behind the wheel. It's not rational; it's just a...feeling."

Noah's lips flattened into a line momentarily. "The feelings I'm currently having are mixed, Em."

"Why?"

He lifted a brow and gripped my chin with his free hand, tipping it up so our faces hovered only inches apart. "You're saying the feeling you get around me is brotherly?" he asked in a husky murmur.

Heat rose to my cheeks as my mind headed straight into the

gutter, replaying the things he said to me last night, how he kissed me and touched me in that bathroom.

I cleared my throat. "No, that's not what I'm saying."

"Good." Noah released my chin, seeming somewhat satisfied by my reply. "Because otherwise, I'd need to redo that kiss to make it clear exactly how you should be thinking about me."

"You could redo it anyway," I said, my lips curving into a smile. Lowering my voice, I added, "We got interrupted yesterday."

"Fucking Sully," Noah grunted. "I know. But that is exactly why I'm not going to kiss you again until I can be sure we won't be disrupted."

Butterflies filled my gut, fluttering with the idea that he planned to kiss me again.

I immediately felt lighter, like I could float right off his plushy first-class seat. Snuggling into Noah's side, I let him ground me again. And then I closed my eyes. But this time, instead of fixating on the plane, I imagined Noah's lips on mine again. And I let that fantasy carry me off, finally catching the sleep that had evaded me last night.

"My two sleepy girls," Noah chuckled as Chloe sagged against him. Meanwhile, I rubbed my eyes. We were waiting for his friend to land and give us a ride home since Noah had ridden with him to the airport. A teammate named Phoenix Jones, or as Noah referred to him, Jonesy. He was the team's infamous kicker, and if I weren't so exhausted, I might have been nervous about meeting him.

Jonesy flashed a larger-than-life smile when he eventually walked up to greet us in the airport. He introduced himself, offering me his ginormous hand to shake. But when I slid my hand into his, he was gentle. A gentle giant.

Jonesy then insisted on pulling his black SUV around to pick us up so we didn't have to walk with our luggage. After parking in the pickup lane, he whipped Chloe's suitcase into the car like it was the weight of a feather before taking mine and doing the same. Noah brushed up against him, muttering something I couldn't catch. But Jonesy nodded and handed over his keys to Noah, who went to open the front passenger door of the car and motioned for me to get in.

"Oh, I can sit with Chloe," I assured him, but Jonesy was already settling into the back seat of the car with a smile on his face.

"Sorry, Gemma. Chloe and I, we got some catching up to do. It's been a minute since I've seen this little twerp."

"I am not a twerp," Chloe giggled as she followed Jonesy, hopping into the car.

"Come on, Em," Noah said, his lips twisting as he listened to the back-and-forth between his friend and his niece as they bickered in the back of the car. "I promised I'd drive you home. Let me drive you home."

This man. He was going to ruin me, and I was going to let him.

I slid into the passenger seat. Noah waited until I buckled my seat belt before closing the door and walking to the driver's side. And then, just as he promised, he drove us home. After a stop at Natalie's to drop off Chloe and a quick thank-you to Jonesy for the ride, Noah and I made it back to his building.

It wasn't until we entered his apartment that I felt my guard finally drop and my body relax.

"Thank you, Noah," I said, turning to look at him in the foyer. I opened my mouth to say more, but I was lost for words. How was I supposed to sum up everything that had happened in the last few days? The dirty touches and words. The sweetness of showing up on the plane. The unknowing of what it all meant. I didn't even know where to start.

But Noah just smiled. Almost shyly. "Thank you for coming to Minnesota."

I nodded, still lost about how to respond.

Noah cleared his voice. "I'm going to shower, I think. Wash away the plane."

I nodded. Again. Mimicked him by clearing my throat. "Yeah, I'll probably do the same."

Noah flashed another timid smile before kicking off his shoes and turning down the hallway to his room and bathroom. I watched him for a second before doing the same.

Showering felt criminally good, and I soaked in it for a long time, letting my mind run around as I thought about the last couple of days. And Noah's reaction when we'd gotten home.

It wasn't like I'd expected him to push me up against the wall and kiss me as soon as we got home, but I was hoping for more than a quick dismissal. I couldn't be upset, though, not after everything Noah had done for me today.

Stepping out of the shower, I dried off and wrapped the towel around me as I wandered back into my connected bedroom. After putting on a clean bra and underwear, I flicked open my suitcase, rummaging through it to find my toiletry bag. But instead, I found a powder blue T-shirt that had a small outline of the state of Minnesota on the front with a note attached.

Thought you might like a souvenir from your time in the North Star State.
Noah will recognize this one if you put it on.
Call it an...experiment.
-Sully

A laugh flew from my lips. He must have snuck the shirt into my luggage while I was eating breakfast.

Just for the hell of it, I threw it on. It fell past my ass, hitting me mid-thigh, and I laughed again. I wasn't sure what Sully meant when he said Noah would recognize it, but I suspected that this was one of Noah's old shirts, and Sully wanted me to tease his brother some more. Although it was definitely a size bigger than the other shirt of his that I wore over the weekend.

When I heard Noah rummaging in the kitchen a moment later, I decided to test the theory. If I needed to tease Noah to get him to loosen up again, I would.

After running my fingers through my damp hair to tame it, I left my room to find my roommate. He stood with his hip leaning against the counter, his eyes on his phone and a glass of water in one hand.

"Something must be pretty fucking funny in..."

His words vanished as soon as he looked up, his eyes landing on me. They immediately turned sharp as they trailed lower over the shirt.

All that shyness from earlier when we got home?

Gone.

He forcefully sat the glass of water down on the counter, and it echoed loudly. But not louder than my heart was beating as Noah said the three words I hadn't expected but was happy to hear, each syllable separated like he had to regain control after uttering even one sound.

"Take. It. Off."

eight years ago
GEMMA

Without thinking, I took a step closer to Noah.

Maybe I was imagining it, but there was a warmth in his eyes that drew me in.

No, not just warmth.

Heat.

"Yeah, I skate at a college closer to home."

Noah nodded and followed my lead, inching forward, too.

Around us, music started playing. People were laughing. I heard Juniper's voice as she snarked at Julian when he returned with the wine. I heard Julian say something mildly flirty back, the tone of which I was sure went straight over Juniper's head.

For once in my life, I didn't care.

"And...where's home again?" he asked, his voice lower now. Soothing and...seductive?

No, that couldn't be.

"About two hours outside of Boston," I said breathily.

His lips had a soft curve to them.

"My sister lives in Boston."

"Maybe you should come visit her sometime."

He lifted a brow, and his grin grew.

"Maybe I should."

CHAPTER TWENTY-TWO

gemma

WHEN I DIDN'T respond right away, Noah repeated himself.

"You heard me, Gemma. Take. The shirt. Off."

His eyes glittered as they raked over me. It was an odd mix of anger and arousal, and I loved how dangerous it looked. Like Noah was one second away from snapping, and I couldn't wait to be on the receiving end of it.

But I didn't fully understand what his problem was. He didn't care when I wore his shirt to bed the other night, so why did he care about this?

Ignoring his demand, I twisted my hips and let the shirt billow out around me. "Why? It fits me perfectly."

"It does not fit you perfectly," Noah argued. "You're drowning in it."

I looked down at the shirt, assessing it. "Yeah, it's a little bigger than your other shirt. But at least this one covers my ass better." I turned around, bending slightly to prove it to him. "See?"

"Goddamnit, Gemma." Noah ran a hand over his face. When I spun back to face him, he gritted his teeth and pushed his next words through them. "All I see is you standing there in my brother's shirt."

Oh, so *that* was why he was pissed. I momentarily doubled over with laughter as understanding dawned. Of course Sully wouldn't want to make his brother's life *easier* on him.

"It's bigger because it's Theo's," Noah added icily. "My mom gave us each a different color to wear when we went to the State Fair one year because she thought it would be cute."

"I bet it *was* cute," I laughed. "Four adult men who love their mom enough to wear matching shirts around in public. Do you have any pictures?"

Noah glared at me, not answering. Instead, he asked, "Why the hell do you have my brother's shirt?"

"Because Sully put it in my suitcase as a souvenir." I tried to wipe the smile from my face, or at least tone it down, but I just couldn't. "I assumed it was yours."

"Fucking Sully," Noah swore. "It's not. Take it off."

I twisted my lips, pretending to consider whether I should.

"If you want a guy's shirt to wear, it'll be mine," Noah added, his voice lethally soft. I could practically feel it caressing my skin.

"You know, Noah...while you're hot when you're jealous, you don't need to be," I said, mimicking his line from the bar.

Noah caught the reference. His lips tipped up in a cocky smirk. "Good. But I still don't like seeing another man's clothes on you. Especially when that man is my brother. Take it off, Em."

"And if I don't?"

Noah crossed his tattooed arms over his bare chest, making his biceps bulge. It made it no less difficult to slow the ache blooming within me.

"Then I'll do it for you," he said, determination set on his face.

I lifted a brow. "I'm not wearing much underneath it."

Noah's eyes flashed at my words, and then they took their time trailing over me, as though if he stared hard enough, he'd be able to see right through the shirt. When his gaze snapped back to my face, he cocked a brow back at me.

"It's your choice, Gemma," he said, his words little more than a hush. I'd never heard anyone say my name so intimately. So reverently. "Walk away and change into different clothes, preferably something that's from my closet...or stay here and find out what happens if you don't."

I wanted to know what would happen.

Even though I knew I was walking straight into a dead end, I'd never forgive myself if I turned away now.

I *needed* to know what would happen.

My fingers toyed with the hem of the shirt, and Noah's eyes zeroed in on the movement. His throat worked as he swallowed.

"I don't know why you think I could walk away from you," I said honestly.

I wondered if he realized that the tension thrumming in his veins danced in mine, too. And while I likely should walk away, I didn't know how.

Noah cursed beneath his breath as he took tentative steps toward me. He knocked my hands away, taking their place, curling his fingers around the hem of the shirt. He breathed my name, our eyes locking. I nodded, letting him know I wanted this. I wanted him so fucking much.

It hurt to breathe the air between us, knowing there *was* air between us. It felt thick, and Noah's movements were slow—as though he were wading through water while he lifted the hem of the shirt.

He looked down, watching. The heat of his gaze warmed my thighs, and then it trailed upward as he peeled the fabric off, revealing more and more skin. Fingertips brushed up my sides, setting fire to my senses. His attention was unwavering as he bared me, and he bit down on his bottom lip, hard enough that I worried he'd draw blood.

Once the shirt was over my head, he threw it on the ground between us. I shook my hair out, letting the damp strands fall around my face.

To my dismay, Noah took several shaky steps back.

"That better?" I asked breathlessly.

I wasn't sure if Noah had heard me. His distraction was clear as he stared at me, gaze wandering over every inch of exposed skin that he could find. My heart beat wildly, my breaths coming quickly. My bra felt too tight, like it was squeezing the air out of me, and I knew my breasts were just a tug from spilling out over the top of it.

Noah noticed, his eyes lingering on my cleavage as he scrubbed a hand over his mouth, looking like he was in a state of disbelief.

"Fuck, Gemma," he swore, still staring at me.

He clearly didn't realize that my knees were seconds from buckling under the weight of that stare. And I needed him to *do* something before I ran back into my room and slammed the door.

I cocked my head to the side. "So...what's gonna happen?"

That got Noah's attention. Those sharp green eyes lifted to mine, and the intensity of his expression momentarily took my breath away. He shoved his fists into his pockets as he took a single step toward me, his movements wooden as though he was trying to hold himself back but failing.

"What's gonna happen?" he repeated, mimicking me by tilting his head to the side in mock consideration. Without looking away from me, he kicked the shirt at his feet, swiping it to the side. "You really wanna know?"

I tipped my head back slightly, watching Noah beneath my lashes. And even though I could barely breathe, I murmured, "I wanna know, Noah."

Noah surprised me by chuckling. He ran a hand through his hair while shaking his head, and I would kill to know what he was thinking. Especially when he groaned and swore under his breath.

"God, Em." He dropped his hand to his side, and his feet started to move. Toward me, closing the distance between us.

"You're gonna be the goddamn death of me, that's what's gonna happen. But fuck it. I don't even care."

As soon as the last word left Noah's lips, he slammed his mouth over mine, and a million butterflies erupted within me.

God. It had barely been twenty-four hours since our last kiss, but it had felt like *forever*. And now Noah wasn't just kissing me. He'd picked me up and cupped his hands beneath my ass as I wrapped my legs around his waist. He was moving, walking, but I couldn't pay attention to that. Not when his lips brushed over mine in sweet little attacks.

Noah didn't put me down until we made it to his room, and then he tipped me back onto his bed, reluctantly letting go. His fingers slid along the length of my legs before finally releasing me. He hovered over the bed, leaning with his hands on either side of my body. Slightly damp hair hung over his face as he took shallow breaths.

"If you don't tell me to stop right now, I'm going to strip you down and do dirty fucking things to you."

I sucked in, my pulse racing with the anticipation of him following through with those words. *Finally.*

"I've been practically begging for you to do dirty things to me, Noah."

Noah flashed me a wicked smile before swooping down to kiss me again. It caught me by surprise, and I gasped into his mouth, which gave him the chance to taste me, letting his tongue stroke mine. And then, just as abruptly as he'd started the kiss, he pulled away.

"Nah, you haven't begged yet," he murmured across my lips. I felt his grin grow. "But you will."

I nipped at his bottom lip. "You'd like that, wouldn't you?"

Noah groaned. I felt his hand find my hip, squeezing hard. "You have no fucking idea."

"Give me an idea," I gasped.

Without missing a beat, Noah's lips returned to mine as he rocked his lower body, letting me feel how hard he already was. I instinctively let my legs part, grinding back into him until I felt that hot spark when we collided perfectly.

I moaned, tipping my head back while shamelessly enjoying the slow spread of heat throughout my body. Noah took the cue, letting his lips drift from my mouth to my neck, sucking a hot trail across my skin. It wasn't until I felt his lips brushing over my stomach that I propped myself up on my elbows so I could see him—see this image for myself, so I could forever catalog it away in my memory.

The gentle swelling of my stomach would probably go unnoticed by most people. But the bump's small size didn't stop Noah from cupping both of his hands around it and pressing gentle kisses across my skin.

This is just sex, I reminded myself. *Just sex.*

Noah was just sweet. And I couldn't confuse that sweetness with anything it wasn't. He was simply a sweet, soft guy who—

"God, I can't wait to bury my face between your perfect fucking thighs," he growled before ripping my underwear from my body. It floated to the ground in pieces.

Okay, maybe I was getting an intermission from sweet, soft Noah.

And I was perfectly okay with that.

"I just knew your pussy would be this pretty," he murmured as his lips flirted with the inside of my thigh. I let my legs fall open wider for him, shocked that I didn't feel even a flutter of nerves. Just a flutter of a million other things.

Noah's lips stopped their exploration right when he reached the apex of my thighs. Instinctually, I lifted my hips, silently begging him to continue, but Noah was too busy staring down at me. Or, more specifically, staring between my legs.

"Holy hell. Look at you," he muttered, sounding like he was talking more to himself than to me. "All wet and ready for me."

"What can I say?" My words were breathless, fighting past the surge of desire. Of lust. Of need. "You're a really good kisser."

"Oh, please, Em." He looked up, our eyes connecting with a

surge of heat. "We both know I don't even need to touch you for your cunt to get this wet for me."

Damn him for being right about that.

"You're cocky in the bedroom."

Not that I was complaining.

Noah proved my point, smirking in a way that was devastatingly attractive. "There have been a lot of things I've been unsure of since you moved in. But you know one thing I'm one hundred percent positive about?"

"What?"

"That I can find your clit." He grinned wolfishly. "And I know what to do with it."

"I'll believe it when I see it."

Noah's smirk didn't waver as he trailed a single finger up my inner thigh before swiping it lightly between my legs. I jolted off the bed at the tease, and Noah swore under his breath before dragging his finger through me again. Harder this time.

I groaned, shocked at how such a simple touch could burn with such intensity. I felt that tiny brush of his finger *everywhere*.

"You're not just gonna see it." Noah slid his fingers back down through my pussy before thrusting one inside me, causing a cry to burst from my lips. "You're going to feel it."

He was right. I felt it. I felt his finger curl inside me while his thumb traced right below the outer lips of my pussy, ghosting around my clit just to mess with me.

"Noah," I gasped. "What are you doing?"

He glanced up, eyes dancing with amusement and heat. "Your clit is more than just that one spot, you know. It's all through here," he murmured, swiping his thumb down to a pleasure point I didn't even know existed. It felt good. But it didn't feel good *enough*.

"But that one spot is the best spot," I argued breathlessly. "Stop mansplaining my anatomy to me."

Noah chuckled as his eyes flicked back down to watch his fingers pump in and out of me leisurely.

"You mean this spot?" he asked before he lowered his face between my legs and pressed a kiss just above my clit.

I shook my head, sure I looked like a desperate mess. "No," I groaned.

Noah laughed, his light scruff brushing against my skin. I shivered, and his free hand clasped my outer thigh in response, rubbing up and down as though he wanted to soak in the feeling of the goose bumps he'd caused.

Then he kissed just below my clit, making me squirm. "What about here?"

"*Noah.*"

"I want to hear you say please, Em." His lips hovered in the same spot as he whispered across sensitive skin. But his eyes flicked up to mine, watching me with a dark expression. "You never ask me for anything. I want to hear you ask for this."

"Please, Noah," I whispered, willing to give him anything he asked for if he just gave me tonight. If he just gave me this. "Please."

The corner of his mouth kicked up as he circled his thumb around my clit, slowly closing in. "Please what?"

"Please show me that you know how to eat a girl out properly."

"Funny." A cheeky smile cracked onto his face. "I've been dying to do just that."

With that, Noah swirled the tip of his tongue over my clit, and I barely withheld a scream, clapping my hand over my mouth to muffle my cries.

"Don't do that." Noah reached up and yanked my arm down, holding it at my side. His voice was gruff and gritty, nothing like the Noah I'd grown used to. But shit, I liked this Noah, too. "I want to fucking hear you, Gemma. If I wanted you to hold in your cries, I would have played with this pretty pussy last night and let you muffle those hot noises with a goddamn pillow. Scream for me, Em."

My throat ran dry from his dirty mouth, and I wondered how

I'd manage to make *any* sound now. But after one more warning glance, Noah returned to his task, using his tongue to toy with my clit, lapping at it while making every stroke harder and more demanding than the last. He fucked his fingers into me at the same pace, and my back arched from the pure bliss of it.

And the sounds...oh, they flew out of me. I didn't need to worry about that. A desperate moan was the first thing to slip between my lips, and Noah groaned *into* my pussy in response. I'd never had a man do that before, never had a man find pleasure from giving it to me.

I *loved* it. Loved that I didn't have to feel guilty or selfish while taking what I really wanted.

"You taste so good," he breathed, sounding dazed, and I didn't doubt for a second that he meant it. Noah sounded as lost to the moment as I felt. "God, you have no idea how long I've wanted to taste you like this."

All I could do was moan. And then he used my moans to figure out the pace and pressure that I liked, and then he honed in on it, flicking his tongue steadily over my clit in a way that had me gasping for air. With every touch, I felt my body wind up tighter, readying for a release that I knew would send me spiraling.

"*Noah*," I groaned, shamelessly rocking my hips up to meet his every lick and every thrust. The need I felt was like wildfire, spreading faster than I could keep up with. I twisted my fingers into his soft, damp hair, using my hold on him to buck higher.

Noah responded by burying his face deeper between my legs and refusing to let up. One of his hands grabbed my outer thigh, gripping it with a desperation I recognized. He steered me straight to the finish line, building up the fire inside me until it exploded, and I had to grip his hair tighter to keep from losing myself completely to the ashes.

Most importantly, though, I screamed. I let his name saturate the air, just like he'd directed.

Noah licked and sucked and used his fingers to fuck me

through my orgasm, not giving up until he'd wrung every last cry and whimper from my body. And only once I collapsed onto the bed with a heavy chest and almost no breath did Noah brush one last kiss across my clit and lift his head.

"That's it, Em," he muttered with a crooked grin, wiping a hand across his chin. But he missed half of the arousal that glistened in his five-o'clock shadow, and I felt a flush work up my body at the sight of Noah crawling up my body, looking mighty satisfied with himself. "God, I like when you're loud for me. And I *love* when you follow my directions like the good fucking girl you are."

My stomach flipped, and something must have shown on my face because Noah let out a husky chuckle.

"You like that praise?" He cocked a brow. "I'll give you all the praise you want, just so long as you keep blushing like that for me."

"What if I did something else for you?" I bit down on my lip, assessing his handsome face. "If you take off your pants, I'll show you exactly what I mean."

The way Noah just worshiped me emboldened me to do the same to him.

But to my utter disappointment, Noah choked on air before tipping his head back with a groan. "I wish, but no."

"No?" I repeated in disbelief.

"This wasn't meant to be about me," he murmured, softness seeping into his expression. "I just thought you needed an example of a man who knows how to properly find your clit."

I frowned. "I think I also need an example of a guy who knows how to fuck me properly."

Noah froze. He stared at me, blinking as though my words had stunned him. I couldn't imagine why, considering how up-front I'd been about wanting him, but he didn't look like he believed it. Like he didn't believe me.

I lowered my voice before speaking again. "When I told you

that I trusted you last night, I wasn't saying that I trust you *not* to touch me. I was telling you that I was trusting you *to* touch me. To do...anything, really. Honestly, Noah. You don't have to worry. I know what this is, and I want it."

"Don't fucking tempt me, Gemma." Noah sat back on his knees with a growl, running his hand through his hair. "I want you more than I even have the words to describe."

I waited until his eyes made it back to my face before I made myself perfectly clear.

"So shut up and take me alr—"

Noah cut me off with a searing kiss, letting me lick my taste from his lips before he slid off the bed and dipped his thumbs into the waistband of his sweatpants.

"Get the fuck over here and show me what you mean, then."

His voice was low, soft...but his eyes glittered with the hardness of diamonds. Or emeralds. His smirk made its return, sliding up his handsome face. God, he was so unfairly handsome.

"If you're as good with your mouth as you claimed the other night, I might even reward you by letting your sweet cunt come around my cock," he added and then punctuated that mouthwatering statement by dropping his pants to the ground.

And my jaw dropped to the floor with them.

"Get on your knees for me."

He didn't have to say it twice. Within seconds, I'd sunk to the ground in front of Noah, struggling to look at anything but his erection. And thinking about how it would likely split me in half.

Noah noticed my preoccupation.

"You'll take it," he murmured, the husky words a mixture of reassurance and promise. "And you'll look so fucking good while you do."

I smiled up at him, feeling heat spread to my cheeks. Noah cupped my face, his thumb grazing my skin in a wandering line. It felt like he'd traced a path through my freckles.

"There's that pretty blush," he said, a reverence to his tone.

"Keep talking like that and you'll see it a lot more," I replied before letting my gaze trail down his bare, muscled body, shame-lessly taking him in. When my eyes returned to his erection, my mouth started to water.

Noah London was a work of fucking art.

He groaned. "I'll talk however you want me to talk, as long as you keep looking at my cock like how you are right now."

"And how's that?"

Noah leaned down, speaking in a soft, sinful hush as his lips flirted with my ear. "Like you're hungry for it."

I really was. I'd imagined us in this position before and was eager to finally watch Noah unravel for me. But a touch of nerves ran through me as I tentatively wrapped my fingers around his hard length.

It only lasted a moment, though. Noah's immediate moan at my touch had my heart racing, propelling me forward. I twisted my hand up his length, enjoying the feel of his silky smooth skin. I rubbed my thumb over his tip, using a bead of precum as a lubri-cant as I slid my hand down and up again.

"I am," I whispered, looking back up at Noah to find him staring at me, eyes blazing.

"Open your mouth, Em." His fingers trailed to my chin, tipping it up. "If you're hungry for my cock, let me feed it to you."

I did as he asked, opening my mouth and sticking my tongue out ever so slightly. With one hand, Noah tangled his fingers into my hair at the back of my head and tugged, making my lips part further. With the other hand, Noah fisted his length, giving it a single pump before sliding it onto my tongue. Then he paused, letting it sit there. Meanwhile, the pulse between my legs grew, and I squirmed.

"Don't worry," he rasped, amusement laced in his tone. "Your pussy will get the same treatment your pretty mouth is getting."

I wasn't able to respond, but my heart leaped into my throat with anticipation, and my lips inadvertently curved around Noah's erection, showing him how ready I was for it.

His eyes wandered my face once before he shook his head

with disbelief. "Fuck, I can't believe this is happening," he grunted before thrusting further in, gasping as my mouth surrounded him.

I moaned at the feel of him, and then I took over, sucking him deeper and deeper before popping him back out between my lips.

"Does it feel real now?" I asked, then hollowed my cheeks and took him further into the back of my throat.

"Oh my fu—" Noah's words broke off in a grunt, but based on how hard he was gripping my hair, I had a feeling I knew what he was going to say. "Gemma, *fuck*."

I pulled him back out of my mouth. A bit of spit dribbled down my chin as I sloppily wrapped my lips around his tip and sucked him back in, slower this time. Meanwhile, I twisted my hand around his base, feeling him swell even larger beneath my touch. When I increased my pace again, bobbing my head, my hair fell in sheets around me. Noah collected it, making a ponytail with his hand and using his grip to direct my movements, encouraging my pace.

Flicking my eyes up to his face, I found him watching me with a clenched jaw and wild gaze. Despite my mouthful, I gave him my best smile, and he responded by rolling his eyes back with a string of curse words.

When his eyes returned to mine, he bit down on a wolfish grin. "I've seen you give me that look in my fucking dreams, but it's so much better in real life."

My stomach flipped, but I didn't have time to think about his words. Not when I had a job to do.

I let Noah thrust deeper, gagging slightly when he hit the back of my throat, but I'd never felt prouder to look up at him with watery eyes. Not when that little gag was causing him to lose it.

I doubled down, lowering my gaze back to his cock to give it my full attention. Like he did with me, I paid close attention to the things he seemed to like, and then I did them repeatedly until Noah's grip on my hair made tears spring to my eyes.

I'd never been happier to let my pain bring him pleasure.

And truth be told, it was bringing me pleasure, too. My inner thighs slicked together, arousal coating them.

"I want to see your mouth filled with my cum," Noah gasped, barely getting his words out. "Do you understand?"

I nodded as I once again pushed myself to the limit with how far back I drew him into my throat.

His hand shifted to my chin again. "Give me your eyes, Gemma."

I did, looking up and finding his heated gaze.

"Tell me you're okay with that," he demanded.

I nodded again, but even more than that, I tried to convey with my eyes just how okay I was. Even when his words were harsh or clipped, Noah knew how to make me feel safe. Comfortable. And tonight, I'd do anything this man asked me to do.

"*God*, yes," Noah grunted, but I wasn't sure if it was in response to my consent or how I gave his tip an extra hard suck before licking the spot right beneath the head. "You're killing me with that mouth, Em. I'm gonna—"

He choked on the last word as he swelled in my mouth and came a second later, shooting his release out with a loud cry. I let it pool on my tongue, careful not to let any slide down my throat. After wringing every last drop from Noah's cock, I slipped it out of my mouth and looked up at him.

His chest heaved while he smirked down at me. He tapped my chin with a single finger and then let it linger along my jawline. "Let's see it."

Tipping my head back, I parted my lips and closed my throat, letting Noah see his release slide down my tongue.

"Shit," he groaned, gaze sizzling as it landed on my mouth. "You are the hottest thing I have ever experienced. Oh my *fucking God*."

I flashed him the sultriest look I could manage while my chest warmed.

"I already know you're good at swallowing," he said, letting his hand trail down to my throat and gently wrapping his fingers around it. He squeezed with just enough pressure to feel my throat work. "Go ahead, gorgeous."

I swallowed. Slowly, making a show of licking my lips afterward and watching as Noah's jaw ticked in response.

"That's a good girl," he murmured.

Fire danced in my veins from the soft praise.

"Get on the bed," he directed with a cocky grin because he knew what he fucking did to me. "I want a better look to see if you blush all over."

I pushed to my feet with tentative movements, my limbs feeling like jelly but also shaking with anticipation. With *need*. My body didn't seem to care that Noah had already gotten me off— and gotten me off *good*. My body only cared for it to happen again.

Noah watched as I sat back on the bed, spreading out for him. His eyes flicked up my body once before he dropped to the mattress, too, crawling over me until his face hovered above mine. We stared at each other for a long, heated moment before Noah abruptly dropped to cover my lips with his, coaxing me to let his tongue in to tangle with mine.

It was a bruising kiss, but I let him have it all, the taste of our arousal mixing between every flick of our tongues. A low growl ripped from Noah's throat as he deepened the kiss, wanting more, needing more. It was precisely how I felt as I wound my hands around his neck: like I wouldn't ever get enough of this feeling.

And for a second—a split second—that realization destroyed me.

Because I would *have* to get enough. Tonight, or maybe a couple of nights if I was lucky, would have to be enough.

But as Noah pulled back from our kiss and whispered how beautiful I was across my lips, I let go of those thoughts. I'd take whatever he was willing to give me and love every minute of it. I'd capture every single butterfly he released inside me, and I'd cherish them while I could.

Noah started nipping his way down my throat, and I gasped at the sensation spreading across my skin from the combination of his hard bites and soft lips.

"You're still wearing a bra," he rasped when he'd made it to the dip by my collarbone. After sucking on the sensitive spot, he pulled back. "I need it off. Now."

A silly giggle slipped out of me as I pushed myself up, letting Noah grumpily reach around my back to unclasp my bra. He was staring at it like it had offended him just by being on my body and in his way.

Once I felt the straps loosen, I shrugged it off, and Noah hastily threw it to the floor before sitting back and staring at me, slack-jawed. He froze mid-movement. All except his eyes, which grew rounder as I fell back onto the bed and let gravity do the work.

"Holy...fuck."

I wasn't sure if Noah even realized the words left his lips. Based on his starry-eyed expression, I wasn't sure if Noah even realized he was still on Earth.

A sly grin worked its way onto my face.

I never imagined I'd be able to make Noah London speechless, and God, it was a damn good feeling.

But I also felt impatient, the pulse between my legs quickening with every moment that passed while Noah's eyes roamed my body. His attention was on me, but mine was focused on how achingly attractive he was. From his tattoos to his sex-mussed hair to all those gloriously defined muscles, Noah was so devastatingly perfect.

And for tonight, he was mine.

"Noah," I breathed, letting my gaze drift to his face. Our eyes met with a clash of desire, and he understood me without needing words.

Dropping back onto the bed, Noah skimmed his lips up my stomach as he took my breasts in his palms, squeezing slightly as though testing the feel of having me in his hands. With a low moan, Noah's mouth found my nipple, and he wrapped his lips around it before moving to the next, sucking and tugging in ways that made my back arch off the bed, crying his name.

"You're a dream, Gemma." His gravelly voice scraped against my skin, making me shiver. "An absolute dream."

I closed my eyes, letting those words wash over me and wondering how much of this could truly be real.

"You don't have to say things like that," I gasped in an attempt to hold on to reality.

I didn't want him to think he had to whisper sweet nothings for this to happen. I wanted him to know that I understood where we stood and why we stood there.

But Noah paused, pulling back and frowning. Something intense, powerful, and raw worked over his expression, taking my breath away. "Yes, I do," he argued. "Because I mean them. I mean everything that comes out of my mouth, especially when it comes to you."

When I couldn't figure out how to respond, Noah spoke again, his husky voice sounding like a goddamn fantasy.

"I have been begging for your number for years, Em," he murmured, his throat working as he struggled to get the words out. "I have been imagining how you would look in my bed for years. I've thought you were a goddamn angel that I couldn't wait to corrupt for fucking *years*. Don't tell me you're not a dream because you are. And I don't *ever* want to wake up."

I blinked up at him, unable to comprehend what he was saying. Unable to *believe* it. But I didn't have too long to think about it because a second later, Noah swooped down for another kiss, and this time, I was ready for him, grabbing his neck and pulling him closer until I could feel all of him. Until our bodies writhed together and our movements became increasingly frantic, desire threatening to wreck us.

"Corrupt me," I begged between kisses. "Show me what you've dreamed of."

Noah's rough laugh grazed my lips. "I don't think I have the control to do everything I want to do. I already feel like I'm seconds from losing it again."

I pulled him closer, letting my lips find his ear, my teeth tugging on the lobe. "Better act fast, then."

"Goddamnit, Gemma," Noah growled before nudging my legs open with his knee and sinking into a position that let his cock— already hard and ready to go again—brush against my clit. "I need—fuck, ah, condom."

"I'm not going to get pregnant twice," I laughed, mostly at how his thoughts came out garbled and scatterbrained. "And I was tested at my first prenatal appointment."

"Right." He dropped his forehead to mine with a gentle chuckle. His hard, bare chest pressed against my soft one, our breaths slowing slightly to move in sync. "I'm good, too. I get tested regularly."

"Then what are you waiting for?" I whispered, rocking my hips up, spurred on by a need I didn't know how to control.

Closing his eyes, he shook his head. "Just trying to mentally prepare myself for how good fucking you bare is going to feel so I don't immediately lose it."

"Maybe I want you to lose it," I countered.

His eyes flashed open again, that brilliant green boring into me. "Remember when I said you're going to be the death of me?" he said, voice scratchy and strained. "I stand by that."

I rolled my eyes while wiggling my body beneath his, desperate to feel the friction between our bodies just a bit more. When I found what I was looking for, feeling his cock rub between my legs perfectly, a hot and electric shock ran through me, momentarily taking my breath away.

"Noah?" I rasped.

He kissed my forehead before murmuring against it. "Yeah?"

"Just fuck me," I begged, thinking he wasn't the only one who might not make it through the night if something didn't happen very soon. "I—I need you."

He pushed onto his hands, satisfaction playing on his lips.

Meanwhile, he tipped his hips down, purposefully dragging his cock through my wet arousal, a look of pure bliss washing over him at the feeling.

"Say it again," he said, the words falling out in a slow roll. As slow as his hips as they moved against mine.

"Fuck me," I groaned.

This was what I got for getting into bed with a cocky player, wasn't it?

He shook his head, torturing me with long, languid strokes between my legs that only made my blood boil hotter. "Not that. The other thing."

"I need you."

It came out whiney, but I didn't care.

His grin was wicked, but his eyes were soft. "Now add my name," he whispered.

"I need you, Noah. Please."

"Love it when you beg," he said gruffly as he slid one of his hands between us to line his cock up. "And I think giving you what you need might just become my favorite thing."

"Please," I whimpered.

I'd beg for him all he wanted. Just so long as he gave me more. Anything to soothe the ache. Fuck, I'd never felt like this before. Jittery and desperate. Noah's weight on top of me was a delicious tease, and just a taste of it had me wanting more. Wanting *everything*.

"I got you," Noah breathed before he inched inside me, and my lips parted with how satisfying it felt. "I love watching that pretty face of yours while you take me," he added when he noted my expression, and his devilish smirk was the icing on the cake as he slid in further. "You feel that, angel? You feel how hard I am for you?"

All I could do was whimper and nod, which made Noah groan. His hand drifted back up my body, stopping to give one of my breasts an appreciative squeeze. "*Fuck*, being inside you...Gemma, you feel so goddamn good."

Watching my reaction, he gradually slid the rest of the way in until he was buried deep. Completely. Entirely. At least, that was my assumption based on how full I felt, how much he'd stretched me with that massive goddamn dick of his.

Noah paused while breathing heavily, and his slow, careful movements made me wonder why he was holding back. Why he was being careful. I didn't want that. I needed to feel. And I needed to feel him.

"I'm good," I panted. "I promise. Don't treat me like I'm fragile. Not tonight, Noah."

"Never." Noah's voice suddenly sounded hoarse, and he pulled out of me in a leisurely draw. "You're so fucking strong, and I know what you can handle."

Did he, though? Because he was so protective by nature, and I didn't want him to hold back. "I don't want you to think that because of the preg—"

Noah's deep, twisted laugh cut me off. "You're making a lot of assumptions tonight, Em. Like that I haven't researched exactly —" He took that moment to thrust back inside me, and I gasped at the pleasure rocketing through me. "—how hard I can safely fuck you. Because I've been wanting this. I've been wanting *you*, even when I shouldn't. *God.*"

I didn't have time to think about the implications of what he was saying before he drew back and drove into me again. Bliss spread through my bones, racketing higher and higher as Noah let me feel every inch of him with his thrusts.

"*Noah.*"

Unbelievable. It felt unbelievable.

"Oh God, yes." The words sounded like they barely escaped his throat. "Again."

"Noah," I cried, and he slammed into me harder. My eyes found his, and they were watching me with an intensity that both ignited and startled me. But as his gaze roamed my face, I realized he wanted to soak it up. He wanted, like he said, to watch my face and see for himself what he could do to me.

And fuck, the things he *could* do to me.

Noah didn't let up. It felt like he was pushing deeper and deeper into me with every stroke, finding undiscovered parts of me. Parts that I wanted him to find over and over again. And when he finally slammed into me so hard that I could practically feel him in my throat, he stilled and grinned down at me.

"I told you."

I was panting. Breathless and gasping for air, but I wanted to know. "What?"

"That you could take it."

He tipped his hips, scraping at my G-spot, and I cried out at the explosion of heat that it caused. It felt like the flicker that happens before the lights go out. A little warning before being reduced to nothing.

"And that you'd look so goddamn pretty while doing it," he added, his words slurring like he was drunk on fucking me. "*Fuck, it's incredible.*"

"So good," I agreed because they were the only words I could muster. "It's so, so good."

"I know," he groaned before tucking his head into my neck.

Wanting him to hit that spot inside me again, I rocked up, meeting him at every slam of his hips. I dragged my fingers down his back, through the sheen of sweat that covered his skin. Then I flattened my palms over his hot skin, urging his body closer to mine. Because despite what Noah had said, he kept a protective bubble of space around my stomach. And right now, I didn't want it.

Almost like he knew what I was trying to do, Noah intervened, distracting me by winding his hands between our bodies and slipping his finger over my clit. The ghost of a scream escaped my lips, and I felt Noah's smile grow against my neck. And then he lifted his head, and I got to see it: that ridiculously attractive smirk of his.

It was a masterful smirk, an acknowledgment that he knew

the recipe he needed to follow to make me fall apart. He rubbed my clit while pumping his cock into me at the perfect angle. I felt that spark I'd been chasing, and Noah urged me toward it, watching as it blossomed into something so much more. So much hotter. Wilder. Inescapable.

"Oh my God," I muttered, feeling like I was on a roller coaster that was about to drop. "Oh my God, Noah."

"Yeah, angel?" He pressed a breathless kiss to my lips that he probably meant to be quick, but I caught his lips and didn't want to let go. So Noah deepened the kiss, and soon, he was ruthlessly fucking my mouth at the same pace he was fucking into me with his cock. "That's it, isn't it?" he breathed against my lips when he finally came up for air. "Come for me, Em. I need to feel you."

"Yes," I cried, and then it quickly became a chant when Noah's strokes all hit *so* perfectly. Bullseyes, all of them. "Yes, yes, yes."

"*Gemma*," Noah groaned, clearly just as lost as me. His movements grew sloppy and imperfect, but the accuracy no longer mattered because I was gone. I was free-falling, floating, crashing.

My orgasm ripped a scream from my throat, and I dug my fingernails into Noah's skin, not thinking of anything other than the mindless pleasure surrounding me. Noah followed my lead, coming with a cry as he stilled above me and gasped for air.

Christ, what a sight. I wanted to see it over and over again.

"Oh my—oh my God," he rasped. "Holy shit, Em. That was...*fuck*."

I nodded breathlessly, agreeing.

Oh. My. God. That was...*fuck*.

Dropping his head back to the crook of my neck, Noah kissed the column of my throat before finding my ear.

"I think I like flooding your pussy with my cum even more than your mouth," he said with a gritty, sexy voice that made my eyes roll back.

"You have to stop doing that," I begged.

"What?" I could practically hear the frown in his voice.

"Ruining me. Ruining all other guys for me."

Noah froze momentarily. And then he snapped his hips, thrusting his semi-hard cock deeper, causing me to suck in with delight.

"Don't talk about other goddamn guys while I'm inside you, Em," he growled. "Tonight, this pussy is mine. Don't you fucking forget it."

I wouldn't forget it. How could I? I was sure I'd be replaying tonight, the night when I belonged to Noah London, for years to come.

So I whispered, "I won't." And there must have been something about my voice because Noah relaxed. I felt his body melt before he slowly resigned and slipped out of me.

I didn't know what would happen next, but Noah made it simple. He always did.

After toppling onto the bed beside me, he drew me closer, wrapping an arm around me like he did two nights ago. Except this time, he wasn't trying to hold anything in. His chest rose and fell quickly against my back as he tried to catch his breath, and his fingers lazily traced over my stomach. I felt those swollen lips of his brush against my temple.

"Are you okay?" he asked.

Soft, sweet Noah was back.

I knew it was dangerous to snuggle into him, but I did it anyway. Noah didn't seem to mind, his soft chuckle ruffling my hair.

"I'm more than okay," I replied after I figured out how to speak again.

"You're comfortable?" he checked, and I laughed.

"Yes, Noah. I'm comfortable."

"Good," he muttered, dropping his head to trail kisses down my neck. He nipped at all the spots he now knew were sensitive, and I wondered what the hell he was trying to do to me. "Because you're staying with me tonight."

I wasn't going to argue with that.

Not when Noah was making it clear he wasn't done with me tonight.

And especially not when I didn't know how to ever be done with him.

Fuck.

CHAPTER TWENTY-THREE

noah

I WOKE TO the smell of Gemma on my sheets.

Summery, sweet, sinful. I spent most of the night with my nose pressed into her hair, which smelled like tiger lilies just as much as it looked like them.

I wanted to wake up to this smell every morning. I wanted to wake up with the fresh memories of her taking my cock in every way I wanted. I wanted to wake up with her whimpers still echoing around me.

I didn't just fuck Gemma Briggs last night. I fucked myself over, too.

Sliding inside her while she looked up at me with those big, blue eyes was possibly the best feeling I'd ever experienced in my entire goddamn life. There was no hope for me to deny our chemistry anymore. Not after knowing how perfect it was when we finally let it play out.

Being with her was so much better than I ever could have imagined. And I'd imagined it a lot. So soft and hot and wet and *Gemma*. The way she'd blossomed under my touch like I'd awoken something dormant in her—that was probably my favorite part of all of it. She looked at me like she'd never felt the things I could make her feel. Like she didn't know they were possible.

I wanted to see that look again.

I wanted to see that look over and over again.

Starting now.

I swung an arm out, looking for the beautiful redhead I'd fucked seven ways to Sunday, long into the night. But when my hand hit nothing but blankets, I frowned into my pillow and opened an eye. And then another when I realized that the other side of the bed was empty.

My mind started to race, wondering where the hell she might have run off to, when I heard the echo of voices trailing down the hallway and into my room.

And not just any voices.

One was Gemma's—I'd recognize that anywhere.

And the other was male.

Jumping out of the bed, I threw on a pair of sweatpants and ran a hand through my hair before going to investigate who was in my goddamn apartment.

"It was so nice of you to watch her, thank you," Gemma said, her voice sickly sweet. Or maybe I was just sickened by it because she wasn't talking that way to me. While still in bed. Where she should be. Preferably underneath me. Or on top of me. Fuck, I could just imagine what she'd look like with her—

"Of course, Gemma."

I made a face. Matt. Matt had just said her name, and everything about it sounded wrong.

"Let me know if there's ever anything you need help with," Gemma offered politely, and I internally groaned at her comment as I quickened my steps.

Why did I have to buy such a fucking huge apartment?

"Well..." Matt started, and I gritted my teeth as I rounded the corner into the foyer and saw Gemma standing at the open door, wearing nothing but my shirt with my dog tucked under her arm.

Seriously? She was standing there in *my* shirt, with *my* dog, and this asshole was still going to try to make a move? Because I

265

knew that was what was about to happen. And that must mean he was pretty fucking dense.

"There's nothing that I need," he went on. "But I'd love to take you to dinner sometime if you'd be interested."

"Oh, I—"

"Hey, man," I interrupted, sliding in next to Gemma and giving Matt a tight smile. His eyes widened with alarm at my sudden arrival. Especially when I wrapped my arm around Gemma's waist, pulled her tight into my side, and then slid my hand over her stomach.

"Hey," he stuttered, his eyes falling to how my fingers spread over Gemma's little bump.

Shit. I hadn't meant to do that. It was just where my hand naturally fell, and now Matt seemed to be making rapid assumptions while he stared at us.

Not that I cared.

As long as those assumptions got him to back the fuck off.

"Oh, I had no idea you were expecting," Matt said, still half-stunned as he lifted his gaze back to Gemma's face.

A nervous little laugh emerged from Gemma's lips as she shrugged. "I've just started to show, so I don't expect people to notice."

Her body was tense beneath my touch, and I moved my thumb in circles, a hopefully soft caress as I tried to convey that I didn't mean to out her or make it obvious. I wasn't sorry for interrupting whatever the fuck was going on when I walked up, but I was sorry for revealing secrets that weren't mine.

Matt nodded woodenly, and I didn't mind the letdown in his expression. It told me he wasn't about to hit on Gemma again, not for a long time.

"Well, congratulations to you both," he said, offering a weak smile.

"Oh—"

"Thank you," I interrupted Gemma with a grin before dropping a kiss on her shoulder. I let my hands drop from around her before putting them out, indicating I could take Winnie. My pup was growing, and I knew it couldn't be comfortable holding a wiggling dog like that.

Gemma obediently passed a happily yipping Winnie to me, and my face was covered with puppy kisses within seconds of having her in my arms. I laughed before setting her on the ground and turning back to Matt.

"Thanks again for helping out, man," I said, trying to keep my tone in check.

"No problem." He nodded, a bit sheepish. "I'm a big fan, so whatever you need to win games, you know?"

I chuckled, thinking it was interesting that he'd never mentioned he was a football fan before.

"I'd be happy to get you tickets to a home game," I said, sticking my foot out as Winnie tried to make a playful escape out the door. She bounced back and ran back down the hallway instead. "As a thank-you. Just let me know which game, and we'll make it happen."

He perked up, a little bit of his disappointment fading. "That'd be amazing. Thanks, London."

I nodded and decided that was enough of this conversation. Especially since Gemma still stood next to me, wearing far too little for my comfort. After saying a quick goodbye, I shut the door before Matt even had the chance to turn away.

Whatever. He could think I was an asshole; I didn't care.

Gemma turned on me the moment the door closed. "I can't believe you just did that," she said with a shake of her head and a reluctant, creeping smile.

"Did what?"

"Implied that you're—" She cut herself off and pushed past me. "I can't even with you, Noah," she laughed.

I followed her down the hallway, enjoying how my shirt lifted just enough to see the curve of her ass as she walked.

"You can't *even* with me?" I repeated. "That's not the way you were acting last night. Do I need to remind you about how you begged for my—"

"Noah!" She turned around with wide eyes, giving me a little shove that caught me off guard enough that I stumbled into her and wrapped her in my arms sloppily.

"Yes?" I whispered in her ear.

"I didn't expect you to be so...so..." Her words came out breathless, labored. Like just the thought of last night made her pulse tick up. I could relate.

I kissed the hollow beneath her ear, sucking a little. I couldn't help it. She just tasted so fucking good, and I wanted more.

"So what, Em?"

"I didn't think you were the type of guy to get so possessive after sleeping with a girl once," she said before moaning when I found that spot that drove her wild, nipping at it. "I think you scared poor Matt."

My lips wandered her skin while I tried to wrap my head around what she'd just said. It made me irrationally pissed. Irrationally because she was absolutely right—I'd never felt possessive over a girl before. Pissed because, for some reason, she was lumping herself in with my hookups as though I was done with her.

"Poor *Matt*?" I repeated after gathering myself, drawing back to raise a brow at her. "He tried to ask you out while you were standing there, half-naked in *my* shirt. Matt deserved to be put in his place. As far as being possessive...that was pretty fucking innocent compared to what I wanted to do."

Her wide blue eyes met mine. "What did you want to do?" she whispered.

"Oh," I said, dropping my voice to a dangerous pitch. "I'm so fucking glad you asked."

After looking over Gemma's shoulder to check on Winnie and see that she'd already made herself at home, curled in a ball on the couch, I spun us around and walked Gemma backward toward the front door.

"First of all, let's get one thing straight," I muttered, enjoying the way Gemma gasped when her back hit the door, and my growing hard-on grazed her stomach as I pressed against her. "You're not just some girl I slept with once."

"What am I?"

What was Gemma?

Fuck, I wished I could answer that question with confidence, but I had no idea how to categorize her. She didn't belong in a box with a label on it.

"Noah, it's okay," she whispered, misunderstanding my momentary silence. "I know."

Why did she keep saying things like that? Why did she know, and I didn't? She seemed so sure about what we were, and I couldn't even begin to wrap my head around it.

"You know what?"

"That this is just sex. Right?" she murmured. "Really, really... good sex."

"Right," I said slowly, ignoring the dip in my stomach at the implication that our connection was merely physical. I should be happy. Relationships weren't the name of my game. There was no way I could promise her what she needed, so I should be relieved. "Just sex," I repeated.

Saying it left a sour taste on my tongue, and Gemma scrunched her nose as though she didn't like the way it sounded coming from my mouth, either.

She cleared her throat. "Like friends with benefits."

Friends. She fucking knew I didn't like that word when it referred to us, and I rolled my eyes.

"Or roommates with benefits," she tried.

"That makes it sound like you moved in just so I could use you for sex," I said flatly, hating to even hear those words aloud.

Gemma shook her head. "No, Noah. If anything, we're using each other. Just like our original deal. I'm here to watch Winnie. We might as well have some fun at the same time."

269

I sighed and shook my head. I should be *elated* right now at what she was proposing, but something didn't sit right.

"Then you tell me," she encouraged when I didn't reply, looking up at me with those blue eyes. "I don't know what I'm doing with my life right now, Noah. I don't know what's going to happen in a few months. But I know that last night..." She sucked in. "I know I liked it."

I sighed, wishing I was good at this. Wishing I knew how to handle this better. But I was out of my depth, and my focus was dwindling as Gemma lifted her hips, purposefully teasing my hard cock with her soft curves.

"If you want a friend with benefits, then it'll be me," I rasped, thinking I'd give her whatever she needed right now because I didn't know what would happen in a few months, either. "As long as you know how much I like you, how much I like fucking you, how much I'm not *done* fucking you, and how I need guys like Matt to know that. And I also need you to admit that the *benefits* last night were more than just really *good*."

"Amazing," she corrected, her voice threadbare, wispy. "Really...really amazing."

Heat filled her eyes as though she was remembering it. Like she was replaying it in her head, the moment I'd slid into her for the first time. Or the moment she'd fallen into a million pieces, my name on her lips. The whole night had been a whirlwind, but I'd remember every fucking second of it for as long as I'd probably live.

"And you only *liked* fucking me?" she asked, her voice dropping as she used my own tactic against me.

I tipped my hips against hers, letting her feel how much even just the memories affected me. "I *loved* fucking you, Em."

"I loved it, too," she whimpered, rocking up to meet me, beat for beat. What a perfect fucking match she was.

"Enough to do it again?"

She nodded eagerly, and I groaned inwardly.

"Then turn around so I can show you exactly what I think about you saying that you're just some girl I fucked once."

Like the good girl she was, Gemma spun and faced the door. Her sex-tangled hair flowed down her back, and I smoothed a hand over it. Despite the messy look, it was silky and smooth, and I finally got to do what I'd thought of so many fucking times.

I wrapped it in my fist and tugged. Gemma's head flung back, her body arching beautifully as she braced her hands on the door. I slipped my free hand beneath her shirt, bunching it up to her hips so that pretty ass was on display for me. I gave it a little smack, testing how Gemma would react.

Her breath hitched, visibly halting before returning to taking quick, unsteady gasps.

God, yes. Our living arrangement was about to get a hell of a lot more fun.

I worked my sweatpants down and over my hips with my one available hand, refusing to release her hair now that I had it in my grip. My dick sprang free, and I let the head trail down the rim of Gemma's ass. She shivered, arching further for me, handing herself over.

So I took the invitation and guided my cock between her legs, dragging the tip through her wet cunt and groaning at the reintroduction. Meanwhile, Gemma squirmed, wanting more, and goddamn did I want to give it to her.

"*Fuck*, Em," I breathed. "You sure you want it like this?"

"I'm sure," she panted, spreading her legs wider to prove her words. "Just—" She broke off with a moan when my dick grazed her clit. "*Please*, Noah."

I chuckled, even though every ounce of need coursing through her body was also destroying mine. It had only been a handful of hours since I'd been inside her, but it felt like an eternity. I *needed* her.

"Are you always this impatient?" I murmured, leaning in to brush my lips along the curve of her ear. She trembled beneath my touch as I slid my hand beneath her shirt, cupping her breast in my palm and squeezing. So perfect. The tits of a fucking angel. "Or is it just for me and my cock?"

Gemma's breath faltered as I teased her entrance, slowly tilting my hips. "Just for you."

"And my cock," I added. A very important part. "Say it."

"And your cock," she repeated obediently, her voice dripping with desire, and I smirked.

"There you go," I murmured and rewarded her by gradually feeding my cock into her dripping pussy. "You want to know what I wanted to do as soon as I saw you standing in front of this door half-naked while another man flirted with you?"

She nodded, seeming unable to talk. Probably because she was holding her breath as I slowly pushed into her blissfully warm body.

"Breathe, beautiful," I reminded, kissing her neck while playing with her breasts, tweaking those pretty nipples. "I'll tell you when you breathe."

When I felt her inhale, her chest expanding beneath my touch, I grinned. She was unbelievable, and right now, she was mine. And if she wanted to hear just how *mine* she was, I'd tell her.

"I wanted to slam the door in his hopeful face and then let him listen while I fucked you against the other side of it."

To make my point extra clear, I slammed all that way into her beautifully tight pussy, groaning from the heat licking up my body. Tightening my grip on her hair as she moaned, I grabbed her hip with my other hand and pulled out, only to thrust inside her again. "You're right, Em. I'm not possessive about girls I sleep with once. But the minute we came together last night, I knew once would never be enough. Not for you, angel."

"Yes," she sighed, melting beneath my touch. Her body was mine to mold. Mine to play like the instrument it was. "Yes, Noah."

Such a sweet fucking sound.

But it wasn't loud enough for me.

"I want to hear you." I picked up the pace, thrusting steadily and letting the sounds of slapping skin fill the hallway. "I want *him* to hear you. Let him hear how fucking off-limits you are."

Gemma whimpered in response, and I shook my head. That wasn't good enough for me.

Deciding she might need extra incentive, I reached around her body and slipped my fingers between her legs. I got momentarily distracted by the feel of my cock slipping in and out of her sweet cunt, but then I found what I was looking for. And when I stroked a finger over her clit, I wasn't disappointed.

"Oh my God," Gemma groaned. Loudly.

I guess she wanted me to work for those sounds.

Luckily, I was more than happy to do that.

"*Noah*," she cried as I thrust deeper with my cock and flicked my finger over that little spot that drove her wild. "Oh my God, Noah."

"That's it, angel," I breathed. "That's exactly it. My name is the only name I want to hear come out of your fucking mouth like that, got it?"

She nodded, and my thrusts grew desperate, needy. Fuck, I wasn't going to make it. My entire body shook with the need for release, and I didn't know if I would make it long enough. But there was no way in hell I'd let this end without wringing an earth-shattering orgasm from Gemma's body.

I gave her hair a little experimental tug, and when she gasped, I gripped it harder, holding on for dear life while she took every single drive of my hips beautifully. Meanwhile, I focused on her clit, drumming my finger over it steadily until I could feel her body tightening against mine.

Her groans grew louder. She started rocking her body, taking everything she could from my cock and my touch. She wanted it, all of it, and fuck, I wanted her to have it. Her fingers curled on the door, searching for something to hold on to, and I knew she was about ready to lose it.

And when she did...she screamed.

Gemma screamed, chanting my name as I fucked her through her release before coming just as hard as she had. If not harder. My cum filled that tight cunt to the brim, and I knew it would be dripping down her legs by the time I pulled out.

Fuck.

I sagged against Gemma's shaky, twitching body and knew she was about to collapse. So before we could fall to the floor, I scooped her into my arms.

"How would you feel about a bath?" I asked, brushing a soft kiss over her lips. God, I didn't know how I'd ever stop kissing her now that I'd started.

She lifted a brow. "Do you think the tub is big enough for two people?"

I nodded with a smirk, walking us back toward my room.

"Big enough for two people."

CHAPTER TWENTY-FOUR

"YOU TOLD ME the bathtub held two people."

Noah chuckled, his breath tickling my bare skin. He crouched behind my back, *outside the tub*. He'd stolen the washcloth from me and was busy dragging it up and down my arm, like he refused to give up touching me completely.

"It does."

"Then why are you out there, and I'm sitting in here?"

Noah didn't respond. Instead, he trailed the washcloth to my chest, gently teasing it over the tips of my breasts beneath the water. They hardened, and I bit down on a moan before snatching the washcloth from him so he couldn't drop even lower.

"You're going to have to get in here if you want more," I said breathlessly.

Noah cursed under his breath and then, to my great disappointment, stood and strode away from the tub.

Well, that backfired.

"I can't get enough of you," Noah groaned, keeping his back to me for a moment before spinning and leaning against the bathroom countertop.

I couldn't get enough of him, either. All I could think about was how ridiculously sexy this man was as he stood there shirt-less with sweatpants riding low on his hips. When he walked up to me while I was talking to Matt earlier, I nearly combusted from the heat of his skin as it brushed against mine.

If I thought Noah was attractive before, it was nothing compared to how I viewed him now that he'd fucked me into a near coma last night. I kept seeing flashes of how his muscles tensed and his eyes rolled back. And right now, his hair was all messy, reminding me of how my hands had sifted through it last night.

And God, it was all *so* hot.

"Then get in," I encouraged.

Noah's eyes drifted over me as I sank back into his massive soaker tub. The bubbles were up to my chin, so I doubted he could see anything other than my head floating above the water, but he seemed satisfied with the situation regardless.

"You're in there because I made a sexy mess out of you," he muttered, finally answering my question from earlier. "And I'm out here because I'm enjoying the view of my pretty roommate."

I sat forward, and Noah's eyes zeroed in on my breasts, peeking out of the water. Smirking, I said, "If you get in the bath-tub, you could enjoy the *feel* of your roommate."

His gaze flicked up to mine. "Pretty."

"What?"

"You dropped the pretty," he said. "I can enjoy the feel of my *pretty* roommate."

I cupped the bubbles in my hand and blew on them, watching as they floated through the air. "You're really stuck on that, aren't you?"

"You're really stuck on ignoring or denying me whenever I try to say how beautiful you are."

I ducked my head, struggling to figure out how to reply. This unfiltered version of Noah had a lot of things to say about me that made my stomach flutter. And I just wasn't used to that. I didn't know how to handle it. Or acknowledge it.

Mostly because I was afraid that acknowledging it would end up hurting me in the end. Noah had made it more than clear that night in the living room fort that he didn't do relationships. He'd looked me in the eyes when he said it, making it feel like a warning.

And while I didn't agree with the reasoning he gave because I knew in my heart that Noah could give someone all the love in the world, I couldn't count on being the one to change his mind. Especially not when it wouldn't just be me he was committing to. I was a two-for-one deal, and if Noah and I delved into more, if I let myself think for even a minute that it *could* be more, I wasn't sure I could handle a broken heart while also navigating single-motherhood.

That's what I should be focusing on, anyway. My mind should be on this baby and everything I still needed to do to get ready for them. This—sitting in Noah London's luxury bathtub—wasn't reality. Even if I was loving every minute of it, this was just a temporary fairy tale. The fact that I was even indulging in it made me feel guilty to the core.

"Gemma," Noah continued without a care in the world for my internal dilemma. "I enjoyed the feel of you last night. And this morning. And if I enjoy the feel of you anymore without giving you a rest, you won't be able to walk at Juniper's bachelorette party."

I laughed, and it echoed in his spacious bathroom. It was all modern lines and sleek fixtures. Not to mention the floor-to-ceiling window that the bathtub sat against, giving me the perfect view of Boston as I soaked.

"Juniper's bachelorette party isn't until next weekend," I protested. "You think you can fuck me hard enough that I won't be able to walk for a week?"

"Careful how you phrase that, angel." The corner of Noah's mouth tilted up as he crossed his arms over his chest. "It almost sounded like a challenge."

I clenched my legs under the water, trying to soothe the

growing ache between them. God, I was insatiable when it came to this man. My body wanted *more*. I suspected it had something to do with the hormones, but also...Noah. Noah London had a lot to do with it, too.

"Maybe it was," I said, looking up at him beneath my lashes as I smiled.

"Gemma," he groaned, tipping his head back and closing his eyes.

"If you're not gonna get in and make yourself useful, why are you hanging around torturing yourself?"

"Because I don't know how to walk away, either." He ran a hand over his face while tipping it back down, flashing his piercing green eyes open to stare longingly at me. My face grew hot, and it had nothing to do with the steaming water. "Clearly, otherwise last night wouldn't have happened."

"I'm glad it happened," I whispered.

Noah groaned. "Fuck, me too."

I could see the indecision in his eyes as he warred with whether to join me in the tub.

I knew what I wanted. I wanted him close. Touching me, preferably. Frankly, I should be concerned with how *badly* I wanted it, with how quickly it was growing into an addiction.

Noah dragged his gaze away from me and looked out the window instead. I wondered what was going on in that head of his, what he was thinking of this...of our situation.

Part of me wasn't sure I wanted to know.

"Have you ever watched the sunrise from here?" I asked, redirecting the conversation into safer territory as I sank back into the tub, letting the suds cover my body. "I bet it would be amazing. A cup of coffee in hand, watching as the light gradually peeked over the cityscape."

"I haven't," he admitted, surprising me. He was always up so early. "But you're welcome to watch the sunrise in my bathroom whenever you want..." He looked back at me, his lips twitching. "In exchange for one request."

I cocked my head to the side. "Is it a dirty request?"

I could almost guarantee that I would say yes to that.

"You tell me." He chuckled. "I want to see your mug collection."

I narrowed my eyes, not believing that was what he really wanted. "Are you sure *that's* the collection you want to see?"

"Is there another option I'm not aware of?" He raised his eyebrows.

"I think you're more than aware of the other option."

He grinned, not denying it. "Fine. I would *also* really like to be introduced to your sex toy collection."

"Hm..." I pursed my lips, pretending to consider his request. "You have to pick. Mugs or sex toys."

"I pick the mugs," he said without even considering it.

Huh. "Surprising."

His expression softened, and I just knew whatever he was about to say would wreck me a bit.

"The mugs tell me about you, Em."

My brows furrowed as I stared at him, unable to find words.

"They tell me the TV shows you like, and the quotes you find funny, and that your favorite color is either green or blue," he went on, making my stomach flip into my chest. "I like that every morning when I see you drinking all that decaf coffee, I learn one new little thing about you. Whereas, if I had to guess, the sex toys would tell me that you like it when that sweet clit of yours gets all the attention." His devilish smirk returned. "But I already knew that."

Yes, he did. And he knew just what to do with that information, too. But I didn't need him getting too cocky on me. That wouldn't do.

I flashed him a teasing look. "Oh, so after one night, you know everything about what I like in the bedroom, huh?"

"Not everything, no." His smirk grew, but his voice dropped to a calm, seductive pitch. One that excited and soothed all at once. "And I hope you know you can tell me if there's something you want that I'm not giving you. But I also like discovering it on my own. I like exploring your body until I figure out what makes you tick."

His eyes drifted across the tub like he had laser vision that could see through the piles of bubbles. Honestly, I wished he did. I liked feeling his gaze on me last night.

Noah's eyes eventually found my face, searching it for...something. I wasn't sure, but I stared back, wanting him to know that I wasn't going to back down from this. I wasn't afraid of it, from what he was saying. And if he wanted to explore my body right now, I would let him.

"Stop looking at me like that, Gemma," he rasped after a minute.

"I'm sorry." I wasn't sorry. "You're just so..." I flicked my eyes over him the way he did to me, needing him to know that he wasn't the only one who recognized the attraction here. If he got to eye-fuck me, I should be allowed to do it back.

"Gemma...cut it out." Noah's jaw ticked as he shifted against the countertop. "Or deal with being unable to walk at Juniper's bachelorette party."

"Fine," I pouted. "I already have enough to worry about with that party."

"Do you think—" he started before biting his lip in thought.

"Do I think?"

"I just..." He rubbed the back of his neck. "Do you really think you can get away with people not noticing?"

"Well, I figure we'll only be together when all of us are at the Bellflower, and then we're going—"

"Wait, what? The girls are going to the Bellflower, too?"

"Yeah." I nodded before rolling my eyes a bit. "Juniper and Julian wanted the whole wedding party to get drinks together before splitting up. Although, I think if it were up to Julian, he would have gone wherever Juniper went."

"He would have," Noah agreed dryly. "But I wasn't talking

about us, Gemma. Although I'm sure keeping my hands off you will be impossible."

"What were you—*oh*."

That.

"Yeah."

"It'll be fine," I said, trying to convince myself just as much as I was trying to convince him. Celebrating my best friend's marriage to my brother would definitely be a lot more fun if I weren't pregnant. *Secretly* pregnant. "The dress I was planning on wearing is loose around my stomach, kinda like the one I wore out the other night. I doubt anyone will notice."

Noah's eyes darkened before he interjected. "If it's like that dress...I'm fucked, Em."

I smirked and then sobered, my thoughts still lingering on the pregnancy.

"After the bachelorette party," I promise. "I'll tell everyone sometime after the party."

Noah considered my words for a moment before nodding. He looked more uncertain than he had in the past whenever I brought up keeping the pregnancy secret. Usually, I had a good read of his thoughts on the matter. But this morning, I couldn't be sure.

"When Julian finds out that you're pregnant," he said after a long pause, "and he finds out you're living here, he's going to try to get you to move out."

I sighed. "I know he is. That's why I wanted to keep it a secret until I had an apartment lined up. But at this rate, I don't know how long I'll be able to hide it. Not with all the wedding events coming up. We're only like a month out from the big day, and I didn't take all that into consideration before."

Noah cleared his throat. "There's no rush, you know."

"No rush?" I repeated. "I thought you wanted me to tell Julian—"

"No rush to move out," he clarified.

"I'm staying until the end of the season," I said, reassuring him that I would stick to our agreement. "Or even if I move out, I'll still watch Winnie whenever you're gone. Or if Natalie needs help with Chloe, I'll be around."

"That's not it." He frowned. "It's that you have enough on your plate without worrying about an apartment and rent. You can stay as long as you want, Em. And Julian can deal with that."

"You're just saying that because the longer I live here, the longer we can have sex."

"If your moving out is our expiration date, then yeah, maybe I am," he said, surprising me with the sharp note in his voice, but then it disappeared as he sighed. "But it's not really that. I just don't want you to be stressed about finding a new place when there's no real reason why you have to move out."

"There's a baby coming, Noah," I whispered because there was definitely a reason to move out. I didn't want to be stressed about apartments, either, but I knew I needed to find one. I needed to get ready for the baby. I needed to find a home for my little lemon.

But Noah just blinked once and said, "I know."

My brows drew together as I attempted to understand the look in his eyes. But a second later, he blinked, and it was gone. Slipping his hands in his pockets, he pushed off the countertop and strolled toward me.

He bent, dropping a kiss on the top of my head.

"I have to head into the gym," he muttered. "I probably should have been there a while ago."

"Okay," I whispered as he pulled away. "If I'm not home when you get back, I'll be at the rink."

Noah groaned abruptly. "Isn't there some way for you to teach those kids how to skate *without* stepping onto the ice?"

"It wouldn't be very effective," I laughed.

"Fine. Just—" He raked his fingers through his hair before shooting me a meaningful look. "Just please be careful."

"Baby and I will be safe, Noah," I said, trying to reassure him with a smile.

He shook his head as he walked to the doorway, a tiny grin playing on his lips. With one foot out of the bathroom, he looked over his shoulder.

"What do you and Baby want for dinner?"

"That's hours from now," I said. "Whatever Baby and I are craving will be totally different by dinner."

Noah turned, facing me again, that smile still on his face. He crossed his arms over his chest, leaning against the doorframe. "Do you have any names in mind, or are you just going to keep calling them Baby?"

I cocked my head to the side, considering his question. And surprised to find I didn't really have an answer. "Baby will have to do for now. I'm hoping it will just...come to me."

"I hope you tell me when it does," he said softly before clearing his throat and adding, "Text me when you figure out what you want for dinner."

Feeling a bit speechless, I didn't get a word out before he walked away. All I managed was a nod.

But because I wasn't going to argue when a hot man was willing to get me dinner, later when I was at the rink and got the sudden urge to eat my weight in spicy food, I texted Noah.

> I need literally anything with buffalo sauce.
> Anything at all.

NOAH: That must be the baby talking.

> Buffalo sauce, Noah.

NOAH: I got it covered. Just get home safe, Em.

> Always.

I was still looking at my phone when another text chimed in.

It was from one of the many people I'd been avoiding.

> DAD: Hey, Gems. How's everything going with
> the new job?

Guilt washed over me. I should call him. I used to talk to my dad on the phone at least once a week, even if it was just a quick check-in. He didn't have a lot of free time, and he had a lot of children to stay in touch with, but he liked hearing our voices. Just for a few minutes.

I'd been dodging his calls because I knew he'd have me spilling everything. Even in those few minutes.

John Briggs had this uncanny ability to see through his children. He'd been the first one to catch onto Julian and Juniper's relationship, and I knew if I gave him the chance, he'd be the first one to catch onto me, too.

> I really like it. It's been a fun change!

> DAD: That's great to hear. Been up to anything
> else fun? Taken any trips or have anything in the
> works?

My stomach flipped, even though I knew it was probably just a coincidence. He knew I used to take trips for work all the time and likely wanted to know if I still did for this new job. That was all.

I swallowed and typed out a response that avoided answering the question about travel because I couldn't outright lie to my dad.

> Just working and getting ready for Juni's
> bachelorette party!

> DAD: You kids have fun. Make sure Julian
> behaves.

Lol you know Juniper will make sure of that.

DAD: Oh, I know.

Sighing, I put my phone away.

And then I wished it was just as easy to put my guilt away, too.

eight years ago
GEMMA

What the hell *was I doing? Insinuating that this man—whose last name I didn't even know—should come visit me after we'd exchanged all of a few words?*

"Here you go, Gems."

Julian's voice jerked me out of whatever trance Noah had put on me. We both sprang apart at the appearance of my brother. And lucky for us, he didn't seem to notice how close we'd gotten. He was too busy shooting glances back at Juniper and running his hand through his hair.

"As Lily so kindly pointed out, the presentation is subpar," *he added, shoving a plastic cup into my hand.* "But the alcohol is good, I promise."

I didn't care about the presentation; I took a big gulp of the wine, needing something to chase down the nerves that Noah was making me feel.

They weren't bad nerves.

They were good nerves.

Too good.

And that was the problem.

287

CHAPTER TWENTY-FIVE

S OCIALIZING WITH THE rest of the wedding party while trying to be a good maid of honor was incredibly difficult when one of the groomsmen wouldn't stop staring at me.

I wasn't sure I'd comprehended a word of what Grayson had said so far as we sat together at a high-top table in the corner of the Bellflower Bar. All of my concentration was currently being used to resist the temptation that was Noah London. Or, more specifically, resisting the urge to *look* at Noah London.

If I risked a glance at Noah right now, who knew what kind of expression would cross my face. And Grayson Everett, star NFL wide receiver and my brother's best man, was sharp as a tack. Luckily, his wife, Nessa, otherwise known as the famous singer-songwriter Wednesday Elevett, drew his attention with something she said, giving me a short reprieve from Grayson's knowing gaze.

A short reprieve that Noah took immediate advantage of, walking past where I sat and swiping my ignored drink off the table. He took a quick gulp before sliding it back in front of me and dropping his hand, letting his fingers graze along my arm before disappearing again.

My skin burned where he'd touched me.

I'd spent every night this week in his bed, and every morning, I spent dawn in his arms. There hadn't been a lot of sleeping involved, leaving me both exhausted *and* horny since today was the first day since we'd returned from Minnesota that I hadn't gotten laid. Noah went into practice early this morning, and I had to finish organizing the details for tonight, leaving little time to fool around.

"Do I need to buy London his own drink?" Grayson chuckled, and it wasn't until that moment that I realized he had seen our interaction.

Shit.

At least Grayson said it quietly.

"No," I said slowly, pushing the drink further away as I processed how else to respond. "No...you don't need to do that."

Grayson frowned, looking down at the drink as though realizing for the first time that I hadn't taken a single sip since one of my sisters set it in front of me. "Do you not like it?"

"It's not that," I said before biting my tongue because it would have been so easy just to say that I didn't really like it. But the people-pleaser, non-complainer in me answered before logic could kick in.

Grayson, still frowning, looked over his shoulder toward Noah again. He was standing at the end of the table between Cameron Bryant, one of Juniper and Julian's colleagues, and Beau Bryant, Cameron's brother-in-law and another one of Julian's college friends.

Noah stood between them, but he was watching *us* over the rim of his own drink.

Shit again.

Grayson's eyes slid back to mine slowly, sweeping over my nearly full drink in the process. He cocked his head to the side, and then, almost as though his subconscious had taken over, his eyes darted to my stomach and back. A sheepish look overcame his face when he realized what he'd done, and I pointedly fluffed my dress, draping it over my knees so it didn't curve over my bump.

Triple shit.

I sighed. "Just ask it," I groaned under my breath.

Grayson's brows lifted. "Nu-uh," he said. "My moms raised me better than to ask any woman that question."

"Can you just pretend the last two minutes didn't happen?" I asked hopefully.

"I can pretend anything you want, Gemma." Grayson rarely drank because he was born with a congenital heart defect, so he pushed his nonalcoholic drink toward me, swapping it out with the glass Janie put in front of me. "But just tell me this...exactly what level of protection is London gonna need from your brother? I need to know what to expect."

I considered, biting down on my lip. "Maybe not quite as much as you think," I admitted.

I suspected that Grayson assumed Noah was responsible for the reason I wasn't drinking. And while I didn't mind the idea of that nearly as much as the truth, it *wasn't* the truth. It would never be the truth.

Grayson narrowed his gaze and lowered his voice. He leaned closer to me, and I followed suit, even as I felt Noah's hot gaze surge stronger. "He hasn't taken his eyes off you since you sat next to me, Gemma. Which, don't get me wrong, isn't surprising. The man's had a crush on you since you walked in the door at our shitty college house nearly eight years ago. But something's different, and you can't tell me otherwise."

"Something's different," I allowed, willing myself not to smile at what he said about Noah. And me. "It's just a long story." I darted my eyes around us, indicating that now wasn't the time to *tell* the long story.

Grayson leaned back with a nod, oddly satisfied with my nonanswer.

"Well, I'll order all the nonalcoholic drinks you want," he muttered out of the corner of his mouth, attempting to be discreet. "No one will think differently of it. They'll certainly think less of it than if you keep letting London steal sips of your drinks for you."

I laughed softly, thanking him, and then he said something that made my heart momentarily stop beating.

"How was Minnesota?" he asked, eyes twinkling.

But before I could answer the question or ask why he was even asking that in the first place, Julian came up and clapped a hand on his shoulder, leaning in to say something in his other ear.

Goddamnit.

Noah must have told him. Right? There was no other explanation. It was probably the reason he was so suspicious about the drinks and Noah in the first place.

I brushed it off, deciding it didn't matter. Grayson didn't seem eager to spill any of my secrets. In fact, for the next several hours, he kept me well supplied with nonalcoholic drinks, which he either slipped to me or Nessa, who handed them over to me without asking a single question.

Considering how many drinks Gianna and Janie kept forcing on me, combined with the cocktail some random guy at the bar insisted on buying me, Grayson and Nessa were lifesavers, switching out the drinks before anyone could notice, and they did it all without batting their eyes.

I wasn't sure whether they were helping me for my sake or the sake of the party, which would surely get derailed if my secret slipped out, but it didn't matter. I owed them.

If my sisters noticed I was still sober after three steady hours of drinking, they didn't say anything. I wasn't worried about Gianna, Janie, and Genevieve; they were too drunk to pay attention to me. I was more concerned about Josie, who was just shy of twenty-one and, therefore, as stone-cold sober as me. But she seemed too engrossed in a conversation with Sofia, Juniper's half sister, to be aware of anything else.

Taking advantage of everyone's preoccupation, I slipped away to find the bathroom. At least no one would second-guess me needing to pee after all the drinks being pushed in my direction.

But there was one person who I didn't account for. One person who wasn't preoccupied with anything or anyone... but me.

As soon as I stepped out of the bathroom, a familiar muscled body pulled me into the dark corner across from it, flipping me around to push me up against the wall. A startled gasp fell from my lips, even though I should have expected this.

"You seem to have a habit of following girls to the bathroom, Noah," I breathed when I found my voice. "If you ask me, it's a bit questionable."

"Just you, angel." He rested his hand on the wall behind me, leaning in. His eyes glowed through the dim lighting. "I just follow you."

I smiled up at him, trying to play it cool despite the fluttering in my stomach. "Should I be concerned about your stalking tendencies?"

He shrugged, his lips tipping up in amusement. "Some call it stalking; others call it worrying."

"Well, I'm fine," I assured him.

"Fuck yeah, you are," he said in a husky murmur, pulling back slightly to let his gaze roam up and down my length. Eventually, it landed where I knew it would: on my cleavage. A soft groan escaped his lips. "You look stunning tonight. I haven't been able to look away from you for more than a minute."

"Noah," I muttered. I had meant for it to sound like a warning. If he kept looking at me and talking to me like that, it would only make the rest of the night harder. Not to mention, someone was going to notice. Well, someone *else*. Besides Grayson. But Noah's hands started drifting up my sides, and his name came out in a sigh instead.

His mouth curved into a wolfish grin as he traced the underside of my breast with his thumb.

"Yeah?"

I melted into his touch, just like I always did. My pulse picked up, and fuck, I wanted more. I always wanted more from him, and he knew it.

"Noah, I—"

My voice broke off as he brushed his thumb higher, grazing my nipple. I pressed my lips together, trying not to let a moan out.

"Cat got your tongue?"

"You're teasing me," I whined, breathless as his thumb still made slow circles around my breast. I could feel the heat of his touch through my dress, lighting me up inside and out.

Noah leaned in until his lips nearly touched mine. His breath grazed my mouth when he spoke, sending a shiver through me. "I don't want to tease you. I want to have you. I want to kiss you until you're gasping for air, Em. But all it takes is a taste of you to get me hard as a fucking rock, so I'm trying to resist."

"Tomorrow," I breathed, my body straining towards his. "We'll be home tomorrow."

"We will." Trailing his lips to my ear, Noah nuzzled in close, nipping my skin in a way that sent little jolts of need through me. "And then I'll give you anything you want," he promised. "Until then...I just need to settle one thing."

"What?"

"I saw that asshole buy you a drink, and it killed me that I couldn't tell him off without people noticing. So I need you to know that while I'm fucking that pretty pussy of yours, no one else better go near it," he growled, pressing me further into the shadows and spurring on my lust. "It's mine, Em. Got it?"

The thought of hooking up with anyone else never crossed my mind, especially not tonight when all my energy was focused on making sure Juniper had a good time. But I'd be lying if I hadn't thought about Noah and what he might do while out with the guys.

"I'll only agree to that if you can promise me the same."

I snuck my hand between us, running my fingers over the

growing bulge in his jeans. But Noah hissed through his teeth and grabbed me by the wrist, yanking my hand away.

"Angel, you can't do that right now. I'm down so bad for you that I'm gonna be in a world of pain until you're back in my bed. Trust me, if you're not touching me tonight, no one is."

"Okay," I whispered, satisfied with his promise. I knew he meant it. Noah might have a reputation as a player, but even more than that, he was loyal, honest, and kind. And goddamnit, I wanted to kiss him.

But to my dismay, he took a step back. "I'm surprised you're still here," he said, clearing his throat. "I thought you and the girls were only going to be here for one or two drinks."

"I thought so, too," I admitted with a wry twist of my lips. "But I can't get Juniper away from my brother."

When I'd left for the bathroom, Juniper had been dancing with Julian, a full drink dangling in her hand and looking like she had no desire to leave. Sofia had the bar's weekend DJ on lock-down, requesting song after song of whatever Juniper wanted. Meanwhile, Genevieve and Janie had been passing out an entire tray of shots to the wedding party.

"It's probably easier this way since it might be hard getting Josie into the other places," I added. "At this point, everywhere else will be closed by the time we make it out of here. I have a feeling our next stop will just be the hotel bar."

"Where are you guys staying again?"

"The Deluge. We have a girls' day planned for tomorrow. I booked us spa appointments at the hotel in the morning, and then we're getting brunch and going to Juniper's favorite book-store. Instead of lingerie, we're all going to buy her smutty books."

Noah's lips twitched, and I could tell he wanted to say something about that but was holding his tongue.

"Hey, it's probably better for her sex life than lingerie," I defended. "Gets the ideas going, ya know?"

Besides, then I didn't have to buy her something lacy that I knew my *brother* would be ripping off.

"I think it's a great idea," Noah said, still fighting a smile.

I shrugged. "I was pretty proud of it."

"You should be. I know how much Juniper loves her books. You're a great friend." Noah brushed his lips across my forehead, and I let my eyes flutter shut, wondering how a kiss on my hairline could get me so...messed up. "Are you getting a massage at the spa?" he asked.

I nodded, unable to form any other words.

"Make sure you let them know about Baby," he said, his hand taking up its usual residence and palming my stomach. "I know you don't want any of the girls to know, but—"

"I let them know when I booked the appointment that I was in my second trimester," I whispered, reassuring him. "They said that was okay."

"Sounds good. I should let you go before someone notices," he said, his lips still a breath from my forehead. "But I don't want to."

I forced my eyes open with a sigh. "I don't want to, either, but you're right. Pretty sure Grayson already put two and two together."

Noah didn't seem as bothered by that information as I suspected, which made me wonder again if he'd told his friend about me coming to Minnesota. Noah took another step back, lifting a shoulder in a slight shrug.

"Grayson might be Julian's best friend, but he won't say anything. He'll do anything to keep the peace and make sure everyone's happy. He urged Julian to make a move with Juniper because he knew it would make him happy. And I'd bet he'd—" He cut himself off, rubbing a hand over his mouth before ending the conversation. "Don't worry about Grayson, Em."

I nodded because I didn't know what else to do or say. "Okay."

He jerked his head to the side with a tiny smile playing on his lips. "Now, go get out there."

"Okay," I said again, forcing my legs to move as I brushed past him.

I didn't expect it to be so hard. I didn't expect to struggle walking away from him without leaning in for a hug or a kiss. I didn't expect the cracking feeling in my chest that crept up on me without warning.

It was just one night apart.

But it was a reminder that there would be more nights apart. With the way things were now, we'd hit our expiration before we knew it. And then there would be a lifetime of them.

Because as much as I was curious if maybe, *just maybe*, we could make this last longer than a few months, especially considering the way Noah had acted tonight and the things Grayson admitted, I knew my reality, my *pregnant* reality, didn't have time for my fantasies.

We never did make it to another bar after leaving the Bellflower. Juniper hadn't wanted to leave the place she knew and loved, and more importantly, she didn't want to leave Julian. Dragging her away from him so we could head to the hotel had been a challenge enough.

"I just really love him, okay?" she said sloppily as she kicked her shoes off on her way into the hotel suite we'd booked for the night. "He's just...so...*ugh*."

"He loves you, too," I said soothingly, holding the door open for the rest of the girls as they filed into the room. "He's been in love with you for over a decade, Junes. We're all just happy you both figured it out finally."

Juniper flopped back onto the bed, her white frilly dress fluffing around her as she stared at the ceiling. I wasn't sure she heard a word I'd just said. "Not to mention, he has a—"

"If you say anything about his dick, I'm gonna have to leave," Janie cut in.

"I'll stay, but I might throw up," Genevieve muttered as she kicked her shoes off next to Juniper's.

Juni lifted her head, a sly grin playing on her face. In her drunken state, it was clear she wanted to say something, but she also didn't want her fiancé's five sisters to be mad at her for divulging dirty secrets about their brother.

"You can tell me," Nessa laughed, flopping onto the bed next to Juniper. "Julian might be my children's godfather, but at least we're not related."

"You can tell me, too," Sofia chimed in, wiggling her brows as she fell onto the bed beside her sister.

Juni grinned at Sofia and Nessa but shook her head as she pushed herself into a sitting position. "I think we should talk about someone's sex life who *isn't* sleeping with someone who most people here are related to."

Nessa sighed. "Count my sex life out. Grayson and I really shouldn't have any more kids, but do you know how challenging that is when the man has a breeding kink?"

Juniper giggled, glancing over at Nessa. "Something tells me you're well taken care of in the bedroom, breeding kink or not."

Nessa had a look on her face that told me she really couldn't argue with that. Juniper, meanwhile, swiveled her gaze to look directly at me.

"What about the rest of you?"

I bit down on my tongue. I wanted to tell her. So badly, I wanted to tell her *everything*. She knew there was something I wasn't saying. She knew it, just like I'd known something was happening between her and Julian when they started working together.

But Sofia jumped in with a dirty joke about her husband, saving me from making a decision. I leaned against the wall and looked at the petite brunette, trying to focus on her storytelling.

Considering how Juniper's eyes were still stuck on me, it was hard. Giving in, I met her gaze, cocking my head to the side as though to ask, "What?"

But she just narrowed her gaze and then flopped back drunkenly on the bed.

Soon.

I'd tell her everything soon.

CHAPTER TWENTY-SIX

noah

I SHOOK MY head as I left the locker room, waving bye to Jonesy before focusing my attention on my phone and the text I just got from Grayson.

> GRAY: I didn't want to bring anything up around Julian last night, but are congratulations in order?

> Depends on what kind of congratulations you're referring to.

> GRAY: You know.

Fuck, I did know.

> GRAY: Gemma wasn't drinking.

My fingers were stiff as I typed the next text.

> It's not mine.
>
> But she is.
>
> For now.
>
> She's been living with me.

To punctuate that thought, another text chimed in as I made it to my car.

> SHE'S JULIAN'S SISTER, NOAH: When are you getting home?

I stared at my phone, thinking I really needed to change Gemma's contact name. The reminder was a little too late, and I didn't need the guilt flooding me every time she texted me.

Especially since she sent a follow-up text with a picture of her naked lower half with a vibrator poised between her legs.

> SHE'S JULIAN'S SISTER, NOAH: If you don't get here soon, I'm taking matters into my own hands.

> > Don't.
> >
> > I'm on my way.

I slid into my car, eager to get home. Despite being dead tired from last night's party, I still had to go to the stadium today. It was damned annoying, considering how badly I wanted to see Gemma. She'd been with the girls all day.

> GRAY: I think I'm gonna need some clarification.

I sighed. The problem? Nothing about our situation was clear.

> > Let me talk to Jules first and then I'll tell you everything. I'm waiting for Gemma to give me the green light. Julian doesn't know about any of it.

> GRAY: Fuck, good luck.

I'd need it. But right now, I didn't want to think about Julian. All my thoughts were reserved for Gemma.

Last night had been the first night in a week that we spent

apart, and while that shouldn't be that big of a deal, it sure as hell felt like it. More specifically, it felt like *torture*.

Torture made worse by the fact that I spent the whole night with the brother of the girl I was fucking. The girl I couldn't stop thinking about. The girl who, at this very moment, was in my apartment, half-naked.

Hopefully, completely naked.

I stepped on the gas, letting the car accelerate at the same rate as my pulse.

I was addicted, and I didn't fucking care. I'd never slept with someone this many times. Yes, it had only been a week, but I'd never even wanted to see someone two nights in a row before. And now, I couldn't think of anything other than spending every goddamn night with Gemma.

Thank the Lord we still had months before our little arrangement was up. Maybe by then, my addiction would have eased. Maybe the excitement would have waned. Maybe my pulse wouldn't tick up like this at the thought of her smile.

That had better be the case.

Otherwise...I was fucked.

Because right now, it felt like I'd never get enough of her, and that downright terrified me.

The interstate lights blurred around me as I sped the rest of the way home. Just as I pulled into the garage, my phone lit up again.

SHE'S JULIAN'S SISTER, NOAH: Hurry.

I swore under my breath as I parked and tucked my full-fledged erection into the waistband of my sweats. I'd thought about Gemma the whole way home, and it showed. The last thing I needed was the building security to see the boner I sported on my way inside.

Rushing into the complex, I damn near sprinted to the elevator before tapping my fingers impatiently as it brought me up to my floor. When the doors opened with a ding, I flew down the hall, completely ignoring whatever snide comment Summer flung at me as she passed.

I held my breath when I entered my apartment, half expecting to hear Gemma's moans as soon as I stepped in the door, just like I did that night after getting home from Florida. But the apartment was quiet except for Winnie's click-clacking paws as she ran over to greet me. I crouched down to pick her up, letting her shower me with puppy kisses as I walked her to my bedroom, where I hoped she'd take a nap. Because I had plans right now that I didn't want interrupted.

Luckily, Winnie's kennel was one of her favorite places to be, and once she was happily tucked away, I kicked my shoes off and padded to Gemma's bedroom, stopping short in her open doorway.

Lying on her stomach, she had her back to me. Or rather, ass to me. I swallowed a groan and leaned against the doorframe, taking in the sight. She had her vibrator twirling in the fingers of one hand and her phone in the other, her thumb flying across the screen as she typed something.

Most importantly, though, she wore this wispy, transparent nightgown that gave me a clear view of her naked body beneath it. The blue, ethereal fabric barely fell over the curve of her ass, and I couldn't wait to push it out of the way so I could—

"Hi."

Considering the dirty picture she sent me less than an hour ago, Gemma sounded surprisingly shy as she noticed me lingering in the doorway.

When I couldn't figure out how to move or speak—too stunned by how incredibly beautiful she looked lying there, Gemma frowned.

"What are you doing?" she asked as she flipped onto her back and pushed herself up on her elbows.

As if that fucking helped.

Now, I was greeted with the view of her tits, barely veiled by the see-through fabric. I could see the perfect outline of her nipples, and my mouth watered. Fucking watered.

"I'm trying to wrap my head around that...thing you're wearing," I rasped.

Gemma laughed, and it rang through the air, beautiful and crisp. "My pajamas?"

"Your pajamas?" I choked out. "That's—I—*fuck*, Em."

She grinned and propped one leg up seductively, sliding her foot toward her ass and letting that flimsy fabric ride up, exposing a tiny glimpse of her pussy. My already stiff cock pulsed, wondering why the hell I was still standing here in the doorway when I could be touching her.

"I thought I should upgrade," she crooned. "I wanted something pretty."

Pretty. Sexy. Stunning. Fucking hot.

Yeah, she'd accomplished that.

But there was something she needed to know.

"Just to set the record straight...those white pajamas you always wear? With the little hearts? You looked pretty and downright fuckable in those, too." I scrubbed a hand over my face. "But this? Em, if you wear that around the apartment, I won't be able to get anything done without ending up inside you."

"Mmm," she hummed. "Sounds good to me."

I chuckled. "Insatiable woman."

"Being horny is basically a pregnancy side effect." She shrugged, and then her lips tilted sideways in a smirk. "What's your excuse?"

"You," I said without thinking about it. "You are the reason I'm so fucking hard. I drove down the interstate with a stiffy after I got that goddamn picture."

She grinned knowingly. "You liked that?"

"Liked it?" I stepped toward it, shoving my hands in my pocket. "God, Gemma. You really have no idea, do you?"

She answered that by giving me a good, long once-over. It felt like permission to do the same, so I let my gaze drift back over her body, appreciating every dip, every curve, every freckle. Everything that made Gemma, *Gemma*.

And then there was that vibrator, still in her hand.

"Are you going to let me watch you use that? You have no idea how many times I've pictured you do that after I heard you that night."

"Maybe another time." A teasing twinkle lit up her eyes as she did the opposite of what I expected, reaching behind her to drop the vibrator in her bedside table drawer. "I don't know if I need the vibrator now that you're here. I have you now."

"You have me," I agreed in a husky murmur. "But I don't think you understand how close I am to losing it. I feel..." I broke off, running a shaky hand through my hair. Seeing her like this was making my heart beat out of my fucking chest. My entire body felt unsteady, and I knew it was because I wasn't touching her yet. I couldn't feel her wrapped around me yet. "I want you so badly that once my hands and lips are on you, I'll only last a few minutes before I'm inside you. And you deserve better foreplay than that, angel. I never said you couldn't use the vibrator. I just wanted to be here to watch."

Gemma raised a brow, but she didn't say a word.

She didn't need to. I saw the wildness in her gaze. Saw how it looked like I felt inside.

I nodded at the nightgown still covering her body.

"Strip for me."

"You sure you want *me* to do it?"

"If I get any closer to you, it's getting ripped off your body. Do you want to keep that pretty thing in one piece?"

She nodded slowly.

"Then strip for me."

Gemma obeyed slowly, lifting the gown's hem and dragging it up her body. She had to raise her hips to pull it up completely, and the way her body shimmied as she peeled the fabric off was un-fucking-believable.

Once the nightgown made its way to her bedroom floor,

Gemma leaned back again on her hands, giving me a fantastic display of her naked body. My cock screamed at me, reminding me of how fast I drove to get here. But how badly I wanted her was the problem. Every inch of me trembled with need, and I felt like all it would take was the littlest touch, and I'd be done for.

"Just so you know..." Gemma started before her voice trailed off when I dragged my shirt over my head in an attempt to regulate my body temperature, which was suddenly out of control.

I had never felt proud before when a woman ogled my body. Not to sound too cocky, but it felt predictable. Almost like they were doing it for show. Or they were doing it because of my name and what I stood for, not for who I was. They were doing it because of what my body represented and not because they liked the man beneath the muscles.

But when Gemma looked at me like that...fuck, it felt like I was on top of the goddamn world. Like I had something I could be proud of. Even if it was just making this woman speechless—the woman I'd fantasized about since I was practically a teenager.

"Just so I know?" I prompted.

I hated to interrupt this little interlude, but damn did I want to know what she was going to say.

Gemma jerked out of her trance. "Just so you know, you could have walked in here, dragged me onto my hands and knees, and fucked me without so much as a hello. I've been ready for you."

She really was going to be the death of me. *Fuck.*

I dropped my pants and underwear to the ground. "You've been ready for me, huh?"

"I've been ready for you," she breathed.

That did it.

That look, that pleading, that pretty face.

I stepped forward to kneel on the end of the bed, and when I spoke, I barely even recognized the deep, strangled voice that came out of me.

"Turn around and grab the headboard."

If Gemma wanted to get fucked on her hands and knees, then Gemma was going to get fucked on her hands and knees.

She scrambled into position precisely like I told her to, placing her hands on the headboard and giving me that perfect ass to look at as she kneeled on the bed.

"Good girl," I breathed, tracing a finger down her spine and watching goose bumps erupt over her skin.

I loved that. Loved seeing how easily I could affect her. She held the same power over me.

Gemma groaned my name, impatient as ever, and a grin slipped onto my lips as I leaned down to lick up her inner thigh. Her legs slid further apart, clearly wanting more. Wanting me to go *higher*.

I happily complied. Gemma's legs trembled as my tongue swept between her legs, her cries saturating the air as I took a minute to toy with her clit. Fuck, she *was* wet. And delicious, making me want to spend days between her legs. I could live here and be a happy fucking man. She tasted so goddamn good. She tasted like...

"*Mine.*"

Gemma rotated her hips in response, trying to get more. "Yes," she whimpered. "Noah, please."

Her pleas had me folding in an instant, kissing my way up her body until I could nip at the shell of her ear.

"I'm here, baby. And I'm going to fuck you hard now," I whispered. "If it's too much—"

"I can take it," she interrupted, glancing back at me over her shoulder. Her eyes blazed with both desire and determination.

"That's my girl." I grinned, pulling back to grab her hips and line myself up. I pumped one hand over my cock once before guiding it between her legs, letting the tip graze her clit because I was addicted to how she whimpered. To how her body squirmed, begging for more. So I gave it to her, slapping my dick hard between her legs and watching as her knees threatened to buckle.

"Better hang on tighter, angel," I warned.

And then I got to slide home.

Fuck, that first thrust inside her body—nothing compared. *Nothing.*

Gemma gasped loudly, and I hoped to hell it was the same feeling for her. It was the feeling I was trying not to think about last night when we were apart. The feeling that plagued me as I drove home with a raging erection.

But it was nothing compared to what was still coming.

I pulled back before slamming into her again, harder this time. Gemma cried out, and I smirked at the sound. *I* made that sound. That sound was just for *me*.

I wanted to hear it again. So I pumped my hips against Gemma's, sliding in and out of her sweet cunt with an unrelenting rhythm. My fingers tightened, digging into her skin as I tried to keep a grip while drowning deeper and deeper inside her. Broken sounds left my lips as heat and pleasure overtook all my senses. I was lost. To all of it. To her.

"Oh my fucking God," I groaned as Gemma's inner walls started fluttering around my cock. "Gemma, fuck, baby."

She threw her head back while taking every single blow. Her fingers remained wrapped around the top of the headboard, and loud pants of desperation left her lips.

Knowing I would lose it soon, I reached around to her front, cupping one breast as it swayed in time with my thrusts. I kneaded it roughly, loving the soft feel of her in contrast with the dirty, hard way we were fucking. Gemma loved it, too, a humming noise leaving her lips as I tweaked a nipple.

So I kept doing it, pushing her over the edge. She gasped, and I felt her tightening, strangling my cock in such a blissful way. I kept my pace steady until she exploded, and then I slapped my hips against hers harder, determined to make her orgasm last. Determined to chase my own release.

When it hit me, I nearly doubled over from the power of it. Pure liquid heat tore through my body as I shuddered uncontrollably.

Holy...holy fuck.

The room spun around me, us, and I had to take a few deep breaths before my vision straightened.

Gemma had dropped her head to the pillow, and she seemed to be doing the same. I watched her back rise and fall as she panted into the bed. Dropping my lips to her spine, I ghosted a few kisses down it.

"You okay?" I whispered. "You took me so well, Em."

She nodded, still not lifting her head.

"I'm okay," she said, the words muffled. "I'm...I'm more than okay, Noah."

Of course she was.

Regretfully, I drew out of her body. And I couldn't help but look down to watch how my cock slid from her dripping pussy. Something in my chest clenched with the sight, and shit, I knew what it was.

Possession.

Gemma was the first woman I'd ever fucked bare. And while I always knew it would feel unbelievable to have sex without the barrier of a condom, I never imagined I'd react like this at seeing her filled with my cum. Holy fuck, it felt like marking her. Like claiming her. And I wanted to do it over and over and over again so that I could have repetitive proof that she was fucking mine.

I stilled at my thoughts.

It was just the sex, making me think like this.

I needed to remember that.

It was just the sex.

It was just sex.

Just. Sex.

CHAPTER TWENTY-SEVEN

N OAH HAD A home game the next week, and as much as I wanted to go watch him, I didn't have anyone to go with.

I mean, I was sure Juniper would have gone with me if I'd asked. Or Julian. Or my dad. Or any of my sisters. But then I'd have to answer a lot of questions about why I wanted to go to a Knights' game on a random Monday night. Especially after I'd been avoiding all of those people. Julian, especially. He'd tried to call a few times since his bachelor party, and I'd dodged them all as I tried to work out a way to tell him I was pregnant.

So with no one to go with to the game and Noah insisting I shouldn't go alone as much as he wanted me there, I was left watching it on TV.

There was something about that, though. I watched this mouthwatering man on TV and then saw him come to life as he walked in the door hours later. I watched him strut around for the cameras in those tight pants before he came home and let me strip his clothes off him.

Yeah, I couldn't *really* complain.

It went on like that for a couple of weeks. We fell into a routine similar to before, with him leaving for games and me going to the rink and watching Winnie.

Sometimes Chloe came home with me after practice, and the three of us—well, four if you included Winnie—had movie nights. And when Noah was out of town, Chloe and I would make more forts while she told me all the secrets of elementary school.

I quickly learned that elementary school sounded *exhausting*. Or maybe it was more that eight-year-olds themselves were exhausting. Sometimes, anyway.

Tonight, I watched my group of eight-year-olds fly around the ice, thinking that maybe—just maybe—Noah was right. Maybe this was a little risky.

Chloe was actually the one who nearly ran into me tonight. She'd been practicing her backward one-foot glide a moment ago when she caught an edge and toppled toward me instead. I'd caught and straightened her back up without incident, but only because I'd been watching carefully while she tried to master the skill. What if I'd had my back turned when it happened, watching another learner? What if while I'd been watching her, someone else lost control?

I wasn't sure why my anxiety around skating had heightened recently, but I couldn't deny that it had. Maybe Noah had just gotten that deep into my head, or maybe it had to do with how my pregnancy felt *different* now. I could feel Baby in a way I hadn't been able to before. Not to mention my reflexes felt more delayed, and my ankles were slightly more swollen than normal.

"I'm sorry, Gemma," Chloe said. Again.

She sounded dejected, and I worked my face into a smile, realizing that while I'd been lost in my thoughts, my expression had likely shown all of them. And the last thing I wanted to do was make Chloe feel bad. She'd been trying so hard to work toward learning her spins.

"Lo, stop apologizing," I said, waving off her worries with a grin. "Let's see you give it another go, huh? You got this."

On the other side of the rink, I heard Sadie give a similar pep talk to a few of our other students. This was one of our biggest groups, so I was glad to be tag teaming this session with her tonight. Keeping track of, coaching, and giving feedback to this many seven- and eight-year-olds as they progressed through their basic skills on the ice was proving to be challenging. Definitely a different experience than working with college students.

"Coach B!" Amber, the little blonde girl that Noah saw practically run me over last month, yelled my name in excitement. "How was that? Did you see that? Here, let me do it again. Okay?" Words continued to tumble out of her before I had a chance to respond to any of them.

"Slow down," I laughed. "I'll be right there, okay? I'm going to watch Chloe, and then I'll be right there to see you rock that spin again for me."

She nodded, delight blazing in her crystal-blue eyes. She was a tiny rocket of energy, and it pushed me to my limits to keep up with her—with all of them—but I loved it.

I watched Chloe nail her glide and then watched Amber do the same with her spin, and before I knew it, it was time to pull everyone off the ice, ending our class time.

Natalie sat on the end of the spectator bleachers, and I gave her a wave as we exited, pointing Chloe in her direction before doing the same for the rest of the skaters, helping them find the adult waiting for them. When everyone was accounted for, I paused to put my skate guards on—a task that was growing a hell of a lot harder to do. I was damn near out of breath by the time I finished and made it over to Noah's sister.

"Chloe did really good today. She's been working so hard," I said, wanting to gush to Natalie while Lo could hear me.

Natalie smiled, but I could tell from her teasing grin she was about to ruin the whole reason I came over here.

"I saw her almost take you—"

"By surprise with how good she's getting, right?" I cut in, trying to give Natalie a look that I hoped she'd understand.

"Yeah, she's doing great," Natalie said warmly, picking right up. Her cheeks indented in amusement as she glanced at her daughter, who sat on the bleachers beside us while she removed her skates. "And how are you doing?" Natalie asked when her attention turned back to me.

"Oh, I'm doing...I'm doing good." I gave her a shaky grin, unsure how to really answer that. I *was* doing good, all things considered. But it was mostly because of her brother. And his talents in the bedroom. Or on the couch. Or in the kitchen.

Because he really *was* a good cook. Among other things.

But I couldn't tell Natalie any of that.

Even though we *had* grown closer. When Noah was gone, I'd grown to rely on his sister to keep my head on straight. Even though I knew she must be ten times more exhausted than I was, Natalie would sit and chat with me when she'd pick Lo up from the apartment or from the rink, like today. And her genuine kindness and no-nonsense attitude made me feel more at ease. More normal. Like it was okay to be unbelievably tired. And worried. And scared about what was ahead of me.

"Noah doesn't think you should be skating anymore," Natalie said, tilting her head to the side thoughtfully.

I blinked, surprised she brought up Noah when we usually skirted around anything to do with her brother. She'd never once asked what was going on between us. Never pried or questioned our relationship. So this was a surprise.

Although not *really* a surprise, considering how often Noah brought up skating. And how he'd rather I wasn't doing it.

"Oh my God," I groaned. "Is he bugging you about it, too, now?"

"He wanted my professional medical opinion about your safety on the ice," Natalie replied, using air quotes as she mimicked her brother.

I rolled my eyes. "What did you tell him?"

"That it isn't exactly my field of expertise. I'm not a skater, nor am I a gynecologist. And if your doctor said it was okay, then I would trust their opinion."

"I'm sure Noah loved that answer."

"He definitely did not," she laughed. Her mouth opened and

closed like she wanted to say—or ask—something else, but Chloe took that opportune moment to stand, skates in her arms, looking like she was ready to go.

"Well, I'll see you both later," I said, more than okay with cutting this conversation short before it ended with questions I didn't know how to answer.

"Say hi to Uncle Noah for me!" Chloe piped in, giving me a look that said she thought she knew *exactly* what was going on.

My chest ached. Because honestly, I wished that what she thought was true.

"I will," I assured her before saying goodbye to Natalie and going to collect my own things.

I wasn't quite ready to head home, though. My mind felt unsettled today, and after I wrestled to get my skates off my slightly swollen feet, I made my way through the rink's complex to the gym, hoping a workout might help both my physical and mental health.

I was determined not to lose myself to this pregnancy. Even if it started to feel uncomfortable. Even if, for some reason, my nose kept bleeding at the oddest times, and I'd swapped nausea for heartburn. Even when the worries started to mount and my bank account wasn't increasing fast enough.

Tossing my stuff by the door, I was happy to find the gym empty. I squatted in front of the floor-to-ceiling mirror, using the resistance bands for a few lateral walks and popping my headphones in.

It felt good to relax into familiar movements and memories as I listened to music from old skating routines. It helped me feel like *me*, even though a whole other human was invading my body. And while I didn't have much energy, I was sure it was more than I'd have after the baby came.

Plus, it was a good distraction from how badly I wanted my roommate.

It was concerning. How much I'd grown accustomed to him. Living with him. Sleeping with him. Kissing him.

I was falling for Noah London.

Enough that I wondered if I should either tell him the truth or end whatever was going on between us.

But I couldn't tell him—not when I didn't know how he felt or what he wanted. Because knowing Noah, he would give me what I wanted, even if it wasn't what *he* wanted, even if it caused him personal sacrifice. And it just wasn't fair to put that kind of pressure on him. He didn't do relationships. Let alone relationships that involved a *baby*. It wasn't fair of me to suddenly ask for more when he'd already given me so much. I should just be happy with what we had. And I was, I really was.

I couldn't tell him the truth.

But I also couldn't end it.

Simply for the fact that it was too *good*. It was so, so good.

But probably more concerning than any of that was how with everything else going on, I'd kept from doing the one thing I promised myself I would: tell my family about my pregnancy.

Because the little bubble I was living in felt really good. Really, really good. I was so scared for it to pop.

I took a deep breath, letting the music fill my ears and memories take me away. But even skating memories couldn't ease my mind. I missed the girls from St. Mav's. And I was worried about them.

After learning I was pregnant, I cut off all contact with them. It was just easier that way. I couldn't bring myself to tell anyone from St. Mav's what had happened with Silas, and I knew there would likely be hell to pay from him if I did. But now that the shock had worn off, guilt was seeping in.

Guilt from ghosting everyone. Guilt from running from a job I loved because a man couldn't keep his dick in his pants. Guilt from the realization that if Silas did what he did to me, he could do it to someone else.

I owed closure, both to myself and my family at that college.

But that meant leaving my comfortable little bubble. The one I was afraid to pop.

I focused on my movements, trying to force everything else out. In my mind, I was performing a Salchow in the middle of the rink, but then a glimpse of Noah in the mirror popped me back into the present. He stood behind me, leaning against an exercise rack.

Why is Noah here?

I ripped off my headphones with a breathless "Hi."

"Hey, angel," he said, his smooth voice taking me back to last night when he murmured dirty things in my ear while I came on his fingers.

It wasn't just his voice, though. Everything about how he looked at me right now had my pulse picking up—the combination of those soft, green eyes and his tense, tight expression.

"How'd you find me?" I asked, letting the resistance bands drop to the floor and stepping out of them.

"I asked that other blonde coach where you were. Sadie, right?"

I nodded, still shocked that he was here. I looked around, double-checking that no one else had slipped into the small gym while I wasn't paying attention. But no, it was just the two of us. We were alone.

"Natalie picked Chloe up from practice," I said, my brows drawing inward as I checked my watch for the time. "Did she not tell you?"

He walked toward me with a casual, relaxed stride. God, he was so effortlessly hot.

"I'm not here for Chloe."

I frowned. Noah had never before come to the rink unless it was to get Chloe.

"I'm here because you weren't home yet," he added as if it were really that simple.

I balked at him for a second. "I was going to come home after my workout."

"I got impatient." He stopped about a foot away and gave the tiniest shrug. His eyes evaded me. "Why didn't you want to work out at the apartment?"

"There's some equipment here that I like to use that you don't have in your gym."

He looked offended by that, his head quickly turning on a swivel as he did a keen inspection, searching the gym for the equipment I might be referring to.

When he couldn't figure it out, he said, "Tell me what it is, and I'll get it for you."

He was kidding, right?

"Noah, don't be ridiculous."

"It's not a big deal, Em," he replied earnestly. "I'm a professional athlete. Expanding my home gym is a logical investment for me to make."

"Okay," I sighed. "I just don't want you buying anything strictly for me when I'm not even going to be living with you two months from now."

Noah stiffened. Just for a moment. I wouldn't have even caught his change in body language if I hadn't gotten so good at reading and watching him.

"And since I only have two months left with you, I want to be greedy," he continued, his voice suddenly sounding rough around the edges. Demanding, like how he spoke in the bedroom. "I want you to work out where I can be with you."

It took me a second to find my voice. "We both know if we work out together, it'll get derailed by sex."

"Does that sound so bad?" Noah smirked, and when I just shook my head with a grin in response, he added, "The first time we worked out together, I nearly lost my shit. You were wearing that same tight little set, and I didn't know how to be around you."

His eyes raked over me, and I realized I *was* wearing the same outfit I had been in his gym that day. I couldn't believe he remembered that.

"Looks like you've figured it out," I laughed, but it came out choked. "How to be around me."

"I'm still losing my shit," he said, lifting a brow. "I just don't care if you see how hard you make me anymore."

I glanced down, and sure enough, Noah had a tent in his sweatpants that made my mouth water.

"And *you* give *me* shit about being insatiable," I teased, trying to ignore the slow coiling of heat in my gut as I turned to look at myself in the mirror. The matching olive-green spandex covering my body was stretched further than it ever had been before. "This set doesn't look as good on me now as it did then."

Noah groaned behind me. "Are you fucking kidding me?"

I cocked my head to the side, still appraising my outfit. And my body—the changes to it. "No?"

I mean...it was obvious.

Out of the corner of my eye, I saw Noah step closer to me in the mirror. He looked determined as he settled his hands on my hips. Leaning in, he brushed his lips down the curve of my neck.

"Noah..." I protested weakly.

"I love watching that pretty flush color in the spaces between your freckles," he murmured. "I like when I know it's because of me."

"You really *are* feeling greedy today," I said, my breaths quickening even though I hadn't moved a muscle since I saw Noah appear behind me.

"Not just today." His grip on my hips tightened as he breathed against my skin. "Always, angel. For you? Always. I don't know if I'll ever get enough of you. So don't you dare say shit like you just did."

My chest tightened at his words because they were exactly how I felt. I always wanted more of him. Always needed more of him. And it was terrifying and exhilarating all at once.

He trailed his lips to my shoulder before his gaze lifted, meeting mine in the mirror. "Remember when you said your tits were only going to get bigger?" he murmured. I nodded, and his

317

lips moved to my ear, murmuring huskily into it. "Well, you were right. And I'm fucking obsessed."

"But—"

"No buts."

They may be bigger, but they were also sensitive and covered with stretch marks.

"But—"

He slapped a hand over my mouth, startling me. It shot a heated awareness through my body—awareness that only Noah knew how to summon. "What did I say, Em?"

I rolled my eyes, and his eyes hardened.

"I think you need a little lesson this afternoon," he declared, all gravel and grit. He dropped his hand to whip off his T-shirt. "Show me your wrists."

My mouth ran dry as I obediently did as he said. I didn't know what the hell he was doing, but I couldn't find it in me to protest. Not when he talked to me like that. And not when he *looked* like that.

His lips twitched, and I could tell he was pleased I'd listened without arguing. "God, you're—" He broke off with a shake of his head, and then his eyes met mine as he took hold of both of my wrists within one of his hands, gripping them together. His gaze sought permission. "Yes?"

"Yes," I gasped, not sure entirely what I was consenting to but knowing I couldn't be any safer than with Noah. He'd been my saving grace over the last few months. He always knew when to let me lead and when I needed a push.

I supposed today he thought I needed a push.

CHAPTER TWENTY-EIGHT

gemma

W ITH A WICKED grin, Noah whipped his shirt in a circle until it made a rope, which he used to tie around my wrists, snapping them together.

"Come here, Em," he murmured, leading me a few steps backward to the multi-use exercise rack he'd been leaning against earlier. "Now, arms up."

I lifted my hands above my head, and Noah looped his shirt around the end of the pull-up handlebar that protruded from the front of the rack. I stood stretched out and helpless as Noah stepped back, admiring his work. And even though he looked pleased as all hell, he said, "We can be done whenever you want. Just tell me. Okay?"

"Okay," I agreed, but his words bounced around in my head.

Done.

I didn't like that word.

I didn't like the idea of being done with Noah. Of us being *done.*

I wondered if he realized how much I'd struggle to find the strength to say those words. Today or in the future.

But my troubled thoughts disappeared when Noah crossed those beautifully tattooed arms over his chest. I clenched my legs at the sight, needing to dull the ache between them before it over-took me because I knew Noah was about to draw this out. He fucking loved to do that.

Noah noticed my reaction, and his grin cocked to the side. "I know you like looking at me, angel, but I want you to look at yourself."

He stepped to the side, giving me a direct view into the mirror. Then, he circled around me until his face hovered over my shoulder. And because it was an incredibly handsome face, my eyes gravitated toward him in the mirror.

"Not at me," he reminded, a soft but lethal edge to his voice. "Look at you. Look how fucking perfect you are."

Knowing he wouldn't stop until I did as he wanted, I flicked my eyes back to my reflection.

"Good," he continued, satisfied. He stood behind me, hands outlining my curves as he spoke. "Now, listen to me when I tell you I wanted you when I saw you in this outfit the first time, but *God*, I want you so much more now."

My eyes widened as they trailed his hands and the path they made over my body. I'd been worried that his interest in me would dwindle. That he—a guy who didn't sleep with people more than once—would think the sex was repetitive. That the changes to my body might affect his attraction.

But here he was saying he wanted me *more*?

"Yes, Em," he reaffirmed, reading my mind. "More. And it fucking pisses me off that you're having a hard time believing that."

I gave in, really looking at the woman in the mirror before me. Her eyes were round and bright. They looked...awake, lit with all the emotions tumbling inside her. The curves of her body were more noticeable than before because she never really had curves. Not like this. And honestly, it felt good. She felt voluptuous, sensual. She felt desired, especially by the man raking his eyes over her greedily.

Noah plucked at my spandex. "I'm dying to peel this off of you. I'd be lying if I said I've never thought about it."

I wasn't sure I'd ever wanted to be naked under Noah's touch more than I did now. But...

"What if someone comes in?" I rasped.

"Locked the door," he said before curling his fingers underneath my sports bra. "No one's coming in. Not until I'm fucking done with you."

"What if there's cameras?" I looked around the room half-heartedly because I didn't really want to find a reason for Noah to stop.

"I'll buy the security tapes off the skating club. I'll spend thousands, millions, I don't care. Just let me touch you, Em."

"Yes," I groaned as a grin split across Noah's face. He yanked the bra over my head, sliding it up my arms before tucking the fabric beneath my fingers. They tingled, but I was able to curl them around the discarded top.

"Hold that so I can touch these pretty tits," he said, his husky voice making my stomach somersault.

I nodded, indicating that I'd hold anything so long as he touched me. His eyes sparked, even the reflection of them making my blood boil. Noah held my gaze in the mirror as he smoothed his hands up my sides and curved them around to cup my breasts. He groaned as he squeezed, flexing his capable fingers.

I stared, captivated, as he tweaked my nipples between his thumbs and middle fingers, rolling them until I cried out. Instinctively, I pulled at my restraints, needing to move, to do something with the energy Noah injected in me with his touch.

His gaze blazed as he watched me squirm against him, helpless. All I could do was stand here and take his slow torture.

He stood behind me with such confidence that I couldn't help but wonder if he'd done something like this with other girls. If he knew just the way to tease me because he'd teased them. Jealousy ripped through me at the thought, but I tried to swallow it. It didn't belong here. I had no right to be jealous. Not really.

Noah frowned, wrapping his arm around my rib cage and pulling me back into him. His hot skin burned against mine.

He nipped at my earlobe. "What's wrong?"

"Nothing," I lied.

Noah's expression grew dark. "I'm not going to do anything but edge you until you tell me."

Fuck, I definitely didn't want that. This was torture enough.

"It's silly," I insisted. "I just...I was thinking that maybe you've done this with other girls, and I—"

"Gemma," he cut me off, his tone sharp. "I have never, not ever, been as desperate for someone as I am for you. If I possessed any self-control around you, I'd have dragged you home first. I would have waited until you were under my roof before tying you up. I would have used your favorite little vibrator to tease your clit until you begged me to fuck you."

He paused, dragging in a breath as his grip tightened around me. "But I don't have that self-control. Not around you, Em. You think this is something I've done before? Fuck no. This is something I'm doing because I fucking need you. But, more importantly, because I want you to see *why* I need you, how *much* I need you. Got it?"

"Got it," I said breathlessly. He'd somehow managed to both reassure me and turn me on even more.

"Good," he grunted before releasing his hold on me and dropping his hands to the waistband of my leggings instead. "Now it's time for these to come off. I can't wait any longer. My fingers are itching to touch you."

His eyes smoldered as he dragged my leggings down my body, and I squirmed, feeling his heat burn hotter with every look he gave me, every touch, and every word.

"Yeah," he said, cocky satisfaction dripping from his voice. "You're wet for me."

I lifted a brow. "How do you know?"

"Oh, I know." He stood, retaking his place behind me. His head appeared above my shoulder, and while my eyes stayed firmly on his face, *his* wandered my reflection. "Oh, *fuck*, look at you."

Then, his hands took over. They roamed my body, squeezing and pinching and caressing as they went. I trembled beneath his touch, pulling at my restraints as desperation coursed within me. I needed to feel him. I needed to have him. I needed more.

And Noah knew it. He knew I needed more, but he wanted to toy with me. His lips tilted when he finally brushed a single finger between my legs, and I damn near screamed when he immediately retreated again.

"You want it?" he asked, his lips grazing my neck. When I didn't answer immediately, he nipped and sucked until my head tipped back with a reluctant sigh.

"Yes," I admitted through clenched teeth. He knew I fucking wanted it.

"Then watch," he commanded, forcing my chin back down with his other hand. My pulse ticked up as I obediently trained my eyes on the mirror, watching his hand. It slowly cupped between my legs, covering my pussy. "Watch me touch you."

"I'm watching," I gasped.

I couldn't look away.

"Good girl," Noah praised. "If you look away—"

"Let me guess, you're going to stop," I mouthed.

Noah's movements paused, stopping just like I suspected he would if I didn't follow his directions. But then he shook his head. I felt his hair rustle against mine.

"No, baby." His voice was low, so deep and delicious that I squirmed, wishing I'd never said anything. "I'm not stopping."

"But then—"

Noah cut off my words with a sharp slap to my clit, shooting pain tinted with pleasure through me. I sucked in, and if it weren't for the shirt tied around my wrists, I never would have stayed upright. As it was, my knees shook, and my toes curled as I groaned. "Oh my *God*, Noah."

"Look away, and this pretty pussy is getting slapped," Noah warned, an edge to his voice.

But his fingers worked in contrast, soothing my aching core as he caressed between my legs with tenderness. Eventually, he let his fingers sink deeper and deeper until I felt one prod my entrance, sliding in. I held my breath as I watched, wishing he'd move faster, wishing he'd give me more.

And wondering if maybe I should look away again.

My eyes drifted to his face, and the sexy grin there told me he'd been waiting for my disobedience. I held his gaze as he delivered another smack to my clit, my jaw dropping with wonder as a flood of sensations wracked my body.

"You're a naughty fucking girl," he murmured in my ear. "Aren't you, Em?"

"Just for you," I admitted with a strained breath.

Because it was the truth.

Just for Noah.

Just for him.

"Fuck, you always know how to tell me what I'm dying to hear," he groaned as he plunged two fingers deep into my pussy. "Just for that, I'll give you what you want, too."

"Yes," I moaned, my limbs turning to jelly as he touched me just as he knew I liked. His thumb rubbed over my clit steadily, and I wasn't sure I could hold myself up much longer. My wrists would be raw by the end of this, but I didn't want to stop. I didn't want any of this to end.

"I got you," he breathed, all-knowing as usual. "I know you won't ask, but I know. I'm always here."

He wrapped his arm around my waist and supported my weight, pulling me against him. He cradled me against his chest, and my head rocked back onto his shoulder, my gaze still locked on our reflection as Noah abruptly cupped my pussy. With two fingers still deep inside me, he used his hold to jerk my hips back into his, grinding his erection into my ass.

"You feel that, baby?" His voice was as hard as his cock. "You feel how fucking bad I want you?"

I nodded because words were beyond my reach at the moment. Oh, I felt him. I felt him, and I *ached* for him.

"Don't forget it," he ordered, the words cutting straight to my core as I heard and understood the desperation in them. God, I understood it. "Don't you ever forget it, Gemma."

"I won't," I whispered and then cried out when Noah continued his blissful torment, finger fucking me until I was writhing in his arms, panting with the need for release. And just like he wanted, I watched. I watched everything that hand of his did as he worked me into an upward spiral that I knew would tear me apart.

"That's it, gorgeous," Noah murmured as I felt my pleasure start to crest. "Fuck, do you see that? Do you see how good you look with my hands all over you? With my fingers inside you?"

"Mmm," I crooned, struggling to speak. All I knew was that I could watch Noah's hands work all day long.

"You're so pretty when you come," he continued, his breath coming in short spurts as his fingers increased their pace between my legs. "Let me see it."

My breath hitched, my whole body tensing. Noah fed murmured praises into my ear as an orgasm ricocheted through me. His grip tightened as I lost the ability to stand altogether, his fingers pumping me through my release.

The second I slumped, spent and exhausted from that unbelievable orgasm, Noah slipped from my body and licked his fingers off with a moan. He swore under his breath before unhooking my hands. They fell in front of me, still bound. The prickles of a thousand tiny needles spread up my arms.

I shivered as Noah untied his shirt, letting it slide from my wrists and drop to the floor. He walked in front of me and lifted my hands, pressing kisses to every inch of skin that was pinched. And then, before I could melt to the ground from the weight of my release and the sweetness of his touch, Noah gently spun me around and guided my steps backward, urging me to sit on the padded bench behind me.

I sat, blinking up at his intense expression, watching how his chest heaved as his gaze wandered over me. I wanted to feel it, wanted to feel how fast his heart beat for me. Because my pulse was out of control, and I wanted to know if it was the same for him.

Noah shuddered when I flattened my hand on his chest, trailing it down his muscled stomach to the waistband of his pants, just above where his erection strained against the stretchy fabric, practically right in front of my face.

"Take me out," Noah demanded before I could tease him any further.

I did as he asked. I wasn't sure if it was an aftereffect of my orgasm or anticipation for the next one, but my hands shook as I hooked my fingers into his waistband and worked his pants down over Noah's hips, revealing his hard cock. The tip was swollen and leaking precum.

"Suck me into your pretty mouth, Em," Noah said, his voice raw. "Get me nice and wet."

I nodded, happy to oblige. I swirled my tongue around his tip, licking the salty evidence of his desire, before slowly sucking him between my lips, taking him deeper at a torturous pace that made an ungodly sound rise from Noah's throat. He murmured my name, letting little praises shower over me as I started to make a sloppy mess on his cock, getting him wet like he wanted.

Just as I was getting into a rhythm, Noah abruptly grabbed me by my hair and yanked me off his cock, using just enough force to make me clench my thighs together in response. Noah's smirk as I looked up at him told me he noticed. Of course he noticed. He always did.

"Lie back," he commanded as my spit dripped from his tip. "Push your gorgeous tits together for me."

Too stuck in a Noah-induced daze to do anything but exactly what he told me to, I fell back, laying out on the bench. I let Noah watch the way my breasts rocked for a moment, enjoying how his eyes tracked my movement, and then pressed them between my palms like he asked.

The heat in Noah's gaze was blistering as he straddled me on the bench, letting his cock trail a mess up my body as he positioned himself above me. Then he paused, shaking his head in disbelief.

"You're unreal, Gemma. Every inch of you. I need you to understand how badly I want *every* inch of you."

I nodded, unable to talk, unable to breathe. I believed him. How could I not after what had just happened?

"I can't even tell you how long I've been dying to see you like this. How long I've been dying to fuck your pretty tits." His eyes raked over me as mine grew wide. "Can I?"

"Yes," I breathed, and Noah didn't hesitate to thrust his cock between my breasts as he groaned loudly.

"*Fuck*, Em." He threw his head back, his eyes closing momentarily before he looked back down at me. With his golden-brown hair flopping over his forehead, he watched as he drew back and thrust again. This time, he nearly hit my throat; something dribbled at the base of it. "Fuck, you always feel so good."

"You should have told me you wanted to do this earlier," I said, my voice soft as I studied the way pleasure worked over his face, realizing I would do anything to make him look like this.

Noah gave a tight nod as he thrust again, sliding easily between my breasts. He rocked back and forth, his hips flexing deliciously. "You're right, but I just knew it would drive me wild and make me lose it, and I have this thing about coming inside of you." Noah reached down, tweaking one of my nipples and making me gasp as he withdrew. "So now we have to stop."

I bit my lip, unsure what I should be encouraging—him continuing so I could watch him lose it from this glorious angle or him stopping so I could feel him inside me again. But before I could make up my mind, Noah's demanding touch vanished, and he leaned down to cover me in kisses. The curve of my neck, the dip near my collarbone, the swell of my breasts.

My stomach.

His lips lingered there, and when his eyes found mine, the intensity in his gaze made me lose my breath.

Without looking away from me, he placed one of his large hands over my bump, spreading it possessively. His eyes lowered to his hand, staring at it.

"I fucking hate that it's his," he said, a bite to his words. "He doesn't deserve to be a dad."

My breath hitched from the rare steel in Noah's tone.

"He's not," I said when I found my voice. "Noah, I—"

He cut me off by moving back up my body, slamming his lips to mine. Which was fine because I wasn't sure where I was going or what I was saying. Probably things I shouldn't.

I moaned, immediately letting his tongue in to sweep against mine. Noah reciprocated, a gruff appreciation vibrating in his throat as he kissed me back just as eagerly, greedily showing me just how much he really did want me. This wasn't a polite kiss or a tender one. This was hunger. Blisteringly raw desire.

Noah's hands cupped the back of my neck, urging me to sit up. I followed his movements in a daze, not wanting to separate, needing his lips and hands on mine. And thankfully, they didn't leave. Noah smoothed his hands down my back until they cupped my ass and picked me up. I wrapped my legs around his waist, even though I wasn't sure I'd be able to hold on, and as though he knew, Noah walked us a few steps to the wall covered in mirrors, anchoring me against it.

I gasped as we collided, and Noah wasted no time finding what he wanted. The head of his cock dragged between my legs as he kissed me, frantic and deep like he couldn't get enough. His skin was feverish, his warmth enveloping me.

And while I knew I was about to get fucked until I saw stars, all I could think about was the way Noah had possessively spread his hand over my stomach. The mixed emotions I saw in his eyes.

My emotions on the matter were clearer, and I—shit, this man. I wanted things I wasn't allowed to want.

"Need," Noah panted between kisses, "you."

"Yes, Daddy," I gasped, my words betraying my thoughts. "Fuck me. *Please.*"

"Oh, *God.*" He groaned before following my orders for once and slamming into me. And then another grumble filled his throat again as he slid deeper, his forehead dropping to mine as his rough breaths ghosted my lips. "*Gemma,*" he growled. "What the—shit, what the fuck are you doing to me?"

I shook my head, clinging onto him for dear life. Clinging to this.

I didn't know. I didn't understand what was happening.

"Jesus fucking Christ," Noah swore again before pounding into me with deep strokes that I felt everywhere. I cried out into the crook of his neck, feeling the vibrations of his groans as he kept going. Never stopping. "Oh my—*shit*, Em."

I tipped my head back, letting it fall against the cool mirror behind me as I memorized how my name sounded when he said it like that. Noah's lips flirted with the column of my neck as his pace quickened. He drove into me repeatedly, slapping his hips against mine, trapping me between his body and the wall. And I was in heaven.

"So wet," Noah murmured, more to himself than to me. "So fucking wet."

My eyes rolled back, and I could hear the smirk in Noah's voice as it slid into my ear.

"You love the feel of my cock, don't you, baby? You like the way it claims that pussy. The way it makes you mine."

"Yes," I admitted because there was nothing else that I could say. "Yes, yes, yes. *Noah.*"

"Are you gonna come for me again, Em?" he gasped, and I could tell he needed me to. He needed me to come so that he could.

I nodded, a whimper escaping my throat as Noah hit that spot within me. And then he did it again. And again, and I was gone. Unraveling. Free-falling. Climaxing harder and faster than I ever imagined possible. Bits of black dotted my vision, and I gasped for air. My fingernails dug into his back, scratching, marking.

"What a good girl," Noah murmured. "That's it. So good. So *fucking* good."

He said the last word with a grunt, violently shuddering as his release threatened to wash over him. His muscles tensed, his jaw clenched, and his beautiful face twisted with passion.

"Yes, baby," I sighed, loving this part when I got to watch him lose all control.

"Fuck," he swore, his voice gritty and rough. "You're gonna take every last drop for me, right?"

I nodded, and that was all he needed to drive into me one last time and fill me to the brim. He pulsed. I could feel it. I could feel his cum slowly dripping out of me, turning me into even more of a mess than I already was. Not that I cared.

I whispered his name, and our gazes connected. His green eyes, usually so calm, were wild. I stroked a hand down his back as my claws retracted, and I tried to catch my breath. His chest heaved against mine while he tried to do the same.

I thought he'd put me down, but he didn't. He pressed me tighter to the wall, driving deeper inside me as he closed his eyes.

"Just give me a second," he muttered. "Just give me another second inside you."

My heart jumped into my throat, and I nodded, even though he couldn't see me. I couldn't find my voice, but he could have all the seconds he wanted.

True to his word, a few moments later, he pulled out and let my feet fall back to the floor. He didn't let go, though, which I was grateful for. I wasn't sure I'd be able to stand on my own. Not without his support.

He wordlessly helped me dress and then deposited me on a bench, pressing a kiss to the top of my head before he found his own clothes to pull back on. My eyes roamed over the scratches on his back, wondering if I should be embarrassed or concerned at how reckless we'd been. But it was hard to regret what just happened.

"Drink some water," Noah directed, his voice hoarse. "You need to make sure you're staying hydrated."

"I fill and drink that huge water bottle you got me every day," I assured him. "I've been doing some research about water intake with pregnancy, so I've been really careful about it."

He gave a curt nod. "Good girl."

I watched Noah clean the gym equipment with far too much interest than it warranted, and by the time he walked back over, I had enough energy to stand on my own. Barely, but I managed.

Noah gave me a once-over, studying my slow movements. His lips tugged upward. "I can carry you to the car if you want."

"Because that wouldn't cause *any* gossip at all," I said, rolling my eyes.

He shrugged. "Maybe I don't care about the gossip."

"I'm fine, Noah." I smiled at him because it was an understatement. He'd destroyed me in the best way possible. "Let's go home?"

He nodded and followed me out of the gym. We walked through a narrow hallway toward the back offices, where the rest of my stuff was, our footsteps echoing in the empty corridor.

Or at least I thought it was empty. But then another pair of footsteps bounced off the walls, and I realized we weren't alone in the hallway at all.

I stopped short when I saw him round the corner, my breath leaving my body. He looked pissed. Oh God, he looked pissed. Determined. His eyes flared, and I knew it was too late. He saw me. He saw Noah. God, what was he even *doing* here?

Noah ran right into me, caught by surprise by my sudden halt. He clearly wasn't paying attention, his arm wrapping around me as we collided. It took him a second to regain balance, and his hand slid down possessively over my stomach when he did.

Fuck.

331

That action alone made Julian stop in his tracks, his gaze dropping to Noah's spread fingers. And to what was beneath them. I felt Noah stiffen as he realized—as he saw who was standing at the other end of the hallway.

When my brother looked up from my stomach, murder was in his wide eyes.

So I wasn't surprised when he looked straight past me to Noah and spat out words I'd been hoping to avoid.

"Oh, I'm going to fucking *kill* you."

eight years ago

NOAH

Julian was clearly distracted.

His eyes constantly moved to Gemma's friend, whose name I couldn't really figure out, considering she'd been called three different things since their arrival.

Meanwhile, Gemma was preoccupied with the drink Julian had just put in her hand, sipping it down like she'd been parched as all hell.

And me? I was busy watching her.

It was a damn shame how perfect she seemed.

A perfect girl deserved a perfect guy, and I was far from that.

I felt when Julian's glare found its way back to me, catching me staring at his sister.

It was probably for the best that he shut this down anyway.

Before I got too close to something too good.

CHAPTER TWENTY-NINE

noah

F UCK, THIS WAS not how I wanted this to go. And not how
Gemma wanted it to go, either.

Within a matter of minutes, I went from feeling on top of the
world to being sick with dread.

Julian stormed down the hallway toward me, and I braced
myself to take a few punches that I deserved. I wouldn't apologize
for everything that had happened with Gemma, but I would apologize for lying to Julian. For keeping this from him. I could see
that beyond anything else in his eyes, there was hurt. Pain.
Distrust. So I'd take whatever hits he had to give.

But just when I was about to step around Gemma to meet
him, she shuffled in front of me.

"Julian, *stop*."

Julian didn't stop. He kept plowing ahead, barely meeting his
sister's gaze.

"Move, Gemma," he warned. "He doesn't get to walk away
scot-free after getting you fucking pregnant."

But Gemma didn't move. Not out of the way. She was very
much *in* the way, shuffling in front of me like a protective shield,
not letting me get around her.

God, these Briggs siblings were stubborn.

Gemma put her hands out, bracing them against Julian's chest as she pushed him back. She stood tall as she faced him, but her voice was small when she spoke. Soft.

Sad.

"He's not the dad, Julian."

Christ, why did it feel like a stab to the chest to hear her say that?

Ten minutes ago, she'd been calling me fucking Daddy while I slammed my cock into her so hard she probably felt it in her throat, and I'd never, ever felt anything like it.

Now, I felt like I was free-falling.

And fast.

Jules froze, angry eyes flicking up to his sister. And then to me. He held my gaze, and all I could do was harden my jaw. I didn't want to confirm that what she was saying was true. I couldn't figure out how to say the words *I'm not the dad*, even though it might save me from getting my ass beaten by one of my best friends.

When my reaction didn't give anything away, Julian raked a hand through his hair and probed harder.

"Who is, then?"

"He's not in the picture," Gemma said flatly. "And he has no interest in changing that."

Julian's expression turned murderous, but at least this time, I knew it wasn't directed at me.

His next question was, though.

"You didn't get my sister pregnant?"

"No," I answered stonily.

Julian didn't look relieved like I thought he might. Probably because the fact remained that even though I hadn't gotten Gemma pregnant, someone had. And I could practically see the gears whirling in that ginger head of his. His calculating eyes wandered over us, no doubt taking in our flushed faces, messy hair, and all the other signs that would give away that we had just had sex.

Best sex of my goddamn life, too. I never imagined I could come that hard.

"You didn't sleep with her?" Julian pressed, staring straight at me because he *knew* the answer.

Guess this little reprieve was over.

RIP my fingers.

Both Gemma and I were silent, and that split second of hesitation was all Julian needed to lose it again.

His face grew into a shade of red that had to be detrimental to his blood pressure as he threw his hands in the air.

"You've been fucking my *pregnant* sister? God, what the— what the *hell*—"

"Julian, stop."

Gemma tried to approach him again, but Julian whirled on his sister.

"Don't tell me to stop, Gems. Don't tell me to let this go. You're *pregnant*." His voice echoed in the hallway, loud enough for anyone in the goddamn building to likely hear. And I could see how it made Gemma's body shake, the slight tremor that didn't go unnoticed. "Jesus Christ, I can't fucking believe this. How the—"

"Julian," I snapped, finally dodging in front of Gemma to get in my friend's face. Because I understood he was pissed and working through some big feelings, but how he was speaking to Gemma wasn't going to work for me. "Watch your fucking mouth when you talk to her. Got it? And lower your goddamn voice. *Now.*"

Julian physically jerked back like I'd punched him, his face wiping blank before he took a deep breath and seemed to pull himself together. He stared at me, his eyes narrowing slightly before he turned on his heel and started pacing. He watched the floor move beneath him as he walked.

"Where do you live?" he asked, shooting Gemma a quick look before training his eyes on his feet again. His tone was calmer, more in check, and I relaxed, stepping aside so he could get the answers from her that he needed. As long as he didn't yell at her, that was fine.

"What?" I heard the breathlessness in Gemma's voice, like she was struggling to process what was happening.

"You dodge all my calls, so I went to your apartment today only to be told you no longer live there. I came here to find you. When did you move out?"

"End of July."

Julian's steps faltered. He stared at Gemma.

"It's *October*," he croaked. "Gems, where—where do you live?"

Guilt continued to swirl in my gut. I could tell just how much the question killed Julian to ask—that he hadn't known where his sister lived for three whole months.

Gemma could tell, too. She was trying so hard to stay poised, to not wither beneath Julian's look, but her expression was so close to crumbling. God, I wanted to wrap my arms around her. I'd never wanted to touch her as badly as I did now, but I didn't know how that would be received when Julian was right there. When he was already so pissed.

Gemma took a deep breath. "I've been living with Noah, Julian."

"You've been—you've been living with *Noah*?" Julian hissed the words as he momentarily paused, stunned as he stared slack-jawed at both of us. And then he continued to pace the width of the small hallway, back and forth as he muttered under his breath. "No fucking way is this real. When I saw my sister in the stands of a football game halfway across the country on fucking national television, I knew there was something she wasn't telling me, but this? This is—"

He broke off, shaking his head.

Shit.

I didn't even think about that. Whenever my family attended my games, especially in a big group like that, they always ended up on some kind of screen, either at the stadium or on TV. I never even thought that someone might see Gemma standing with them.

And based on Gemma's reaction, she'd never thought of it, either.

Gemma brought her hand to her mouth, her eyes wide. "I was...what?"

"They panned over to show Noah London's family, and wouldn't you know, my sister was right in the middle of them," Julian grumbled, talking to his feet. "Funny, I don't remember her mentioning anything about going on a trip with one of my best friends."

"I don't...understand," Gemma stuttered. "That was weeks ago. Why are you...why now?"

"Weeks ago," Julian repeated with a humorless laugh before he lifted his hurt gaze. "It was *weeks* ago. And I would never have known if I hadn't watched the recording of the game today."

"You record my games?" I cut in, surprised.

Julian's eyes flicked to me, brows furrowing together. "Of course I record your games. I don't always catch them live, but I watch all of them. Every single one."

Fuck, he just had to add to the guilt, didn't he? I needed him to stop looking at me like that. Like he did when he was my captain in college and I did something fucking foolish for him only to be disappointed in me.

His look turned into a glare.

"I didn't realize you were going home after all of them to sleep with my sister behind my back."

"Cut it out, Jules. I'm sorry, okay? I'm sorry I didn't tell you. I'm sorry I've been a shitty sister." Gemma stepped toward him, and even though I could hear the tears clogged in her throat, she jabbed a finger in his chest like the little fighter she was. "But do I need to remind you that you were the one to sleep with my best friend first? You remember that, right? You remember sneaking around with her and not telling me, right? You remember how *I* reacted?"

Julian had the presence of mind to look sheepish at Gemma's accusation. But only for a second, and then a flare reignited in his gaze.

"But you *knew*, Gemma."

She scoffed. "I suspected something was going on between the two of you, but I didn't *know*."

"No." Julian shook his head, his voice gentler because he was about to talk about Juni. "No, that's not what I meant. You knew I was in love with her. You knew she was endgame for me. I wasn't using her; we weren't just sleeping around. We were trying to find our footing as a couple before telling our family." His eyes drifted to me. "Is that what's happening here?"

His question dropped into my gut like a rock. I didn't know how to answer that, didn't know how to say the thing that would make this all better. And the worst part? Julian knew. He knew I'd always been too afraid of my own goddamn feelings. He knew we weren't finding our footing as a couple because that would mean I'd have to commit to being one.

And I'd never done that. Not since I'd known him.

But that didn't mean I couldn't. Didn't mean I wouldn't. Especially for the woman next to me.

I opened my mouth to say something, *anything*, that would convince Julian what this actually was—even if I was still wrapping my head around it—but Gemma spoke first.

"Julian." Gemma's voice was soft and nervous, and I looked at her only to see a sheen in her eyes. They looked glassy, and fuck, it tore at me inside. "Please. Stop. You're being unfair. I never expected that from Noah, and he never expected that from me."

My heart sank.

Of course she didn't.

Of fucking course she didn't expect anything from me.

Of course she didn't think I was relationship material.

I was just some guy who could fuck her until she screamed and made all those pretty little sounds that meant nothing at the end of the night.

Except they didn't feel like nothing to me. Sometimes when she breathed my name, it felt a whole lot like *more*.

"I'm an adult," Gemma continued. "Capable of making adult decisions."

Julian sucked in, chewing on his cheek as he considered his sister.

"I know you're an adult." His words were just as soft. "But just like you knew me, I also know *you*."

I hated how he was talking like *I* didn't know her. Like I had no idea what Gemma's wants and needs and feelings were. Like I wasn't the one who'd been there for her for the past three months.

And then, almost like she could read my mind, Gemma went to bat for me again. She was pleading for Julian to understand something I didn't even comprehend.

"Noah's done so much for me, Julian. He's gone to my appointments, held my hair through my weeks of morning sickness, and gave me a place to live when I couldn't afford my old place anymore. You don't understand the full situation. I owe him more than I know how to put into words."

She checked back at me, her eyes imploring, and I supposed it should make me feel good to hear how grateful she was. But I felt empty inside. Especially when she looked back at her brother and added, "I know he's your friend, but he's also become mine."

Friend.

There was that fucking word again.

I didn't want to be Gemma Briggs' fucking friend.

Julian knew it, too. He looked from Gemma to me, noting how my jaw clenched.

But I couldn't say anything, not without launching into a whole new conversation. A conversation I definitely didn't want to have in front of Julian. So I stepped forward, wrapping an arm around Gemma's back and gripping her side like I'd done so many times before. Then I leveled with Julian, saying the one honest thing I could.

"I would do anything for her...anything."

Julian's eyes wandered my face, and I didn't know what he saw there, but I had to swallow hard when I noticed the pity leak into his expression. Remorse.

"Noah..." he started, but I didn't trust what he would say, so I cut him off.

"She's done so much for me, too," I said. "She's been watching Winnie. That's partly why she moved in. And she came to Minnesota because Nat couldn't come at the last minute, but my niece still wanted to go to my game with my family. Gemma volunteered to fly with Chloe instead."

Julian frowned, looking back at his sister. "You volunteered... to fly?"

Gemma cleared her throat. "Well, I didn't want Chloe to miss the game."

For the first time since Julian appeared in front of us, his lips twitched with a smile.

And then it vanished a second later.

"Why didn't you tell me, Gems?" he asked, sounding resigned. Sad. "Forget about sneaking around with London. I'll talk to him later." He glanced at me before addressing Gemma again, opening his arms, palms up in a sign of surrender. "But why didn't you tell me I'm going to be an uncle? I could have helped. With everything."

Gemma stepped toward him, and I reluctantly let go of her. I supposed I'd have to get used to sharing her more now.

"Because I was scared," Gemma whispered, choking on the words. "I was scared of what everyone would say. I was scared to let everyone down. I'm...I'm scared, Julian." She walked forward into Julian's awaiting arms, and I knew, even as she cried, a part of her was healing. This secret had been killing her inside. It had been killing *me*, so I could only imagine what it had done to her.

"I'm sorry, Gems. Fuck, I'm so sorry." Julian wrapped his arms around his sister, holding her tight. He ducked his head, murmuring something in her ear as she buried her face in his chest. She nodded, squeezing him tighter. Her shoulders shook as tiny sobs released from her throat, muffled by Julian's shirt. "It's gonna be okay," Julian breathed. "I promise it's gonna be okay."

Julian propped his chin on her head. He held my gaze over Gemma's head for a long, hard moment, and I knew he was looking right through me.

"Thank you for taking care of her." He took a deep breath. "Even if it was behind my back."

His words held little heat. The anger had seeped out of him.

"Always." I hadn't been lying; I'd do anything for Gemma Briggs. "And thank you for apologizing to her. Because I don't ever want to hear you talk to her like that ever again. Got it, Jules?"

A flash of shame showed on Julian's face as he nodded. His gaze held mine, and relief washed over me because I knew we understood each other. Yeah, he'd just been lashing out and trying to prove a point like the fucking lawyer in him, but hearing him say what he did to her and imply that I'd been using her had cut straight to my goddamn core.

It was never like that.

Julian tightened his hold on his sister, his eyes flicking down to her and then back to me.

"Do you know who did this?" he asked.

I nodded gravely.

Murder reentered Julian's eyes.

"We're gonna pay him a visit, right?"

I crossed my arms over my chest and nodded again.

Because fucking *finally*. I'd been waiting for this.

Julian nodded back, his lips zipped tight. I could tell he was holding his tongue on Gemma's account. He wanted to know more. He wanted to know everything. But Gemma was still sniffling in his arms, and talking about that sperm donor was the last thing she needed right now.

"Em," I said softly and watched as Julian's eyes widened at the nickname that had become so normal for me. For us.

Or maybe his reaction was for my tone. For everything he heard in my voice.

Fuck it, I didn't care.

Gemma lifted her head, looking back at me with watery, exhausted eyes.

"Let's go home," I said before my eyes momentarily flicked to my friend. "Julian can come, too, but let's get you home."

"I—" Julian's attempt to say something on behalf of his sister was cut short by my glare. I didn't know what was going on between Gemma and me, but I knew one thing with absolute certainty: if Julian thought he was going to take her from me, he was dead fucking wrong.

To my immense relief, Gemma gave me a wobbly smile.

"Okay. Let's go."

I kept waiting for her to say *home* like she did when we were leaving the gym twenty minutes ago. Let's go *home*.

But she never did.

CHAPTER THIRTY

noah

I WASN'T SURE what was more shocking: that Julian let me walk away with Gemma unscathed or that he only asked Gemma once if she wanted to move in with him and Juniper. Once she declined, he nodded and let it go. Let *her* go. With me. Back to my apartment. He didn't even try to come with.

Maybe he'd realized it was too late for an intervention. Perhaps he'd seen the truth in my eyes—that I would fucking fight him if he tried to take her away from me now.

Either way, I was relieved. But I wasn't delusional that things would be the same. I felt it in the air, in Gemma's quiet unease, as we drove back to my apartment. Julian had voiced things that couldn't be ignored. But it was Gemma's pleading voice, her reaction, that I couldn't get out of my head.

I never expected that from Noah.

The line kept repeating, over and over.

When we silently walked in the door of my apartment, Gemma made for her room. I followed for a few steps and then stopped, watching her leave me behind. She glanced over her shoulder as though she could feel my heavy gaze. A mix of emotions coated her expression, and I wished, more than anything, that I could get inside her head.

"I think I just need..." she started before trailing off when she saw the look on my face. She stood in the kitchen, turning to face me, but half her body was still angled toward her bedroom like she was ready to make a break for it.

I waited for her to say more.

What do you need, baby?

Gemma cleared her throat. "I have people I should...probably call."

I nodded, even though I knew that wasn't what she'd been about to say a minute ago. "I think that's a good idea."

"Do you think..." She wrapped her arms around herself in a lonely hug I desperately wanted to invade. "I should probably start looking for apartments, huh? Just so I have something lined up."

No.

Fuck no.

The fact that she would even ask that made my chest crack open.

My lips parted, reassuring words on my tongue, ones that would make it more than clear what I thought about her moving out. But then *her* words echoed in my head again.

I never expected that from Noah.

She'd expected a place to crash for a few months. She'd expected sex. She'd expected a goddamn *friend*. She didn't expect anything more. Did she want more? There was only one way to find out.

"Is that what you want?"

I'd already told her that there was no rush to move out. And I'd meant it.

Gemma chewed on her bottom lip before answering with a nonanswer. "It's probably for the best."

Was it, though? The thought of Gemma moving out did not feel remotely like something that could be described as *the best.* In fact, it felt very much like the opposite. And Gemma didn't exactly look excited by the thought, either. But maybe that was just a reflection of the afternoon, of the exhaustion that seemed to set in after she'd hugged Julian one more time and turned to face me with dried tears on her cheeks.

I pressed my lips together, not knowing what to say. She looked like she expected me to say more, but how could that be? So much for No-Expectation-Noah.

It made me want to rip my hair out, unable to decide if I wanted to prove her wrong or prove her right.

I knew I had a reputation. I knew I'd floated through my adult life while living a no-strings-attached lifestyle. I knew I wasn't the most dependable person, knew my schedule was unpredictable and busy. I knew I didn't have relationship experience or much to show for myself outside of money and football, but Christ, had the last few months meant nothing to her? Had I not proven that I was at least a *little* committed to her, to this, to us?

I hadn't said the words. I realized that. But I'd *lived* and *breathed* Gemma Briggs for the last month. Did she not see that?

Gemma's eyes scanned my face, and I knew I was doing a terrible job of hiding my emotions. I was trying not to be pissed, trying not to show I was pissed, especially because I knew how emotional the last couple of hours had been for her. But fuck, I was struggling.

"I'm sorry that Julian found out that way," she said softly. "That he said the things that he did."

I swallowed the lump that had made its way into my throat. "Me too."

"I meant what I said, though. To Julian." She let her arms fall to the side, and there was something about the action that felt so...helpless. Or maybe helplessness was just what stirred up inside me as I stood a few paces from her, watching everything crumble around us. "You don't hold any obligation toward me. I know you warned me that you don't do relationships, and I know I'm the last person you'd break that rule for."

The *last* person?

Gemma Briggs was the *only* fucking person I'd ever considered breaking *any* rules for. Didn't matter what they were. If it meant she'd cut it the fuck out and get back over here into my arms, I'd break any rule.

I shoved my hands into my pockets as I frowned. "Why would you think that?"

She pursed her lips like she didn't want to tell, but that wasn't going to work for me.

"Why the *hell* do you think you'd be the last person, Em?" I pressed.

"Come on, Noah..." she hedged, giving me a look I didn't quite understand.

"No." I took a step forward. "Tell me. I need to know."

"What guy wants a girl who's pregnant with another man's baby?" She threw her hands up, nearly choking on the question before following it up with a humorless laugh. I could see that sheen in her eyes again, and I ground my teeth together at the sight. At what she'd said.

"Did you not listen today?" I punched the words out through gritted teeth, balling my hands into fists in my pockets. "Do we need to replay this afternoon? I've *been* wanting you."

"Noah, stop." Gemma dropped her head, shaking it. "I know you've been wanting me. But just for..."

"Sex," I finished for her when she couldn't seem to do it. "Right?"

The word dropped between us like an anvil.

She blinked, not saying a word. And holy shit, that silence hurt. That was what she really thought of me? Of this? Sure, we'd agreed to it. But weeks had passed since then, and I couldn't believe that none of it had meant anything to her.

"Is that what it felt like today?" I asked, my voice cold and stony. "When I had you up against the wall? It was just another fuck, right?"

I pressed my lips together as I tried to read between the lines. Because I needed to know. I needed to know if we'd just been fucking today. It hadn't *felt* like just fucking, and I didn't know what I would do if she hadn't felt that, too. Because I'd never experienced anything like that. Anything like her.

Pain lanced through Gemma's eyes. "Don't make me answer that."

"No, if that's how you really feel, then I need to hear you say it." When she just blinked at me, I added desperately, "Because it was...Gemma, it was more. *You* are so much more to me than that. How can you not see that by now? I don't know what's happening or where to go from here, but you *know* it was more."

"I know," she whispered in the smallest voice. But I didn't care, because those two words meant there was still hope.

I sighed, feeling ragged and raw. "Then why? Why do you keep trying to reduce us to less than that?"

"Because." Her voice was tired, so tired, and I just wanted to wrap her up and bring her back to bed with me. But I knew that wouldn't solve anything right now. "I didn't want you to think that I went into this arrangement with the illusion that I could change who you think you are. I respect your boundaries and will never expect you to give me more than you are willing or able. And one time, you told me sex was all you *could* give. But if something's changed for you..."

She shook her head like she couldn't even fathom that something *had* changed, which killed me. "Of course it feels like more to me. Of course *you* feel like more to me. You feel like *everything*. But Noah, *I'm* more. I come with so much more than just me. And it's okay if that's too much...more for you. It really is okay."

I swallowed, soaking in her words.

I'm more.

Yeah, she was.

She was more. She was the only woman I'd ever felt this wild about. She was brilliant, gorgeous, funny, talented, and yeah, she was about to be a mom. She wasn't just more. She was everything.

I knew, without a doubt, that I wanted her. That I'd been committed to her since before I even realized it. That this had always been more than sex for me. But Gemma was right; this wasn't just about her and me. It was about being a *parent*. And all I could think about was my family's shock when they thought that I was going to be a dad—as if it were out of the realm of possibility for Noah London, serial playboy, to settle down and have a kid.

Was I really ready for *everything*? For all the *more* that she was talking about?

God, I wanted to be ready. I wanted this. I wanted it and her so fucking bad, even if maybe I shouldn't. Even if I wasn't the right person for the role. With everything happening in her life, Gemma needed someone who knew how the hell to be a dad, someone who was experienced in relationships, and right now, I felt like I was failing her.

"Stop looking at me like that," Gemma pleaded while I was still trying to put my thoughts into words. "I know you don't know where to go from here, but I just don't think that's something I can tell you. I can't...put that on you. You need to decide that for yourself."

I raked my hand through my hair. Every part of my body ached with the need to reassure her, but for the first time since she'd moved in, I didn't know how. Not after everything that had been said today. She was scared, and meanwhile, all I could think about was that this was why I always kept things casual with girls. Because I hated the idea of letting them down. Of being someone that people couldn't expect things from. Of not giving them what they deserved.

And Gemma Briggs and Baby? They deserved the world. They deserved the best. The best version of me. The version of me that Gemma didn't have any doubts in. The version of me that Gemma *would* have expectations for.

"You don't have to decide right now," she whispered, and the crack in her voice broke my fucking heart. "I told myself that I would be okay with however this ended, and I will be. I'm okay, Noah." She offered a small, wobbly smile as she tried to prove to me that I didn't owe her anything. That she was okay with walking away with nothing.

I didn't believe her. And even if she was okay with it, *I* wasn't.

Ended. She said the word *ended* like I was going somewhere. Like we were over.

Fuck that. We hadn't even begun—not really. And that was my fault, something I needed to fix.

Gemma walked away after she gave me her reassurances that actually felt like little stabs to the chest.

And I let her.

CHAPTER THIRTY-ONE

gemma

J UNIPER STARED AT me, slack-jawed, as she tried to comprehend everything I had just told her.

We sat in her apartment, which, despite my brother living here, too, looked totally Juni-fied. A bookshelf stood in the corner, filled with books and plants, a cake tray with cupcakes decorated the kitchen table, and a bunch of colorful cushions were scattered on the green couch beside us.

Juniper's mouth opened. And then closed. And then opened again.

"When Julian told me we needed to talk, I didn't think..." She pursed her lips momentarily, her watery brown eyes landing on me. "Gems, I—I don't know what to say. Oh, God, I should have—"

"You should have done nothing," I interrupted. "*I* should have told you."

A single tear slipped down Juniper's cheek, and a lump formed in my throat. I'd cried so much after I walked away from Noah, leaving me to spend the night alone for the first time in weeks, and I wasn't sure I had any more tears left in me. But as soon as another tear dropped from Juniper's lash line, I had to choke down a sob.

Especially when she threw her arms around me and murmured, "I wish you did."

"I didn't want Julian to know yet." I hugged her back, my words muffled against her shoulder. "And I couldn't ask you to keep that secret from him."

Juni squeezed me tighter before reluctantly letting go. Her eyes were sad, and her lips parted like she was about to say that she would have, that she would have kept the secret.

Except we both knew she couldn't.

Because it would have hurt Julian to no end. I hated causing Julian pain, hated seeing his reaction yesterday when he realized what I'd been keeping from him. But that pain would have been so much worse if he realized that Juniper had been lying to him, too.

I might be Juni's best friend, but my brother had her heart. I was okay with that. I understood.

I couldn't imagine keeping secrets from Noah.

Besides the ones I already had been.

Juniper straightened, asking the question I'd been expecting.

"Do you want to move in with Julian and me?" she suggested before hesitating and adding, "At least until you figure out whatever is going on between you and Noah, of course."

I sighed, shaking my head. "Thanks, but it's okay, Junes. I don't think I could handle living with the two of you." Juniper opened her mouth, and I rushed on before she could try to convince me that she wouldn't be disgusting with my brother. "And I've already started to hunt for apartments. I'm sure I'll find one soon, but until then, I should really stay with Noah. I promised him I'd watch Winnie, and it's just easier when I'm living there."

Juniper's eyes wandered my face as though she was trying to decide if she should push harder for me to change my mind. But ultimately, she let it go.

"Okay, if you're sure."

I mustered a smile, flashing it at her. "I'm sure."

I wasn't sure. Being around Noah the last couple of days while I wasn't sure where we stood had been torture, and I knew I'd continue to live in torture until I moved out. But at the same time, the idea of leaving earlier than I'd planned gutted me. I didn't want to leave. God, I *really* didn't. Especially when it felt like things between Noah and I were unresolved.

It felt like home. *He* felt like home.

Juniper nodded and then snapped into action mode. "So what do you need now? What can I do?"

I toyed with the ends of my hair, my stomach churning. "Would you want to come with me to my appointment next week?" I asked.

"Absolutely." Juniper nodded eagerly, ready to take on any request I threw her way. "What else?"

"I..." I shook my head. "I don't know. I think that's all for now."

While I loved Juniper, she was staring at me, waiting for instructions. I didn't have those. I didn't know what the hell I was doing. Every day was one step at a time, and while I *was* figuring out how to navigate it, I had no clue what came next.

Noah, on the other hand, had never asked me what my plans were. He had never expected me to know what I was doing. He just stepped in alongside me, took my hand, and walked one step at a time with me.

"Did anyone go with you to your appointments before?" Juniper asked, breaking into my thoughts in the worst possible way—like she could see them revolving around my roommate.

"Noah did," I answered with a sigh.

Juniper's expression softened, and she slid her hand over mine. She wasn't surprised when I told her I was sleeping with Noah. Out of all the bombs I'd dropped on her this morning, she'd reacted the least to that one.

"Of course he did."

Of course he did.

"I told him he didn't have to, but he insisted."

"I'm not surprised." Juniper squeezed my hand before looking at me, curiosity written all over her face. "Was that before or after you started to get hot and heavy with him?"

"It was before," I answered. "He was really supportive from the beginning, from the first time I showed up at his apartment and promptly sprinted to his bathroom because of morning sickness. He rubbed my back while I threw up more times than I could count and held my hand during the first ultrasound and started obsessing over cooking meals with lots of folic acid. I swear he's done more research about pregnancy health than I have. He *hates* that I'm still skating." A wistful smile twisted on my lips at the memories. "And he always insists on driving me everywhere."

Juniper raised a brow. "And you let him?"

I shrugged, glancing away from her knowing look. "He's a good driver. And a nice guy."

"Gemma..." she started, and I steeled myself for whatever lecture she was about to give me. "Noah *is* a nice guy. But you're not describing a nice guy. You're describing a man who is in—"

"Don't say it," I begged, my eyes seeking hers.

I couldn't hear it, not when I wasn't sure I could have it.

Juniper pressed her lips together at my command, but her gaze told me what she was going to say. She sighed, tucking a golden-brown hair behind her ear.

"Fine," she allowed. "Then tell me how *you* feel about *him*."

"I like him...so much." I shook my head because the words were so pitiful compared to the truth. "But I just don't know, Junes."

Juniper's brows drew together. "But why? Is it because of how Julian reacted? I know he probably overreacted, but I can promise you he's already over it now that he understands the full picture."

"It's not about Julian," I said, which was ironic considering that the conversation with Julian was what had destroyed everything. But only because it *exposed* everything. Everything that Noah and I weren't saying.

"Then what?"

I looked at her with a pleading gaze. "Isn't it obvious?"

Juniper blinked at me. Once. Twice. I could see the gears working in her head as she cocked it sideways. She knew I'd never exactly been shy about going after what I wanted. But that was before, and things were different now. Well, one thing was different now.

"It's because of the baby."

She whispered the words. A statement, not a question. Because she knew me.

I nodded. "Noah doesn't think he's the kind of man who can give a girl love. A relationship. A future. That's what he said. And even though I don't believe him, it would be foolishly hopeful to expect him to change his mind for me. Especially when it's not *just* me in the picture. I refuse to put that kind of pressure on him by confessing just how much I—"

I snapped my mouth shut, but the words still rang in my head.

If I told Noah what I wanted, he'd bend over backward to give it to me. If I told him I didn't want to move out, he'd probably let me stay with him forever. If I told him I needed help with the baby, he'd fill into a role that wasn't his just because he felt like he was supposed to do that.

The thing about Noah was that he was so worried that he'd let people down that he couldn't even see how much he catered to everyone else before worrying about himself.

I couldn't tell him what I really wanted.

"Gemma," Juniper said gently, pulling me out of my thoughts. "After everything you've told me, I wouldn't be surprised if Noah wants that baby nearly as much as he wants you."

Her words filled my chest with all that foolish hope I knew I shouldn't trust. I wasn't sure Noah really felt that way, but my heart squeezed with longing anyway.

"Do you know if it's a boy or a girl yet?" Juniper asked, switching the topic because she could probably see the roller coaster I was riding inside. It did the trick. I perked up a little, nervous energy running through my veins. The excited kind.

"No." I gave her a tiny smile. "But I think we might be able to find out next week."

Juniper dropped my hand as she squealed, clapping with excitement, which made my smile grow. A different kind of hope blossomed in my stomach. A kind that had nothing to do with Noah and more to do with the knowledge that I was going to be okay. I might be raising this child as a single mom, but I wouldn't be alone. I had Juniper. And Julian.

And the rest of my family...who I still needed to tell. After my conversation with Noah, I hadn't had the energy.

"Have you talked to your sisters?" Juniper asked, reading my mind once again.

I shook my head before giving her a sheepish glance. "Could you sit with me while I call them?"

Juniper took my hand in hers again, gripping hard.

"I'm not going anywhere."

The next person I had to talk to was Silas; I couldn't put it off any longer. Ideally, I wanted to talk to him before going to the doctor next week.

Hoping she'd forgive me for completely ghosting her after I quit, I messaged Kayla, one of the other skating coaches at St. Mav's. I'd been so shocked after learning I was pregnant that I didn't realize until recently how much I'd really lost when I left the collegiate skating world. It was more than a job—it was also relationships like the one I had with Kayla.

She was nicer than I probably deserved when she replied, giving me the information I wanted to know: what was on Silas' work calendar for this week. All the coaches had access to it as a means of scheduling meetings when necessary.

And I certainly planned to schedule a meeting. A surprise one.

I also made plans to meet up with Kayla. It was time to let her know what happened. Mainly to make sure it didn't happen to anyone else and to let her know about the letter I'd recently sent to human resources at St. Mav's before she found out from anyone else.

The sun peeked into the apartment through the living room windows as I walked out of my bedroom. Noah was up, standing in the kitchen and looking at something on his laptop. As soon as he heard me, he snapped it shut and pushed it away like he didn't want me to see what he was doing.

I frowned but didn't say anything as I walked past him to make breakfast. He started doing the same. He put an egg on the stove, and I poured milk into my cereal. He eyed my bowl, and I could tell he wanted to offer to make more food for me because that's what he always did, but he'd been hesitant with his words ever since the other day. Like he was trying desperately to come up with the right ones, and I so wished I could help him. But I just couldn't.

I should never have let it get to this point, but the falling happened so quickly. And it wasn't fair to expect Noah to catch me.

"I might not be here when you get home later," I said when I couldn't handle the silent tension between us.

Noah's head jerked up, his eyes wild with something akin to panic. "What?"

"I'll be home later than I usually am on Tuesdays," I clarified and watched Noah visibly relax before stiffening again when my next words came out. "I'm going over to St. Maverick's after skating."

"Why?"

"I need to talk to Silas."

Slowly turning the burner off, Noah pushed the frying pan to the back of the stovetop and gave me his full attention. "About what?"

I cleared my throat, trying to act like I wasn't internally panicking about this meeting. "I want to grill him about his medical history before my doctor's appointment."

Noah's brows drew together. I could tell he was trying to control his expression—just like I was. "Can't you do that over the phone?"

"I could, but I don't want to risk him dodging me."

I'd thought about it. A lot. Yes, I could call him. That sure sounded easier. When he didn't pick up, it would give me an excuse—say I tried and leave it at that. But I wanted—needed—to know everything I could about my baby. And I also needed the kind of closure that involved facing him one last time. And doing it on campus felt right.

"I know he'll be in the office this afternoon," I added. "I'm just going to stop by."

"*Fuck* no." Noah took two steps toward me before halting in his tracks. It was like he'd forgotten that he wasn't touching me anymore. I hated that. "Are you kidding me?"

"Definitely not kidding," I said flatly, even though my heart rate picked up. It was climbing like a mountain because Noah was two steps closer to me, which was closer than he had been in a few days.

"I'll go," Noah insisted. His jaw was set. "I'll get any information you need from him while you stay home."

I let my gaze meet his, pleading with him to understand. "I need to do this, Noah."

He stared back at me, crossing his arms over his chest. He wasn't going to keep me from going, and he knew that. It pissed him off, but he knew it.

"Okay, but there's no way in hell you're doing it alone," he said, breaking our staredown by running a hand over his face. "Julian and I were already planning to pay that asshole a visit. I'll let Jules know that we're doing it today."

"Noah..." I started, unsure if putting Julian in the same room as Silas was a good idea. Or Noah, for that matter.

Noah was shaking his head, though. He didn't want to hear my protests.

"You're not," he said, his voice strangled. "You're not going there alone. I don't want that man anywhere near you, but if you need to talk to him, fine. I'm coming with. I don't fucking trust Silas Taylor."

"You don't know anything about him," I argued weakly.

Noah's nostrils flared as he leveled his hot gaze on me. "I know enough."

"Okay," I allowed, my voice barely more than a whisper. "But let me talk to Julian about it."

Noah gave me a look like he didn't think I'd follow through with that.

"I will," I insisted. "There are some...legal considerations I should really go over with him."

Noah's eyes danced around my face, trying to read between the lines.

And then he came right out and asked it. "Did you consent that night?"

I didn't answer him for a long moment. Partly because it felt like my throat was squeezing in the truth, not wanting it to get out. But partly because I didn't know the answer. Wasn't even sure if the truth was real.

"I'm not...sure. I think so, but I'm not sure," I said before looking away, unable to handle the intensity of Noah's expression. I released a shaky breath, trying not to let my mind wander to the fuzzy memories of that night. "I wasn't entirely sober."

"Then you didn't," Noah growled, and I glanced back to find him looking murderous. Even more than Julian had in the hallway at the rink. "I'm going to fucking kill him," he muttered.

That was what I was worried about.

"Can you at least wait until after I talk to him?" I asked, even though I knew it was probably foolish to hope I'd get in a word with Julian and Noah present. "In fact, I'm going to need you to promise you'll follow my lead."

359

Surprisingly, Noah nodded. "You do what you need to do, Em. I'll take care of the rest."

My breath caught in my throat at his response. So simple but so perfect, and exactly what I needed. This man. God, I adored him. He was everything. When had he become everything?

It wasn't that hard to figure out. Not considering how much he'd done for me. Like I told Blake that day at the football game, Noah London was the best man I'd ever known. He deserved to have everything that he wanted. Even if what he wanted long term didn't include me.

We'd reached a sort of impasse, and I didn't know what to do about it.

"I'll pick you up from the rink when your class is done," Noah said, clearly determined to not let me slip off to campus without him. "Julian can either meet us there or at St. Maverick's."

I nodded as my stomach turned.

The last person I wanted to see today was Silas Taylor.

But I was admittedly glad not to be going alone.

I was about to walk away to finish my undoubtedly soggy cereal in my room when Noah stopped me.

"Hey, Em?"

I looked back over my shoulder.

"Do you..." He scrubbed a hand over his face. "Have you read any books?"

"Any books?" I repeated, confused. "I usually read whatever Juniper's new obsession is, but I'm not totally sure those books would be up your alley."

"No," he said hoarsely. "That's not what I meant. I was wondering if you had any recommendations for...never mind."

I stared at him, hoping he'd change his mind and finish the sentence, but Noah returned his attention to his egg, which I was sure was as cold as my cereal was soggy.

So, once again, I walked away.

eight years ago
NOAH

"You're still here," Julian said flatly, a slight edge to his voice.

"I'm still here," I said lightly.

He cocked his head to the side. "Why?"

I shrugged. "Just keeping your sister company while you went to get her a drink."

Julian's shoulders dropped, relaxing just slightly. Not completely, though. Because I knew he caught me staring at her. And I knew he knew what I was thinking.

He didn't have to worry about me, though. I understood Gemma Briggs was off-limits.

Maybe one day, he would give me the green light.

But until then, I'd behave around his angel of a sister.

CHAPTER THIRTY-TWO

noah

J ULIAN AND I flanked Gemma as she led the way to Silas Taylor's office.

She walked confidently, but I didn't miss how she pushed her hands into her pockets to keep them from trembling. The thing was, it was hard to tell if she was shaking because of nerves or because of anger.

Gemma had things to say. I could tell. She'd wanted to have this meeting in person on purpose, and a part of me couldn't wait to watch her put this man in his place. He deserved every little thing about to come his way—tenfold.

Silas' expression was priceless as Gemma waltzed into his office, me and Julian right behind her. Outrage flickered over his face before it was replaced by indignation. And something else. Panic. Fear.

And that was all before he realized Julian and I stood at her sides, looming over him at his ridiculously large desk. His eyes widened as he fumbled for something to say, especially when his gaze caught on my face, recognition flaring.

"Hello, Silas," Gemma drawled, reeling his attention back in. Her voice wavered, but it was slight and masked by the sarcasm

362

her tone dripped in. "Hope you don't mind that we dropped in unannounced, but we need to chat."

His mouth gaped like a fish until he pulled himself together. "When I said I wanted to chat, this was the *exact* thing I wanted to avoid. You can't simply show up—"

Gemma cut him off, nodding toward Julian. "As you might be able to guess, this is my brother. Julian Briggs, attorney at law."

Silas' jaw tightened, and it only worsened when Gemma gestured toward me.

"And this is Noah London."

No title, no nothing, just Noah London.

Fuck.

I didn't like the idea of being Gemma's friend, but I hated being her nothing a hell of a lot more.

It hadn't been the same between us, and it was the worst form of torture. I knew she expected me to *say* something, *do* something, *fix* everything. But then a part of me couldn't get over the way she told Julian she never expected *anything* from me.

I didn't let that stop me from trying, though. I still didn't know what the hell I was doing, but I figured picking up a few books and learning whatever I could about being a parent was a good way to start if I wanted to be with someone who was about to become one. I figured researching cribs and playpens and high chairs might help if I wanted Gemma to believe me when I said Baby had a home in my apartment. That she did. They both did.

I didn't really know what I was doing. But I was trying to figure it out so that maybe when we broached the conversation of our relationship again, she'd realize that she could expect things from me.

And in the meantime, I was here. Because I wouldn't let anything take away the satisfaction of the sight before me. All the blood drained from Silas' face as he turned into a ghost. He pushed to his feet, fully intending to spew something, but Gemma cut him off.

"There are a few things we need to discuss," she continued.

"So I suggest you sit down." When Silas remained poised, seeming to debate his best course of action, Gemma cleared her throat. "If you don't, I'm sure Julian and Noah would love to make you. Considering they played college football together for several years, they're remarkably well versed in teamwork. They're also *very* well-connected in collegiate sports, to people I'm sure would be interested to learn about our little story."

God, this girl. My lips twitched, her comment about me forgotten. She could say whatever she wanted as long as she took this asshole out in the process.

Silas sat his ass back in his chair, looking like he would rather throw it than sit in it. He lowered robotically, as though he had to consider every movement and control it. Keep it in check. His slowness gave me a chance to look him over.

I'd assumed that Silas Taylor was older than Gemma, based solely on his position as a collegiate athletic director. But I wasn't prepared for this man to be old enough to have salt-and-pepper streaks in his dark hair. The picture I found online must have been old because he'd looked a lot younger then.

I frowned, looking over the rest of him, my fists balling at the thought of him touching her. He had the look of a retired athlete, broad shoulders with height on his side—that is, I assumed he'd be tall if Gemma allowed him to stand—but he also looked like his desk job had made him into a lazy version of himself.

"Did you at least make sure no one saw you come in?" he hissed, bushy black brows drawing together.

Gemma shrugged. "That's not really my problem."

Something flared in Silas' eye, and Julian and I instinctively moved closer to Gemma. It did the trick. Silas' expression turned stony as he glared at us. It was tame compared to the flash of anger I saw a second ago, and my stomach turned as I wondered what could have happened had Gemma shown up here alone.

"Fine." Silas leaned forward on his desk, his too-small suit straining with the position. "What the hell do you want?"

This guy had a lot of audacity to talk to Gemma like that after what he did to her. It took everything in me not to step in on her behalf and remind him how to fucking behave. I could tell Julian was itching, too. But Gemma had the floor, and I couldn't take it from her. Not yet. She told me I had to wait, so I was waiting.

I hated that I was waiting a step behind her, though. I hated that I wasn't next to her, holding her hand. I really fucking hated that. I wanted Silas Taylor to understand that if he wanted to get to Gemma or that baby, he'd be going through me. Not just today but for a long time.

"Firstly, medical records," Gemma snapped, drawing me out of the place my mind had just gone. I shook my head, needing to focus. "I need your complete medical history for my baby's records."

My—not our. For some reason, that satisfied the hell out of me. To hear her exclude him.

Silas nodded slowly, and I didn't miss the slight relief that made his shoulders snag. As though he thought that Gemma had been about to drop something worse on him.

I knew, though, that the conversation wasn't over.

"I can do that," Silas agreed. "I'll have a copy of any family medical history sent over to you."

"I need it by Friday," Gemma said flatly. "I have an appointment next week."

Silas only paused a second before nodding. "I'll make it happen."

Gemma nodded back, and I noticed her relax a little. That had been the most important reason for her coming here, and he'd agreed without issue.

"If you don't, I'll be back," Gemma promised. "And I'll make *sure* people see me."

Silas glared. "What else do you want? Is it money?"

"I don't need your money," Gemma said softly.

No, she didn't. She could have all of mine. I'd ensure that child had anything they could ever need or want.

"I know you probably thought that just because I quit and

disappeared, you wouldn't have to worry about me. But while I don't want your money or your involvement or to even look at your face more than I have to, I do want you to know that there are consequences for your actions."

Rage filtered over Silas' face. "It's not my fault you spread your—"

"If you say one bad thing about her, I will fucking end you," I stepped in, refusing to let this man spew any of his goddamn bullshit. Gemma might be calm, but I was anything but as I slammed my hands down on his desk and pinned Silas with a glare. I didn't realize it was possible to hate someone this badly, but God, did I want to destroy him. "I'd watch your fucking mouth if you want to keep all your teeth."

Silas seethed but ultimately remained silent. He stared at me with a look of betrayal, and I found it somewhat rewarding. Meanwhile, Gemma took a shaky breath behind me, and I refocused, pushing off Silas' desk and returning to her side, all while red-hot rage burned through my veins.

"You're right," Gemma said, looking straight at Silas. "It's not *entirely* your fault that I spread my legs. But the fact remains that you, my boss, bought me one too many drinks. And you, my boss, brought me back to your apartment. And you, my boss, slept with me even though I wasn't fully sober. And you, my boss, got me pregnant."

Hearing her say the words aloud made me regret not punching his lights out a moment ago. Fuck this guy.

But I focused my attention on Gemma instead. She ran a hand over her stomach, emphasizing the small bump. She wore a tight dress today. It was black with long sleeves to combat the fall air, and it showed off every curve of Gemma's body, including the most important one.

I physically ached with the need to touch her. The possessive urge to wrap my arms around her and splay my hands over her stomach terrified me. It terrified me, but it also overwhelmed me. *Consumed* me. But all I could do right now was just stare at

Gemma as I stood beside her. She was beyond beautiful, and I hated that Silas even got to look at her.

I had a feeling Julian agreed. He crossed his arms over his chest, clenching them tightly to keep his anger in check. I could practically see the steam rising out of his ears. I was equally pissed, but at least I'd had months to come to terms with what had happened to Gemma. He'd only known for a matter of days.

Silas' mind was whirring, his wheels backpedaling. "Look, Gemma—"

"So now two things are going to happen," she continued, glossing over his attempt to make a point she didn't care to hear. "One, I want it in writing that I will maintain sole custody of my child."

"I already told you I have no interest—"

"*In writing,*" Gemma ground out before continuing. "Two, you might hear that I've resubmitted my letter of resignation to include the true reason for my sudden departure from St. Maverick's. I thought the university might be interested to hear how you're sleeping with the young, drunk coaches on your staff. You know, in case they wanted to keep an eye on that kind of behavior. I would hate for it to become a pattern, Silas. Make sure that it doesn't."

"You—" Silas choked on the rest of his words as he jumped to his feet. He'd been standing for less than a second when Julian stepped forward to reach out and clap a hand on his shoulder, roughly pushing him into his chair again.

Silas seethed, trying to shake Julian's grip off. Julian didn't let go, squeezing his shoulder hard enough that Silas made a strangled noise. I took a step forward, ready to back Julian up if Silas made a move. I'd be *more* than happy to lend a hand.

But then Gemma cleared her throat, and we both backed down. Julian looked disappointed as he released his hold on Silas, and he continued to hover near the athletic director's desk, keeping a keen eye on him.

Meanwhile, I inched closer to Gemma. I didn't care if things were weird between us; I needed to be near her right now. I needed her to know I was there.

For that reason, when Gemma turned to walk out of the office, leaving Silas to sputter to her back, I turned and walked out with her. I heard Julian's low voice as he hurled both legal and physical threats at Silas, and I thought I even heard a yelp of pain, but I left the intimidation to him, even if it slightly pained me to do so. I'd hear if he needed help, and it didn't sound like he did.

I stayed at Gemma's side. Where I belonged.

She shook her hands as she walked, releasing the pent-up energy and nerves. When we rounded the corner, she paused, slumping against the wall. Deep, unsteady breaths racked her body, and she squeezed her eyes shut for a long moment.

"Thank you," she whispered. She opened her eyes but kept them trained on her feet. "For coming. You didn't need to."

"Yes," I said lowly, wishing she would look at me. "I did, angel."

I *very* much needed to come. I needed this today almost as much as she did. Needed to see her walk all over him. Needed to make sure he didn't lay a goddamn finger on her. Needed to make my presence known so Taylor didn't get any ideas.

I felt my throat tighten, and my hands balled into fists. She shouldn't have to thank me like that—like I was doing her a favor. She should know that I would always be there, and I wouldn't ever ask for anything in return.

Gemma's breath hitched, and then she held on to it. I knew enough about this girl to know she was trying not to cry, but I wanted her to know I would be here to catch her tears if she did. Instinctively, I started to reach out, unable to battle the innate need to comfort her. But Gemma stiffened, and I wasn't sure if it was because I moved to touch her or because Julian's footsteps echoed in the hallway behind us.

Either way, I dropped my hand, gritting my teeth until the physical pain eclipsed the stabbing sensation in my chest.

Gemma took a slow step away before refocusing on the path ahead. With a sad glance, she took off, leaving me behind.

I sighed just as Julian rounded the corner. He practically barreled into me as he huffed through the hallway, stopping short as his eyes shifted from me to Gemma. Curiosity replaced the anger in his eyes.

"Come on," I muttered before following his sister.

I didn't want to answer any of his questions right now.

Even as we were leaving, Gemma walked with purpose across campus, her boots clicking on the cobblestone. Her copper locks flew in the breeze as she led the way, her pace quickening as though she wanted a little space. I gave it to her, even though it pained me.

And it opened me up to questioning from fucking Julian once Gemma was out of earshot. The questioning I'd been hoping to avoid.

"How many times?"

"What?" I glanced over at him, disbelief in my voice. Was he really asking what I thought he was asking?

"How many times," Julian repeated, overenunciating the words. "How many times did you sleep with my sister?"

I shook my head. We weren't having this conversation. "Don't you have other things to worry about with a wedding coming up in a week?"

"Just answer the question."

"You really don't want me to do that."

"You're right," Julian grunted grumpily. "But I just want to confirm that it was more than once."

More than once was one way to put it.

"And why would you want to do that?"

"Because you never hook up with a girl more than once," Julian said, and the suddenly light tone of his voice both confused and pissed me off.

"Shut up," I snapped, stopping short to glare at him. "Gemma wasn't a fucking hookup."

But Julian just smirked as he rocked to a halt next to me. "When you're ready to talk through some shit, let me know."

I scowled, growing more irritated by the second. "You want to know all the ways I slept with your sister? Because that could be a long conversation."

A muscle in Julian's jaw jumped, but he didn't take the bait.

"Quit the act, London." His tone was suddenly severe, but there was also a hint of understanding. Of support. That was the thing about Julian. Sometimes he came out brash, but he loved hard. And he felt it was his responsibility to ensure everyone was cared for. I knew that, but I wasn't used to him talking to *me* this way. "You can tell everyone you're a player, and yeah, you have a history of sleeping around sometimes, but you have never in your life *played* a goddamn soul. I know you, man. Do *you* know you?"

"I..."

Words escaped me as I tried to figure out what he was asking.

Julian's expression softened, and then the corner of his mouth tipped up again. This was the last look I'd expected to see on him after everything he'd uncovered recently, but maybe the timing of his wedding next week had worked in my favor.

"Let me know if you need help figuring it out," he said before leveling his blue gaze with mine. "I'm sorry about how I reacted at the rink. I didn't realize at first."

"Didn't realize?" I repeated even though my stomach somersaulted.

Julian clapped a hand on my shoulder, looking mighty pleased with himself. "That you're in love with her."

A second later, he shoved his hands in his pockets and strolled after his sister.

His sister that I was absolutely in love with.

Oh, *fuck*.

I hated to admit when Julian was right about something, but he was undeniably right about this.

I'd fallen in love with his sister.

And I'd fallen *hard*.

CHAPTER THIRTY-THREE

noah

I SAT ON the couch, staring into space. A pinkish light filled the apartment as the sun rose over the city. A book sat open on my lap—one Nat had recommended when I asked her—but I'd stopped focusing on the paragraphs about child development a while ago. Winnie had decided it was too early to wake up, so she was still snoring on her dog bed in the corner. A scalding cup of coffee damn near burned my hand as I held it, but I was numb to the pain.

I wasn't even sure why I'd poured myself a cup.

It was decaf.

I didn't drink decaf.

A few minutes later, Gemma slipped out the bedroom door in a way that told me two things. One, she didn't see that I was sitting here. And two, she didn't expect me to be sitting here. She was trying to be quiet, trying not to wake me.

But I was wide-awake. Even though it was my off day and I could have slept in, I was wide-awake. It hadn't exactly been easy to sleep lately. Not when I'd gotten so used to the feeling of her next to me, and now she was gone.

Gemma tiptoed over to the coffeepot and cocked her head to the side when she realized it was full.

"It's decaf," I said, wanting to make sure she knew she could have some.

She jumped, her hand flying to her chest as she spun to face me. Remembering the book in my lap, I pushed it off, burying it in between the cushions of the couch so Gemma wouldn't see. Her tired eyes landed on me, and her shoulders dropped, tension releasing.

I liked that. I liked being a person she could relax around. That she didn't have to have her guard up. I didn't just want to be *a* person, though. I wanted to be *her* person.

"Thanks." Gemma flashed me a small smile before going to a box outside her bedroom and plucking a mug from it for her coffee. I hated that box. I wasn't sure why it had been sitting there the last few days, and I was worried to find out. I glared at it.

Gemma seemed to notice. "I'm trying to get organized. This is all the stuff I'm thinking about selling or donating to make room for baby things. I can move them if they're bothering you, though."

I frowned, her words twisting my gut into a knot.

"They're not bothering me."

But something else was. Pushing off the couch, I walked to the stack of boxes and peered over the top of the one Gemma had just grabbed a mug from. And sure enough, it was filled with mugs. All of the mugs she'd kept hidden in her bedroom for the past few months. The ones that were precious enough that she hadn't even wanted to put them in my kitchen cabinets.

"You can't sell these," I said, my frown deepening as I faced her.

Gemma leaned against the kitchen countertop, the mug of coffee at her lips. It had pretty orange and pink flowers painted on it, reminding me of her hair and the color that tinged her cheeks whenever I made her blush.

"I've done some looking around. At apartments. But I can probably only afford a studio," she said softly, slowly taking a sip

372

and placing the mug on the countertop. "There won't be a lot of space for things I don't need."

"Gemma—" I started, but her phone rang, cutting me off.

"Hey, are you here?" she asked, answering the phone. I watched as she bit on her bottom lip, nerves evident as she waited for the reply. Then, she nodded. "Okay, I'll be right down."

"Who's here?" I asked when she hung up the phone.

I wanted to know who was taking my place today.

"Juni," Gemma replied.

I'd never been annoyed with Juniper St. James before today. No, jealous. I was *jealous* of her.

Gemma's eyes skated over mine as though she didn't dare look me in the eyes as she walked gingerly to the front door. She slipped her feet into her shoes and grabbed her jacket off the hook before I couldn't bear it anymore.

"Gemma," I said, even though my voice was raw.

She looked up. She looked at me. Our eyes finally connected, and my breath vanished. Longing lingered in her gaze, and I suspected she'd been avoiding me because she hadn't wanted me to see it.

"I have an appointment," she said, assuming I wanted to know where she was going. "And Juni wants to chat and get coffee at Georgia's first."

"Gemma," I murmured again because I needed her to stop talking. I didn't want to hear about the appointment she was going to without me or the apartments she'd been looking at moving into that weren't mine or the places she was thinking about donating her mugs. I didn't want to hear it. "Gemma, I know you're going to an appointment."

I stood and closed the distance between us, watching as Gemma sucked in a breath, holding it as I neared her.

"I have your calendar, remember?" I added because she was looking at me with wide, surprised eyes. I stopped a foot away from her. Just a foot, but it felt like a mile.

"I remember," she whispered before stepping forward.

I took it as an invitation, making the final move so I could touch her, gently at first, my fingertips only grazing her arms. But when her body swayed toward mine, I slid my palms up to her shoulders before I finally held her face between my hands, angling it up toward me. Beautiful, blue eyes connected with mine, and my heart jolted.

"It's Tuesday, Em."

She'd scheduled the appointment on a Tuesday. She'd scheduled it so I could come.

"You deserve to have a day off, Noah," Gemma said weakly, giving a forced smile.

I sighed. "But I'm awake for a reason."

"It's okay," she assured me. Or at least, she tried to assure me. My stomach dropped further with every word out of her sweet mouth. "You don't have to. Juniper was excited to come."

I nodded, even though it pained me to do it. "She'll probably be better at...all of the baby stuff than I was."

Gemma pursed her lips, and I wondered if she was trying not to agree with me. If she didn't want to hurt my feelings.

"Don't do that," she said finally.

"What?" I tipped my forehead against hers, reveling in the feel of having her so close again. Her eyelids fluttered shut.

"Say words that make me want to convince you of things I shouldn't," she breathed. Her lips were so close. So close to mine, and it was unbelievable how badly I wanted to taste them again.

"Like what?"

"Noah, please," she begged in the smallest voice.

I released a shaky breath and gave up, lifting my head to kiss Gemma on the forehead. She leaned into it, clearly as reluctant as me to walk away again. My lips traveled to her hairline, and I closed my eyes, soaking her in. "I expect an update when you get back," I murmured against her soft hair.

She nodded and then slipped out of my grasp, muttering something about how she had to go.

Feeling her slip away had never felt more terrifying. At the moment, the only thing keeping me grounded was the way she paused at the door, glancing back.

"You were good at it." I watched her throat work as she swallowed hard. "You were really good at it, Noah."

And then I watched her walk out the door, repeating her words over and over in my head, hoping they were even a little bit true. The way Gemma said them...she seemed so sure. I wanted to be as sure as her.

I'd noticed that about Gemma lately. She was maneuvering her way through her pregnancy with more assurance, more determination, and I admired her for it so fucking much. I knew sometimes she might not feel it on the inside—how good of a job she was doing—but she was doing it.

She shouldn't have to do it alone, though.

I didn't want that for her, but even more than that, I wanted more and more to do it with her. It wasn't just about supporting Gemma anymore. I didn't want to go to the doctor appointment today because I didn't want her to be alone. I wanted to go because I wanted to *be there*.

Because I didn't just want Gemma Briggs.

I wanted...*more*.

I walked back over to the couch, my mind reeling.

I picked up my phone, typing in the location of Gemma's hospital. It was only a couple of miles away, but with all the damn one-ways in Boston, I needed to have a route plotted ahead of time for when the time came.

Because it would come.

Baby was coming.

And I wasn't going anywhere. I wanted her too much to ever be able to walk away. I wanted *them*—so much. I'd actually never wanted anything more.

Now, I just needed to convince Gemma of that, too.

Counterproductive to my plans, I didn't see Gemma for the rest of the week.

I mean, I *saw* her, but she was always dashing in and out the door. All her free time was devoted to helping Juniper with the wedding this weekend, but even so—it felt like she was avoiding me. She'd spent the whole day with Juniper on Tuesday, not coming home until late, and even then, all she said about the appointment was that it was *good*.

To make matters worse, I had a Thursday night game in LA, where Grayson kicked my ass. If I had to suffer an embarrassing loss, I'd rather it be because one of my best friends was a goddamn legend over anything else, but still. I hated losing, and I hated being away from Gemma. I hated that she was working her ass off to prepare for the wedding, and I wasn't around to help. And because of my pissy mood, Jonesy had been on my ass all week about what was happening.

By the time I saw Gemma again, it was Juniper and Julian's wedding rehearsal. I walked into the hotel to see her wearing that blue dress, the same one she'd had on when we kissed for the first time, and I nearly lost my mind. I barely made it through dinner. The toasts, the celebration, the sight of Gemma in that blue dress —it was a whirlwind.

There was no way she hadn't done that on purpose. Fuck, what was she trying to do to me? My self-control was already so close to snapping, and then she had to show up in the one thing that would torture me until I was back in bed with my hand wrapped around my cock.

Since almost all my friends were married, I'd gotten my own room at the hotel where the ceremony and reception was the following day. We weren't that far from my apartment, but I wanted to be around in case of any last-minute wedding emergencies.

There weren't any. Which I supposed should be a good thing, but it left me alone to stew once everyone crashed. I stared at the ceiling in my room, contemplating if I should go find Gemma. But

I convinced myself that tonight wasn't the night. Tonight was for her, Juniper, and the other girls as they prepared for tomorrow's wedding.

But damn, it made for a lonely evening. One I probably deserved.

And one with little sleep, too.

The next morning, I helped Julian and the rest of the groomsmen set up the ceremony space. Julian was a terrifying ball of emotion, switching between barking orders and staring wistfully at his surroundings with a goofy, ridiculous smile.

After he'd given the okay, we returned to our rooms to shower and dress. And just as I was struggling with my tie, my brother called. I only had a few minutes before I had to meet Jules again, but Blake rarely called. So I answered, putting it on speaker as I fixed my tie and tried to get my hair to cooperate.

"What's up?"

"Hey, man," Blake answered. "Do you have a minute?"

"Just a couple," I said. "I have to finish getting ready for Julian's wedding."

"Oh, is that today?" Blake's surprise drifted into a chuckle. "Does he know that you're sleeping with his sister yet?"

I sighed, deciding it wasn't worth pretending. I never told Blake that Gemma and I were sleeping together, but if he wanted confirmation, I'd give it to him.

"He knows that I *was* sleeping with his sister."

"Was?" Blake repeated before I cut him off, ignoring the question in his voice.

"And do you know why he found out?"

"Uhh..." Blake sounded hesitant, like he wasn't sure he really wanted to know. "Why?"

"She was on TV. You were, too. At the Minnesota game. Julian saw it."

"Shit," Blake hissed, his low breath indicating he could probably guess how that conversation with Julian went.

But the conversation wasn't what I wanted to talk about.

"I went to find that clip, you know," I continued. "Of you and Gemma. Because I wanted to see what Julian saw when he watched the replay. And the two of you were *awfully* close. Care to share what you were so intent on talking about?"

To my immense irritation, Blake started to laugh. Of course he laughed.

"You," he answered between chuckles.

Oh, well, that explained why he was laughing. Because that answer was a fucking joke.

Giving up on my hair, I glared into the mirror, pretending I was glaring at my brother.

"Dissecting my plays, were you?"

"In a way," Blake admitted. "I was dissecting your plays at getting Gemma and realizing none of them had been successful."

God, he was annoying sometimes.

"It was obvious you weren't together, but it was equally obvious that you were both obsessed with each other," he added. "Which brought me to the conclusion that you must not have actually tried. You weren't making *any* plays."

"You don't understand," I grumbled.

"I don't," he said forcefully, going all big brother on me. "I really don't. Because Gemma watched you play that game with stars in her eyes. And not the kind of stars that other people look at you with. They were the kind that told me she'd still be looking at you like that even if you were winning a game at a community center and not a billion-dollar football stadium. She told me you were one of the best guys she's ever known and then looked at you like you hung the moon."

"*One* of the best?" I replied, choking past the emotion that his words evoked. If I didn't hold on to something other than pain, I didn't know how I'd make it through today. Even if it was jealousy.

Blake laughed again. "She said she was related to the other ones."

"I don't know what she's talking about...I'm definitely better

378

than Julian," I scoffed, letting a protective layer of sarcasm drip into my voice. And then something made me pause. "You asked? About the other guys?"

Blake was quiet for a second.

"I asked."

"Why?"

"Because I was scoping out your competition. And when I realized you didn't have competition, I wondered what the hell you were waiting for."

"Well, there's the fact that her brother is one of my best friends."

"That's not why."

I rolled my eyes as I fussed with my tie again. "What the fuck are you talking about?"

"You're not afraid of Julian," he said, exasperation filtering through the speaker. "I remember you telling me how you took the girl he's *in love with* out on a date just to mess with him. If you were afraid of Julian, you would never have even *talked* to his girl, let alone asked his sister to move in with you. You're not afraid of Julian."

I swallowed. Fuck, he was right. "I'm not afraid of Julian."

Weighty silence hung between us as Blake gave me a chance to come to terms with the real reason. The reason I already knew, and I'd been wrestling with all week.

"What if I'm not good at it?" I finally voiced, walking away from the mirror. Looking at myself wasn't helping right now.

"You'll be good at it." Blake paused. "And you'll be an even better dad."

My breath hitched. *Dad.*

"I don't want to be the guy who's never around and just acts like money can make up for not being there," I said, voice straining from all the emotion I was struggling to place. "I don't want to be that dad, that boyfriend, that son or brother."

"You're not," he insisted. "We know you're busy. But we know that you won't always be this busy. We know you try to come back when you can. And you make sacrifices to do it. You're a good brother, Noah." He sighed. "You're better than the rest of us, honestly. Because it shouldn't always be up to you. Planes fly both ways. I should be out there visiting you all more. In fact..."

"What?"

"Well, the reason I called you is actually because I have an interview."

"An interview?"

I wasn't making the connection.

"In Boston," he clarified. "I have an interview in Boston."

I froze, not sure I was hearing him correctly. "You're moving here?"

"If the hospital hires me, then...yeah. I guess I probably am."

"You work at the best hospital in the world," I said in disbelief.

Blake hadn't been able to shut up about his job when he first landed it. He was a cardiologist at the Mayo Clinic, a hospital widely regarded as one of *the* places to be a cardiologist.

He sighed again. "Well, Boston has something that Mayo can't offer me."

I wanted to ask what, but Blake kept talking.

"Do you think I could stay with you when I'm in town? The interview is at the end of this month."

"Of course," I said, still a little stunned.

"Great," he replied. "I look forward to seeing you and Gemma. I'll plan to stay two nights, so if you need help building a crib, I'll have time."

"Blake—"

"Have fun with the wedding!" he interrupted before promptly hanging up.

Goddamn him.

He sometimes drove me to my wits' end, but I still smiled as I straightened my tie, left the hotel room, and walked down the hallway. As much as I wanted to sift through my thoughts, now wasn't the time to try to parse out everything Blake had said, not when I had a groom to rein in.

Julian's voice could probably be heard throughout the entire hotel.

"Open the door, Gemma!"

I rounded the corner to find Julian glaring at a door, looking like he was trying to set it on fire.

"Why?" Gemma's voice filtered through the wood, and my smile grew.

"Because I want to see my wife," Julian grunted.

"She's not your wife yet," Gemma yelled back, and Julian's frown deepened as he let his forehead drop against the door.

"Just open the fucking door, Gemma," Julian groaned, and I shook my head with a laugh. It was unbelievable that for *years*, Julian really thought he would successfully live his life without giving in to loving Juniper.

Then again, I'd learned recently denial was a bitch.

"No, she's still getting ready." Gemma cracked the door open, peering out to glare at Julian. And just that tiniest glimpse of her made my heart skip. "You can see her at the first look."

"I'm impatient."

Julian gave the door a little push. It looked harmless, but then Juniper's voice called, "Careful! You'll hurt the maid of honor if you're not careful, Jules."

That had my steps quickening.

"I don't care if it's your wedding day," I snapped, sliding in beside Julian. "If you knock over your pregnant sister, I will kick your goddamn ass."

There was a pause while Julian raised his brows, smiling knowingly at me. He was annoying today. Did we really have to celebrate him?

"Noah, come in here!" Juniper shouted, and Julian's expression dropped, irritation washing over him. "I need to talk to you."

Julian glared at the door. "You're going to let him in and not me?"

"Yep, that would be correct," Juni answered, and Julian cursed under his breath.

I couldn't help but laugh as Julian regretfully stepped back to let me slip into the bridal suite. I paused in the doorway, awestruck at seeing Gemma in her flowery bridesmaid dress, and she had to grab my tie and yank me further into the room so she could close the door and keep Julian from sneaking in behind me.

That little tug on my tie did things to my cock. She could yank me around as much as she wanted. In our bed. Later. Hopefully soon. Really soon. Because I couldn't do this thing we were doing for much longer. I needed her badly.

Gemma stepped back, but then she froze, too. I wasn't sure what made her still or what she was looking at, but I was looking at her. She was breathtaking. The flowery dress fell to the floor, the fabric soft as it framed her curves. She looked like a Grecian goddess. Like someone should get her a halo because she was a goddamn angel. *Fuck, baby.*

I wanted to immediately request a re-order in the lineup for the ceremony today because I didn't want anyone else walking down the aisle with her. I didn't want anyone touching her. I didn't want anyone looking at her. I wanted her to be mine. All fucking mine.

I wasn't sure how long I stared at Gemma before someone cleared their throat.

"What's up?" I said as I dragged my gaze away from Gemma and faced Juniper. She sat in front of a mirror with a smile on her face and a white robe tied around her waist, her hairdresser standing at her side as she curled her golden-brown hair into waves.

"I was wondering if you could do me a huge favor," Juniper said as I walked toward her. "I left Julian's present in my car, and—"

A banging at the door interrupted her, and she sighed. "Gemma, can you go keep Julian company so he doesn't cause damage to the property?"

Gemma shook her head with a roll of her eyes but went into the hallway anyway. I felt the minute her presence disappeared, and then I heard her banter pick up with Julian on the other side of the door.

"Look, I can tell Gemma isn't feeling great today," Juniper said as soon as Gemma was gone.

My stomach dropped as panic rose. "What do you mean? What's wrong? Is it the baby? Do I need to take her to the—"

"No, no," Juniper rushed to wave all my worries away. She looked panicked that she'd made *me* panic. "She's fine. She's totally fine. Just feeling a little uncomfortable in her own skin, I think. I can only imagine carrying another life inside you would do that."

"I think she looks beautiful," I said honestly, staring at the door where she disappeared. "She looks beautiful carrying that little life. I wouldn't change anything about her, except for that baby to be—"

I bit down on my tongue before I could say *mine*.

I'd never said that aloud.

Juniper lowered her voice, understanding filling it. "You might not biologically be that baby's father, but you've supported Gemma in a hundred ways he hasn't. Thank you for that."

I slowly turned to meet her gaze again and gave a brief nod to acknowledge what she said. If I spoke, I might lose it.

"She can't tell you," Juniper added thoughtfully.

I cocked my head to the side. *What?*

Juniper's brown eyes bored into mine. "Gemma rarely asks anyone for anything."

A humorless laugh slipped from me. "Trust me, I know."

"I'm sure you do. I'm sure she didn't even ask you to so much as hold her hand at her doctor's appointment, even though I'm sure she needed it."

I shook my head because she was damn right about that.

"How was the appointment this week?" I asked, desperate to know.

Juniper gave me this sort of sad, knowing smile. "You should ask Gemma about it."

"I did, but she's been busy this week. Busy avoiding me."

It sounded petty, but I didn't care. I missed her so goddamn much.

"Noah..." Juni sighed. "She can't be around you because she can't tell you what you want to hear. She can't tell you what she wants to tell you. Because then she'd be *asking* you for a whole lot. *Way* more than hand-holding at doctor's appointments, and she can't even do that."

"But I want to give her all of it," I admitted, feeling raw and exhausted. "I want to give her everything. Way more than hand-holding at doctor's appointments."

Juniper smiled. And it wasn't sad anymore. "Then tell her."

It sounded so simple, but the idea made my breath hitch. "I plan on it. After the wedding."

Juni cocked her head to the side. "Why wait?"

I thought that would be obvious. "Because it's your wedding day, Juniper. She's busy. It's not a good—"

"I want my best friend to be happy on my wedding day," Juniper said calmly. "And right now, she isn't. Not the way I know she could be. Besides, she's all ready. She was the first one to get her hair and makeup done. She's just waiting around for everyone else."

My heart skipped a beat at Juniper's words, at her implication. More than one beat. So many beats. So many that it had to be dangerous, right? This wildness in my chest had to mean this was a bad idea, but the thought of telling Gemma everything felt *so right*.

The thought of having Gemma felt so right.

The thought of having that baby felt so right.

So unbelievably right.

But more than anything, the idea of Gemma being unhappy wrecked me inside. And if Juniper thought I could change that... I'd risk it all.

I spun on my heel, taking off before remembering why Juniper asked me to come in here in the first place. I twisted back around, breathless.

"You needed Julian's present?"

Juni shook her head. "I have the present." A sly grin worked onto her face. "Go find Gemma."

She didn't have to tell me twice.

CHAPTER THIRTY-FOUR

noah

I FOUND GEMMA on the roof.

Julian pointed me in the right direction, which only reaffirmed I was making the right choice. The only choice I *could* make at this point.

Gemma stood beneath the glass panels of a greenhouse that the hotel had converted into a rooftop bar, and tonight, it was where Juniper and Julian would be getting married. I wasn't sure how they found this place, but it was hard to deny the magic that lingered here, an oasis amidst a concrete jungle. Strings of floating lights lined a path they'd walk down, and I followed it, looking for my own loves.

Gemma walked up and down the aisles of chairs, straightening them unnecessarily. Everything was already perfect, even though there were several hours until the ceremony still.

Julian and Juniper wanted to get married at night.

She moved with grace and ease, reminding me once again of something—or someone—unearthly, heavenly. The flowers surrounding her matched the late-fall landscape, blossoms of deep red and burnt orange. The glowing petals highlighted her curled hair, which flowed around her shoulders like a gorgeous curtain.

My heart caught in my throat. The chill in the air had nothing on the chill that ran down my spine when I looked at her.

This wasn't attraction. This emotion I felt when I looked at Gemma Briggs...it wasn't just attraction. I wasn't sure when it had become so much more, when it had blossomed into this unnerving need to be near her all the time, to care for her, to protect her, but I knew it wouldn't be fading anytime soon.

And I couldn't hold back telling her any longer.

"Hi, Em."

She stilled at the sound of my voice, of her name that was just for me. Her head lifted slowly. She moved like she half expected it to be a dream, like I wouldn't really be here when she looked in my direction.

But I was here.

I'd always be here.

Her breath visibly hitched when her eyes landed on me.

"Noah," she whispered.

Her voice lilted at the end of my name, though. A question lingered there. She wanted to know what I was doing here. I wanted to know why she thought I'd be anywhere else.

I walked toward her. It took everything in me to take it slow when all I wanted to do was run to her. But the torture of the last couple of weeks had been my fault. She was the one who was pregnant and scared, and yeah, maybe she'd said some things that had triggered my insecurities and doubts, but I never should have let that keep me from seeing the truth.

Now, I had some making up to do. And I wasn't going to rush it.

Gemma watched me approach with curiosity and anticipation in her eyes. Vines curled up the walls of the glassy greenhouse, and I ran my fingers over them as I strode toward her, weaving between skinny tables overflowing with potted flowers.

"How long do you think it took for all of this to grow?" I asked softly.

She laughed, and nerves coated the pretty sound. "That's more of a Juniper question."

I nodded. I didn't really need to know the answer to that. I was much more interested in other things that were growing. Like the feelings I got whenever I looked at her. And that little bump she carried, the one I was falling in love with, too. And us...just us. But before I could talk about any of that, I needed to clarify how goddamn regretful I was.

"I'm sorry."

She cocked her head to the side, and I shoved my hands into the pockets of my dress pants.

"I'm sorry it took me so long to wake up and grow into the kind of man you deserve. But I'm here now, hoping it isn't too late."

She started to shake her head, so I cut her off with honesty.

"I hate that you didn't feel like you could ask me for more and I'd give it to you. All I want is to give you the world. I want to be that man. I've been learning how to be that man. Especially over the last couple of weeks, Em. Because not being with you has been destroying me."

Everything I was about to say would be coated in honesty, no matter what. If she rejected me, then so be it. But I couldn't hold anything in anymore.

My feet had stopped moving. It hurt not to close the distance between us, but even though I'd touched every inch of her in the past month, I felt like somewhere in the last week, I lost permission to be the one who got to hold her. God, I wanted it back.

"I should have set things straight long ago," I admitted hoarsely. "We're not friends, Gemma. With benefits, without benefits—it doesn't matter. We're not friends. We never were, and we never will be. I don't care about you like a friend. I don't think about you like a friend. Never have."

Gemma looked at me, her eyes watery. "I know that now. But I didn't know what to think," she said in a small voice. "You looked me in the eyes that night in the fort and told me you didn't date.

And I wanted you in whatever way I could have you, even if you didn't want to date me or be with me. Even if you didn't want me like that."

It hurt to swallow. Emotion scraped my throat with every breath. The fact that she'd been walking around thinking I didn't *want* her? Fuck, that killed me.

"I said that I wasn't the kind of guy girls date," I acknowledged because I knew it was true. "But I'd like to change that. I want to be that guy, Em, because I want you like that. I want you like that so fucking bad."

Her eyes grew round and wide, big blue windows into the prettiest soul I'd ever seen. Her lips parted, but several heavy moments passed before she managed to slip my name out of her mouth.

"Noah..."

"Ask me," I said, daring to take one step toward her. "I want you to know that you can ask me for anything, Gemma. From now on, anything you ask for—it's yours. Ask me."

"I can't," she choked out.

"You can't? Or you don't want to?"

"I can't," she repeated.

"Why not?"

I knew why, especially after that conversation with Juniper, but I needed her to say it so I could make my feelings on the matter clear.

"I told you. I'm so much...*more*, Noah. I can't just ask you to be with *me*," she whispered. "It's not just me."

I nodded reassuringly. "I know. And I still want you to ask me."

"Do you know?" she asked, wrapping her arms around herself. She looked like she needed the biggest hug, and I couldn't wait to give it to her. "Do you know how big that is?"

"I know exactly how big it is." My eyes found hers, and I prayed she'd be able to see everything in my gaze. How much I meant that, this, everything. "Now, ask me."

She sucked in, squeezing herself tighter. "Are you sure?"

"Goddamnit, Gemma." I raked a hand through my hair, starting to feel desperate. She couldn't see it. She couldn't see it, and I needed her to understand. "I'm sure, angel. I'm so fucking sure. And do you want to know why?"

She nodded, and I let my arm drop back to my side and pleaded with my eyes for her to see the truth as I said it.

"Em...I'm in love with you. I'm so desperately in love with you. You, and every part of you. *Every* part. And while, believe me, I'm utterly terrified and more scared than I ever have been in my entire life, I've also never been more sure of anything. I love you so goddamn much. Now, *ask me.*"

Gemma's breath hitched as her arms loosened around her, slowly falling to her sides. We stood there like mirrors, only feet apart. And I waited for what felt like an eternity as I watched tears well in the lashes of Gemma's eyes.

Her lips started to spread, and it was the slowest, most agonizing smile I'd ever experienced. But even as she smiled at me, she stayed silent, cocking her head to the side as though assessing me and my words.

"If you ask me if I'm sure that I love you, I swear to God, I'm going to lose it," I rasped. "That's not what I want you to ask."

She shook her head, copper curls bouncing around her face. "I know it's not," she said, a laugh hiccuping out of her.

She better know.

"Okay," she began, pausing to wipe away the tears that had started to fall even as she grinned. Meanwhile, I held my breath, waiting to hear more. "Noah, do you..." Her words caught in her throat, and she had to clear it before continuing. "Do you think we could be more? More than roommates and more than friends? Because that's...that's what I want, too. I want it so, so bad."

"Fuck being friends," I grunted. "I dare you to call me your friend one more time and see what happens."

Another laugh escaped her. Her obvious happiness brought my own smile out. It crept over my face until it was hard to contain. I couldn't hold anything in anymore, and my feet started moving, unable to stay still. Gemma's eyes sparkled as I closed the distance between us, welcoming me back.

"I wouldn't dare me if I were you," she giggled. "I'm way too curious for that."

I rolled my eyes. "Shut up," I whispered, slipping my arm around her waist and tugging her into me. She flew into my chest in a way that felt so right, her hands automatically snaking around my neck. God, it felt amazing. This felt amazing.

"Make me," she whispered back, tipping her head back to look up at me.

I grinned, more than happy to give her what she wanted, slamming my lips to hers.

Gemma immediately groaned my name, sending more shivers down my spine, and I melted into her. Fuck, I'd missed this. The feel of her, the taste of her, the sounds she made. Everything. It hadn't even been that long, but I'd missed her so much.

"We can be more, baby," I breathed against her lips. "We can be everything."

"Good because I love you," she whispered. "More than I even understand. I'm so in love with you, Noah."

I groaned, kissing her harder as a wave of euphoria nearly knocked me over. The only thing keeping me grounded was her—her lips on mine, her arms around me, her body against my chest. God, what was she doing to me? I'd dreamed of Gemma millions of times, but I never dreamed I'd hear her say that.

And now I needed to hear her repeat it.

I ripped my lips from hers. "You *what*?"

She looked up at me with shining eyes. "I love you, Noah. Stop acting surprised. I've *been* in love with you. I was just too afraid to admit it. Even to myself. Because I thought—"

She clamped her mouth shut, and I felt like I was suddenly sifting through an ocean of guilt.

"I should have made sure you knew," I said, hoping she heard the sincerity in my voice. I pulled back, tucking a lock of hair behind her ear. "All those times when I told you how much I wanted you, I meant I wanted *you*. More specifically, I want to be *with* you. It was never just sex. Not for me, Gemma. And if I'm honest..."

I paused, not wanting to ruin this moment.

"I want you to be honest," Gemma said earnestly.

I sighed. "It hurt, Em. It hurt that you expected so little of me when it came down to it. It felt like you didn't think I was good enough to give you more. Like I wasn't good enough for all the parts of you." I let my hand drop, curving down her sides, my fingers lingering over her bump.

Her jaw half dropped, and her eyes traced my face, her pain evident in them. "Never. Oh, Noah. *Never.*"

My heart leaped into my throat as Gemma slipped her hand beneath my suit coat, placing it on my chest.

"I've never thought of you the way you think of yourself," she said, her words strong. "When I look at you, all I see is the best man I'll ever know. You are the best man I have ever known, Noah. And for that reason, I wanted you to know you didn't owe me anything. The last thing I wanted was for you to commit to me because you felt you had to. Or before you were ready. To give me more because you felt guilty or responsible or pitied me instead of—"

"I don't pity you, Gemma," I interrupted with a frown. "I know you don't need me or any man."

"But I want you," she whispered. "I want to be *with* you. And I just needed to know it was what *you* wanted, too."

"I promise I want that, too. I really do, Em. The next few months will be busy, and I'll have football getting in the way of us, but—"

"I don't think it'll get in the way," she insisted. Because she knew me so well, and she knew what I was worried about. "It hasn't gotten in the way so far. And I can come to more of your games and events. I think as long as I can be with you, I'd fly anywhere."

I raised a brow. "You don't have to fly for me, baby."

"I want to," she whispered. "I want to try. If you want me with you, that is."

I nodded, covering her hand with mine. "Fuck, of course I do. I've hated leaving you. All season long, I've hated it. I miss you so goddamn much when I have away games."

Gemma's eyes widened as though she'd never realized, and I knew I had so much I needed to tell her, so many words and thoughts and feelings I'd kept to myself over the last few months. And she needed to know everything now.

"I fell in love with football because it was the one thing I was good at," I said honestly. "It felt like everyone else in my family was good at things I didn't even begin to understand, but damn, I could throw a football. So I held on to that, the feeling of being useful at something, and for a time, I *only* focused on that. I distanced myself from everything else—all those other things I felt useless at. And then, at some point, people started looking at me like I was one-dimensional."

Gemma's expression started crumbling, but I wasn't done. I hadn't said the most important thing yet.

"I started to believe it, too," I admitted. "That football was all I was good at. But I think I could become a man who is damn good at loving you, too."

"I don't think you need to become anything." She cupped my face with her free hand, forcing me to see her conviction. "I think you're already that man, Noah. I think you always have been. You're a good player but an even better person. An amazing brother, son, and friend."

My breath momentarily caught in my throat. "What about boyfriend?"

I wanted a hell of a lot more than that, but it would work for now.

She grinned, letting her fingers slide off my cheek and wrapping her arm around my neck again. "That, too."

And then, just to make matters incredibly clear, I added, "You're not moving out."

Her brows rose, and I interrupted before she could question it —me—again.

"I'm serious, Gemma. You're not selling your mugs. You're not looking for a new place. You're not moving out."

"I'm pregnant," she said pointedly, as if she thought I didn't fucking know that. "There's a baby coming."

I looked at her and said what I did when she sat in my bathtub that morning. "I know." I leaned down to deliver a soft kiss before murmuring against her lips. "And once we move into the same bedroom, we'll have more than enough space for our nursery. I've been researching cribs, and I've narrowed it down to three that are highly rated, but if there's a different one you want, I—"

"Noah. You *what*?" I felt her soft gasp against my mouth and kissed her again to interrupt any possible argument. Except this time, I got a little carried away, dragging my tongue along the seam of her lips until she let me in to taste her. It made it impossible to pull away, but I knew I had to. Because I knew I had to make sure she knew how serious I was.

"I'm well aware you're a two-for-one deal," I said when we came up for air. "But that sounds like the best fucking deal I've ever heard."

Gemma leaned back, clearly stunned. Her hand slipped from mine, moving to cover her mouth.

"Are you sure?"

"I told you not to ask me that," I groaned, knocking her hand away. I refused to allow any space or anything between us, chasing her lips back down to nip at them. "I'm sure, angel. And if you even think about going to one more doctor's appointment without me, I'm going to lose my goddamn mind."

She bit down on a tiny but sad smile. "I love Juniper, but it just wasn't the same without you this week."

I slid my hand between us until I found the gentle swell of her belly again. I spread my palm over it like I'd done so many other times. Except this time, I fully accepted the possession that'd been growing within me.

Mine.

I didn't say it yet because, ultimately, it was Gemma's decision what role she wanted me to play in her child's life. But if she gave me a chance, I'd love this baby like it was my own.

"I want you to tell me everything I missed," I said. "And I mean *everything*."

She nodded as she leaned into me, her body molding to mine. "Can I tell you later? I think we've talked enough for now."

Perfect. She was so perfect.

"Yes—"

Gemma didn't wait for me to say more before she tugged me down for another gravity-defying kiss that made me feel like I was floating. She groaned into my mouth as she took control, sneaking her tongue into my mouth, teasing me in a way I wasn't sure I could handle right now. But it was the best kiss of my life, and I didn't know how to stop it, either.

"Gemma," I moaned, desperately needing more. Without breaking our kiss, I walked her backward until her ass hit the edge of a table. Then I gripped her waist and lifted her on top of it, sitting her in an empty space between potted flowers and winding vines and stepping between her legs. She wrapped them around my hips, pulling me closer, and I couldn't resist leaning in to feel all of her. "*Fuck*, baby."

As if I wasn't already losing it, Gemma started running her hands all over me, letting her fingers explore my body as if she'd forgotten what I felt like. And all the while, our lips remained locked in a heated, fierce kiss that I never wanted to end.

"You look *so* good in this suit," Gemma gasped into my mouth, tugging on the lapels of my black suit coat. "So good that I want to rip it off you."

"Funny," I muttered, smoothing my hand up her body until

my fingers flirted with her cleavage. "That's kinda how I feel about this dress, gorgeous girl."

"Do it," Gemma encouraged, and that's how I knew she was just as lost as me. She had to know that if I ruined her maid of honor dress for her best friend and brother's wedding, we'd both get an earful. And Gemma would never do anything that might jeopardize this important day.

"Later," I chuckled, reluctantly breaking our kiss. Gemma immediately pouted at the loss of my lips, so I decided to taste her neck instead, nibbling up to find her ear. "Later, I promise."

"But I need you," she whimpered, knowing I struggled to resist her.

Fuck me.

"Gemma, please," I growled into the crook of her neck. "You know I want to fuck you right now, so hard that you scream my name while I fill you up. I want to watch you walk down that aisle later while my cum drips from your cunt beneath this pretty dress. But you know what I want even more than that? To watch you spend the rest of the night thinking about what it's going to feel like when I slide inside you again. I want to know that you're getting wetter and wetter for me until I get you alone again."

"I think we can make both things happen," Gemma gasped, arching against me.

Fuck, I forgot how insatiable she was.

Reluctantly, I stepped back, forcing my feet to move. Gemma glared at me until her eyes dropped to my prominent erection, and then she couldn't help but smirk, looking awfully satisfied with herself.

I raked my hand through my hair, taking a steadying breath. "I'm not afraid of Julian, but I do respect him enough not to fuck his sister before his wedding ceremony and have both of us show up looking like a mess for the photos in a bit."

To my surprise, Gemma's lips tipped up. "See?" Her grin grew. "The best man I've ever known."

396

I raised one brow. "Don't expect me to be such a gentleman later tonight."

Gemma grabbed my tie, using the leverage to pull herself off the table of flowers. She grinned seductively, and I wondered how the hell I was going to make it through my friend's wedding while I tried to hide a hard-on for his sister.

"I can't wait," Gemma whispered.

I couldn't, either.

eight years ago
GEMMA

Silent communication passed between Noah and Julian, and I suspected I knew what it was. Especially since Noah took another step back, giving me space.

I almost frowned before I caught myself.

I didn't need either of them to know how weirdly attached I'd gotten to someone I'd just met. Or how much I could feel the distance he just put between us.

I couldn't help but feel...let down.

Maybe eventually, I'd have the confidence to go for what I wanted, but it wasn't today.

Today, I'd let the butterflies he gave me go and hope that someday I'd see them again.

CHAPTER THIRTY-FIVE

TODAY HAD TO be the best day of my life.

Ironically, it had to be the best day of my brother and best friend's life, too. Or the best night, rather. The inky sky bled through the glass greenhouse ceiling as dusk turned to night, and the moon popped out, full and bright.

Regardless, paying attention to the nuptials was incredibly hard when my mind was racing from my conversation with Noah. I kept replaying everything he said, still struggling to fully believe it all.

Swallowing past the lump in my throat, I watched my brother and best friend exchange their wedding vows. I knew we'd be here one day, but that didn't make it any less astounding to see it actually happen, and I was so unbelievably happy for them.

When the newlywed couple took off down the aisle for the recessional, I linked arms with Grayson before following them. A second later, I felt Noah's eyes on my back as he and Sofia followed us.

How? How was I supposed to make it through the rest of the night feeling his hot gaze like that?

I shook my head, knowing I needed to focus on Juniper and Julian. For crying out loud, my brother just married my best friend. I shouldn't be thinking about Noah or anything that wasn't making this wedding the best one ever.

But then again, the couple in question didn't bother to slow their pace on their way down the aisle, instead immediately disappearing back into the hotel.

Of course.

"Did we already lose the bride and groom?" Noah asked, pulling up next to me with Sofia in tow.

"Where did they go?" Gianna questioned as soon as she walked up with Cameron.

"I don't think we want to know," I laughed as I felt Noah's arm wrap around me. His fingers danced across my back until settling on my hip, causing heat to hurtle through my body. We hadn't talked about whether or not we would be public with our relationship tonight, but apparently, Noah had made his mind up about that.

Not that I minded.

Gianna clapped a hand over her mouth when she realized what Noah had done. Very non-discreet, too. Then Genevieve did the same when she walked up, and then the rest of my sisters surrounded us a moment later. And all of them, every single one, were looking at Noah and me, passing intuitive looks between them.

They hadn't been entirely surprised when I told them about Noah and our situation. I guess Noah and I had *not* been subtle at the bachelorette party, and Julian was the only person who really didn't notice anything. And that was only because he'd been glued to Juniper all night.

My sisters *had* been surprised about the pregnancy, though. But instead of pity, shock, or disgrace like I'd worried, the surprise was filled with a happiness I hadn't expected. Joy. Excitement. Gushing. Definitely some swearing at Silas Taylor, but also this all-encompassing love for their future niece or nephew. We still weren't sure which it would be because, as it turned out, I just...

hadn't been ready to know yet. There had been something missing at my last appointment.

Or someone.

Ultimately, my sisters knew I wanted to be a mom, and while this wasn't the traditional way to go about it, they were still happy for me. And I'd needed that. I really had.

Meanwhile, Noah didn't back down from the sudden attention. His hand remained on my hip, and I could feel it inching toward my stomach, which filled with butterflies at his touch. This man really did want to lay claim to this baby, didn't he? It was hard to wrap my head around it, but it was true, and my heart felt like it would thump right out of my chest.

I smiled at my sisters, a confirmation smile, and then let Noah lead me into the hotel before the crush of guests filed out of the greenhouse.

"I'm sorry," Noah muttered as we made our way to the reception hall on the hotel's main level. "I'm just so done hiding the fact that you're mine. God, I'm so excited that I get to hold you in public now. And spoil you whenever I fucking want."

I gave him a warning look. "Noah, you already spoil me."

He threw his head back and laughed before opening the door to the reception hall for me. "No, I've taken care of you, and I think I've treated you well, but I have *not* spoiled you." I walked through the door, and he followed, raising a brow in curiosity. "Your old apartment was in the suburbs, and you liked it better than living in the city, didn't you?"

I shook my head, even though he was partly right. I'd never loved city life, but it had grown on me recently. "I don't know what you're thinking, but stop."

"A house in the suburbs would have room for Winnie to play," Noah continued. "And Baby."

My heart flew into my throat, but I knew this conversation was ridiculous. We'd been dating for all of a few hours.

"Noah, I know you love your apartment. We do *not* have to move."

"I do love it," he replied honestly. "Which is why I'm not *really* proposing moving."

My brows furrowed. "What are you proposing, then?"

"Buying you a house. *Us* a house. A second residence," he said flippantly. "Thought that was obvious."

"Oh my God," I started before I saw my dad walking toward us and immediately zipped my lips. I'd deal with Noah and his excessive spoiling later.

My parents' reaction to the news about the pregnancy had been different from anyone else's. John Briggs was quiet after I spilled the truth. So was my mom. Too shocked for words. Eventually, my dad nodded, cleared his throat, and asked a few calm, logistical questions. One of which was if I wanted to move home.

It had been tempting; I couldn't lie. More tempting than living with Julian and Juniper or any of my sisters when they'd asked. My parents knew how to care for a baby and raise a child. They'd done it six times. But returning home felt like stepping backward just when I'd started to feel more comfortable moving forward. Besides, it would mean finding yet another new job.

"Now I know why I saw my daughter in the stands of a Minnesota game on TV."

My dad sauntered the rest of the way toward us, one hand in his pocket as he grew a half-smile. He put his other hand out to greet Noah, and my new boyfriend took it with ease, all while keeping his grip on me intact.

I should have known my dad would have seen me on TV, too.

"Considering we destroyed Minnesota in the endzone, I'd call that game a Knights' game, sir."

"You're right," my dad chuckled before releasing Noah's hand. "And I've told you before to call me John. That doesn't change now that you're dating my daughter." I lifted my brow in surprise, and my dad noticed, adding, "That *is* what's happening, isn't it?"

"Yeah, Dad," I said with a light laugh. "That's what's happening."

My dad nodded, satisfaction coating his features. "Good."

I glanced over at Noah, and I could see his expression relax. I hadn't even considered that he might be nervous about my dad's reaction. Maybe he'd thought my dad would disapprove, considering his reputation.

But my dad had always liked Noah. He talked about him all the time when we watched Knights games together, about how, out of all of Julian's friends, Noah was one of his favorites. I assumed it was just because Noah played for my dad's favorite NFL team or because Noah liked to talk shop about his motorcycle with my dad, but either way, he'd never said a bad thing about him.

And I suspected Noah needed to hear my dad say that. Needed to hear him say *good*.

"She doesn't want to move home," my dad continued, "so take care of her when she's being stubborn, okay?"

I started to roll my eyes, but Noah's smooth voice stopped me.

"I'll take care of both of them, John."

Both of them.

"Good." If my dad sounded satisfied before, it was nothing compared to how assured he sounded now. "Now, I think you kids have to get lined up for that grand entrance or whatever they call it."

Noah glanced at his watch and nodded, a smile playing on his lips. "You're right. Let's go, Em."

He started to tug me back toward the reception hall entrance, but before I turned around completely, I caught my dad's eye and smiled. Wordlessly, he grinned back.

I walked out of the elegantly decorated, floral-covered reception hall to run straight into Juniper.

Juniper looking like she'd been freshly fucked.

By my brother.

"Oh my God, Juni," I groaned.

"What?" Juniper looked alarmed as she faced me, like she really had no idea what I was talking about.

I glared at Julian, whose satisfied smirk made me want to gag. "Really? You couldn't have waited until after dinner?"

He shrugged. "My wife was asking for it."

"Julian!" Both Juniper and Janie hissed his name simultaneously.

I shook my head, struggling not to smile, even though my brother was absolutely ridiculous. "Come on, Junes," I said, grabbing her hand. "Let's go fix your hair."

Julian tried to intervene. "I can do that—"

"No." I whirled on him, shaking a finger in his face. "You're not allowed alone with your wife again until *at least* after dinner. Otherwise, we'll never make it to the first dance."

My scowl did nothing to Julian's grin. Which I supposed was good. I was happy he was happy.

"Hurry up," Noah whispered in my ear before brushing a soft kiss against my skin. A delicious shiver wracked my body. "I'll go tell the DJ to wait a few minutes."

Noah's proximity made my stomach flip, but my attention was on my brother, watching as his expression morphed, his brows lifting straight into his hairline. And if I wasn't mistaken, his smile widened just a hair.

"London," Julian called before Noah could leave on his errand. I felt him still behind me.

"Anything you're about to say, I already know. The threats aren't necessary. Trust me," Noah said over my shoulder.

Julian cocked his head to the side. "I was just going to say I'm proud of you."

Noah was silent except for a quick intake of breath. Then, he cleared his throat. But before he could reply, Julian added lightly, "But also, I'm going to kick your ass if you hurt her."

"Oh, shut up." I could *hear* Noah roll his eyes. But I also heard amusement. Happiness. "I'm not going to, and you know it. Now, excuse me while I go tell the DJ to wait for my girlfriend to fix your wife's hair."

Noah disappeared back into the reception hall, and I started tugging Juniper away, ready to answer her million questions about what had happened in the last few hours.

As we passed Julian, I saw him mouthing the word Noah had just said.

Wife.

Meanwhile, I was stuck on the other word.

Girlfriend.

Yeah, tonight really was the very best night.

And the best part was that it was far from over.

The feeling of Noah's touch lingering on my skin and his promises from earlier were a hot, heart-thumping reminder of that.

CHAPTER THIRTY-SIX

A FTER A LONG night of celebrating and struggling to keep our hands off each other, Noah and I stumbled into his hotel room in the early morning hours. We kicked off our shoes as we entered, and then, as soon as the door slammed behind us, Noah's lips were on mine. And *God*, did they feel good.

"Do you know—" He panted the words between kisses. "How hard—" A nip at my bottom lip. "It is to control myself—" His tongue flicked inside my mouth. "Around you?"

I nodded absently before throwing my arms around his neck and deepening the kiss. I did know. I had an excellent idea because, for the whole night, I'd struggled not to throw myself at Noah every time he so much as looked at me. And then the dance started, and Noah's hands were on me, and I started counting down the minutes until we were alone again.

"At least we didn't have to pretend," I gasped against his lips.

"No, but I definitely had to pretend I wasn't thinking about what you look like under that dress." Noah's hands slid down my back to my ass. "Do you know how many times I almost smacked this in front of your dad?"

He demonstrated, smacking my ass with enough force to make the ache grow between my legs. I moaned into his mouth, feeling my knees buckle with the weight of wanting him. *Needing* him.

"Noah, please," I begged. "Don't make me wait any longer."

"Oh, *baby*," he groaned. "I'm sorry I made you wait at all. Fuck, I've missed you."

"I've missed you, too," I whispered before abruptly pushing Noah back on the bed.

I missed him, and I wanted him. Now.

Noah looked momentarily stunned as he bounced onto the mattress, but then his eyes blazed with a surge of heat and arousal. He smirked at me while loosening his tie.

What. A. Sight.

I could get used to seeing Noah London in a suit.

I could also get used to seeing Noah London take *off* a suit, and Noah's mind seemed to be in a similar place as mine.

"You gonna take that off for me?" he asked, his gaze raking down my body. "You're drop-dead gorgeous in that dress, but I know you'll look even better once it's on the floor."

"You want it off?" I asked, cocking my head to the side as I found the zipper on the side seam of the dress.

Noah leaned forward, watching me with eager interest. "Badly."

"How badly?"

"Name your price. I'll gladly pay it."

"I don't want your money, Noah."

He'd never insinuated that I did, but I might as well clear that up now, especially with all his talk earlier of spoiling me. His money had never played any role in my interest in him.

"I know you don't." He grinned knowingly. "So tell me, Em. What's the price?"

"Undress for me first."

Noah grinned sexily as he slotted his finger into the knot of his tie and undid it, yanking on one end until it snaked out of his collar. He tossed it to the ground, and I gave him a once-over.

"You're not gonna need that tonight?" I questioned. The last time we'd been together had been burned into my brain for eternity. My hands tied above my head, the mirror, the trust.

"Not tonight, angel," he murmured, shrugging off his suit jacket. I could tell by how he looked at me that he remembered our last time, too. "I need your hands touching me tonight. I've been deprived of them."

"I'll touch you wherever you want, Noah. I'll do anything you want."

His throat worked as he swallowed. "Be careful what you say, Em."

"I mean it."

"So many fantasies," he husked, his fingers slowly moving down his shirt, undoing one button at a time. "I have so many fantasies of you we still haven't played out."

"Which fantasy are we doing tonight?" I asked, watching as he stripped his shirt off completely, exposing his muscled chest and tattooed forearms.

"I want you on top of me," he answered automatically, unbuckling his belt. He whipped it out and threw it to the ground with the rest of his clothes. "It seems so simple, but we haven't done it. There was a moment in time there when I thought I was going to have to live the rest of my life without getting to see you ride my cock."

"We can't have that," I said, my breath hitching as Noah unbuttoned his pants and slid them off, dropping his underwear to the ground in the same movement. Then he leaned back on the bed, naked and proudly aroused. I couldn't help but stare at his erection, noting just *how* hard he was for me.

"No, we can't," Noah agreed, his voice silky soft. "I need to see you on top of me. I really, *really* need it."

I stepped toward him, my body shaking at his words, images filling my head. Images I desperately wanted to create in real life.

"Take the dress off," Noah commanded. "Now. Or I'm ripping it."

"Hey," I protested, refocusing on the zipper on the side seam of my gown. "This dress was expensive."

Noah's lips twitched. "Your boyfriend's worth eight figures. I wouldn't worry about it."

My mouth ran dry at the idea of that much money, but I refused to give him the satisfaction of shocking me.

"Not quite a billionaire yet, Mr. London?" I tsked.

He shook his head with a throaty chuckle, but then his slight smile faded into a look of concentration as I slipped the strap of my dress off my shoulder and let the fabric fall to the floor. It pooled around my feet, and a muscle twitched in Noah's jaw as he realized that I hadn't been wearing anything underneath the dress all night. It had been tailored well enough that I hadn't needed to. Plus, the last thing I wanted was for my underwear lines to show in all the photos.

"You were naked under that?" he choked.

"Naked and wet," I said with a flirty grin.

He shook his head, his smile growing to match mine. "Good girl. Now, get over here so I can feel *how* wet."

He didn't have to ask me twice. Taking two steps forward, I slid onto his lap, straddling him as he sat on the edge of the bed. His hard cock rutted between my legs, and I immediately started shamelessly grinding against it. God *yes*, this—I'd needed this. Noah's hands molded to my waist, encouraging my movements before he curved them to my front and cupped my breasts.

"Missed these," he murmured before smoothing one hand down my stomach and slipping it between my legs. "And I definitely missed this."

Our combined groans echoed off the four walls of the boutique hotel room as Noah's fingers slid easily through my wet pussy. There was no resistance when he thrust one finger inside me and then another, making me gasp.

"Em." Noah dropped his head to my shoulder, breathing hard into it. "Em, the feel of you and those noises you're making are going to push me overboard. I'm going to come before I even get inside you."

"That sounds kinda hot," I breathed, and Noah lifted his head to kiss me hard and fast.

"Stop," he commanded thickly. "I told you how I want you tonight, and it's not that."

"Then lie back so I can fuck you."

Noah pulled back to stare at me, his lips parting like he was awestruck. Then he shook his head with a devilish grin. "I'm going to fuck that dirty mouth later."

"Can't wait," I laughed.

Noah slid from under me, scooting back onto the bed before reclining against the massive stack of hotel pillows. I kneeled on the end of the mattress, appreciating the sight, and when my eyes met his, I realized he'd been doing the same.

"Come here." He crooked his finger, motioning for me to come to him. "Crawl."

Smirking, I dropped to my hands. Noah's vision sparked, and I kept my eyes on him as I slowly crawled up the bed toward him. My hair was snarled from a night of dancing, and my heavy wedding makeup had likely smeared or wiped off, but Noah didn't seem to care. He watched me, a man transfixed. And his direct, heated attention made my blood simmer.

Soon, I was back in position, hovering over Noah's erection with his hands on my waist. I felt his eyes as they traced every inch of me, watching closely as I reached between my legs to run my hand up and down his length, fisting his base when I found it.

That jerked Noah out of his trance, his fingertips digging into my skin. "Fuck, baby," he groaned. "You gotta be careful. I told you I'm already close."

"I want you," I whispered, dragging my free hand over his chest. I raked my nails, leaving marks. He *had* said he wanted my hands all over him.

"Take me," he encouraged, his voice sounding guttural and

deep. So deep I could easily get lost in it. Drown in it. "Take all of me because I know you can."

A flush worked over me at his words, and I positioned Noah's cock until I felt him pushing at my entrance. Noah leaned forward, wrapping his lips around my nipple, sucking and tugging in a way that made me whine with desperation. Unable to bear the wait any longer, I eased down onto him. My lips parted, my breath vanishing as he filled me in the most delicious way. *Stretched* me. Let me experience the perfect bliss that was the intersection of pain and pleasure.

"I forgot how big you are," I gasped.

Noah released my nipple from his mouth and leaned back again, his eyes glittering. "You didn't forget, angel. It's all you've been thinking about all night. Probably longer. You dream about taking me in that tight pussy, don't you?"

"Yes," I admitted with a sigh as I dropped down.

"Good girl," he praised, lifting his hips to ensure we were completely locked together. Our eyes locked, too. Tension pulsed in the room as Noah dropped his voice and said, "Now, ride Daddy's cock."

Noah London was going to ruin me, and I was going to let him. Because I knew now that he would be there to pick up all the pieces he was about to shatter me into. He'd be there, and he wouldn't leave. This was real. This was us.

I rotated my hips, experimenting with the position. Noah watched patiently, his eyes full of smug heat as he took in my awe-filled expression.

"Feels good to take all of me, doesn't it?" he asked.

"Feels unbelievable," I said, practically breathless.

And then I tossed my head back...and started to *ride.*

"Unbelievable," Noah whispered, his raw voice washing over me. "*You* are unbelievable, Gemma. You *feel* unbelievable. You *look* unbelievable. It's—"

He broke off, choking when I slid up his length and slammed back down. I loved watching his reaction. His jaw clenching and eyes widening. His whole body tensed in the most beautiful way as a whimper slipped out of him.

"Gemma, please," he rasped, and a thrill trickled through me at hearing him beg. I relented, speeding up my thrusts, riding Noah harder as pleasure spread through my body like slow, sweet molasses. Noah's fingers started playing with my clit, and I felt feverish as sweat trickled down my back and my legs trembled. "It's so much better," he breathed.

"What?"

"It's so much better than I imagined." His eyes were full of something I couldn't believe I hadn't noticed before. Or maybe I had, and I was too afraid to acknowledge it in case he never did. "You are so much better than anything I have ever experienced."

I bore my hips down, wanting to feel as much of this man as I possibly could. I wanted to mold us together in every possible way until all I felt was *him*.

Noah reached up, cupping my face with a firm grip. His piercing green eyes met mine, and I couldn't look away. I sank deeper and deeper until the feeling burning inside me had nothing to do with our hips as they smacked against each other. Still, I slammed down extra hard because I needed more, and Noah made a sexy, gruff noise in the back of his throat.

"I love you," he groaned, saying the words his eyes had been telling me. "*God*, I love you, Gemma. You know that, right?"

"I know," I said, my voice rising as I neared an undeniable climax, spurred on by the reminder that he *loved* me. My breaths came in quick pants as I told him the truth. "I love you, too. I love you so much, Noah."

Noah dropped his hand back into the sheets, fisting them as he swore under his breath.

"Again."

I didn't have to ask what he meant.

"I love you, Noah," I moaned, bracing my hands on Noah's chest and using the leverage to work his cock over faster. Harder. Better.

His eyes fluttered shut momentarily, and when he opened them again, I could tell how much he was struggling.

"I want to spill inside you so badly, but I need you to come, Em." His words broke through rough gasps as his hips continued to work against mine. "Come for me."

I looked down, eyes traveling over every inch of him. He was the most gorgeous man I'd ever seen, and I had no idea how we'd ended up in this situation, but I'd never take it for granted. Not ever.

Especially not when the sex was this goddamn good. *Fuck.*

"*Gemma.*" He was desperate, more and more by the second.

But so was I.

I wanted so badly to unravel into Noah's arms and to feel him do the same. I wanted it, and the tight tension coiling in my gut told me I was about to get it. Pleasure unfurled inside me, reaching every corner of my body until it exploded, dousing me in a storm of sensations.

I cried Noah's name and then stilled, too destroyed by my orgasm to move. But he kept driving up into me, fucking me through my climax until he reached his with a hoarse shout that resembled my name.

"Oh my God," I gasped as I fell on top of him. "Oh my God, Noah."

His gentle touch slid up my back as I felt his heart beat wildly in his chest, pounding against mine. "I know. I know, baby."

He said the words like he had known. He'd known all along that this was how it was supposed to be for us. And for some reason, that was so comforting.

I slid off Noah, landing on his side. He wrapped around me, fitting snugly to my body as he transformed into my big spoon. His arm looped over my side, and I traced my fingertips over the fine inked lines of a lily near his wrist. We faced the window in his hotel room, and pinkish light reflected in the glass. It outlined the skyscrapers as the city got its first glimpses of dawn.

Noah kissed my neck before sliding his lips to my ear. "Julian told me that Juniper wanted their wedding ceremony to be at night because all those late nights they spent together at their office was what made them realize how goddamn gone they were for each other."

I glanced over my shoulder to find Noah staring absently out the window. Then, almost as though he realized I was looking, his bright eyes shifted to me.

"I think when I get married," he said softly, "I want to get married at dawn."

"But no one's awake at dawn," I laughed, even though the words nearly got stuck in my throat, tangled in the emotion there.

He didn't laugh. He held my gaze. Firm and steady. Sure.

"You are. You always are." His hand drifted over my side to my stomach, spreading his fingers possessively like he'd done so many times before. "And I have a feeling you'll be the only one who matters."

"Noah..." My mouth gaped as I struggled to find words. "You... we haven't even gone on a date yet."

But that didn't matter, and we both knew it.

"Let's fix that." A gradual grin split onto his face. "Gemma Briggs, will you go out with me?"

My heart swelled in my chest.

"I'd love to. I think I have Tuesday open."

"Funny." Noah leaned forward to kiss me. "So do I."

CHAPTER THIRTY-SEVEN

gemma

NOAH RENTED OUT an entire pottery painting place for our first date so I could paint my own set of mugs. To say it was the sweetest thing that anyone had ever done for me was a gross understatement, especially considering that Noah decided to paint a little ceramic puppy that looked like Winnie because he wanted to start decorating the nursery.

A few blissful weeks had passed, and now it was Tuesday again, and we were back at the doctor's office, sitting in the waiting room while someone on the other side clearly tried to be discreet about taking a picture of us.

"Ignore them," Noah muttered beneath his breath. He grabbed my hand, intertwining our fingers together. I leaned my head on his shoulder because I truly didn't care if they took pictures. As long as Noah didn't care.

"I'm not going to deny it," he said softly after a minute.

I looked up at him. "What?"

He met my gaze, and I was taken aback at how fierce his expression was. "People are going to see us together, post pictures, and assume that's my baby. And I'm not going to deny it. I don't want to deny it. They're going to say that I've only settled down, that we're only dating because I got you pregnant, and while that pisses me the fuck off, I'd rather people believe something false than think, for even one minute, that you and that baby aren't *mine*."

I stared at him, feeling momentarily speechless. But once I got ahold of myself, there was really only one way to respond.

"We are yours, Noah."

A smile played on his lips at my words. "I don't intend to lie. I'm not going to outright say something that's not true. But I don't want anyone to doubt who the man is in your life and that child's life."

"*Our* child," I corrected in a whisper.

Noah sucked in, stilling. "Our child, Em?"

I nodded, swallowing past the thickness in my throat. I knew I was probably going to cry today, but I didn't want to do it in the waiting room. "As long as that's what you want."

A hushed curse slipped through Noah's lips as his hand smoothed over my stomach. "I want that so fucking much. I love you. God, I love you. And I will love our child with everything that I am. Okay?" I nodded as I tried to keep the tears in, and Noah's eyes darted around us before he added, "I promise to try to shield you and Baby from it, but there might be times you end up on TV again or photographed without even realizing it. Are *you* okay with that?"

My lips curled into a grin as I placed my hand over his on my stomach.

"Noah, I've been living with you for months. I've always known that people might see us and assume things, and I only ever cared on your behalf. I didn't want to put you in a compromising situation. But me? You're asking if I care that the world knows you're mine? That you're off the market and exclusively in *my* bed?" My grin grew, and Noah's gaze glittered as he listened to me. "Yeah, Noah. I'm pretty okay with that."

"You're so fucking hot when you talk like that," he said, lowering his voice. The tone of it made me shiver.

"Gemma?"

A nurse calling my name startled both of us. My cheeks reddened; I'd definitely been about to jump my boyfriend in the clinic waiting room, and it was probably obvious.

Noah cleared his throat before standing and taking me by the hand, giving it a squeeze.

And then he smiled at me knowingly, and I nearly melted on the spot.

God, I loved him.

"It's a girl."

Did this woman say what I think she just said? A girl? I was having a baby girl? As in a living, breathin—

"Oh my God." Noah's choked voice cut into my thoughts. "She's going to look just like you, isn't she?"

"It's very possible the baby will have Mom's traits, but there's no guarantee," the sonographer said politely, and Noah's eyes flicked from her to the image on the screen, almost like he was pissed that she dared to speak the truth.

"She's going to look like you," he whispered stubbornly, leaning close enough to kiss my cheek.

She was going to look like me. Well, *maybe* she was going to look like me. But either way, she was real. She was coming—a living, breathing part of me, and I already loved her so much. Emotion swelled in my chest, and I looked over to see Noah's shiny eyes, a clue that he was feeling the same way.

Every time I looked at him and witnessed my feelings reflected in him, I almost lost my breath. I never imagined I'd experience this. But he really did love me, didn't he? He loved me, and he loved our little girl. I could see that, clear as day and as sure as the sun rising at dawn.

"You're going to have to think of a name," he muttered,

reaching out to brush away a stray tear that had escaped my lash line.

"No." I shook my head. "*We're* going to have to think of a name."

A grin spread over his face before he leaned back, looking dazed and content. "Can't fucking wait."

"A girl," I whispered, more to myself than anything.

"A girl," Noah breathed back, just as awed as me. "Our baby girl."

I smiled at him before glancing around the room, trying to take deep breaths. We were back in the same place we'd been weeks earlier, sitting side by side once again.

So much had changed since then.

I should've known from the minute Noah insisted on coming with me to my doctor appointments that he was in it for the long haul. And even more than that, I should have realized that there was no way in hell I would get through this pregnancy and room-mate situation without falling in love with him.

There was now a nursery in the apartment. Blake stayed with us for a few days when he came to Boston for an interview, and the brothers put together a crib while I watched with a bowl of ice cream in hand. They bickered at each other the entire time, but it reminded me of my own siblings, and I couldn't help but smile.

I hoped Blake got the job. It would be good for Noah to have more of his family around, and despite my initial impression of him, Blake really was a nice guy. Before leaving, he gave me his number, making me promise that I'd text him if I had any medical questions about the baby or whatever else.

That made Noah happy. With the football season in full swing, he wasn't home much, and he was worried. To put it lightly. And giving me easy access to his doctor siblings seemed to make him feel better.

"Does everything look okay?" Noah's anxious voice brought me out of my thoughts. "Anything we need to worry about? Mom and Baby both."

The sonographer suppressed a small smile as she glanced at Noah.

He was cute; I couldn't blame her. Who would have ever thought that this tattooed, hot shot of a football player was so goddamn adorable once you peeled back his layers?

I'd always known that Noah was an amazing man, but even still, he'd blown me away in the past month with his love and support.

"The doctor will review the results with you at your appointment."

Noah's mouth curved into an abrupt frown. "You can't just tell us, like, right now?"

"Noah," I laughed. "Our appointment is in half an hour."

He shot me a glare that was truly ineffective. It looked more like a pout. "That's a long time to go while thinking about the answer to that question."

I rolled my eyes, but lovingly. "You weren't worrying about that question an hour ago."

"Says who?" He raised a brow. "I'm always worried about you and Baby. Why do you think I damn near carried you off the ice last night?"

Noah saw me nearly take a stumble on the ice last night at practice, and when I stepped off the rink, I found him pacing around the perimeter of it. I wasn't sure if I'd ever seen him strung so tight, and if there hadn't been people watching, I was positive he would have thrown me over his shoulder and marched me straight out of there.

I opened my mouth to say something, but Noah looked straight at the amused sonographer and said, "She flies around an ice rink on tiny blades for a living, and I'm just supposed to be *okay* with that?"

"You get tackled by linebackers for a living, and *I'm* just supposed to be okay with that?" I shot back. "That's far more terrifying to have to watch once a week."

Noah turned back to face me, and his voice softened. "I'm not carrying our child, angel."

Our child.

I wasn't sure I would ever get over that, but I couldn't wait to find out.

"Dr. Amos can further discuss restrictions if Mom would like to have that conversation," the sonographer cut in, and I could tell she was trying to keep a straight face while also maintaining professionalism.

I sighed as I looked at Noah. "I've already talked about it with Dr. Amos, but I can bring it up again today if it would make you feel better."

"Yes," Noah said definitively. "It would make me feel better."

I poked a finger into his hard chest. "But you're not allowed to argue with her if you don't like what she says."

Noah threw his hands up. "Fine."

Roughly thirty minutes later, Noah and I followed a nurse back to a different patient room. When Dr. Amos arrived, she greeted me before her eyes immediately skirted to Noah.

"Good to see you again, Mr. London."

So she *had* recognized him the first time he was here. Her brows rose slightly, and I could tell she wanted to ask questions about his reappearance but was holding her tongue.

"It's good to see you, too, Dr. Amos," Noah replied with a nod. He didn't seem put off by the way she'd acknowledged him. In fact, he appeared more than comfortable in the seat beside me. Maybe a touch tense, but I knew it was only because he was anxious to hear more about how Baby was doing.

"I was wondering if you'd be back," Dr. Amos said, almost more to herself, as she sat in front of her computer and began clicking around to presumably bring up my file.

"I'm back," Noah confirmed. "And I'll be back for every appointment after this."

Dr. Amos smiled to herself. "Glad to hear it."

"You might be less glad when you realize how many questions he has," I laughed, and Dr. Amos chuckled as she tore her attention away from the computer monitor and swiveled in her chair to face us.

"That's what I'm here for," she said, opening her palms up in a welcoming gesture. "To answer any questions that Mom and..." She paused as her gaze landed on Noah.

"Dad," he supplied, so confidently that I had to bite down on a smile. "I'm still not going to be able to provide any information about Baby's medical history because that, unfortunately, will never be tied to me. But you can call me Dad."

She grinned warmly and finished her sentence. "...Any questions that Mom and Dad have."

"Excellent." Noah clasped his hands together. "So, how do you *really* feel about pregnant women ice skating?"

CHAPTER THIRTY-EIGHT

noah

"E VERYONE WILL UNDERSTAND if you want to stay home," I said as I walked behind Gemma in the mirror.

We stood in our bedroom as she tried to figure out what to wear to my playoff game tomorrow. Now that she was almost in her third trimester, the Knights jersey she usually wore while watching my games no longer fit over her bump, and she'd been frowning into the mirror for over a minute.

I wasn't so concerned about the jersey as I was about everything else. I'd been worried enough about Gemma when she came to my Minnesota game; now she was much further along, I was head over heels in love with her and Baby, and I found it increasingly hard to let them out of my sight.

"Noah." She sighed. "There is no way in hell that I'm going to miss the—oh my *God*." She broke off with a groan of contentment as I cupped my hands under her bump and lifted, giving her relief from carrying the weight.

She smiled at me in the mirror as she leaned back against my chest, letting me support her in more ways than one.

"Stop trying to distract me," she said, but her voice was a lot less strong now that my hands were on her. "I'm not going to change my mind."

"I just worry about you, Em," I said softly, kissing the top of her head. "It will be a lot of walking and big crowds and rowdiness, and what if—"

"Everything is going to be fine." She cut me off before I could work myself up with hypotheticals.

But no matter what she said, I couldn't help the concerns from swirling. "I just wish I could be there *with* you."

"I know, baby," she laughed, and my insides flipped at the little term of endearment. "But that kinda defeats the whole purpose, right? We're there to watch you on the field. And you're going to do great."

I smoothed my hands on the underside of her belly, still supporting its weight. But I remained quiet, thinking, worrying, and she sighed.

"Julian will be there," she pointed out. "And Natalie and Chloe. And *all* your brothers. And *all* my sisters. Both of our parents, too. I think I'll have plenty of people around me if I need anything."

I scoffed. "Julian is going to be far too busy making sure the rest of your sisters are safe from the London boys."

It was just another reason I wished I could be in the stands with them. I wanted to be there to watch the chaos that would undoubtedly be the collision of the Londons and the Briggs. I'd warned my brothers to keep their shit together or risk Julian's wrath, but I doubted they'd heed my advice.

Gemma laughed. "I told Julian he had to behave."

"When has that ever worked?"

"He listens to me more than he listens to most people," she said. "I'd bet I'm second after Juniper."

My lips twisted—a combination of irritation and amusement. "I'm not going to convince you, am I?"

"Not a chance," she confirmed.

It was for the best. Because in the end, I selfishly wanted Gemma there. I wanted her to be with our family in the stands. I had this feeling that tomorrow was going to be one of the best days of my life, regardless of whether we won or lost. Just the fact that everyone was going to be there, together, watching in real time. I couldn't describe the feeling it gave me, but fuck, it was a good one.

"Then come on." Releasing her stomach, I grabbed Gemma's hand instead, leading her to my walk-in closet. "Let's find you something to wear. I need my girl wearing my number if she's gonna be at my game."

"I've been wearing your number for years," she confessed with a shy smile.

"And I've wanted you to be my girl for years." I kissed her temple, murmuring the next words across her skin. "Seems kinda perfect, huh?"

"Not kinda," she whispered. "It is. It's perfect, Noah."

Absolutely perfect.

As I suspected, the playoff game was unbelievable in the best way.

Somehow, my brothers survived meeting Julian (and his sisters).

Gemma was well taken care of by all our siblings and looked so damn good with my name and number on her back.

And we won the game.

We didn't win the ones after it, though, which meant that the London-Briggs takeover game had been my last one of the season. It was disappointing, to say the least, but I could hardly be mad about it. Our team played a hell of a season, and now I got to be here. At home with Gemma. And Baby.

"Is Baby girl ready for her bedtime story?"

Gemma turned on her side as I dove into bed next to her, grabbing a pillow and propping my head on it so I was face-to-stomach with her.

"Oof." Gemma slid her hand over her belly, rubbing soothingly. "That was a big kick. I think that means she's ready for the story."

My heart leaped into my throat as I snuck my hand beneath Gemma's pajama shirt—one of my old football tees—and waited to see if Baby would move again for me. "Did she really kick?"

"She always kicks when she hears Dad's voice."

I'd been getting used to that word—Dad. But whenever Gemma called me that, I fucking melted. I wanted to be a dad—I really did. But one of my favorite parts of that title was how it linked me to the other half, to Baby's mom. To Gemma. That we were in this together. That we were a family.

Gemma's fingers trailed down my arm, as far as she could reach from this position, and I knew what she was looking for. I lifted my arm so she could see my new tattoo, just above my elbow, where a pair of angel wings had been permanently etched into my skin. Just like she was permanently etched into my goddamn being.

I loved how much she loved it. How much she sought it out, trailing her fingertips over it.

So I let her do that while I brushed my lips over Gemma's stomach, clearing my throat and whispering to our daughter.

"Tonight's story is about the night I met your mom."

Gemma's breath hitched audibly as she stroked my damp hair, similar to how I'd threaded my fingers through her gingery locks in the shower just before this.

Taking care of Gemma in these last few weeks of her pregnancy was my favorite thing. She'd finally given in to it, letting me dote on her and pamper her and treat her like a fucking queen. *My* queen. I couldn't carry the load for her, but I could carry her and love on her in every way I knew how.

Gemma didn't complain much, but I could tell how uncomfortable she was. How ready she was for Baby to be born. She was restless. It likely had to do with not skating anymore, and thank fuck for that. She hadn't been skating for the last two months, finally agreeing to hang up her skates until after the birth.

"I was a sophomore in college when your mom showed up at the house I lived in with your uncle Julian," I said softly, letting the memories take me back to that moment. Goose bumps covered my skin as it replayed in my head. "She walked in the door, and I remember thinking she was the prettiest girl I'd ever seen in my entire life."

Gemma's fingers stilled in my hair, but I didn't look at her. Not yet.

"But after Uncle Julian recovered from seeing Aunt Juniper walk in behind your mom, he gave me a look like he knew exactly what I was thinking. He didn't want me to so much as *talk* to your mom. But even though he was my roommate, one of my best friends, and my team captain...I ignored him."

A laugh rang through the air, and I glanced to see Gemma's eyes shining as she looked down at me. I smiled at her, warmth filling my chest, before returning to my story.

"I stole your mom away as soon as I got the chance. Uncle Julian started arguing with Aunt Juniper because that was how they used to flirt with each other before they got their heads out of their asses—"

"*You* told *me* I couldn't swear during story time," Gemma cut in, and I cleared my throat apologetically.

"Sorry. Anyway, Uncle Julian was...distracted. And that was when I swooped in because I just knew I had to talk to her. Even if she was my friend's off-limits sister."

"Maybe you wanted to talk to me *because* I was your friend's off-limits sister." Gemma continued tangling her fingers in my hair, playing with it in a way that was both soothing and a bit arousing. If she started tugging on it...fuck, I'd be all over her. "Maybe you just liked to cause trouble, Mr. London."

"If I liked trouble that much, I would have kissed you that night, Em." I rolled my eyes. "Don't you dare downplay my attraction to you."

She raised a brow. "So because you *were* attracted to me, you *didn't* kiss me?"

"I didn't kiss you because I liked you. A lot, angel. Come on, you know that."

Gemma's gaze remained steadily on me as she soaked in my words. Then, she wordlessly tipped her head to the side, resting it on the pile of pillows. She smiled a gentle smile.

She did know—that was what that face told me.

But Baby didn't know, so I turned my focus back to my story.

"See, I wasn't much of anyone at the time. Just a second-string quarterback from Minnesota who somehow got a scholarship to a Division I California college. But your mom didn't seem to care. She smiled at me like I was...*someone*. And I knew. I knew then and there that I would never have a shot with her. Not like a *real* shot. She deserved things I didn't think I could give her, and that's why I didn't even try to kiss her. But that didn't stop me from soaking up every bit of her that I could that night. Even while your uncle Julian glared at me."

"You're overexaggerating," Gemma said. "I'm sure Julian didn't care that much that you were talking to me."

"Baby, there is no doubt in my mind that it was clear as day on my face that I wanted to do much more than talk to you. Trust me, Julian did not like that I was making a pass at his sister right in front of him."

"I do remember you being a bit of a flirt," she giggled.

"I was trying really fucking hard to play it cool."

She brushed my hair back from my face unnecessarily. "Considering I spent the next few years with a silly little crush on you, I'd say you succeeded."

"A *little* crush, Em?"

A secretive smile indented her cheeks. "There's a reason I liked watching football with my dad whenever I was home."

"Always did like John Briggs."

Her hand slid down to cup my face. "He likes you, too."

Baby kicked, clearly reminding me that I hadn't finished my story. Unfortunately, though, there wasn't much more to say about that night. Gemma slipped away as the night wore on, sticking to Juniper's side. And then, the following day, she was gone.

"Demanding little girl," I chuckled, brushing my lips over Gemma's stomach again. "She's definitely a Briggs."

"I don't know..." Gemma cocked her head to the other side thoughtfully. "I think she's more of a London-Briggs."

My gaze flicked to Gemma's in disbelief. I stared at her, trying to figure out if those were just words she said offhandedly. But when she spoke, she sounded...nervous.

"How would you..." She cleared her throat. "How would you feel about that?"

Christ, was she really asking that question? I felt...I felt unbelievable. *Speechless.* So damn happy. So damn lucky.

"How would I *feel* about that?" I repeated when I found my voice.

"Yeah," Gemma murmured, and I had to sit up and face her. I needed to see her correctly, needed to take in every bit of this moment.

"I would feel...really, *really* good about that, Gemma. Fuck, I love you. And I love her. And I—I just—"

She leaned forward, kissing me into silence. "I love you, too," she whispered across my lips. "But are you sure?"

"Oh, yeah." My lips stretched wide in a smile so big it nearly hurt. But it was the best kind of pain. "Oh, *hell* yeah."

My mind started to turn, the gears whirring. Because as elated as I was for our daughter to have my last name, I really wanted her mom to have it, too. Fuck, I wanted that. But blurting out an unplanned proposal wasn't the way to do it.

My and Gemma's journey had been decidedly *un*planned. Nothing about us was traditional. And while I knew Gemma wouldn't care if I proposed to her while we sat in bed, telling bedtime stories to Baby, I wanted to be deliberate about this. I wanted her to know this wasn't something offhanded. It was something I'd thought endlessly about.

I wanted her to know I'd never been more serious about wanting to marry her.

So I tucked my thoughts about making her into a London-Briggs or a London or even a Briggs with a Mrs. in front of it into the back of my mind, and I put Baby's name in the front of my mind instead. Her name—the one we'd spent so long picking out—plus my name. And Gemma's.

It was perfect.

"London-Briggs had a nice ring to it, doesn't it?"

"*I* think so," Gemma said, struggling just as hard as me to contain her happiness. "But let's ask her."

"What do you think, sweetheart?" I placed both my hands on Gemma's belly. "Do you want to be a London-Briggs?"

It took a few seconds, but then we got the confirmation we were looking for in the form of a kick.

And everything was right in the world.

CHAPTER THIRTY-NINE

noah

EM : My water nrike.

What?

OH

EM : Beoke

EM : BROKE sorry my hands are shaking

I'm on my way.

Almost there, baby.

Just sit down with Winnie and take a deep breath, Em.

EM : I sat down and Winnie laid on top of Baby so I can't move anyway.

Winnie is excited to meet her, too.

I'm in the elevator.

EM : I just want to apologize in advance for screaming at you during labor. I love you. 🩶

I love you, angel. And you know I like it when you scream my name.

EM : It's not going to the that kind of scream, baby.

I think I'm going to be sick.

JONESY: You're not the one who's pushing a baby out of their body. Get it together, London.

You don't think I know that? Why do you think I'm texting you? Gemma sure as hell doesn't need to know how much I'm freaking out.

JONESY: You're gonna be a great dad, man. Gemma and that baby are lucky to have you.

Was that so hard?

JONESY: Sorry, I wasn't sure which angle to go for.

JONESY: Next time I'll skip the tough love, my bad.

JONESY: I meant it when I said you're going to be a great dad, though.

JONESY: Whole team is hella excited for you.

Thanks, Jones.

Can you please both get your asses over here? I don't trust anything that's happening right now.

BLAKE: Everything is going to be fine. I'm
finishing up my rounds, but then I'll be there.

BLAKE: I thought you liked Dr. Amos.

I do. But she isn't my sibling.

NAT: I'm touched, baby brother.

BLAKE: You do know we're not highly trained in
delivering babies like Dr. Amos is, right?

Small details.

Just get here.

Now.

NAT: Gemma is going to be fine. So is the baby.
Everything will be okay, Noah.

NAT: But I'm coming.

NAT: Wouldn't miss the birth of my niece.

I'm so excited to meet her.

BLAKE: We're so happy for you, man.

BLAKE: And so excited to meet her, too.

Since when does Delaney work in Boston?

BLAKE: What? She doesn't. She's still in
cardiology at Mayo.

Huh. Thought I just saw her. Nerves must be
making me see things.

NAT: Get off your phone and pay attention to
your girlfriend, Noah.

BRIGGSY: Let me in.

No. If anyone is coming in, it's Juniper.

BRIGGSY: If Juniper comes in, I come in.

No one's coming into this hospital room.

BRIGGSY: I heard you invited your siblings in.

They're doctors. You're not. But then Gemma vetoed it anyway. She said I was being ridiculous.

BRIGGSY: Is she okay?

She's okay. I promise. I got her, Julian.

BRIGGSY: I know you do.

MOM: Can't wait to meet my new grandbaby. Send pix asap!!!!

MOM: Love you and Gemma.

We love you too, Mom.

DAVE THE REALTOR: The sellers got back to us with a counteroffer. I sent the details to your email, but we need to act fast.

DAVE THE REALTOR: So... did you get a chance to look it over?

DAVE THE REALTOR: What should I tell them?

My girlfriend's in labor. Give them whatever they're asking for. I don't care.

DAVE THE REALTOR: It's a done deal.

DAVE THE REALTOR: Congratulations!

JUNIPER: Tell Gems I love her, and she's got this!

JUNIPER: I love both of you!

JUNIPER: All three of you!

Gemma says she loves you and not to let Jules see these texts.

JUNIPER: He's too busy pacing the waiting room.

GRAY: Deep breaths, Noah. Deep breaths.

Does it ever get less scary?

GRAY: Never. But it does get more amazing.

JOHN: You should know there's no one else I'd rather have at my daughter's side.

I'm not ever leaving her side, John.

> I was going to do this in person, but you should know I plan to ask your daughter to marry me.

JOHN: I already knew. Good.

SULLY: It's not too late to name her Sullivan.

SULLY: I would also accept a middle name.

SULLY: People end up getting called by their middle names all the time.

> Sul, I'm kinda busy. You already interrupted our first kiss, you don't need to interrupt the birth of our first child, too.

SULLY: I'm just having FOMO.

SULLY: Blake and Natalie get to be there.

> You can move here too, you know.

SULLY: Tempting.

SULLY: Also, was that really your first kiss? You lived with her for months in that penthouse of yours and waited until you were in a bar bathroom in Minnesota to make a move before taking her back to our parents' house?

> Goodbye, Sully.

SULLY: No, come back!!!

SULLY: I want to know everything!!

SULLY: How dilated is she??

THEO: I'm really happy for you, man.

THEO: And I can't wait to visit so I can meet her.

> Do you want to come visit so you meet my daughter or so you see her aunt again?

THEO: Gemma told you about the football game, huh?

> That you couldn't stop ogling her sister? Yeah, she mentioned.

THEO: Did she also mention she was going to share her sister's number?

NAT: Mom says I'm not old enough to babysit the baby.

NAT: Tell her I'm old enough, Uncle Noah.

> Just give it a couple more years, Lo.

> Hi everyone. It was a long night, but Delilah Dawn London-Briggs was born at 6:45 this morning, weighing 8lbs 3oz. She looks like her mom, who is very tired but very happy.

We both are.

GEMMA

"I S THAT NOT the most attractive thing you've ever seen in your entire life?"

I leaned against the countertop in our apartment, salivating as I watched Noah stride across the living room with Delilah strapped to his chest in the baby carrier. Cradling the back of her head with his palm, he bounced slightly while brushing his lips over her head and the wisps of tiny, gingery curls.

"Mmm," Juniper replied, and I jerked out of my trance to look over and find Juni salivating over someone else.

My brother.

Gross.

Julian stood by the huge windows overlooking Boston, saying something to Noah about football. I could only hear snippets of what they were talking about from across the apartment, but I also wasn't really trying to pay attention. All my attention went to my daughter and how the man I loved couldn't stop doting on her. The man who was her father in every sense of the word except for legally, and even that was in the process. We were just waiting for the paperwork to be finalized.

I loved watching them. I could do it all day, every day. Noah was going to spoil her just as much as he spoiled me, and while that might be a problem in the future, I'd been soaking in the bliss of it lately.

Loving Noah London was such a blessing; having him in my life had changed it in ways I couldn't even comprehend. He was the perfect partner, and I loved him so incredibly much.

I loved her so much, too.

God, I couldn't even put into words how much I adored her, how much my life revolved around her, how difficult it was to tear my eyes away from her. Even though it meant I was exhausted half the time.

Okay, all the time.

My brother's face lit up as he stuck his finger out for Delilah to wrap her little hand around. Crouching to her eye level, he murmured something to her, and my heart swelled.

Meanwhile, I glanced to find Juniper with her mouth hanging open, seconds away from drooling. I tapped her chin, and she jerked to attention, blushing furiously.

"Sorry, it's just—"

"You ready, Em?"

Noah turned toward us, flashing a crooked grin that made me wonder what, exactly, he had up his sleeves for today.

It was our first date since Delilah had been born and the first time that both of us would be away from her. I'd gone out for quick errands, but Noah always stayed behind. Or vice versa.

So *no*, I wasn't exactly ready.

I wasn't sure I'd ever be ready to leave her, even for a few hours. But I'd just breastfed her, it was only midafternoon, and Julian and Juniper would take care of her. Everything would be okay. For a couple of hours.

So I nodded. Tentatively. Slowly.

Noah chuckled, clearly reading my mind.

"She'll be just fine, Gems," Julian soothed before putting his hands out to take her from Noah. "Here."

Noah looked my brother up and down wordlessly.

"Oh, come on. Not you, too," Julian said with a roll of his eyes.

Then, he crouched back down to kiss Delilah's head. "Baby girl wants to hang out with Uncle Julian tonight, doesn't she?"

Delilah smiled cheekily, betraying both Noah and me. It should annoy me—like it clearly annoyed Noah—but something about it *did* put me at ease. I was lucky to have a brother who I knew would, without a doubt, never let anything happen to his niece. Between the two men in front of me, my poor girl would have one hell of a time trying to date when she grew up.

"It was really nice of you two to come over so we could go out," I said, wanting to break the tension between my boyfriend and brother. Usually, it was my brother looking at my boyfriend like he wanted to strangle him, so while this was a bit of a turn-around, Noah and I had plans.

"Of course!" Juniper chimed in as Noah relented and slid Delilah out of the carrier, handing her to Julian.

Winnie, sensing that her new best friend was on the move, ran over to Julian, dancing happily around his heels at the chance to say hi to Delilah. She waited impatiently as Noah and Julian transferred the carrier to Julian so he could tuck Delilah against his chest instead.

"It'll be good practice for us," Julian said with a smile and a wink at Juniper, and I stilled.

"Wait, are you..." Slowly, I looked between Jules and Juni. Both of them beamed at me. Julian's grin was unrestrained, ridiculously happy, and overbearing. Meanwhile, Juniper tried to hide her grin behind a half-hearted glare at Julian.

"I thought we weren't going to say anything tonight," she muttered.

"Sorry, Juni baby," Julian said, looking entirely *not* sorry. He walked toward us, sidling up beside his wife and smoothing his hand over her stomach in the same way Noah used to do to me all the time.

Juniper didn't *really* look upset that the news had been spilled as she sank into Julian's embrace, and my lips stretched into a wide, nearly painful smile.

"Oh my God!" I squealed, clapping my hands together excitedly. "Oh, I'm so happy for you guys. And Delilah will have a cousin—"

"Cousins," Julian cut in immediately, and Noah laughed as he strode over, wrapping his own arms around my waist.

"Already planning for the next one?" He chuckled as his lips brushed my cheek. A shiver ran through me at his touch, as simple as it was.

Julian shook his head. "No, not exactly..."

He grinned again, his hand still splayed possessively over Juniper's stomach. Juniper smiled back at him and then up at me, and when I saw the slight nerves running through her expression, I realized—

"You're having *twins*?"

Both of them nodded enthusiastically, and I clapped a hand over my mouth to keep from screaming. Noah gripped Julian on the shoulder, wishing him congratulations and muttering that he really *would* need the practice. I hugged Juniper—once, twice, and a third time—before Noah eventually dragged me out the door. But not before giving a million kisses to Delilah and promising her we'd be back in just a short bit.

"It'll be okay," Noah said as we got into the elevator. I wasn't sure if he'd noticed how tears welled along my lashes or if he just *knew*, but I sighed and leaned into his touch as he wrapped himself around me.

"It's just—" I wiped at my lash line, trying not to smudge my makeup. I hadn't put makeup on in weeks. I didn't want to mess it up in the first five minutes of our date. "It's just a lot. A lot of emotions."

"I know, angel," Noah whispered, his voice the gentle, reassuring caress I needed right now.

"But I'm so happy," I said, even though it sounded like I was holding back tears. "I'm so happy, Noah. For them. For us. I don't want you to think—"

"I know that, too," he replied, and I could hear the smile in his voice.

He knew. He always knew.

"I'm hoping I can make you even happier tonight," he murmured as the elevator doors dinged, and he took me by the hand, leading me through the parking garage to his corner.

Yes, Noah had a whole corner. He needed one, considering how many damn vehicles he owned.

Today, he led me to one I'd never gotten to experience.

One I'd always *wanted* to experience. Even though it made my nerves tighten, it was almost deliciously so.

"Can I take you for a ride?"

Noah stood behind me, his lips grazing the curve of my ear. The simple touch made goose bumps erupt all over my body.

It had been too long since I'd really gotten to enjoy his touch. Like *really* enjoy it. Savor it, like I used to. I'd been cleared to have sex for two weeks now, but Noah gave me worried looks whenever I brought it up.

If he was any other man, I might grow anxious that he'd lost his attraction for me. But Noah's worried looks would be followed by hungry ones. His body would grow rigid and his eyes dark, and I knew it had absolutely nothing to do with how much he wanted me.

"It's about time," I said with a laugh, walking over to trail my fingertips along the seam of the bike's seat.

I saw Noah shake his head out of the corner of my eye. "Sorry I didn't want my pregnant girlfriend to get on a motorcycle."

"I haven't been pregnant for a couple months."

"We've been a little busy, Em." He grinned, which floored me. Because we'd been so busy and tired and overwhelmed, but this man was still smiling at me like he wouldn't have it any other way. And for someone to choose not only me but my daughter— our daughter—like that? It was unbelievable. "So you want to go for a ride or what?"

He went into the trunk of his car, grabbing a helmet to pass to me. I took it with a smirk.

"Is the bike the only thing I'm going to get to ride today?"

Noah groaned as he snatched the helmet back and put it on my head himself, making sure it was snug before buckling it beneath my chin. Then he leaned in to mutter, "If you talk dirty on this date, I'm not going to fucking make it. So be a good girl for me, and I'll make it worth it at the end of the day."

I bit down on my lip in reply because I couldn't make any promises that I'd be a good girl, not when it had been so long since I'd had him. But I'd try. A little bit, anyway.

Noah shook his head with a cocky grin before striding to his bike and mounting it. My mouth ran dry as I watched him. He wore jeans, a white tee, and a leather jacket that I could practically see his muscles straining through, and my body couldn't help but react to how goddamn good he looked.

I mean, Noah always looked good. For example, he looked really good with our daughter strapped to his chest. But seeing him cock a finger and beckon me over to his motorcycle reminded me of the playful charm that first attracted me to this man. And it made me realize just how far we'd come in the last year.

Following Noah's directions, I slid onto the bike behind him and circled my arms around his chest. My body molded to his, his closeness keeping any anxiety I might have at bay. Noah ran his hands over my forearms, memorizing the feel of this moment, before giving a reassuring squeeze where my hands were clasped.

"If you want me to pull over at any point, just tap on my chest. 'Kay, Em?"

"Okay," I agreed. "But I trust you."

"And I take having your trust seriously. More seriously than anything," he said before running through all the safety tips I needed to know, like to look in the direction of the turns but not to lean over the bike and that it was normal to feel off-kilter at times. He told me not to worry and to hold on.

So that was what I did. I nodded, hugging him tighter to show him how much I appreciated that. How much I appreciated him. And then we were on our way. The bike hummed beneath my legs, and Noah's body warmed me in such a delicious way. The combination of it all churned the heat inside me.

I'd already asked Noah a million times what his plans were for today. He just kept telling me he wanted it to be a surprise, and while I didn't mind a surprise every now and again, I couldn't help but wish he could have given me some small crumbs to go off of.

Especially when we started driving out of the city, and I couldn't help but think that every mile we flew down the road was another mile away from our daughter.

Luckily, though, barely twenty minutes passed before Noah's pace slowed, and I wondered if we were getting closer.

Except we were in a neighborhood.

Which was an odd place for a date.

My confusion grew as Noah drove the motorcycle straight into the driveway of a beautiful home with blue siding and a red door. It was gorgeous, probably built within the last ten years, and perfectly maintained. But again, a strange place for a date.

He got off the bike first, clearly less stunned and confused than I was. His lips curved as he looked at me and swore beneath his breath.

"Fuck, I knew you'd look good on my bike. I've been waiting for this day."

"And you've been very patient, too." I smiled as I dismounted from the motorcycle. "I'll reward you for it later. I'll even reward you *on* the bike if you—"

"Gemma," Noah groaned, throwing his head back with apparent frustration.

I swallowed my laughter as I whipped the helmet off and shook my hair out, hoping my curls were still somewhat intact. When I looked back up, Noah was staring at me, his mouth slightly ajar.

"You are—" He broke off with another shake of his head and

then took two steps forward to slam his lips to mine. The kiss sent desire hurtling through me. It was a hard kiss, but Noah filled it with the same longing and desperation that existed within me, and all too soon, he pulled away.

"Come on," he muttered, letting his lips brush over mine once more before leading me toward the house.

"Whose house is this?"

Noah looked over his shoulder at me as we approached the front door, his smile tilted. And in that moment, I knew.

It was our house.

Oh my God, it was our house, wasn't it?

I stopped, my hand flying to my mouth. Tears sprang to my eyes. "Noah..."

Noah halted, turning to knock my hand away. "Not yet, baby. You can't cry yet."

"But—"

"We haven't even gotten to the best part yet. Come on," he repeated softly. "Let me show you around our house."

"Our house?"

I couldn't believe the words even as I said them. *Our house?*

"Yeah," he breathed, gently moving the hair out of my face. His finger twirled around one of my curls, following it down the side of my face. "For me and you and Lilah and Win. What do you think about that? We'll still keep the apartment, but I wanted you to have this. I wanted us to have this."

I didn't have the words to respond.

He'd joked about this. One time. At Juniper and Julian's wedding, but that was months ago. And I didn't think he'd actually—

"Let me at least show it to you before you say no."

He thought I was going to say *no?*

I mean, yes, it was too extravagant, too much, too beautiful, too everything for me to possibly accept such a gesture.

But it was also too perfect for me to say no to. Delilah

deserved a big yard to play in with Winnie. And when I thought of the girls, there would only ever be one correct answer.

So I followed Noah wordlessly through the front doors, letting him guide me into a gorgeous foyer with endless natural light seeping through the big windows above the front door. A staircase curved up to the second floor, but Noah led me past it, deeper into the house, until we stood in a dazzling kitchen. A massive bouquet of flowers sat in the center of a marble-top island. They were tiger lilies, a deep orange in color with pretty speckles dotting the petals.

"I don't know if I've ever told you this," Noah said, breaking through my silent admiration, "but your hair...the color has always reminded me of these." He pointed to the flowers. "So fucking beautiful. And when I bought this home, I knew I wanted it to be full of...you. Everything that reminded me of you and everything that you love."

"You," I choked, looking at him and seeing all the love in his eyes that made my heart squeeze. "You are what I love, Noah. I hope you know that. I don't need anything else."

"I know." He nodded like he really did know. "But Em, you almost moved out of my apartment and threw away some of your favorite things because you didn't think you had enough space for them. So I want you to know there will always be space for you here. There will always be space for you in my life. You and Delilah."

A joyful laugh burst through my lips just as tears once again threatened to fall. "You think there's room for all my mugs here?"

"I know there's room," Noah said, his grin suddenly so wide I thought his lips might crack. He stuffed his hands in his jeans pockets, almost shy-like, and nodded toward the cupboards in the kitchen. "Why don't you go take a look for yourself?"

Something about how he said it made my heart skip a beat, but I couldn't place why, so I walked past him to the kitchen cupboards and started flinging them open.

I gasped.

My mugs were already here.

At least, a lot of them were.

And in the middle of the collection was one new one.

On it, there were four words.

And my heart didn't just skip a beat; it shot straight into overdrive.

I gasped as I whirled around to face Noah, only to find him on the ground.

On one knee.

"I know," he rasped, emotion clogging his throat just as clearly as tears shone in my eyes. "I know it's only been a year since you moved in with me. But honestly, I should have said this sooner, angel: I *never* want you to move out. I want to live with you and be with you and grow with you and learn how to parent with you. I want you forever, Em. And I just hope to hell you want me forever, too."

"I do," I whispered, nodding aggressively to hopefully make up for the fact that I barely had a voice. My throat tightened as I tried to keep from completely bursting into tears. "I do, Noah."

"Yeah?" His smile grew adorably, like a part of him couldn't believe it was real. But at the same time, he popped open a box that I just realized was in his hand. I'd been too focused on his face and memorizing everything I saw there.

"Yes," I confirmed, my eyes widening when I saw the most beautiful diamond ring I'd *ever* seen. "Yes, yes, yes!"

"So does that mean you'll marry me?" he asked, hopefulness in his gaze. "Because fuck, I wanna marry you. That's all I want, Gemma Briggs. All I want is to marry you. Will you let me?"

"Yes!" I cried again, bouncing on my feet because I so desperately wanted him to stand back up so I could throw my arms around him.

Noah stood and reached for me, trying to grab my hand as he laughed. "Then stand still so I can put this ring on your finger where it fucking belongs."

Somehow, I managed to contain myself long enough for Noah

to slip the ring on my finger, where it was—no surprise—a perfect fit. He stared at it for a moment, and I stared at him, staring at it. Finally, once he was satisfied with how the ring looked on my finger, he stood.

I didn't waste a second before flinging myself at him. And Noah didn't waste a second before kissing me.

Heat wrapped around us as our lips collided, our tongues tangled, and our hands grasped at each other. Noah picked me up, setting me on the edge of the countertop so I could wrap my legs around his hips, tugging him close. My heart raced with the adrenaline of the moment, and I didn't know how to slow it. I wasn't sure it ever *would* slow.

But I didn't care right now. All I cared about was Noah.

"Need you," I gasped, and Noah groaned because he knew exactly what I wanted as I slid my hands beneath his jacket and shrugged it off him.

"Are you sure you're ready?" he asked despite his own arousal pressing between my legs.

"I'm ready," I assured him between frenzied kisses. "I've been ready, Noah. You're the one who keeps pushing it off."

"I didn't want to hurt you. Or rush you. And there are plenty of other ways I know how to satisfy you without being inside you."

God, wasn't that the truth.

"I know," I whimpered. "But right now, I need *you*."

Noah took a step back, fishing a condom out of his wallet, and I frowned. When he looked up, he noticed.

"What?"

"We've never used a condom before."

"We've never fucked when you weren't pregnant before," he said, lifting a brow.

"I'm on birth control," I said, wondering if I hadn't told him that. But I was pretty sure that I had.

"Good." Noah nodded, even as he unbuckled his pants.

It was my turn to raise a brow as something sank slightly in my stomach.

"Is it that...worrisome for you? That I might get pregnant again?"

Noah stilled, meeting my gaze. "Of course, baby. Your body needs time to rest. Heal. And the last time you got pregnant, you weren't in control. I never, ever want to take away your control for something like that. It should be something you decide. So for now, we'll use all the protection."

I swallowed, his words easing the feeling inside me. "*We* decide, right? Unless you don't think you'd ever want..."

My voice trailed off because I suddenly realized this wasn't a topic we'd broached. And maybe we should have. Because I knew what I wanted, but perhaps it wasn't what he wanted.

Noah's eyes grew wide as he realized what I was saying, and then a bark of laughter slipped through his lips. "Oh fuck, Gemma. You have no idea."

He shook his head with a growing grin, and I couldn't help but reciprocate his expression as he continued what he was doing, unzipping his pants and sheathing his cock with the condom. Then, he slid his hands up my legs and hooked his fingers in the sides of my leggings, yanking them down with my help as I lifted my hips.

Noah pulled me closer to the edge of the countertop before slipping a finger between my legs and sliding my underwear to the side so he could toy with my clit. I gasped, and he leaned closer. Close enough that his warm breath fanned across my skin.

"I want more with you, Gemma. And that includes more kids." He spoke in a low, gravelly tone. It made me arch my body toward him, seeking...more. "And when the time is right, there is nothing I will enjoy more than fucking you until you're pregnant with my child. So don't think for a second that's not what I want. But you and your health will always come first. Okay?"

I wasn't sure how he always made caring for me sound so sexy, but Lord, I was a mess.

"Okay, Noah." I wrapped my legs tighter around him. "I love you. You know that, right?"

He grinned, and the cockiness of it was tinged with softness. "I know, angel. I love you, too."

"I know," I whispered. "Now, fuck me like you don't."

Noah half laughed, half groaned, but he didn't listen.

"Let's take it slow," he said, even though I could tell by the slight shake of his body that *taking it slow* was the last thing he wanted. "I don't want to hurt you."

"I don't think you could ever hurt me, Noah," I said, gasping as he slowly worked one finger inside me. I held my breath, surprised at how...different it felt. Despite what I just said, I couldn't deny the twinge of pain that accompanied Noah's touch, and I bit down on my lip.

"Ah," Noah murmured. "Don't lie to me, Em. I need you to be honest with me about this. Promise."

He curled his finger, hitting that spot inside me he knew I loved, and I swallowed a cry. When he pulled out and then repeated the motion a little faster, heat tore through me, masking the pain from before.

"I promise," I agreed breathily. "Just keep...keep doing that."

"I will, angel." Noah's lips caressed my skin, kissing across my cheek, my jaw, and then down my neck. "I won't stop until you're drenched for me, and I know you can take it."

And he didn't. Noah kept going until I was begging him to fuck me. And even then, he lined us up and gradually pushed into me, inch by inch, murmuring a mixture of dirty promises and loving encouragement. We were both so lost, lost in the over-whelming feeling of our connection. It had been so long. So long since I'd gotten to feel him inside me like this, and God, I'd missed it.

"Fuck, I missed you," Noah moaned, echoing my thoughts. He stilled once he'd thrust all the way in, letting me adjust to the size of him again. It was...a lot, but it was also perfect. Every twinge eventually subsided into a pulsing pleasure, and all I could do was nod, unable to speak.

"You good?" Noah whispered the words against my forehead.

"So good," I managed. "Amazing."

I felt Noah's lips curve against my skin before he pulled out and drove back home again. "That's my girl."

His girl. I was his girl, and Noah made sure I knew it as he fucked me in the kitchen of our new home. Every stroke drove deeper, making the realization set in that this was our new reality, and there was nothing in the world that made me happier.

Noah kept going and going, his pants grazing my skin and setting my world on fire. He didn't stop until I was a sweaty, gasping mess, begging him for release. And when he finally gave it to me, he let go, too.

I wasn't sure how long had passed while we lay together on the kitchen floor, surrounded by our discarded clothes and matching smiles. But I didn't care. All I wanted was this.

Well, and—

"Knock, knock!"

I bolted upright at the sound of my brother's voice.

"Julian! You can't just barge in," Juniper hissed. "What if they're *busy*?"

"They better not be fucking *busy*," my brother grunted, but the first footsteps I heard didn't go any further.

"We're busy!" Noah called, but he didn't sound surprised. No, instead, he looked over at me with a shy smile. "I thought you might want Lilah to be here and see the new house, too."

Tears sprang to my eyes again because that was exactly what I wanted and exactly what was missing from this moment. I rushed to fix my clothes while Noah did the same, and once we were all situated again, I ran to the front door, where Julian stood holding Delilah.

"Congratulations, Gems," he said, pulling me into a hug. "Hope you don't mind having your housewarming and engagement party all at once."

I looked up at him with a confused frown. "What do you—?"

Movement from outside caught my attention, and I looked past Julian to see the whole family standing on the stoop.

"Surprise!" Janie and Gianna shouted while Chloe screamed, "Congratulations!" while jumping in front of her uncle Blake.

I stood there, stunned, as Noah ushered our guests in. There were hugs and tears and laughs, and just when I thought I might pass out from the joy of it all, Noah tugged my hand and dragged me up the stairs of our new home. At some point, he'd acquired our daughter and passed her to me. He knew what I wanted.

"Let them set up the party," he murmured. "I want to show the two of you something."

He led me to a bedroom that was clearly meant for Delilah. There was a wall of board books, a dresser with a stuffed baby loon sitting on top, and a crib already set up in the corner. My throat tightened, watching through watery vision as Noah walked over to the windows. There wasn't much to see out of them except for a few trees and the distant skyline of Boston, but Noah paused there.

"I wanted to make sure Delilah's room faced the east. I know there are probably many mornings that I'll be awake to see the sunrise over the next few years, and I want to watch them all. With her. With you. I'm ready, Gemma. If I haven't proved it by now, I want you to know."

I gripped our daughter tighter in my arms and then slid into his.

"You've more than proved it," I said. "You've never needed to convince me, Noah. I've always known the kind of man you are. But I just hope I've convinced you, too."

"Convinced me of what?"

"That there's no one else I'd rather be awake at dawn with, Noah. No one else."

He grinned like I knew he would.

"I know."

acknowledgments

LIKE GEMMA, I am navigating a stage in life where I'm embracing a fresh start, a new path, and in a way, this book is at the center of it. It has truly been a joy to write, but I have so much thanks to share for the help I've been given along the way.

To my readers, first and foremost, thank you for being here. Thank you to those who have shown me endless support from the beginning and thank you to those who took a chance on supporting me by reading today.

To Nate, your endless encouragement is what keeps me going. Thank you for picking up all the balls that I've dropped while juggling my way through this past year. I'd never be here without you.

To Caitlin, my personal-assistant-best-friend-extraordinaire, thank you for listening to every single detail about this release that there could possibly be. And thank you for helping to make it the best that it could be.

Kelsey and Reilly, my alpha readers. I never would have gotten to the end of the first draft without you. Thank you for listening to my voice notes and rambling thoughts and giving me a direction to go with it. You were so instrumental to getting me here.

To the best group of beta readers: Deidre, Kristin, Hanna, Madison, Emma, Alyssa, Nikki, Sevval, Belinda, and Arielle. It was incredible the way each of you were able to provide me with unique feedback that truly shaped the final version of Gemma and Noah's story. Thank you so much.

To Maxie, one of the first people I messaged when the idea of this book came to me. Thank you for reassuring me that, yes, pregnant figure skaters exist and then going out of your way to message every one of them that you knew. Noah would prefer they all get off the ice, but Gemma sure appreciated the input.

Sandra and Bailee, thank you for your editing expertise and all the help you provided in preparing for publishing!

To Alie, I'm so lucky to have gotten to know an artist as talented as you. Thank you for continuing to bring my characters to life and always being willing to dive into a new project with me.

To my fellow authors and friends in the book community, I'm so honored to get to experience and navigate this space with you. Thank you for always being here.

To my friends and co-workers who have been nothing but supportive as I transition into this new author era, I appreciate you more than you'll ever know.

And to my family, thank you for always being there and for cheering me on in whatever passions I stumble into. Hopefully this one takes me further than my dance performance in "Flight of the Bumblebee."

about the author

AMELIE RHYS is a romance author with a love for writing swoony stories packed with tension and heat. When she's not daydreaming about fictional characters, Amelie loves to travel new places (so she can write about them) and find new coffee shops and bookstores (so she can curl up and read in them). Amelie also likes spending time at the lake with her family. She lives in Minnesota with her husband and two rescue dogs.

instagram.com/amelierhys.author

Printed in Great Britain
by Amazon

44002145R00263